Other Works by David A. Wells

The Sovereign of the Seven Isles

- THINBLADE
- SOVEREIGN STONE
- MINDBENDER
- BLOOD OF THE EARTH
- CURSED BONES
- LINKERSHIM
- REISHI ADEPT

The Dragon's Egg

Dragonfall: Book One

by

David A. Wells

THE DRAGON'S EGG

Copyright © 2015 by David A. Wells

Edited by Carol L. Wells

This is a work of fiction. Characters, events and organizations in this novel are creations of the author's imagination.

www.DragonfallTrilogy.com

The Dragon's Egg

Prologue

Seventy-five years ago, the dragons fell from the sky. We thought they were just meteorites—six terrifying explosions rang the world like a bell. When the dust settled, we went on with our lives as though nothing had happened.

More than a decade later, five of the eggs hatched. The dragons that emerged were small and weak. They kept to the shadows, working in secret to persuade people to do their bidding, offering magic as payment and reward. Years passed ... and still we didn't notice the evil growing in our midst.

The war began suddenly. Survivors called it the 'apocalypse'—nine billion people killed in an afternoon.

Then the dragons revealed themselves, burning huge swaths of what remained, taunting and mocking and murdering the survivors.

Four leaders arose: The Wizard, the Dragon Rider, the Monk, and the Dragon Slayer. Allied with the rebel dragon, they waged war for years until they too were defeated, scattered, or killed.

When the war ended, only one dragon remained ... but that single dragon was enough to plunge the world into tyranny.

Chapter 1

Benjamin hoisted a sack of flour over his shoulder with a grunt.

"Do you think the markers will hold?" Zack asked, sitting on a table against the wall of the store, kicking his feet back and forth.

"Probably," Ben said, carrying the sack down the hall to the storeroom, ducking slightly to get it under the top of the doorframe.

"But what if they don't?" Zack asked when Ben returned and began selecting other items from the supply cart, distributing them to their appointed places on the shelves occupying the front of his grandfather's store.

"Then the stalkers will get into town and more people will die," Ben said, eyeing the bucket of nails on the cart and opting instead for three bolts of fabric.

"I hope the markers hold," Zack said.

"Why wouldn't they hold?" a female voice demanded.

Ben turned toward the front door, coming to an abrupt stop. The bolts of fabric balanced on his shoulder kept turning and fell clattering to the floor, in spite of a somewhat flailing, and entirely failed effort to catch just one of them. He took a deep breath and centered himself.

Zack didn't even notice the commotion that Ben had caused ... his eyes were firmly fixed on the woman filling the frame of the door, his mouth open, his feet frozen in mid-kick.

"I asked you a question," she said as she entered, trailing two more Dragon Guard behind her. All three wore black armor, all three were armed with swords and dragon-fire rifles, and all three were scarred with dragon runes. Identical symbols stood out on the left cheek of each. But the woman had another, more complex scar on her right cheek as well.

Hopping off the table, Zack flushed and swallowed hard, held firmly in place by the woman's glaring blue eyes.

"Can I help you?" Ben asked, stepping over the mess he'd made.

She slowly turned her gaze on him. "Do you doubt the Dragon Guard as well?"

Ben shrugged, just a hint of teenage flippancy in the gesture. "You haven't been here that long, but the stalkers have stopped coming into town since you put your markers up. That says something."

She appraised him for a moment before walking farther into the store.

Zack backed up against the table as she passed.

"Did you need something?" Ben asked.

"Who owns this store?"

"My grandfather," he said, gesturing over his shoulder with his thumb. "He's down at the dock unloading a supply shipment with my brother. Would you like me to go get him?"

She didn't answer, instead pulling her long blond braid over her shoulder and fiddling with it as she slowly walked the length of the counter, scanning the shelves along the way. At the far end of the counter, she cocked her head, turning back toward Ben and pointing through the open door into the studio where he and his grandfather practiced tai chi.

"Why do you have a sword?"

Ben frowned, confused for a moment. "Oh, that's just a wooden practice sword."

"Yes, but why do you have it?"

"Some of the exercises I do require a sword," he said. "My grandfather says that a sword can focus the mind more sharply than anything else."

She almost smiled, but opted instead for a grunt.

Before she could ask her next question, the side door swung open, and an older man stood just outside for a moment, scanning the room in a glance before entering with a cautious smile. He stepped lightly over the bolts of fabric on the floor.

"Good afternoon," he said. "My name is Cyril Smith. I'm the proprietor of this establishment. What can we do for you today?"

The woman seemed to lose interest in Ben and Zack as if they had never been of any importance. She eyed Cyril up and down before nodding to herself.

"I'm Dominus Nash, commander of the K Falls Dragon Guard detachment. Beginning today, all merchants are ordered to accept silver drakes in payment for goods or services at the posted exchange rates."

"But there's hardly any silver in those coins," Ben said. "They look more like tech metal."

Both Cyril and Nash shot him a withering glare—it was the fear in his grandfather's eyes that silenced him.

"Finish your work," his grandfather said, gesturing to the bolts of fabric on the floor before turning back to Nash. "As long as everyone else is using your coin, I'm happy to take 'em."

"See that you do," she said. "Refusing to accept a drake in payment will be considered a crime."

Cyril nodded gravely. "Well, thank you for taking the time to make sure we were informed of the law. You won't have any problems here, Dominus." He paused, then asked, "Did you have an order you wished to place today?"

She regarded him for a moment before slowly shaking her head. "No," she said, scanning the store again before striding out the door. The other two Dragon Guard filed out behind her without a word.

Zack seemed to deflate like a balloon, letting out a long stream of air as if he'd been holding his breath the entire time. Cyril ignored him, watching the Dragon Guard make their way into the next store along the waterfront marketplace. All hint of the shopkeeper eager to make a sale was gone. In its place was a hardness that Ben had rarely seen on his gentle old grandfather's face.

"Maybe the stalkers would be better than them," Zack said.

"They're a package deal," Cyril said, quietly enough that Ben could hear him but Zack couldn't.

Zack suddenly stood up on his tiptoes to look over a shelf and out the front window.

Ben followed his gaze and saw a flash of blond hair. He felt a rush of excitement, then his mouth went dry.

"Here comes Britney," Zack said. As she came into full view through the window, he mumbled, "She's so pretty." When she reached the front door, he seemed to snap out of a trance and said, "I gotta go." Then he disappeared out the side door.

Cyril became his kindly old self again and smiled at Ben. "I'll see if I can stall Frank for a few minutes," he said, heading back outside. "He mentioned that he was broke this morning. I'm sure the promise of today's wage will hold his interest for a bit."

Ben heard his grandfather's voice in the background, but his attention was already fixed on the beautiful young woman walking through the door. Britney Harper had been coming into the shop every Tuesday for the past several months to deliver her mother's list. And every Tuesday, Ben told himself that today would be the day he would make his move … but then she would arrive, and all of his carefully practiced lines would vanish along with his courage.

"Hi, Britney. How are you today?"

"I'm well, thank you," she said politely, rummaging through her bag and withdrawing a somewhat crumpled piece of paper. She seemed a bit distracted.

"Is everything all right?" Ben asked.

"Yeah, everything's fine. My parents are just really stressed out about the dinner party they're throwing tonight for the new Dragon Guard commander and the priest. Apparently, it has to be perfect or the world will end."

A hint of nervousness rippled through Ben's gentle laughter, but Britney didn't seem to notice.

"My father's firm is the first in town to be granted license to be heard by the dragon court," she said proudly.

"I bet that'll be good for business."

"My father thinks so … enough to hire me as an assistant in his office, anyway."

Ben smiled broadly. "Congratulations. You must be really excited."

"I am, but I'm also nervous. My father is very demanding and I can't stand the thought of him being disappointed in me."

"That could never happen," Ben said softly.

She snorted. "You don't know my father."

"No, but I know you."

She smiled graciously, then smoothed out her list and laid it on the counter.

"Oh, I have something for you," Ben said suddenly.

Britney frowned, a bit confused.

He retrieved a small bag from under the counter and handed it to her. "I remember you saying that you loved grapes, so I set some aside for you."

She looked in the bag. "Well, that was thoughtful. How much are they?"

"Oh no, they're a gift."

"Really? Are you sure?"

"I'm positive. Try one."

She looked at him like she was breaking the rules, then took a dark purple grape from the bag and popped it into her mouth. She closed her eyes as she bit into it.

"Mmm, that's so good."

Ben just stood there, smiling like an idiot.

"Thank you, Ben. You're always so nice. I wish I could stay and chat for a while, but my mother's really in a hurry to get these supplies."

He heard her words, but it took him a moment to tear his eyes away from her. When he came to his senses, he picked up the list and looked it over quickly, nodding to himself.

"I think we have all of the items you want. I'll put the order together and deliver it this afternoon."

She grimaced slightly. "My mother asked if you could make delivery as soon as possible. She needs some of the ingredients right away."

Ben frowned and started to say something.

"I know it's a lot to ask," she said, before he could speak.

"Okay. I'll see if my grandfather can watch the store for me."

"I'd be happy to deliver your order," Frank said from the side door, "on one condition."

Ben's buoyant mood deflated.

Franklin walked up to Britney and flashed his all-too-perfect smile. "I'm Frank," he said, extending his hand.

"I'm Britney," she said, looking up at him with her big blue eyes.

He took her hand and slowly brought it to his lips, kissing her knuckles gently as if it were the most natural thing in the world, then lowering her hand without letting go.

Her face flushed and she giggled.

Ben watched helplessly.

"Now I understand why my brother always wants to work the store in the morning," Frank said, leaning in closer to look at her necklace. "That's a really beautiful piece of jewelry."

She blinked a few times, her free hand going to the gold charm hanging around her neck.

"My father gave it to me almost two years ago for my sixteenth birthday. It's my favorite."

"Proof positive that you have excellent taste," Frank said, eyeing her like prey as he gently and ever so subtly pulled her a few inches closer.

She swallowed hard, still looking up at him with dreamy eyes. After a moment, she seemed to snap out of her trance, gently pulling her hand away. "My mother's going to kill me if I don't get those supplies home soon."

Frank shrugged. "As soon as Ben puts the order together, I'll be happy to deliver it … on the condition that you walk with me."

She nodded, her eyes losing focus again.

"Well then … come on, Ben, you heard the lady, she's in a hurry."

Ben stood there, struggling with the frustration building in his belly. When Britney looked at him expectantly, he nodded and went to work gathering the items on the list and loading them onto a pushcart. Frank didn't bother to help, not that Ben expected him to. Instead, he spent the time telling Britney stories that had her laughing.

After Ben finished loading the order, he wheeled the cart out of the supply room and into the front of the store.

"Ah, there he is. That didn't take too long," Frank said. "We'll get these right home for you."

"Thank you so much, Frank. You're a lifesaver," she said, laying her hand easily on his forearm.

"I'm always happy to help a beautiful woman," he said, flashing his smile again. "Please, after you." He gestured toward the door.

She giggled, heading outside without so much as a glance at Ben.

He stood there watching her go, knowing exactly what was going to happen next.

Frank turned and gave him a grin that said, "I win." Ben schooled his expression, studiously ignoring his brother. The flicker of disappointment on Frank's face before he turned to leave was Ben's only consolation.

He watched until Frank and Britney were out of sight, then he went to the studio and picked up his practice sword.

Chapter 2

Frank angled the cart to avoid a large puddle in the road where the asphalt had cracked and worn away over many years of inattention. The morning chill of the early spring day was just fading under the sunlight.

"I always love the way the clouds push up against the hills all the way around town," Britney said.

Frank frowned for just a moment as he looked up at the big white and grey clouds ringing the punchbowl valley, all crowding against the surrounding hills that stood like sentinels, guarding the town from the rain.

Frank selected a smile that said he was in awe of the sight and put it on like a mask.

"I know exactly what you mean," he said, softly, as if caught up in the grandeur of nature's beauty. "It always makes me feel safe when the clouds back up against the mountains like that. It's almost like this valley is protected from the storm that's raging across the rest of the world."

She nodded, smiling up at the bright sky. "Now that the Dragon Guard are here, we'll be safe," she said. "The markers are working. There hasn't been a stalker in town for weeks."

"I have to admit, I am sleeping better now."

She nodded again, falling silent for a moment while Frank maneuvered the cart's wheels over a section of the road that had cracked and was jutting up several inches, forming a curb that ran diagonally across the width of the street.

"I saw one once," Britney whispered.

"A stalker?"

She nodded, looking over at him with the ghost of fear in her eyes.

Frank steered the cart to bring him just slightly closer to her and waited for her to continue.

"It looked like a coyote," she said, "but there was something so wrong about it. It was gaunt and dark and its eyes were black as night."

She went quiet, trembling a bit.

Frank gently put his hand on her back. "Hey, you're safe now. We don't have to talk about this if you don't want to."

She shook off the chill and smiled at him.

"I was in my room looking out the window down into my neighbor's yard. He was working in his garden, just pulling weeds, when it bounded over his fence. It saw me first, looked right at me, right *through* me with those black, dead eyes. But then, my neighbor gasped when he saw it and it turned on him. It was so fast and vicious. It leapt on him, knocked him to the ground and tore his throat out in a second. I just stood there, frozen with fear." She paused to shiver, shaking her head with dismay. "It was like the stalker was frantic, like it was desperate to kill the man, like it couldn't stand the idea that there was a living being anywhere near it. Then it looked right at me again, fresh blood coating its snout. I knew I was going to die, I just knew it.

"But then the hunters came. One of them shot it in the ribs. The bullet went clean through, spraying black blood all over the fence. Even with a hole through its chest, it turned toward the hunters and charged. God, it was so fast. It leapt at the closest man, but he managed to bring his pitchfork up just in time and drove all three tines into the thing's chest. He fell over backwards, pushing the stalker to the side so it wouldn't land on top of him. It hit the ground, still snarling and snapping, trying to get back up. One of the hunters grabbed the handle of the pitchfork and held the thing down while another man started chopping at it over and over again with an axe.

"I didn't sleep for a week after that."

They walked in silence for a few blocks before Britney pulled the grapes out of her bag and offered some to Frank.

"Wow, those are hard to come by, and expensive too," he said as he tossed one into his mouth.

"Ben gave them to me as a gift," she said. "It was very thoughtful of him."

Frank pursed his lips and looked down, shaking his head.

"What's wrong?"

"Oh, it's nothing, Britney. I'll take care of it."

She frowned at him. "Take care of what?"

"Really, I shouldn't say anything."

She stopped him with a hand on his arm, turning him to look at her. "Well, now you have to tell me."

He hesitated for a moment. "It's just that my grandfather is struggling to keep his store open, and Ben keeps giving things away."

"Oh no ..."

"I shouldn't have said anything. My grandfather is a proud man. He'd be mortified if he knew that I'd told you this. Please don't say anything."

"Of course not. Your grandfather has always been so nice to me. I feel terrible. You have to let me pay for these."

"No, I couldn't. This isn't your doing."

She dug into her bag and came up with two drakes, holding them out to Frank.

He shook his head, holding up both hands, palms out. "You don't have to do this. I'll fix it. I've been doing odd jobs on the side for a while now to cover for Ben's misguided generosity. I don't blame him. He means well ... he just doesn't have much business sense."

She looked at him sternly. "Nonsense. I insist," she said, taking his hand and putting the two coins into his palm, then closing his fingers around them. "Give these to your grandfather."

He looked down sadly for a moment before looking back at her. "Are you sure? I mean, I didn't want to make you feel bad. I shouldn't have said anything."

"Of course you should have … you're protecting your family. Don't ever apologize for that."

Frank closed his eyes and bowed his head for a moment before nodding and slipping the coins into his pocket. "You're right. Thank you. I'll make sure my grandfather gets these."

"Good, and you should talk to your brother about this."

Frank nodded again before turning back to the cart.

"We shouldn't keep your mother waiting on these supplies."

They walked in silence for a few moments, moving to the side of the road so a horse-drawn wagon could pass over the broken and uneven pavement.

"So, what's the occasion?" Frank asked, nodding toward the supply cart.

"Oh, my father has just been accepted as an advocate by the Dragon Guard. He's throwing them a dinner party to celebrate."

"Well, that is exciting," Frank said with his most charming smile.

She nodded. "He's going to hire me as an assistant to help with all the new business."

"Wow, he must be so proud of you."

She grimaced, looking down at the road. "I don't know about that. I mean, I know he loves me, but I think he really wanted a son."

"Don't be silly. I'm sure he thinks the world of you."

"It's just … I can't stand the idea that I might disappoint him."

Frank chuckled, shaking his head. "I can't imagine that ever happening."

"You don't know my father. He's driven, and very demanding."

"Sounds like he's a businessman who wants to succeed so he can take care of his family. Can't blame a man for that."

"Oh, I don't blame him for anything. It's just that I really want to earn his respect, you know?"

"You will. I have complete confidence in you."

She blushed slightly. "I wish I did."

"Not everyone can be naturally confident," Frank said. "But you can learn to be."

"I hope you're right," she said.

"Of course, I'm right," he said with his cockiest grin.

She giggled, pointing to a big house just up the road.

"This is it," she said. "We'll take the supplies around back to the servants' entrance."

Frank took in the house—two stories and at least five bedrooms. It was well maintained and clean, unlike so many of the houses and buildings in town that had been abandoned during the Dragon War and allowed to deteriorate.

"Nice place. Your father must do well for himself."

"He makes good money, but he's always at work."

"Well, now that he's going to hire you, you'll be able to spend more time with him."

"I hadn't thought about that. It will be nice to see him more often."

Frank stopped the cart outside the back door. "I should probably load these in by hand. My cart wheels are muddy, and I don't want to track dirt into your mother's kitchen."

"I'm glad to hear it," a middle-aged woman said from the doorway. "I just got my kitchen clean from the mud the dairyman tracked in."

"Hello, Mother," Britney said. "Frank was kind enough to make delivery right away."

Britney's mother looked Frank over and glanced at her daughter, nodding ever so slightly to herself.

Frank offered his best smile, but then quickly replaced it with a deferential nod when she didn't smile back.

"Mrs. Harper, it's a pleasure to meet you," he said, as earnestly as he could manage. "Where would you like me to put your order?" He picked up a parcel from the cart and waited for her answer.

She appraised him again for several moments before waving for him to follow her into the kitchen, where several servants were busy making preparations for the dinner party. She led him to a storeroom and pointed to an empty table.

"Put everything there. My staff will sort through it," she said, stepping aside to let him by.

Frank was careful to place the items on the table gently and precisely, studiously ignoring Mrs. Harper's scrutiny and going about the task with care and diligence. He worked quickly and had the cart unloaded in a matter of minutes, all under the watchful eye of Britney's mother.

After the last trip, he checked all of the items, verifying that everything on the list was accounted for. Then he turned toward the door.

"You're not the usual delivery boy," Mrs. Harper said.

"No ma'am, that would be my brother Ben. He watches the store in the morning and normally makes his deliveries in the afternoon. But Britney said you were in a hurry, so I offered to make a special trip."

She pursed her lips, as if she were looking for a reason to disapprove but couldn't find one. "Well, I appreciate the extra effort. Here's a coin for your trouble."

"Oh, thank you, ma'am, I couldn't take that. I'm just doing my job."

She gave him a withering glare. "Let me give you a piece of advice, young man. When someone offers you a kindness, accept it graciously."

Frank looked down sheepishly for a moment. "My apologies, ma'am. I didn't mean to offend. Thank you so much for the gratuity."

"That's better," she said, dropping the slightly bluish coin into his hand.

"Thank you again, ma'am ... for your business and for your kindness," Frank said. Then he turned to Britney. "I enjoyed walking with you. I wish there was some way we could continue our conversation."

"Me too," Britney said with a smile.

"Well, in that case," Frank said, turning back to Mrs. Harper, "There's a diner not too far from here that makes the best apple pie in town. May I ask permission to take your daughter to lunch? It would give me something worthwhile to spend this coin on."

Mrs. Harper frowned, pursing her lips again.

"Please, Mother. All of my chores are done."

She looked from Britney to Frank and back. "Very well, but come home straightaway. I have more for you to do this afternoon."

Britney leaned in and kissed her mother on the cheek, momentarily dispelling some of the woman's sternness as she offered her daughter a genuine smile.

"I'll walk her home right after lunch, ma'am. You have my word."

"See that you do," she said, donning her mask of authority again.

Chapter 3

Ben sat on a bench in front of the store, absentmindedly rolling his lucky coin between his fingers, from one to the next and then back again. He stopped and held the gold wafer by its knurled edges, looking at the image of North America stamped on its face with the letters NACC across the top and the year 2098 across the bottom.

His grandfather had given identical coins to both of his grandsons on their twelfth birthday. Frank had spent his within a week. Ben thought back with a mixture of guilt and satisfaction to the last time Frank had tried to steal his. That day marked the last fistfight they'd ever had. Ben had always taken pride in his self-control, but he'd lost his temper that day and demonstrated to Frank just how uneven a match they had become. Since then, Frank had been far more cautious in his efforts to test Ben's forbearance.

As he looked at the coin, he found himself wondering if it was time to teach his brother another lesson, but dismissed the thought just as quickly. For all his faults, Frank was still his brother.

Homer padded up and put his chin on Ben's knee, looking up at him with his big brown eyes. Ben smiled at his dog, a brown-and-brindle mutt that could vanish into the shadows like he was a part of the night.

"You want me to pee on his leg?" Homer asked.

Ben chuckled, scratching him on the head. "No, just stay away from him. I don't want him trying to hurt you again."

Homer had been Ben's best friend for his entire life. As long as he could remember, Homer had been there, watching over him. He had already lived longer than any normal dog, yet he looked like he was only about a year past the puppy phase.

That would have been enough to make Ben wonder about Homer's origins, but the fact that he could talk was what really set him apart from other animals. It wasn't that he could actually speak, but Ben could hear what he had to say, and Homer could hear Ben too, provided they were close enough to one another, anyway.

As a young child, Ben had taken it for granted that animals could talk to people with their thoughts. It was only later that he realized just how special Homer really was. At Homer's urging, Ben had kept their secret from everyone, even his grandfather, though he suspected that Cyril knew.

"I can take care of myself," Homer said, "and Frank's got it coming. You really like her, I can tell."

Ben shook his head, looking down at the dirt.

Homer grumbled out loud as he curled up at Ben's feet. "Sun feels good."

Ben nodded, smiling down at him.

"Ah, there you are," Cyril said from the doorway, pausing before taking a seat next to him. "He did it again, huh?"

Ben nodded, looking over at his grandfather. "It'd be one thing if he actually liked her."

Cyril sighed helplessly, falling silent for a few moments. "One day you're going to meet a woman who'll be able to see right through both of you. He won't stand a chance with her."

"Why can't that woman be Britney?" Ben whispered.

Cyril fell silent again.

Ben waited. He knew his grandfather well enough to know when he was working through his thoughts, taking care to choose just the right words.

"I know you don't want to hear this, but I'm glad it's not Britney."

"Why?" Ben asked, bristling at his grandfather's disapproval.

"Because her family's in bed with the wyrm," Cyril whispered, looking around cautiously.

"So? The dragon is here to stay. The resistance lost. We might as well learn to live with that. At least Britney's family is making the best of it."

Cyril withdrew into himself for a moment, closing his eyes, bowing his head and becoming very quiet.

Homer whined almost inaudibly, looking up at them both.

"Tell me your impressions of Dominus Nash," Cyril said.

Ben's brow furled as he thought about his earlier encounter. "I didn't like her. She acted like we were property, not people."

"So, would you be willing to learn to live with that?"

"No," Ben said after a few moments of reflection.

"The wyrm and his minions are evil, and evil never lasts for long. It takes time for the abuses to pile up to the point where average people will risk their lives to make a stand against it, but it always happens. All through history, evil people have risen to positions of power, and every time they bring about their own demise. Unfortunately, they usually cause untold suffering before they fall. The dragon is no different."

"The dragon has magic. How can you fight that? All of the tech from the world before Dragonfall was useless against them."

"That's not entirely true," Cyril said. "Remember your history. There were five dragons, and now there is only one. Tech played a part in that fight.

"But more importantly, the dragons didn't destroy the world with magic, they destroyed it with our own weapons—tech weapons. And even then, they didn't use magic, at least not directly. They used bribery, extortion, and blackmail to turn a relatively small handful of people in just the right positions against the rest of the world."

Ben shook his head sadly. "I've never understood that part of the story. How could anyone do what they did? They helped slaughter nine billion people, and for what? So they could rule over a broken world?"

"The wolves among us will always choose power over humanity."

Ben sighed helplessly.

Cyril waited.

"I know what you've taught me is true—objectively at least. But there's a part of me that just can't accept that there are people in the world who would do such things."

"Ah ... you've just stumbled into one of humanity's greatest conundrums. It's difficult, maybe even impossible, for a good person to fully comprehend the inner workings of an evil person's mind. Lacking that comprehension, most people assume that everyone else sees the world in the same way that they do. As a result, far too many people are easily taken in by the carefully crafted deceptions and lies that are told so convincingly by those who crave power."

"So how do you persuade people to fight against something that they don't even believe exists?"

"You don't. There are no words that can make a person believe something that they don't want to believe."

"Then how can evil ever be defeated? I mean, if people won't even believe it exists, then how can they be convinced to take up arms against it?"

"They can't. It's never the mass of people who make the difference, Ben. It's always a small group—those who can see evil for what it is and who are willing to risk everything to stand against it. And more often than not, they pay a heavy price."

Homer barked suddenly, drawing their attention.

"What is it?" Ben asked.

"I smell Imogen ... and horses."

A moment later, Ben heard the hoofbeats, coming hard and fast. He stood to see the Highwayman coming around the corner, followed close behind by Imogen. While technically his aunt—Imogen was more like a sister. He hadn't seen her since she'd run off to Rogue City two years ago to marry Enzo Gervais.

He could almost feel his grandfather's emotional turmoil. Cyril hid it well, but Ben knew that he missed his daughter terribly.

The look of anguish on Imogen's face, coupled with the mask of cold anger worn by the Highwayman, was enough to freeze Ben in place. A surreal detachment washed over him, holding him in thrall. He could hear the kindly voice of his grandfather in the back of his mind: 'Turning points come to us all—events and the choices they offer. The better part of wisdom is learning to recognize those moments when they happen.' Ben couldn't help but feel that this was one of those moments.

Imogen dismounted, her anguish transforming into tears as she rushed to her father.

"I'm so sorry, Daddy," she sobbed into his chest.

"It's okay, you're home now. That's all that matters."

She shook her head, pulling away from him so she could look him in the eye.

"They took my baby," she said, putting her forehead to his chest again and weeping uncontrollably.

For the second time in as many hours, Ben saw a kind of hardness in his grandfather's expression that only served to magnify his own fear.

Still holding his daughter, Cyril looked to John Durt, a lean, competent man.

"Are you being pursued?"

"Probably," the Highwayman said. "But they're not close."

Cyril nodded to himself. "Come inside, both of you. Ben, tend to the horses."

It was only at the mention of his name that Imogen noticed him standing there, rooted to the ground. She pulled away from her father.

"Hey, Baby Brother," she said through her tears.

"Hey, Big Sister," he said, giving her a hug. "It's good to see you."

She nodded tightly, tears flowing down her face.

"Come, we haven't much time," Cyril said, taking Imogen by the arm and leading her into the store.

"Go with them and listen," Ben said to Homer.

Cyril locked the front door, put the closed sign in the window, and drew the curtains, all of which only served to punctuate the gravity of the situation. Ben couldn't remember Cyril ever closing the store in the middle of the day.

A moment later, his curiosity overcame his trepidation and he quickly led the horses behind the store and into the fenced backyard. He removed their saddles and turned the animals loose to graze on the lush green grass.

After making sure the gate was locked, he raced inside and upstairs to the living quarters, stopping like he'd hit a wall when he reached the landing. The room was deathly quiet, save for Imogen's quiet sobbing. She sat with her face in her hands. John stood next to the window looking down over the front yard. Cyril stood stock-still in the center of the room, a mixture of sadness and fury warping the features of his face.

"What's happened?" Ben asked Homer.

"Enzo took Imogen's baby and gave it to the priest."

Ben stood there, stunned by what he'd just learned, trying to process exactly what it meant, but unable to make sense of it for lack of information. He felt like he was missing something, some vital understanding that would make everything clear.

"Imogen, look at me," Cyril said. "When did this happen?"

"Two days ago," she said, wiping her nose and sniffing back fresh tears.

"How old is your child?"

"He's only eight weeks. He needs me."

Cyril clenched his jaw, taking a deep breath and letting it out slowly. "What did Enzo say when he took him?"

"He said everything would be all right, that we could always have another baby."

Cyril closed his eyes and turned away, taking a few aimless steps before coming full circle to face his daughter again. "This is very important," he said. "I need you to tell me exactly how you felt before he came to take your baby, how you felt while he was taking the child, and how you felt after he'd left with him."

She frowned, her brow furrowing deeply as realization seemed to creep into her mind.

"Before, I was happy, all the time. But looking back at it now, it seems almost like a dream—like I could only see the good things. When he told me he was taking our son, I didn't understand at first. And then I did. It felt like something broke inside of me. All of the love I had for Enzo vanished in an instant and was replaced with revulsion. I never even liked him. I'm not sure why I married him." She looked up at her father helplessly. "What's happening to me?"

Cyril pulled a chair in front of his daughter and sat down, taking her hands in his.

"None of this is your fault," he said. "You've been under a spell."

John's head snapped from the window to Imogen in an instant, anger and hope in his eyes, though he remained silent.

"I don't understand," she said.

"I should have seen it," Cyril said, shaking his head and closing his eyes. "When he first started courting you, your disinterest was blindingly obvious. But then, very suddenly, you fell for him. I talked myself into believing that he'd won you over. But he hadn't. Instead, he'd made a deal with the devil, and your baby was the price."

"What will they do to my son?" she whispered.

"I don't know, but I don't think he's in any immediate danger."

Cyril went to the window, staring off into the distance, lost in thought.

John glanced at Imogen. Seeing her face in her hands again, he put a hand on Cyril's shoulder.

"I've heard stories—"

"I know," Cyril whispered, holding John with his eyes.

He nodded, turning back to the window.

"So what are we going to do?" Ben blurted into the uncomfortable silence.

Cyril turned to face his grandson, as if noticing his presence for the first time. His face went from hard to gentle. "We're going to get Imogen's baby back."

She looked up, hope mingling with tears in her eyes for a brief moment before despair overcame her again.

"The priest is too powerful. He has magic and a whole company of Dragon Guard. We wouldn't stand a chance against him."

"Not if we fight fair," Cyril said.

"Time's up," John said, picking up his bow and throwing his quiver over his shoulder. "Your husband is here, and he's got half a dozen men with him."

"Do you still have your pistol?" Cyril asked.

John shook his head, his eyes never leaving Enzo. "I stashed it outside the markers after the Dragon Guard burned out Old Man Johnson for refusing to give up his shotgun."

Cyril nodded, looking out the window at his unwelcome son-in-law. He turned abruptly and went into his bedroom. A few moments later he returned with a bundle wrapped in leather. Ben could do little more than blink when Cyril unrolled it onto the table, revealing two identical swords, complete with scabbards and belts. He handed one to Ben, then took the other for himself, strapping it easily around his waist.

Ben drew the blade. It was light and sharp—the pale grey metal just slightly iridescent.

John whistled. "Tech metal—nice."

"This has the same weight and balance as my practice sword," Ben said, testing the weapon against the air before him. "I mean, exactly the same."

There was a loud banging on the front door.

"I know you're in there," Enzo yelled. "And I know you have my wife. Give her back to me and I won't report you to the Dragon Guard."

Imogen bolted to her feet and stomped to the window, her face going red with fury. She fumbled with the lock for a moment before throwing it open.

"I hate you!" she screamed. "And I'm not your wife anymore!"

"Oh darling, I know this is hard for you," Enzo said. "Come home with me and I'll make it all better. We'll have another baby. Everything will be like it was. I promise."

"Nothing will ever be the same again."

"You are my wife," he said, an edge in his voice. "You belong to me. Remember your oath? Remember the words you spoke in front of the priest? You can't take those words back—not ever. You're bound to me, if not by love, then by law. Only death can sever that."

"That can be arranged," John said, drawing an arrow and nocking it.

"Stay out of this, Highwayman," Enzo said. "With the Dragon Guard patrolling the roads, your standing is falling fast. You'd do well to look to your own future instead of meddling in my marriage."

Cyril looked down at Gervais. "My daughter doesn't want to see you right now. It would be best if you left."

"That's not going to happen, old man. She's coming with me if I have to break your door down and tie her to a horse."

"That would be a mistake, Enzo. Give her time to calm down. We can talk about this tomorrow."

"No! She's coming home with me now."

"I'll never go back there with you," Imogen said.

"Just come home with me," Enzo said, his demeanor going from angry to caring in an instant. "We'll go see the priest. He'll make things like they were. You can be happy again."

"Never!" she shouted.

"You heard her," Cyril said. "It's time for you to leave."

"I will have my wife," Enzo said. "And you can't stop me."

"I can try," Cyril said.

"There's only two of you. I have six men. You don't stand a chance. Give her back and no one will get hurt."

Ben stepped up to the window.

Enzo chuckled, looking to one of his men. "Oh shit, they have a boy, too."

His men laughed.

"Last chance," Enzo said.

"It's funny you should say that," Cyril said. "I was about to make you the same offer."

Enzo shook his head and motioned toward the door.

At the sound of glass breaking, Cyril bolted for the stairs. "Remember your lessons," he said to Ben without slowing.

John followed right behind him.

Chapter 4

Ben hesitated, but only for a moment before following John down to the first floor. By the time he reached the front of the store, his grandfather was facing off against a large man holding an axe handle.

"What are you going to do, old man?" the man said, swinging his club at Cyril's sword in an attempt to disarm him.

Ben had sparred with his grandfather a thousand times, but always with wooden swords, and always without any hint of anger. This was something else.

Cyril dropped the point of his blade, allowing the axe handle to pass down in front of him without resistance. The momentum pulled the man off-balance and left him with his arm across his body. Cyril whipped his blade around and stabbed him in the shoulder, eliciting a cry of pain and causing him to drop his club. His sudden anger turned to fear when he saw the bloody tip of Cyril's sword not six inches from his face. Cyril walked him backward, crowding the men behind him out into the front yard.

"You'll pay for this, old man," Enzo shouted past his men.

Ben saw one of the thugs coming around the side of the store and quickly locked the door, backing away when the man started trying to break it down. Then he heard the distinctive twang of a bowstring followed by a wail of pain. John had sent an arrow over Cyril's shoulder and into Enzo's archer, dropping the man to his knees before he could loose an arrow at Cyril.

"The next man to attack will die," Cyril said.

In that moment, Ben realized that these wouldn't be the first men his grandfather had killed.

"He can't take you all!" Enzo yelled to his men. "Attack!"

His men didn't move. A few of them glanced back at Enzo like he was crazy.

"Why don't *you* step forward, Enzo?" Cyril said. "Fight your own battle instead of hiring others to do it for you."

"I have him," John said, bowstring drawn to his cheek. "Just say the word."

"You've lost, Enzo," Cyril said. "You can either leave right now, or my friend will put an arrow through you."

"You're not paying me enough for this shit," one of his men said, sheathing his knife and taking a step back. Others murmured in agreement. Uncertainty flickered across Enzo's narrow face.

A moment later, the sound of galloping horses reached them, and his arrogance returned in full force. "You're mistaken, old man," Enzo said triumphantly. "You're the one who's just lost everything."

Dominus Nash and six Dragon Guard rode into the yard, trailing another of Enzo's henchmen. The guardsmen drew their dragon-fire rifles as they spread out to surround everyone.

Nash reined in her horse and scanned the scene. Her eyes narrowed when she saw Cyril holding a blade stained with blood. "Weapons down or burn," she said.

Cyril nodded, slowly laying his sword on the ground.

John leaned his bow against the wall.

"Dominus," Enzo said with a subservient bow, "I'm here to retrieve my wife. Her father is holding her against her will."

"That's a lie!" Imogen said, pushing past Cyril and into the yard. "I came home to get away from him." She pointed at Enzo as if she were accusing him of murder.

"And these men?" Nash motioned to the two wounded thugs.

"Victims of an unwarranted attack," Enzo said, easing his horse closer to Nash. "I just want my wife back. She was kidnapped by the Highwayman and brought here against her will."

"You lying bastard!" Imogen said, starting forward until Cyril stopped her with a hand on her arm.

"Are you his wife?" Nash demanded.

"Not anymore," Imogen said. "I don't ever want to see him again."

"Were you married by the priest?"

"We were indeed," Enzo said. "It was such a beautiful ceremony. I just want her to come home."

Nash seemed to be considering the situation.

"Perhaps if we could speak in private," Enzo said, pulling his coat aside and revealing a gold dragon broach pinned to his shirt.

Her demeanor changed in an instant.

"I'd be happy to hear you out," she said, dismounting and walking toward the road with Enzo.

Ben watched through the window as they talked for a moment. After Enzo handed her a small leather pouch, they returned.

"The woman will go home with her husband," Nash said.

"No!" Imogen shouted. "I'm not going anywhere with him."

Nash looked at her for a moment like she was a curiosity, then strode up to her and backhanded her across the cheek.

Imogen fell sprawling to the ground.

Cyril reached for his sword but the nearest Dragon Guard pointed his rifle at him.

"If your hand touches metal, you will burn," Nash said. "Detain the rest," she said, casually motioning to Cyril, John, and Ben. She turned away from them like they were of no consequence.

A Dragon Guard grabbed Cyril by the back of the shirt and pulled him onto the ground. His eyes never left Imogen as one of Enzo's henchmen lifted her onto a horse and mounted up behind her.

John surrendered when another Dragon Guard pointed his rifle at him and ordered him from the store.

Ben stood frozen with disbelief and fear as another Dragon Guard pointed his large-bore rifle at him.

"Drop the blade, boy."

He seemed to remember all at once that he was holding a sword and let go of it like it was a snake, letting it clatter to the floor. A moment later he was hauled out into the yard and thrown to the ground. A big man wrenched his arms behind his back and bound them tightly.

All three were tied together with a rope that was attached to the saddle of the nearest Dragon Guard. Ben felt an odd sense of detachment come over him. His whole life had just changed in an instant. It didn't even seem real—except for the pain of the ropes cutting into his wrists. That was all too real.

"What should I do?" Homer asked.

"I don't know yet," Ben said. "Stay in the shadows and don't let them catch you."

Homer whimpered and hid in the bushes.

As they set out toward the Dragon Guard headquarters, a thousand questions tumbled through Ben's mind, but he didn't dare speak for fear of reprisal.

Not two blocks down the road, Rufus Hound came around the corner. He was a big man with a pockmarked face and a penchant for whores and bar fights. Ben thought the man was a bully—the fact that he was Frank's drinking buddy probably had something to do with that. Hound walked into the middle of the road and stopped with his hands on his hips, causing Nash to rein in her horse.

"What's going on here?" Hound demanded.

"None of your concern," Nash said. "Stand aside or I'll have you bound as well."

Hound didn't budge, looking past Nash to Cyril. Cyril shook his head ever so slightly. Looking farther back, he saw Imogen, her face bloody and her arms bound behind her back. His face hardened and he looked back to Cyril. Again, Cyril shook his head almost imperceptibly.

"I know these men," Hound said, somewhat less confrontationally. "What did they do?"

"None of your concern," Nash said, leaning toward him pointedly.

Hound looked at her directly and a crooked smile slowly spread across his face. "I bet you're a handful in the sack," he said.

"What did you just say to me?" Nash said incredulously.

"What? A guy can't compliment a good-looking woman," Hound said, looking past the Dragon Guard again. "I was just looking for Frank—wanted to see if he was going drinking tonight."

"He's making a delivery to the Harpers," Cyril said.

"Quiet!" Nash snapped, fully back in her element again.

"Fair enough," Hound said, wandering over to the side of the road. "If you ever want some company, the name's Rufus Hound—you know, like the dog." He punctuated his offer with a smile that was anything but subtle.

She glared at him. He smiled back until she turned away, spurring her horse forward.

His smile vanished a second later, replaced with the kind of seriousness reserved for important work. He looked to Cyril, who nodded. Hound turned toward the road leading to the Harpers' house without another word and set out at a brisk pace.

Ben's mind was spinning. More than anything, he wanted to ask his grandfather questions about what had just happened. He'd seen Enzo give Dominus Nash a purse right before everything had turned against them. Objectively, he knew that Nash had been bribed, but for some reason he couldn't reconcile that fact with his sense of morality. Law was supposed to be fair and impartial, not for sale.

He walked miserably past the onlookers muttering his grandfather's name in hushed tones. Whatever the final outcome of this day, Ben knew that his family's reputation, and therefore his family's business, had just been destroyed. A welling sense of injustice began to build in his belly.

They were taken up the hill overlooking K Falls to a large and relatively new estate that had been confiscated by the Dragon Guard as their headquarters and barracks. Workers were busy finishing renovations clearly intended to make the place more secure and defensible.

"Take them to holding and schedule a transport to Rogue City for tomorrow," Nash said to one of her subordinates.

They were led to a small building away from the manor house and locked in a cell. Once inside, their bindings were removed by the jailer.

"What's going to happen to us?" Ben asked through the bars.

The jailer ignored him with a bemused grunt, ambling back to his small office. He closed the door and peered through the window at them for a moment before returning to his paperwork.

Cyril went to a bench against the stone wall and sat down, putting his face in his hands for a moment.

John began a careful but casual inspection of their cell.

"What are we going to do?" Ben asked in a harsh whisper.

"For now, we wait," Cyril said, sitting back and resting his head against the wall.

"Wait for what?"

"To see what they do next," Cyril said. "This cell is pretty solidly built, so I doubt we could break out without drawing attention. Besides, there may be an opportunity to bribe one of the Dragon Guard when they transport us."

John looked skeptically over his shoulder at Cyril.

"I know it's a long shot, but it beats trying to fight our way out without weapons."

John nodded, seeming to consider Cyril's words but offering none of his own.

"Why are they taking us to Rogue City?" Ben asked.

"That's where the priest is," Cyril said. "He's the regional governor and judge. He'll decide our fate."

"What will they do to us?"

"That's hard to say, but it won't be good."

Ben fell silent, staring at the ground for a few minutes while he thought about the events of the day. "This is all so wrong," he said. "How can they do this to us? We were just protecting Imogen. And everybody saw Nash take Enzo's money. I thought the law was supposed to protect people."

"It is," Cyril said. "Just not the people you think it's supposed to protect."

"What's that mean?"

"Think about it for a moment and then you tell me."

Ben frowned, his anger starting to well up inside him again. "It didn't protect anybody," he said with a look of disgust.

"On the contrary … it protected Enzo."

"But he sold Imogen's baby and attacked our home," Ben said. "He's the criminal—we're innocent."

Cyril smiled sadly, closing his eyes and leaning his head back against the wall.

Ben stood there staring at his grandfather, waiting for some further explanation. When none was forthcoming, he threw his arms up in exasperation. "Why would the law protect him and not us?"

Cyril opened his eyes and held his grandson for a moment with a stern look before answering. "Because he paid them."

Ben opened his mouth to say something, but stopped, turning away from his grandfather.

"Hey!" he shouted to the jailer.

The man looked up, just his eyes and his balding head visible through the window.

"We didn't do anything wrong," Ben yelled, loudly enough to be heard through the window.

"Stop it!" Cyril snapped, coming to his feet. "You can't reason with these people and trying to will only get us into more trouble."

"But—"

"No 'buts' … these people serve the wyrm. He's a tyrant and a monster who wants to rule over everyone, everywhere, so every single thing these people do is done to further that end and nothing else."

Ben stood mute, trying to reconcile his conscience with the truth of reality.

"After we're out, then what?" John asked, leaning his back against the bars.

"I'm going to get my daughter and my grandson," Cyril said.

John nodded approvingly, then stretched out on a bench and closed his eyes.

"How are we going to do that?" Ben asked.

Cyril just smiled mirthlessly. He returned to the bench, lying down and closing his eyes as well.

"Why won't you tell me your plan?" Ben asked, whispering again.

"To protect you," Cyril said, opening his eyes and forestalling more questions with a look. "You should get some rest." He motioned to the vacant bench along the side wall.

Ben huffed, shaking his head. When Cyril closed his eyes again, Ben sat down. Less than a minute passed before another question came to mind.

"What was that all about with Hound anyway?"

"Rufus is going to find Frank and tell him about our arrest," Cyril said without opening his eyes.

"A lot of good that'll do," Ben muttered.

"Your brother can always be trusted to do what he thinks is best for him," Cyril said. "It won't take him long to figure out that we don't have a future here. After that, he and Rufus will take steps to help us because Frank knows he's far better off with us than he would be on his own."

"But why would Hound help us? He's a thug and a bully."

Cyril chuckled. "I can't argue with that, but he's not evil … and he is a good man in a fight."

"That still doesn't explain why he'd risk his neck for us."

"Someday I'll tell you why, but not today."

Ben sighed with exasperation.

Cyril opened his eyes again. "Once we're free, we're going to be on the run. You're going to need your rest. Lie down and stop asking questions."

He did as he was told, albeit reluctantly. He was lying on the bench, staring at the ceiling when he heard someone enter the front door of the building. Ben sat up, then got to his feet and went to the bars when a man approached the cell. The brand on his left cheek said he was Dragon Guard, but he wasn't wearing the distinctive black armor that Nash and her soldiers wore. Instead, he was dressed in a deep-red tunic with a dragon rune emblazoned in gold over the left side of his chest.

The man looked through the bars at each of them like they were meat. "Name?"

"We didn't do anything wrong," Ben said.

Cyril came to his feet and was at Ben's side in a matter of moments.

"Boy, we can do this one of two ways," the man said. "You can answer my questions or I can beat the answers out of you."

"That won't be necessary," Cyril said amiably, taking Ben by the elbow and silencing him with a firm grip. "My grandson's name is Benjamin Boyce. My name is Cyril Smith."

The Dragon Guard wrote both names down on his clipboard.

"And you?"

"John Durt," the Highwayman said, without opening his eyes.

The Dragon Guard looked at him and snorted softly before writing his name down and turning away from the cell.

"Pardon me, sir," Cyril said, waiting for the man to turn back to them. "We're unfamiliar with the system of justice provided by the dragon. Would you tell us how this process works?"

The man sighed wearily, then shrugged. "You'll be taken to the priest. He will hear the charges against you and dispense justice."

"What form is justice likely to take?"

"You'll probably be sold to House Adara and put to work on the railroad."

"You mean like slaves?" Ben said, despite the grip his grandfather had on his arm.

"Exactly like slaves," he said. "And you should be thankful that there's work for you to do. If there wasn't, you'd probably burn for this."

"For what? We didn't do anything wrong," Ben said, wrenching his arm away from Cyril and gripping the bars.

The Dragon Guard looked at his clipboard and frowned. "Says here that you abducted a woman of high standing and held her against her will."

"That's a lie! She's family. She came home to us."

He shrugged indifferently. "That's not what it says here." He waved his clipboard at them and left without another word.

Cyril turned Ben toward him and looked him in the eye with a measure of sternness that was usually reserved for the most serious transgressions.

"You have to stop," he said. "Reason and morality have no power here. Truth matters for nothing with these people. All you're doing is antagonizing them. You're liable to get yourself beaten."

"If you knew these people were so bad, then why did we stay here? Why didn't we leave before they took over?"

Cyril shrugged helplessly. "Imogen," he said, returning to the bench. "I couldn't stand the thought that she might come home and find us gone."

Ben closed his eyes and nodded to himself. At least he could understand that part of his grandfather's reasoning. He went back to the bench and lay down without another word.

Chapter 5

When Frank saw Hound coming through the door of the diner, he knew at a glance that something was wrong. Under normal circumstances, Rufus would have smiled with mischief at seeing Frank with Britney, but today his face was all business.

"What's wrong?" Britney asked when Frank stopped telling his story.

"Oh, a friend of mine just walked in," he said, never looking away from Hound. "Would you mind if I had a word with him?"

"Of course not," she said, turning around to see Frank's friend.

He squeezed her hand to bring her attention back to him. "I won't be but a minute."

She smiled, waggling a fork at him. "Don't be too long or there won't be any pie left for you."

He got up and headed toward Hound. "What's going on?" he asked.

Rufus stepped outside, motioning for Frank to follow him. He said quietly, "Your grandfather and brother have been arrested by the Dragon Guard."

"What for?"

"Not sure, but I saw Imogen being taken away by that dandy of a husband she's got. Looked like she'd been beaten."

Frank frowned, shaking his head slightly. "None of this makes any sense."

"Sense or not, Cyril and Ben are locked up on top of the hill," Hound said. "I've been watching the wyrm's men since they got here. They usually take their prisoners to Rogue City. I figure that's our best chance to break them out."

"Whoa ... you want to attack the Dragon Guard?"

"How else are we going to get them out?"

Frank looked over his shoulder through the diner's window at Britney, holding up a finger.

She nodded with a smile.

"I have an idea that doesn't involve getting lit on fire," Frank said. "I know a guy who has standing with the Dragon Guard. He's in town and he owes me a favor. With his help, I bet I can get them released."

"Uh huh," Hound said.

"Once they're out, my grandfather will want to go after Imogen. You go to the house and get some supplies together and load the coal hopper on the boat. We'll make better time on the water than on the road. Maybe we can get some horses at Rocky Point."

"You sure about this, Frank?"

"I really think it's our best option."

"All right. But if your plan doesn't work, we'll do it my way."

"Agreed."

Rufus watched him return to the table before heading off toward the store.

Frank sat down with his best mask of concern.

"What's wrong?" Britney asked.

He shook his head. "It's nothing for you to worry about."

She took his hand and squeezed it. "Look at me," she said.

He looked up after a moment's hesitation.

"Tell me."

He sighed, shaking his head in dismay. "My grandfather and brother were just arrested."

"What for?" Her hand tightened around his.

"I'm not really sure. Honestly, it all sounds like a big misunderstanding, but I won't know for certain until I go up the hill and talk to the Dragon Guard." He looked back down at the table.

"Your grandfather and Ben have always been so nice to me. I can't imagine what they might have done."

Frank just shook his head, wiping his face clean before looking up at her.

"I guess Imogen was back in town and her husband came to get her," he said. "Rufus said she looked like she'd been beaten."

"Oh God. That's horrible."

"Yeah, but it might explain what happened."

"Well ... tell me," Britney said after he fell silent again.

"It's just that ... well, Ben has a temper. If he thought that someone had hurt Imogen, he probably beat them up. Imogen's husband, Enzo, is from a respected family in Rogue City. If Ben roughed him up—"

"That's hard for me to imagine. Ben has always been so gentle and soft-spoken."

Frank nodded. "Most of the time he is." He went silent again.

"What are you going to do?"

Frank shrugged helplessly. "I'm not sure. The Dragon Guard won't even hear me out because I don't have standing."

After a few moments, Britney said, "I do."

Frank looked up, confusion and hope in his watery eyes. "I don't understand."

"My father is an advocate recognized by the Dragon Guard."

He took her hands, shaking his head. "Britney, I couldn't ask you to get involved in this."

"But I want to help."

He looked back down at the table, seeming to work through an inner struggle. "Maybe ..." he said, shaking his head a moment later and falling silent.

"We could talk to my father."

Frank winced. "He's a busy man, Britney. I'd hate to take such a trivial matter to him. Besides, we probably couldn't afford his rates."

"There must be something we can do."

"If I could just talk to them, I'm sure I could straighten this whole thing out," Frank said. "But without standing, I won't even get through the door."

"Like I said, I have standing," Britney said, digging into her purse and withdrawing a small dragon broach. "My father gave me this."

"You would help me?"

She took his hands in hers. "Of course."

"It would mean everything to me, Britney. They're the only family I've got."

"Well, let's go then," she said with a smile.

"Thank you," Frank said. "Let me go pay the bill."

He fished two silver drakes from his pocket and laid them on the counter. The cashier frowned at the slightly iridescent coins but took them without a word.

On their way up the hill, Frank fell silent.

Britney walked quietly by his side for several minutes. Then she said, "You must be so worried."

He nodded, seeming to snap out of a trance. "I'm sorry. I didn't mean to ignore you."

"I understand. You're worried about your family. It's only natural."

He smiled at her, taking her hand as they walked. "I bet your father will be so proud of you."

"What do you mean?"

"Well, this is your first case. Once he sees how well you handle it, I'm sure he'll be impressed."

She smiled. "Do you really think so?"

"I'm certain of it."

Once they reached the compound gate, or what passed for a gate in the absence of a completed wall, Frank stopped and turned Britney toward him.

"Are you sure about this?"

"I am if you are."

He nodded and they approached the guard. Britney showed her dragon broach, and the bored-looking man waved them inside without a word.

"That looks like the place," Frank said, guiding her toward the holding building. He opened the door and followed her inside.

There was a long counter separating the front of the room from the office area beyond. Three desks faced the counter with a single door behind them. A man dressed in a deep-red tunic sat at the middle desk doing paperwork. He didn't look up when they entered and continued to ignore them when they stopped at the counter.

"Excuse me, sir," Britney said.

He kept writing without looking up.

She started to say something else but stopped when Frank touched her arm. They waited for nearly a minute before the man looked up.

"State your business."

Britney showed her broach, and the man got to his feet, forcing a smile as he came around the desk to the counter. "How may I be of assistance, miss?"

"My name is Britney Harper."

Before Britney could continue, Frank interjected smoothly, "I'm Franklin Boyce. I'm told you have my grandfather and brother in custody."

The man retrieved a clipboard from his desk. After a moment he nodded. "Three men were brought in this morning: Benjamin Boyce, Cyril Smith, and John Durt."

"May I ask the charges?" Frank said.

"Kidnapping one Imogen Gervais."

"That just doesn't make any sense," Britney said. "Imogen is Cyril's daughter."

The man shrugged indifferently.

"I'm sure we can clear this up," Britney said. "Is there any way we can have them released?"

He sighed and went back to his desk, looking through a number of papers before finding the one he wanted.

"What did you say your name is again?"

"Harper ... Britney Harper."

"Says here that your family has standing," he said. "If you're willing to vouch for them and guarantee that they'll show up for trial in Rogue City, I can let them go."

Britney hesitated, looking at Frank with a hint of fear.

"Thank you so much, Britney," he said. "I can't tell you how much this means to me."

"Maybe I should ask my father before we do this," she said.

Frank's face fell, his charming smile transforming into a mask of despair in a moment. "I understand," he said. "I don't want to get you in trouble with your father. It's just ... well, I hate the idea of my grandfather spending the night in a jail cell."

She looked torn.

"Like you said," he continued, "this is all just a misunderstanding. I wouldn't want to bother your father when you could take care of it with a signature."

He waited for her to wrestle with her indecision until she took a breath to speak.

"It would mean so much to me," he whispered before she could object again.

She nodded, wincing a little and turning to the Dragon Guard.

"I'll vouch for them," she said.

The Dragon Guard looked from her to Frank and back to her again, then shrugged, pulling a stack of papers from under the counter.

"This will take a few minutes," he said, beginning to fill out the forms.

After the first three documents and several minutes, Frank started to fidget.

"Is there a problem?" the Dragon Guard said.

"No, not really," Frank said. "Is there any chance you could let them out while we complete the paperwork? I mean, it's just a formality now, right?" He looked down at the counter. The man's eyes followed. When he saw the silver drake, he nodded, slipping the coin into his pocket without a word and leafing through the papers already signed by Britney.

"Take this to the jailer and he'll release them."

"Will you be all right without me for a few minutes?" Frank asked.

"Of course," Britney said with a smile. "Go get your family."

"Thank you. You're an angel. I don't know how I can ever repay you."

"I'll think of something," she said, smiling more brightly.

Frank gave her hand a squeeze and returned her smile, lingering for a moment and holding her eyes with his before making his way around the counter and through the door to the back of the building. He scanned the room, smiling to himself when he saw the side door leading out into the compound's yard.

The jailer came out of his office when he saw him. "What's your business here?"

"Oh, I have a release order for these three," Frank said, handing the paper over.

Cyril, Ben, and John came to their feet but remained silent. The jailer scanned the document, took it into his office and stamped it, then retrieved the keys from a peg on the wall and opened the cell door.

"Looks like you're free to go," he said, handing Cyril the release order. "Show this to the guard at the gate."

Cyril nodded politely.

"Let's go out this way," Frank said, heading for the side door. All three followed silently but warily.

Once they were through the front gate and a block away from the compound, Cyril stopped. "How did you get us out?" he asked.

"I know a guy with standing who owed me a favor," Frank said with a shrug.

Cyril nodded, scrutinizing his grandson for a moment.

"Rufus is preparing the boat and gathering supplies," Frank said. "We have to hurry if we want to catch up with Imogen."

Cyril bit the inside of his lip and nodded again, turning back down the hill and heading for home at a brisk pace. They walked in silence for most of the way.

When they reached the bottom of the hill, Cyril looked at the Highwayman and asked, "Do you think they'll stop for the night?"

John nodded. "Just about have to. Lake of the Woods would be my guess."

"Can we make it there by dark?"

"Doubt it," John said. "More like midnight."

"That'll have to do," Cyril said, picking up the pace.

Chapter 6

When they arrived at the store, Zack was sitting on the bench out front petting Homer. He got to his feet so quickly that he left the ground by an inch.

"What happened? Where did you go? How come your door is broken?"

Cyril silenced him with a raised hand and a stern look.

"Thank you for looking after the store, but you should really go home now."

Zack frowned, crestfallen. "I found swords and a bow … and blood," he said. "What happened?"

"I'll tell you later," Ben said.

"What did you do with the weapons?" Cyril asked.

"I put them behind the counter."

"Good man." Cyril patted him on the shoulder. "I know you're curious, but you really need to go home now."

Zack looked to Ben helplessly. His frown grew even deeper when Ben nodded.

"You don't want any part of this," Ben said.

"But—"

Frank put his arm around Zack's shoulder and walked him toward the road. "Whatever we tell you would just get you in trouble," he said. "But I'll make you a deal. If you go straight home and don't tell anyone you saw us, a few days from now I'll tell you everything that happened."

When he started to protest, Frank silenced him with a disapproving look. "That's the deal, Zack. You go home right now and I'll tell you everything in a few days. Take it or leave it."

Zack nodded reluctantly, walking away slowly with his head down.

"What did you say to him?" Ben asked as Frank returned to the store.

"The truth. What else?"

Ben watched him walk into the store, then followed him.

"We have to hurry," Cyril said, emptying the cash box into a leather purse. "Gather what you need. We won't be coming back."

"Why not?" Frank said.

"We're going to take Imogen from those men—by force if necessary. I doubt the Dragon Guard will be terribly welcoming after that."

"Where will we go?" Frank said.

"Probably north," Cyril said, handing Ben his sword.

Frank noticed the blade already strapped to Cyril's waist. "Where did you get those?" he asked with a frown.

Cyril ignored him as he leafed through a ledger. He removed a sealed letter and slipped it into his pocket. "We have to move quickly. Go get your things—only what you need." He headed for the stairs at the back of the building.

"Where's *my* sword?" Frank called out after his grandfather. When Cyril didn't answer, Frank followed him in a hurry.

Ben sighed and headed for his room.

"Why does he get a sword and I don't?" Frank demanded once they were upstairs.

Cyril turned and took a step toward his grandson, his jaw clenched. "Ben knows how to use a sword—you never bothered to learn. Now go get your things, we don't have time for this." He turned away without another word, leaving Frank fuming.

While he packed his bag, Ben heard Frank trying to argue with their grandfather. The conversation was pretty one-sided since Cyril didn't bother to engage. Ben emerged from his room with his pack a moment before Cyril returned to the main room with his gear and a bag for Imogen.

Frank stood in the doorway of Cyril's room watching his grandfather walk away.

"Come on, Frank," Ben said. "We don't have much time."

He shook his head. "It's not fair. If you get a sword, I should get one too."

"I suspect you'll get your wish before this is over," Ben said, turning for the stairs before Frank could protest. He reached the dock just as Hound was taking Cyril's bag onboard.

"Surprised they didn't take this," John said, looking at his finely crafted recurve bow.

"I expected our blades to be gone as well," Cyril said.

"They don't like 'em, but they aren't outlawed … yet anyway," Hound said. "Just tech weapons, like this." He pulled back his long coat to reveal an old-fashioned revolver strapped to his hip.

"Not sure that qualifies as a tech weapon," John said with a grin.

"Low-tech is the new high-tech," Hound said. "I can make bullets for this. Try reloading a plasma rifle these days."

John nodded, conceding the point.

"Besides, I also have Bertha," Hound said with his crooked smile.

"Who's Bertha?" Ben asked.

"She's my shotgun, complete with a variety of rounds, not the least of which is a couple of grenades." He started to reach into his bag, but stopped when Cyril put a hand on his arm.

"Maybe it would be best if Bertha remained out of sight for now."

Hound nodded, scanning the lakeshore marketplace. There were plenty of dock workers within view.

"Probably wise," he said. "I'll show you later, kid."

Homer padded up to the boat and whined. "You know I don't like the water," he said.

"Yeah, but this is the only way to catch up with Imogen."

Homer grumbled before jumping into the boat and finding a spot out of the way to curl up. "If I fall in, I'm going to shake off all over you," he said, closing his eyes.

"We ready?" Hound asked.

"Waiting on Frank," Cyril said, looking toward the store.

Frank emerged a minute later, walking toward the boat without any hint of urgency.

Ben shook his head and sat down.

"You better move like you got a purpose," Hound yelled. "We're on a timeline here."

Frank didn't put much effort into it but he did pick up the pace. Hound helped him aboard and then shoved off a moment later.

"Whoa, can't you let me get settled first?"

"Apparently not," Hound said, pointing to the driver's seat. "Why don't you take us out ... Captain?"

Frank hesitated for a moment before taking his place at the controls. "Is the coal hopper full?"

"She's ready to go," Hound said.

"Let's make best speed for Rocky Point," Cyril said.

Frank glared at him, but nodded, opening the air intakes wide. The old steam-powered engine started to belch smoke into the air as the boat slowly gained speed. Within a few minutes, they were powering up the shoreline of the lake that K Falls took its name from.

Ben managed to hold his tongue until they were in open water. Finally he said, "So what's the plan?"

Cyril shrugged. "Our course will be dictated more by events and circumstances than any plan we might make."

Ben sighed.

"We'll get horses at Rocky Point and head for Rogue City," Cyril said. "Once we catch up with them, we'll take Imogen back and flee north."

"But how?"

"That's where the events and circumstances come in," Cyril said.

Ben frowned, taking a moment to scratch Homer's ears.

"What about Enzo?"

"What about him?"

Ben looked up at his grandfather and set his jaw. "We should kill him."

Cyril nodded, seeming to consider Ben's words.

"And would you be the one to end his life? Will you let him mark your soul? Is he really worth that?"

"He deserves it," Ben said.

"Perhaps he does," Cyril said. "But that has little bearing on the guilt you would suffer for having killed him."

Frank snorted derisively, but said nothing.

"So we just let him get away with what he's done?"

Cyril shrugged.

"That doesn't seem right."

"What Enzo has done is wrong," Cyril said. "Should we compound his crime with one of our own?"

"How is justice a crime?"

"Justice isn't—killing often is. Don't be so hasty to take what you can never return."

"But—"

Cyril stopped him with a raised hand. "I'm not trying to defend Enzo. His actions are indefensible. I'm trying to protect you."

"From what?"

Cyril smiled gently, marshalling his thoughts. "Throughout history, soldiers have been commanded to kill innocent people. Most of these men were just ordinary people—until they took innocent lives. Once they'd killed the defenseless, they likely felt crushing guilt and remorse for the crime they had committed, only to be commanded by their leaders to repeat their crime again and again. Each time they stepped over the line of their conscience, the line moved, until one day it simply vanished altogether. I don't want to see you start down that path."

"What if Enzo tries to kill one of us?"

"Killing in defense is different than murder," Cyril said. "It may be that we will kill Enzo ... but that's not our purpose."

"Once we have Imogen, won't he just come after her?"

"Probably, but I doubt he'll be willing to pursue us past the markers."

Ben looked startled, blinking a few times before the reality of their situation settled on him.

"What about the stalkers?" Frank asked before Ben could.

"We'll deal with them as they come," Cyril said.

"Those things aren't even alive," Frank said. "How do you kill something that's already dead?"

"I've done it," Hound said.

"You never told me that," Frank said.

"I've never told you a lot of things."

"So how did you kill it?"

"Bertha," Hound said with an offhanded shrug.

"A lot of good that does me," Frank said. "I don't even have a sword."

"I doubt a sword would do you any good," Hound said. "I watched a man impale a stalker on his blade only to have it land on top of him and rip his throat out. Then the damn thing turned on me with the blade still sticking right through it."

"What did you do?"

"I shot it with Bertha," Hound said like he was talking to an idiot child. "Force-fed the thing a shotgun grenade. Lucky shot, too. Hit it right in the mouth. It didn't get back up after that."

"What kind of stalker was it?" Ben asked.

"Mountain lion."

Homer whined.

"What about Imogen's baby?" Ben asked, absentmindedly patting Homer on the head.

"We'll come back for him," Cyril said.

"Wait ... Imogen has a baby?" Frank said.

Cyril nodded. "Enzo sold her son to the priest."

"Whoa ... I wouldn't want to be Enzo right about now," Frank said. "Imogen will probably kill him before we get there."

Cyril closed his eyes and bowed his head. "That is a distinct possibility."

"If the baby is in Rogue City, then why are we planning to go north outside the markers?" Frank asked. "Wouldn't it be better to stay on the road?"

"And face who-knows-how-many Dragon Guard?" Cyril asked. "No, we have a better chance in the wild."

"I'm not sure I buy that," Frank said. "At least the Dragon Guard are alive."

"True, but they're organized and they're well armed," Cyril said. "Stalkers are few and far between. I'd rather avoid a fight if we can."

Frank shook his head, turning his attention back to piloting the boat as they approached Rocky Point. The place was bustling with shipments from Rogue City being loaded onto boats for the final leg to K Falls. Frank eased the boat up to the dock attached to Cyril's warehouse. Rufus and John secured the lines while Frank closed the air intake, smothering the fire in the belly of the steam engine.

The building wasn't large but it was well built with stone walls and stout steel doors. Cyril scanned the docks, looking at the various carts and wagons being loaded and unloaded, before ushering everyone inside and closing the door behind them.

The faint odor of sulfur filled the air as he struck a match and lit a lamp. Shelves lined the walls, while pallets of dry goods stored in neat rows occupied the center of the building's cement floor.

"It's about three hours on foot to Lake of the Woods," Cyril said. "If we can get some horses, we can be there in an hour or so."

"Horses cost money," Frank said.

"Indeed they do," Cyril said with a smile, rummaging through a tool box on one of the shelves and coming up with a hammer. He went to the far corner of the room and counted several stone blocks to the right and several more up from the floor. After checking his count, he hit the wall a few times until the block began to crack. He removed several chunks of stone, then reached inside and retrieved a small plastic tube. Its end caps were screwed on tightly and sealed in place with a bead of glue. He wedged the tube between two nearby pallets and hit it with the hammer until it split open, revealing a heavy leather bag inside.

"You've had that the whole time?" Frank asked.

Without answering, Cyril removed several gold coins and handed them to Ben.

"You and John go see if you can buy some horses. Frank, I need you and Rufus to fill the boat's hopper and make her ready ... we might need her in a few days."

"Why would you keep all that money to yourself?" Frank demanded. "We could have used it."

"For what, exactly?" Cyril asked, stepping toward his grandson. "You have always had food, shelter, and clothing. How might you have spent my money?"

Frank clenched his jaw and frowned but remained silent.

"Listen well," Cyril said. "The coming days will be difficult enough without you constantly questioning things you have no right to question."

Frank composed himself and shook his head sadly. "I've worked every day to keep your store afloat for a pittance of a wage," he said. "I spent my last coin to get you out of jail and still you don't trust me with important family business. I guess I just don't understand. I mean, I know Ben is your favorite, but I'm still your grandson."

Ben shook his head and headed for the door, trailing John and Homer with him.

"We don't have time for this, Frank," Cyril said. "Go make the boat ready while I see about finding you a weapon."

"What kind of—"

Cyril stopped him with a raised hand and a stern look. "The boat."

"Come on, Frank," Hound said, taking him by the arm and turning him away from Cyril. "We have work to do."

Frank went with Hound more because of the firm grip on his arm than anything else. Once outside, he snorted in disgust. "I don't know why he had to keep all that gold hidden from me," he said, heading toward the boat.

"Probably 'cuz he didn't want you to drink it," Hound said with a look of mischief.

"Doesn't seem right. All this time, my grandfather's had money that we could have put to good use."

"By 'we' you mean 'you,' and by 'good use' you mean 'blowing it on whores and whisky,' right?"

Frank couldn't help but smile. "I would've shared."

"I'm pretty sure that's why Cyril kept it a secret," Hound said. "Now, help me tie off these lines more securely and get that coal hopper open."

Frank hesitated just long enough to draw a glare from Hound before going to work. Once the boat was secured, they returned to the warehouse and started loading a cart with coal from the storage bin in the corner. Two trips later, with the hopper nearly full, the sound of a horse on the road filtered through the fir trees.

"Looks like your brother's friend," Hound said when Zack came into view.

"I'd better go find out what he wants before my grandfather sees him," Frank said, leaving Hound to finish with the boat.

Frank trotted up the dock, waving for Zack to stop before he reached the warehouse. The boy and his horse were both winded.

"What are you doing here?" Frank whispered harshly, taking the reins and leading the horse back up the road and out of view.

"The Dragon Guard are looking for you," Zack said in a rush, a bit too loudly for Frank's taste.

"What are you talking about?" he asked, motioning for Zack to dismount.

"I didn't go home like you said. I hid in the bushes and watched you load your boat and head north."

"And?" Frank asked, looking around warily while Zack caught his breath.

"The Dragon Guard showed up a while later and found me. They wanted to know where you went—said that you broke out of jail."

"Oh shit," Frank said, scanning the road for any hint of pursuit. "What did you tell them?"

"Nothing ... at least not very much. You wouldn't tell me what happened so there wasn't much I could tell."

"What, exactly, did you tell them?"

"Just that you left by boat."

"Goddamn it, Zack."

"What did you want me to do? The Dragon Guard scare the hell out of me."

"Did they say anything else?"

"No, not really, just that Britney got arrested for helping you escape."

Frank grabbed his hair with both hands and turned away from Zack before turning back quickly and taking him by the shoulders.

"You have to go. Right now!"

"But I came all this way to warn you. I want to know what's going on."

"No, you have to go."

"But why?"

"For starters, because if my grandfather sees you, he's going to kick your ass."

"But, I just want to help."

"Trust me when I tell you, you don't want any part of this. Just go home."

"What about Britney? If you come back, they'll probably let her go."

"Britney will be all right," Frank said. "Her father is an important man. Look, Imogen came home to get away from her husband because he beats her. He bribed the Dragon Guard to arrest my grandfather and brother, then tied Imogen up for the trip back to Rogue City. We're going after her. That's all I can tell you right now."

"Oh ... I like Imogen. She's pretty."

Frank closed his eyes and sighed. "If you come with us, the Dragon Guard will be after you too."

"I hadn't thought about it like that."

"I have to get back to the dock. Just remember, if my grandfather sees you, he'll knock you on your ass."

Zack nodded dejectedly and took the reins. After a few steps, he looked back, but continued on toward K Falls when he saw Frank watching him.

"What did he want?" Hound asked when Frank returned to the boat.

"To be included."

Hound snorted and shook his head. "The kid has no idea."

Frank did a quick inspection of the boat before taking the key and heading back to the warehouse.

Cyril had a small pile of supplies waiting for them. "Top off your packs," he said. "We might have to make do in the wild for several days."

He pointed to a bundle atop another pallet. Frank frowned as he unrolled it and found a sturdy leather belt with a long knife and a hatchet that looked more like a tomahawk upon further inspection.

"What am I supposed to do with these?" Frank asked.

"You wanted a weapon. I just gave you two."

"May I?" Hound said, taking the hatchet without waiting for Frank to give permission. He stepped outside and hurled it at a big cedar thirty feet away, burying the blade deeply into the heavy bark. "Not bad," he said. "With a bit of practice, you might be dangerous with that thing."

"Huh," Frank said. "I didn't know an axe could be thrown like that." He went to the tree and struggled for a moment to extract his new weapon, finally putting his foot against the trunk and nearly falling when the blade came free.

Ben and John returned a few moments later.

"No one would sell," Ben said.

"Damn," Cyril said. "I guess we're on foot. Load your packs up and we'll head out. Oh, did you remember to drop that letter into the post for me?"

"Yes," Ben said, nodding. "Who's up in the Deschutes Territory?"

"Just an old friend," Cyril said.

Chapter 7

"How often do the Dragon Guard patrol this road?" Cyril asked as they set out.

"Once a day," John said, adjusting his pack.

"It's pretty close to evening … it's a good bet they've already come this way," Cyril said. "If we hear horses, everyone get into the woods and hide."

The road was cracked and broken. A strangely angular spider's web of light green moss decorated both sides of the pavement like the filigreed hem of a robe. Bits of moss clung to the cracks in the middle of the road where the cart wheels and horse hoofs had missed them.

Firs and cedars lined the sides of the road, filling the crisp air with a sweet fresh smell. The undergrowth was sparse and littered with fallen trees in various stages of decomposition. Boulders, pockmarked with lichen, were scattered across the forest floor.

"Is that a marker?" Ben asked, stopping to point through the trees.

John peered into the forest and nodded, turning back to the road without a word.

Ben lingered for a moment. The marker was nothing more than a stone pillar six feet tall and two feet around. He trotted to catch up when the rest of the party kept walking.

"Doesn't look like much. I wonder how they keep the stalkers out."

"Magic," John said.

"Well, I know that. But how?"

"The markers are enchanted by the priests," Cyril said. "Each one bears a series of dragon runes on the far side. The stalkers can sense them."

Ben fell silent, looking at a tree with clumps of thick green moss on one side.

"I like the way the forest smells," Homer said.

Ben smiled at his dog. Homer was always pleased by the simple things.

While they walked, Ben thought about magic and the dragon. He had so many questions, but he knew that answers would not be forthcoming. Growing up, he'd hounded his grandfather with his curiosity about everything. Cyril had always been willing to indulge his questions on just about every topic … except magic.

Ben always felt, almost intuitively, that Cyril knew more about the subject than he would say. But all his grandfather had ever offered was that magic wouldn't be magic if we understood it—it would be science.

In light of recent events, he decided to try again.

"How does magic work, Grandpa?"

Cyril looked over to his grandson and smiled sadly, nodding to himself as if some prerequisite had been met. He took a few moments to formulate his thoughts, as was his habit when Ben asked questions with particularly complicated answers.

"Magic is largely a function of the presence of dragons, though not exclusively so. In fact, every culture in human history has stories of wizards and witches."

Hound snorted dismissively.

"You doubt the existence of magic?" Cyril asked.

"Well, not now," Hound said. "I buy the part about the dragons, but myths and legends are just that."

"Perhaps I would agree if we were talking about a handful of stories," Cyril said, "but we aren't. When every culture in the world for thousands of years has handed down similar stories, it becomes more difficult to dismiss the underlying concept."

"If magic was here before the dragons, then why wasn't it commonplace?" Hound asked.

"Because it requires a level of will that most people simply don't have," Cyril said.

Ben felt a tingle of dread in his spine, but he couldn't quite place why. "What does willpower have to do with magic?" he asked.

"Everything," Cyril said. "Will is the very essence of magic."

"I thought dragons were the essence of magic," Frank said.

"In one sense they are. Dragons have a different relationship with reality than we do," Cyril said. "A dragon can perceive and interact with other planes of existence and with the beings that live there. Dragon magic is largely the product of those interactions and the bargains made with the denizens of those worlds."

"Then how do the priests cast spells?" Ben asked.

"That is the crux of the matter, isn't it?" Cyril said. "As it turns out, any conscious being with sufficient will and knowledge has the ability to cast spells when in the proximity of a dragon or a dragon artifact."

"You mean I could cast spells if I had a dragon artifact?" Frank asked, suddenly very interested in the direction the conversation was going.

"What's a dragon artifact?" Hound asked.

"Any part of a dragon, from scale to bone to blood, is an artifact. And yes, with the right knowledge anyone can use magic—if they have an artifact."

"So if I find a pile of dragon shit, that makes me a wizard?" Hound said.

Cyril chuckled, shaking his head. "No. Though I have heard stories of people using excrement to wield magic, it rarely turns out well for them. Besides, you don't have the knowledge. Without that, attempting to bargain with beings from other realms is usually fatal."

"So how did the real Wizard do it?" Ben asked. "How did he fight the dragons with magic?"

Cyril fell silent, shrugging and shaking his head.

Homer barked softly. "I smell horses."

"We have to get off the road," Ben said.

Cyril looked to his grandson and nodded agreement without a word, heading through the trees toward a cluster of boulders entirely overgrown with moss.

"Why?" Frank said. "We're the only ones here."

"Listen," John said, cocking his head into the gentle breeze. "Horses, maybe six or seven. Step lightly. We don't want to leave them a trail."

Everyone crouched behind the boulders. Ben found himself holding his breath as the clip-clop of horses grew louder.

John lay down on his belly, peeking around a boulder, a fallen fir bough draped over his head.

Frank started to poke his head up to get a look, but Hound pulled him back down and admonished him with a glare. In the space of two minutes the horses had passed and the sound of hoof on broken pavement was fading into the distance.

John sat up and frowned. "I wonder why they have your friend."

All eyes turned to the Highwayman.

"Zack was riding with one of the Dragon Guard. His hands were tied to the saddle horn."

Cyril closed his eyes and shook his head.

"Why would they have Zack?" Ben asked.

Hound looked at Frank with a withering glare.

"What?" Frank said.

"Are you going to tell them or am I?"

"Oh, that," Frank said, offhandedly. "Zack followed us to Rocky Point. I sent him home."

"What?" Ben said.

"Why didn't you tell me?" Cyril said. "And what, exactly, did you tell him?"

"I didn't see the point in telling you," Frank said. "I told him to go home and he left—nothing to tell."

"What did you tell him, Frank?" Cyril demanded.

Frank shrugged helplessly, shaking his head, his hands up and open.

"And why would they even be following us?" Ben asked.

"Maybe they're not," Frank said.

"Nash was leading them," John said. "Seems like too much of a coincidence."

"What did you tell Zack?" Cyril asked again.

"Nothing, really. Just that we were going to get Imogen back."

"Damn it, Frank. Why do you think I kept Zack in the dark?"

"I had to tell him something to get him to leave, so I told him the truth," Frank said.

"That still doesn't explain why they're following us in the first place," Ben said.

"How should I know? Are we going to stand here and argue or go get Imogen? We're losing daylight."

"What aren't you telling us?" Cyril said.

"Nothing!" Frank said, turning away angrily and heading back to the road.

"He's right about the light," John said, looking at the sky.

"How much farther?" Cyril asked.

"Couple hours, more in the dark."

They caught up to Frank a few minutes later. He was walking fast and breathing heavily from the exertion.

Cyril stopped him with a hand on his arm, turning him around when he tried to pull away. "Listen to me. We're in great danger here. Our lives are at risk. You can't be keeping things from us."

"I didn't think it was important," Frank said.

"Maybe it is, maybe is isn't," Cyril said. "Either way, we need to know."

"All right," Frank said, holding his hands up in surrender. "Can we go now?"

Cyril scrutinized him for a moment before nodding.

As the light fell, the forest seemed to close in. All of the sounds that added to the sense of natural beauty during the day transformed the night into a threatening and foreboding place. Shadows cast by the sliver of moonlight seemed to move of their own volition. Ben was already nervous when a howl of frustration and rage shattered what little calm he had left. It sounded like a wolf at first but became a scream of such unnatural fury and pain that Ben froze to the spot.

"What the hell was that?" Frank whispered.

"Stalker," John said.

Homer whined softly.

"What do we do?" Ben said.

"Nothing," John said. "We're inside the markers."

"How much farther?" Cyril asked.

"An hour or so."

"We'll make better time with some light," Cyril said as he took a candle lantern out of his pack.

"Won't that give us away?" Frank asked.

"Not until we get closer."

As they moved through the night, the dim glow of Cyril's lamp did little to calm Ben's nerves. He replayed the sound of the stalker in his mind, trying to reconcile his understanding of reality with the wholly alien shriek of the beast in the darkness.

He jumped when Cyril put a hand on his shoulder.

"Dwelling on it won't help."

"I know, but I don't know how to un-hear that sound."

"So don't try. Simply recognize it for what it is."

"That's just it," Ben said. "Nothing of this world is supposed to make a noise like that."

"And therein lies its power to evoke fear," Cyril said. "The stalkers may look like animals, but they're not. The unnatural quality of their shriek is the product of dark and terrible magic—and so is the fear you feel when you hear it."

"Are you trying to tell me that was a spell we just heard?" Hound asked.

"Not a spell, but magic nonetheless."

"How do you know all of this?" Frank asked.

Cyril shrugged. "I'm an old man. I lived through the Dragon War."

"You never talk about it," Ben said.

"No, I don't."

"Quiet," John said, stopping them with the urgency of his whisper. "We're getting close."

Cyril snuffed out his light, plunging the world into darkness so inky black that Ben felt a flutter of fear. He swallowed hard and willed himself to focus on his breathing, centering himself with one of the many meditative exercises that his grandfather had taught him over the years. Several slow deep breaths later, his fear receded. He smiled to himself in the dark, noting how well the technique actually worked.

"See the light?" John asked.

"I do," Homer said. "I smell horses too … and food."

"We're getting close," Ben said, his eyes adjusting enough to see the flicker of firelight through the trees.

"Slow and quiet," Cyril said. "We'll stick to the south edge of the road until we get closer, then we'll move into the forest."

As they crept along and drew nearer to the Lake of the Woods waypoint, they could see the growing light from several fires and torches. When they rounded a bend in the road, the campground came into clear view not five hundred feet away.

Cyril motioned for John to lead them into the forest. They moved even more slowly, taking pains to avoid making noise. When they came to a fallen log just inside the wood line, they stopped.

From their position they could see the Dragon Guard barracks off to the side of the camp. The small building was built of stone with stout doors. A low wall ringing the roof provided cover for the two sentinels standing watch.

Three parties were camped in the area, each circled around blazing fire pits. Two had wagons or carts parked nearby. Cyril pointed to the third.

John nodded, scanning the wood line and pointing to a string of boulders scattered just inside the trees at a point close to the camp in question. He set out without a word, moving into the cover of the forest's shadows, slipping through the night like a ghost.

Ben found himself struggling to move quietly. Every step seemed to find a dry twig or branch. Fortunately, the occupants of the camp were sufficiently preoccupied that they didn't notice.

When they reached the boulders, John pointed through the dim firelight. All eyes fell on Imogen. She was sitting with her back to a hitching post just outside the warmth of the fire. Her hands were bound to the post, a blanket was draped over her shoulders. Enzo and one of his men were sitting closer to the flames, talking quietly while the rest of his men appeared to be sleeping.

"I can probably get close without being noticed," John whispered.

"Then what?" Frank asked.

"Then we fight," Hound said.

"I'd prefer to cut her loose and slip away without notice," Cyril said, scanning the campground.

They watched as Enzo got up from the fire and stretched. He squatted down in front of Imogen and said, "As much as I'd like to share my bed with you tonight, you're in far too foul a mood." He adjusted the blanket around her shoulders and smiled. "Are you warm enough, my darling?"

"Go to hell," she snapped.

He shook his head sadly. "We were so happy. I hate that you can't get past this."

"Get past this? Are you fucking kidding me? You stole my baby!"

The Dragon Guard atop the barracks looked over toward them as their conversation became more heated but made no move to intervene.

"He was *our* baby, and his loss pains me as much as it does you."

"Liar! Everything about you is a lie. But the biggest lie of all is the idea that I ever loved you. What I felt for you was a fraud, just like you. It was nothing but smoke and mirrors—a spell cast by your precious priest."

Enzo smiled, nodding agreement. "And you'll feel exactly the same way again, right after the priest works his magic on you. By day after tomorrow, this will all be a distant memory and we can get back to our life together."

"Not if I gut you before then," Imogen said.

"Which is precisely why you are going to spend the night tied to a post instead of in my bed," he said, patting her cheek and laughing at her attempt to bite his hand as he snatched it out of harm's way.

"Keep an eye on her," he said to his man before crawling into his tent.

John whispered, "I can take the man at the fire from here."

"No," Cyril said. "Let's wait awhile—let things get quiet."

"We could go get her and be out of their camp before they knew what hit them," Frank said.

"Perhaps," Cyril said, nodding. "But I'm concerned about Nash. She's here somewhere."

"You thinking trap?" Hound asked, scanning the camp with renewed interest.

Cyril nodded, settling in to watch.

"If she's even here, she probably doesn't care about us," Frank said.

Cyril stared at Frank until he began to fidget. "She wouldn't have had Zack tied to a horse unless she was after us," he said, "which raises the question: How exactly did you get us out of jail?"

"I told you, I know a guy who owed me a favor."

"Looks like the guard is getting sleepy," John said, drawing everyone's attention back to the camp.

"I have an idea," Ben said, offering his knife to Homer. "Take this to Imogen," he said silently. "Go get Imogen, boy," he said aloud.

"You know I hate it when you talk to me like a dog," Homer said, taking the knife by the handle and vanishing into the darkness.

"You're going to risk everything on your stupid dog?" Frank asked.

"He's not stupid," Ben muttered.

A few moments later, Homer seemingly materialized from the shadows, quietly placing the hilt of the knife in Imogen's hand.

She lifted her head and craned her neck to see behind her, smiling broadly when Homer licked her cheek. Then she scanned the campground to see if anyone was watching. Satisfied that Enzo's man was dozing by the warmth of the low fire, she went to work cutting the ropes binding her hands. A minute later she was free.

She started moving in a low crouch toward Enzo's tent.

"Stop her," Ben said.

Homer took Imogen's pant leg in his teeth and tugged. She stopped, frowning at him.

He wiggled, wagging his tail and turning toward the wood line.

Cyril stood up and motioned for her to come to him.

She hesitated for a moment, looking back at the tent, then to the man nodding by the fire before finally following Homer.

When she reached the forest, Cyril took her in his arms, hugging her without a word.

She looked around, smiling at her family. "You're all here."

"Where else would we be?" Ben said.

"Will you help me kill Enzo?"

"I will," John whispered.

Cyril held her at arm's length and shook his head gravely. "I know you have cause to want his death, but we have more pressing concerns right now."

"Like what?"

"Like your baby," Cyril said, holding her eyes. "If we attack Enzo, the Dragon Guard will be alerted and we'll be in a fight we probably can't win. We have to escape without notice if we are to have any chance of rescuing my youngest grandson."

She frowned but nodded.

"Good girl. Let's go," he said, motioning for John to lead the way.

They hadn't made it thirty steps into the forest when Enzo's man took notice of her absence.

"She's gone!" he shouted.

Ben stopped to look back, just barely able to see him through the trees.

The man looked around wildly and shouted again. "Wake up, the bitch is gone!"

Enzo came stumbling out of his tent.

"Don't call her that … she's still my wife," he admonished him. "And you were supposed to be watching her!" He picked up the severed bindings and held them in front of the man's face. "They're cut. She had help. Alert the Dragon Guard."

Ben turned away from the camp and hurried to catch up with the others.

"Where to?" John asked.

"North," Cyril said. "We have to get past the markers before they see us."

"Wasn't that stalker to the north?" Frank asked.

"Yes, I believe it was," Cyril said.

"Why would we go toward that thing?" Frank asked, stopping in his tracks.

"Because that is precisely the path they will not expect us to take," Cyril said without stopping.

When everyone else continued without hesitation, Frank hurried to catch up.

They reached the road just as a Dragon Guard mounted on horseback came around the bend, his dragon-fire rifle held in one hand like a lance, a tongue of blue flame a foot long burning from the barrel like the fire from a cutting torch. He saw them and charged with a battle cry.

"Take the horse," Cyril said.

John loosed his arrow.

The horse squealed in surprised pain and terror, rearing back and nearly throwing the Dragon Guard. His rifle discharged, sending a cone of bluish flame a hundred feet into the air and igniting the fir boughs on either side of the road with a whoosh, flooding the area with orange light.

"Run!" Cyril said.

The horse reared again, then toppled over, throwing the Dragon Guard to the uneven pavement.

Ben didn't look back. He focused on moving with as much speed as he could muster through the forest without tripping and falling on his face. He didn't even see the markers as they fled into the wilds, heading first due north up into the hills and then turning west and traveling parallel to the road.

Angry shouts filtered through the trees from the road below. The fire burned itself out within a few minutes, leaving only a column of smoke rising into the night sky to mark the place where they had nearly been burned to death.

"Where are we going?" Frank asked.

"If I remember correctly, the old Pacific Crest Trail intersects with the road just east of Lake of the Woods," Cyril said.

"That's right," John said. "It's a bit overgrown these days, but it's still an easier path than cutting a trail."

"Then what?" Frank asked.

"We go north" Cyril said. "I have a friend who lives on Mazama's south slope. He'll give us shelter."

"That's at least a full day on foot," John said.

"More like two, given the terrain," Cyril said. "Keep an eye out for a good place to stop for the night."

Chapter 8

"Did you hear that?" Frank whispered.

"Probably nothing," John said.

They had taken shelter under a thick stand of young fir trees crowded up against a cluster of boulders embedded in the side of a hill. It was cramped and cold, but Ben found himself dozing off, exhausted from the exertion and emotional ordeal of the day. The fear in Frank's voice woke him up in an instant. He waited, listening to the darkness for any hint of danger.

"What's out there?" he asked Homer.

Homer sniffed the air for a moment. "Nothing dangerous."

Ben tried to relax, focusing on his breathing to slow his racing heart. Within a few minutes he was calm enough to sleep, but his mind had started working again, turning over all of the possible dangers that they faced, invariably going to the worst-case scenario almost immediately. When he realized that he was working himself into a needless state of fear, he began to practice one of the meditations that his grandfather had taught him.

He pictured his lucky coin.

He had learned that when he quieted his mind and narrowed his focus to a single object, it never failed to leave him feeling calm and centered—provided he succeeded in keeping his mind fixed to the image of the coin.

At first, he had struggled to prevent his mind from wandering, but over time and with much practice, he'd learned to hold his attention steady. As simple a practice as it was, Ben found that he'd developed the ability to concentrate on a subject to the exclusion of all else—something that gave him insight that others seemed to lack. Often he would find that he lost all sense of self when he brought his mind to bear on a given object.

His grandfather called it "grace"—that state of being where subject and object became one. Ben had experienced it a few times, or at least he thought he had. It was an odd sensation since he only became aware that he'd achieved it after the fact.

When he'd told his grandfather about the experience the first time it had happened, Cyril had smiled with a knowing sense of pride. That alone was enough to propel him to continue the practice.

Now, many years later, he visualized the coin simply to calm his nerves and center his mind in the hopes that he might get a few hours of sleep before dawn and the grueling trek ahead of them.

He woke with a start, the fading image of his coin still in his mind. Everyone else had been startled awake as well. He could just make out the fear on their faces in the dim light of the coming day.

A howl in the distance transformed into an inhuman shriek.

"It's answering the horn," Hound said.

"Is that what woke us?" Cyril asked.

Hound nodded. "Sounded like it came from Lake of the Woods."

"What are you talking about?" Frank asked.

"The Dragon Guard are calling a stalker to them."

"What?" Frank said, his eyes going wide with renewed fear. Ben took a deep breath to settle his own nerves.

"I wondered about that," Cyril said, gathering his bedroll. "We have to move."

"Wondered about what?" Imogen asked.

"Whether the Dragon Guard could command the stalkers. Seems they can."

"What are we going to do?" Frank asked.

"Run," Cyril said.

"Sounds like that one used to be a wolf," John said. "Won't take long for it to pick up our scent."

"I know," Cyril said, hoisting his pack. "Gather your things. We don't have much time."

Ben didn't hesitate, hastily securing his blanket to his pack. He didn't know what his grandfather had planned, but he was certain that Cyril had something in mind. He was equally certain that any plan was better than nothing.

One by one, they emerged from the thicket into the gloaming of pre-dawn, equal measures of fear and fatigue on each and every face.

"We should get back inside the markers," Frank said. "It's our only hope."

"Like hell it is," Hound said, hoisting Bertha up like a trophy fish.

"You want to fight a stalker?!" Frank said. "Are you crazy?"

"Don't be a pussy," Hound said. "I got two grenade rounds and a few other surprises. So long as I see it coming, that thing doesn't stand a chance."

Frank opened his mouth to say something but nothing came out.

"Lead the way, John," Cyril said.

Finding his voice again, Frank said, "We have to get back inside the markers."

"Wouldn't do any good," Imogen said, her big brown eyes alight with the fear that everyone was feeling.

"Why not?"

She shook her head as if reconciling a memory with her inability to grasp the significance of it at the time. "I don't know why it didn't set off the alarm bells," she muttered, almost to herself.

Cyril looked at her, encouraging her to continue with a gesture.

"When Enzo and I were married, the priest had a stalker lying in the corner of the room, like a pet. It was a full-grown mountain lion, which would have terrified me if I'd been in my right mind. Thinking back, it was so much more frightening than just a big cat would've been. It was wrong in so many ways—its eyes were completely black, and it was gaunt, like it hadn't eaten in weeks." She shivered, closing her eyes tightly. "I can't explain it, but there was a darkness to it, an unnatural quality that makes my skin crawl just thinking about it."

"All the more reason to get inside the markers," Frank said.

"Don't you see?" Imogen said, opening her eyes and fixing them on Frank. "The stalkers obey the Dragon Guard. They can pass inside the markers when commanded."

Frank's jaw dropped, a look of horror spreading over his face.

Ben sympathized with his brother. He'd known that they were in trouble from the moment the Dragon Guard had taken them, but the full extent of their plight was just beginning to settle in, and it was terrifying.

But along with the fear, a sense of moral outrage began to build within him. He'd never put the two together. Now it seemed so monstrously clear—the stalkers were agents of the dragon, created for the purpose of terrorizing people into accepting the protection, and hence the rulership, of the dragon and his minions.

"Seems like the real question we have to ask is will they set the stalker loose to hunt us on its own or will they use it to lead a squad to us?" Hound said.

"That probably depends on how intent they are in returning Imogen to Enzo," Cyril said.

"His family is powerful in Rogue City," she said. "The priest—" She stopped talking, her eyes losing focus as horror and disgust spread across her face.

"What is it?" Cyril asked.

"The priest … he's not human. At least not anymore," she said. "Why didn't I see it before?"

"You did, it just didn't matter to you at the time because his magic was clouding your mind," Cyril said.

"What do you mean, he's not human?" Frank asked.

"His eyes were bright yellow and catlike, his fingernails were claws, and his skin was scaled like a snake's."

Cyril nodded. "A side effect of drinking dragon's blood. The priests become mules, transformed into something more than human but less than dragon. It sounds like this one is in the early stages of the transformation, which is fortunate for us, all things considered."

"How can that possibly be good?" Frank asked.

"As the transformation progresses, his power will grow. Right now, he's still more human than dragon. That'll make him easier to defeat, if it comes to that."

"You want to fight him? Didn't you hear Imogen? He has a stalker for a pet," Frank said, clearly exasperated.

"He also has my grandson," Cyril said.

Frank was again rendered speechless.

Ben considered the forces arrayed against them and measured them against the life of his newborn nephew ... and he found clarity. He knew that he would do whatever was necessary to help Imogen get her baby back. It wasn't even a choice. The child was family. The child was innocent and helpless. But more than all of that, his conscience demanded it of him. Through all of the fear and doubt, a calm gentle voice offered him the one honorable path before him ... and Ben resolved to walk that path, no matter the cost.

"What's his name?" he asked softly.

All eyes turned to him.

Imogen blinked tears onto her cheeks. "Robert," she whispered.

Cyril closed his eyes tightly, nodding to himself with a sad little smile. "Lead the way, John. We have work to do."

John set out through the sparse forest, picking a path that was at once easy to follow and hard to track. If their pursuers were human, they would have a hard time of it ... a wolf was another matter, and a stalker something else entirely.

Ben had heard stories about the creatures when they first started hunting in the area around K Falls. They could smell and see and hear better than any living animal. They were fast and tireless, vicious and relentless. Once a stalker was on the hunt, its prey could either kill it, find refuge within the markers, or be run down and ripped apart. Until now, it had always seemed odd to Ben that they didn't eat their kill. New understanding of their true purpose cleared up that point of confusion.

A howl ripped through the morning air, half wolf and half something else. This time, it came from the south. Everyone stepped up the pace. An hour after full light, they came to the trail and turned north. While the path was easier to negotiate than the forest, it was also steeper, ascending toward the east face of Mount McLaughlin.

"Why do you think the old man has been holding out on us?" Frank quietly asked Ben while they walked.

Ben shrugged and adjusted his pack. "I'm sure he has his reasons."

"He obviously knows more about magic than he ever let on. What possible reason could he have for keeping that from us? We must have asked a thousand questions about it over the years."

Ben shook his head, though he had a few ideas. Magic was just the sort of thing that Frank would be drawn to—easy power. For Ben, magic had always been a source of wonder and mystery, but he honestly wasn't sure what he'd do with it if he possessed it. Until yesterday, he'd never wanted or needed anything enough to warrant the use of such power.

"He was probably just trying to protect us," he said.

"Step it up," Hound said from behind them.

The trail rounded a bend and the ground fell away to the right. A steep slope of jagged rocks and boulders defined the landscape for several hundred feet to the forest floor below. To the left, the slope continued up toward the mountain.

Loose rocks littered the narrow trail, making the path treacherous. One wrong step and it would be a several-hundred-foot tumble to the bottom.

Another howl shattered the morning calm, much closer this time.

Ben froze. He wanted to run, to flee the danger, but thankfully he couldn't move. He had to remind himself to breathe, slowly and deeply.

"Out of the way!" Frank shouted from behind, panic and terror rushing his words as he shoved Ben, toppling him toward the edge. It seemed as if the world tipped over, the level ground hundreds of feet below rushing at him with terrifying clarity and detail. The moment stretched on, expanding in his mind, a thousand thoughts filling his awareness—all of them ending with a briefly painful, head-over-heels race to the ground, culminating in his inescapable death.

And then, just as quickly, he was yanked back from the brink and thrown against the upward side of the slope. Safe. Hound had grabbed his pack with one hand and tossed him like a doll on his way to stop Frank from his panicked flight.

Cyril beat him to it. Spinning around and seeing his grandson rushing toward him with unbridled fear, he set himself and struck Frank with the palm of his hand in the center of the chest right where the ribs meet the stomach, paralyzing his diaphragm and stunning him into instant submission. Then he followed through, knocking Frank backward with his shoulder and laying him down against the upward side of the path. He stepped over him and raced to Ben.

He said nothing, instead holding Ben's eyes for a moment and nodding to himself with a quiet sigh of relief. He stood abruptly, drawing his sword and motioning back the way they'd come. Hound unslung Bertha with a grim smile and brought the weapon to his shoulder. Ben tracked the direction of the barrel and his fear spiked again.

The stalker, a big grey wolf with black eyes and patches of mangy fur all over its body, was loping up the trail toward them, a single-minded need to kill seeming to radiate from its very presence.

But then it stopped, well out of range of Hound's shotgun—a fact that only served to heighten its frightfulness. It barked a few times, savagely and intensely. Each time, a sharp crack filled the air, and each time, fear flooded into Ben's stomach. Each bark, a statement of horrible intent.

It tipped its head back and howled, tearing into the calm air and into Ben's sanity, sending birds scattering and silencing the rest of the forest inhabitants.

"Why doesn't it attack?" Hound said, even his voice a bit unsteady.

"Because it knows that you'll kill it if it does," Cyril said.

"How can a wolf be that smart?" Imogen asked, her voice trembling.

"It's not a wolf—at least not anymore," Cyril said.

"You hit me," Frank croaked, still struggling to regain his breath.

"You panicked," Cyril said, without turning away from the stalker.

"And you almost knocked me off the edge," Ben said, shooting his brother a look.

"I didn't have any choice," Frank said, without looking up.

Ben ignored him, dropping his pack and drawing his sword.

"I don't like that thing," Homer said, from behind Ben. "It smells like it's dead. Dead things shouldn't be running around."

"Can't argue with that."

The twang of a bowstring announced John's attack. The arrow sailed true, hitting the creature in the haunch, driving deeply through it, the bladed head emerging just next to its tail, the feathered shaft jutting at an angle from its rump. The stalker snarled and barked, not in pain or fear, but with rage and unsatisfied bloodlust—but these barks didn't send shockwaves of fear through Ben like the others had. He frowned to himself, filing yet another question away for later reflection.

"Don't waste your arrows," Cyril said.

Hound slung Bertha and snatched up a rock the size of an apple, tossing it a foot into the air to gauge its weight before hurling it at the stalker with surprising accuracy. It bounced off the thing's head and elicited a growling snarl that brought every hair on Ben's body to rigid attention.

Hound picked up another rock and started toward the creature.

"Rufus!" Cyril snapped, but Hound ignored him.

Cyril followed, sword raised and at the ready.

The stalker came quickly, bounding toward Rufus with alarming speed. He threw the rock, a direct strike to the eye, sending a spray of blood onto the nearby rocks ... but the impact didn't even slow the beast down. Ben was mesmerized by its speed. It closed the distance before Hound could bring Bertha up and around, leaping at him with jaws snapping, crashing into him and knocking him back onto the trail. When the stalker landed on top of him, Hound managed to save himself from a quick death by jamming the stock of his shotgun into the beast's mouth.

As Rufus fell backward, Cyril danced lightly out of the way, whipping his sword around and stabbing the creature through the ribs and out the other side of the chest, pulling his blade out a moment later as he braced his foot against the beast's neck. It didn't seem to notice the grievous wound. Its single-minded focus was directed at Hound. A man of lesser strength wouldn't have been able to resist such a ferocious attack, but Hound matched the creature with a rage of his own, holding Bertha's stock in its mouth as he struggled to heave the beast off of him.

It began clawing at Hound's chest like a dog digging for a bone, tearing long gouges into his hardened leather breastplate until blood seeped through. Rufus shouted out in pain, his determination faltering with a slip of his focus. As the stalker bore down on Bertha, her stock began to crush and splinter, the creature's jaws coming dangerously close to Hound's face.

Ben reached the thing, half unaware of what he was doing, driven by a frantic need to protect his grandfather and Hound, half terrified by his own actions, and wholly propelled by his training and instinct. He stabbed the beast in the eye, a clean, hard thrust that drove the blade into its head and out the back of its skull. When the creature flinched away from the attack, Ben's sword slipped from his grasp. Cyril kicked the stalker in the side, forcing it to lose its balance and teeter over the edge of the trail. Hound rolled, using the shotgun to leverage the beast, and sent it tumbling down the boulder-strewn slope several hundred feet to the bottom, taking Ben's sword with it.

"Holy shit," Hound said, flopping onto his back. "Next time you tell me to stop, I think I might actually listen."

Cyril held out his hand and helped him to his feet.

Hound stood there, inspecting Bertha and shaking his head in disgust. "Look what that thing did to you, Girl," he muttered, blood trickling from the deep scratches on his chest.

"Never mind your shotgun," Cyril said. "Take off your armor. Your wounds need tending. There's no telling what kind of filth a beast like that has under its nails."

Frowning, Hound gently set his shotgun down and unbuckled his leather armor. The gouges were just deep enough to bleed. Cyril opened his pack and went to work cleaning and bandaging the wounds. Hound didn't flinch or complain, though Ben could tell from the tension in his face that it hurt.

"Can you walk?" Cyril asked when he'd finished.

Hound just smirked and got to his feet, albeit a bit unsteadily. He inspected his shotgun again, shaking his head sadly.

"Frank, I'm going to need that hatchet of yours."

"What for?"

Hound glared at him until he reluctantly handed over the axe. Several strokes later, Bertha's stock was gone, a crude, but serviceable pistol grip in its place. He handed Frank the axe and went to work restringing Bertha's strap.

"We should be going," John said, pointing down the slope.

Ben wasn't sure what he was seeing until John handed him a monocular. He put it to his eye and felt his heartbeat accelerate as he watched the stalker lope into the woods, headed in the direction that they were going. It still had his sword sticking clear through its head.

"How is that possible?" Ben asked, handing Cyril the small telescope.

"It isn't alive," Cyril said.

"Then how can we possibly kill it?" Frank asked.

"First, you don't run away like a pussy," Hound said.

Frank clenched his jaw. "What was I supposed to do?"

"You almost knocked your brother off the edge," Cyril said. "You have to control your fear better than that."

"Look, I'm sorry Ben was in the way, but I had to get away from that thing."

Homer whined, subtle mockery in the tone.

"Time to go," John said. "The Dragon Guard are probably close."

"Good," Hound said. "Something I can kill that'll actually die."

"I'd rather not get lit on fire if we can help it," Cyril said. "Also, this isn't the best battlefield."

"Maybe it is," Ben said, pointing toward a section of the upward slope littered with scree and lots of large rocks. "If we go a ways farther, we can circle back along that ridge and ambush them with a rockslide."

"I like it," Hound said. "Much rather make a stand than run headlong into that stalker."

"And what's your contingency?" Cyril asked.

Ben frowned.

"If the rockslide fails, then what?"

"We'd have the high ground," John said.

"True enough," Cyril said. "But they have superior weapons."

"Bertha's still got some fight left in her," Hound said.

"I don't doubt that, but John's arrows won't penetrate their armor and Ben is without a sword. Also, we don't know how close they are, if they're even following us at all. Perhaps a better course would be to trigger a rockslide and be on our way. If we're lucky, the debris will make the trail too treacherous to traverse."

"Either way, we should get off this slope," Imogen said.

"Can't argue with that," Hound said.

Chapter 9

John set out again, moving at a brisk pace. Ben found that he had to focus on walking lest he step on an errant stone and twist his ankle. He was glad for the distraction, given recent events.

He felt naked without his sword, vulnerable. Admittedly, it hadn't done him much good, but it did make him feel like he had a fighting chance. Without it, he was at the enemy's mercy.

When they reached the far side of the scree field and came to a small stand of trees, Ben eyed a sapling. It was a small straight tree with a set of branches forking away at the same knot.

"Frank, let me borrow your axe," he said.

Frank frowned, hesitating for a moment before handing over his hatchet.

Ben quickly began cutting away at the tree until he had the rough outline of a boar spear—a long spear with a crossbeam that would stop a boar from pushing its way up the shaft.

He handed his brother the axe and then went to work with his knife, stripping away the twigs and sharpening the center branch and the two smaller branches, which were now only six inches long and formed a stop point at the eighteen-inch mark of the stout spike.

Hound nodded approvingly after Ben had finished creating his makeshift weapon. "Not bad for a kid," he said with a mocking smile.

Ben ignored him.

"Looks like we can get to the ridgeline right there," John said, pointing up the trail.

Cyril looked at the sky and then scanned the path to the top of the scree field. "If we do this, we won't make much more distance today."

"Not sure we have a choice," John said, handing Cyril his monocular and pointing across the expanse.

After a quick look, Cyril returned the monocular and let out a long sigh. "We have to hurry," he said. "That patch of rocks is our best bet." He pointed to a collection of a dozen or so large boulders all piled in a jumble jutting up from the steep slope. "We'll move up the ridgeline and then come straight down behind those rocks. John, you lead."

Durt set out without a word. It was a harsh pace, especially considering the elevation gain. Each step forward seemed to take them only half a step up. Ben found himself struggling to overcome the burn in his legs and the difficulty he was having keeping his lungs filled with air.

Cyril stopped, breathing heavily as well. Everyone else took the opportunity to put their hands on their knees and regain control over their breathing.

"We have to hurry," John said, pointing back the way they'd come. A string of six men were now clearly visible, their black armor standing out in stark relief to the whitish-grey of the rocky slope in sunlight.

They reached the base of the spur and the terrain shifted from a steep climb over grassy dirt into a more gradual ascent up the rocky ridgeline. As they gained altitude, they had to slow down to ensure they didn't take a bad step. A fall down one side would send them sliding to the trail and into the approaching enemy. A fall down the other side would drop them off a cliff into a narrow ravine fifty feet below.

Ben watched his footing while he tried to master his labored breathing. Before he knew it, Cyril and John had stopped, first scanning the enemy and then the slope they would have to descend to reach the boulders.

"I doubt they can see us here, but they'll probably notice if we disturb the scree," John said.

"Say we make it down there, then what?" Frank said. "Even if we can wipe them out with a rockslide, how are we going to get down afterwards?"

"I'm not sure we have a choice," Ben said. "If we wait here, they'll probably see us, but if we all go at once, then they'll just a see a rockslide on an unstable slope."

"He's right," Cyril said. "Together then?" He put out his hands to Imogen and Frank.

"This is crazy," Frank muttered.

Ben took Imogen's free hand.

"You ready?" he said to Homer.

"Would it matter?"

"Not really," Ben said, and then they went, stepping onto the scree slope and sliding on a wave of loose stone. It happened fast, much more quickly than Ben imagined it would, with one of the consequences being a painful crash at the bottom when they came to an abrupt halt against the cluster of boulders amid a shower of clattering stones.

"Anyone hurt?" Cyril asked before standing.

Ben checked his extremities and found that he was pretty beat up, but unbroken.

He looked to Homer. "You okay?"

"My feet hurt," his dog said.

Ben chuckled to himself as he stumbled to his feet on the loose and uneven debris. He was happy to see that the stone formation completely shielded them from view.

"Goddamn it, that hurt!" Frank said.

"Not so loud," Cyril said.

"You all right?" John asked Imogen as he helped her to her feet.

She nodded with a pained and somewhat forced smile. A trickle of blood ran down her forehead and around her eye.

Ben slipped up to the top of a boulder and looked for the Dragon Guard. Finding them a few minutes away, he started looking at the stability of the big rocks, hoping to find one he thought they might be able to dislodge. On the side closest to the approaching enemy, he found nothing promising, but the far side yielded better results.

A menhir stood like a statue, separated from the nearby stones by a foot of daylight. It was at least twenty feet tall and looked to be about twelve feet around at the top. It was balanced on a stone a couple of feet across, worn away by ages of wind and water. Below the small monolith lay a field of smaller stones and then the path.

Ben looked at Hound and pointed to a shelf eight or ten feet up the sheer stone wall. "Help me get up there," he said.

Hound eyed the shelf and shrugged, getting into place and offering his hands, fingers interlaced together. Ben steadied himself with a hand on Hound's shoulder, then put his foot into his hands. As he stepped up, Hound nearly launched him into the air, propelling him to the shelf in a blink. He struggled for a moment to gain a handhold, and then another. Once he'd swung his legs up onto solid ground, he reached down and took his spear from Cyril and braced himself to help his grandfather up. They made their way to the top of the stone outcropping along a precarious but relatively clear path of steps and shelves, crouching low as they moved carefully across the top boulder to the trigger stone. It was completely separated from the rest of the stones on all sides, its only solid connection with the world at the single point where it balanced on the small stone underneath it.

"It's perfect," Cyril said, assessing the progress of the Dragon Guard. "If we trigger now, they might just turn back."

"Or we might lose our best chance to end their pursuit," Ben said.

Cyril grimaced and looked down, nodding ever so slightly to himself.

"I don't understand," Ben said. "You trained me to be ruthless in battle, to strike fast and hard, to never let up once I have the enemy wounded. Ever since I can remember, I've learned about war and violence from you. Now that I'm faced with a real enemy in a real battle, you hesitate to kill at every turn. Why?"

Cyril shrugged helplessly. "Because killing is so final. I don't want that stain on your conscience."

"Why not? They deserve it."

"'Deserve' is a judgment. Killing someone because you deem that they deserve it places you in an untenable moral position."

"They're not going to stop," Ben said.

"No, they're not. That's why I'm up here with you. Killing for defense, especially defense against evil, is morally justifiable. These Dragon Guard are the enemy, they're evil, and they intend to kill or enslave us." He stopped, holding Ben with his eyes. "Always be absolutely certain you know why someone needs to die before you kill them. Killing in defense, you can live with. But kill an innocent and you'll discover the true meaning of the word 'hell.'"

Cyril sat down and put his feet against the trigger stone. Gentle pressure didn't budge it. Firmer pressure caused a few pebbles to come free, showering the cliff face with a clattering rain of stone.

"I think we can topple it if I push and you use your spear as a lever," Cyril said. "Stay low until they're right where we want them."

The Dragon Guard moved torturously slow, crawling across the expansive scar in the side of Mount McLaughlin. Ben saw sunlight flash on a golden braid of hair. Nash was the last person in the file.

He started to feel anxious, anticipating the outcome, fearing a thousand possible disasters, catching himself in the futile and distracting practice and then chiding himself for losing focus. He looked over at Cyril. His grandfather was calm and steady, his eyes locked on the enemy, his breathing slow and easy.

Ben glanced down toward the Dragon Guard as they entered the slide area. He held his breath, waiting for Cyril to give the order ... but it didn't come.

Instead, his grandfather braced himself and gave a heaving shove with both legs against the precariously balanced stone. It swayed, sending another shower of pebbles down the slope and drawing Nash's attention. A moment later, a sharp cracking noise reverberated away from the mountain and the trigger stone began to topple.

"Retreat!" Nash shouted.

The stone moved with agonizing slowness, leaning away from them like a tree bowing in the wind. Then there was a louder cracking sound and the entire menhir fell forward and down a dozen feet in an instant, a mosaic of fissures spreading across its surface in a second. The giant pillar fell away, the top end gathering speed as it traced an arc to the ground below.

And then it hit.

The earth shook with a single jolt, pitching Ben forward. He landed on his knees, then fell onto his chest, his head going over the edge of the shelf. For all the world, it felt as if the ground below was pulling on him, drawing him toward it. With a surge of panic, he scrambled away from the precipice. Cyril grabbed him and dragged him farther back.

The trigger stone exploded into a thousand pieces ranging in size from an apple to a horse, all picking up speed as they tumbled haphazardly down the slope toward the trail, gathering scree and dislodging boulders along the way.

Ben and Cyril approached the edge as closely as they dared to watch what they had wrought. A chaotic cacophony filled the late morning air as dozens of boulders bounced and bounded to the forest floor, liberating stone and scree with each impact.

Small sections of broken shale began to slide. Then one by one, they bumped into others and grew into a larger slide, until, all at once, an entire section of the mountain dislodged and began to move with increasing speed and energy toward the trees below.

The Dragon Guard tried to flee the onslaught. All but one were swept away in the storm of stone, carried to their graves, buried under thousands of tons of rock in a matter of a single minute's time.

For two hundred feet, the slope was scarred bare, stripped of all vestiges of the trail and leaving the way entirely impassable.

"I'd say your plan worked rather well," Cyril said.

"Except for the part where you triggered the avalanche without me," Ben said.

Cyril shrugged unapologetically and started to make his way down.

"I'll find you!" Nash's voice floated up to them on the breeze. "I'll see you burn!"

"She'll have a hard time picking up our trail now," Cyril said.

"Until she finds another stalker," Ben muttered.

"There is that. We should go."

Ben swung over the face of the shelf and pushed off, dropping to the ground amidst his family and friends.

"That was really loud," Homer said. "You could've warned me."

"Sorry."

"Nash sounded happy," Hound said, a smile creeping up one side of his mouth.

"Yeah, I probably should've waited until she got closer," Cyril said. "Fortunately, she's alone and she's on the far side of the slide. I doubt we'll see her again."

Hound snorted. "I'll take that bet. That bitch is pissed." He smiled like he knew something about it. "She ain't never gonna stop now."

"Is there a trail that leads around this?" Cyril asked John, gesturing to the rocky mountain face.

John considered the question for a few moments, finally shaking his head. "None that would be fast enough for her to catch up with us."

"Good," Cyril said. "She'll probably return to Lake of the Woods for reinforcements. Let's see about getting back to the trail without joining our friends at the bottom."

Several hundred feet of steep, scree-covered slope lay between the boulders and the edge of the scar. The trail was two hundred feet below, down highly unstable terrain.

"This is kind of a dumb place to be," Homer said.

Ben snorted, looking sidelong at his dog, then frowning to himself as he began to see the situation from Homer's perspective.

"Can you make it without falling?"

"Depends on how much the ground moves."

Ben started to worry.

"Why don't we just go back up to the ridge?" Frank asked, attempting to climb the steep, and already unstable slope that they'd slid down to get to the boulders in the first place. He made it nearly a dozen feet before the ground beneath his feet gave way, sweeping his legs out from under him. He fell face-first and slid back down to the outcropping.

"Goddamn it!" he shouted, scrambling to his feet.

"Keep your voice down," Cyril said. "We don't need to attract any more trouble than we already have."

"Fine. What's your plan?"

"I think we can tie a rope off to that rock," Cyril said, pointing to a small boulder jutting three feet out of the scree. "From there we can slide to that cluster of rocks below, which gets us a hundred feet closer to the trail."

"Then what?" Frank asked, looking out over the proposed route and shaking his head. "If we make it there, we'll be stuck. Besides, how are you going to get a rope over to that rock in the first place?"

"I'll take it," John said.

"Are you crazy? You'll fall for sure," Frank said.

"I'll be fine."

Frank opened his mouth, closed it abruptly and turned away, shaking his head.

"I don't see the next step either," Ben said.

Cyril shrugged helplessly. "It's the only viable path."

Ben blinked a few times, reality dawning on him quite suddenly. There was no other way and they couldn't stay where they were.

"Tie off to that stone there," Cyril said. "It looks solid enough."

Once the rope was secured to the stone, John tied it around his waist. Hound took up the slack, wrapping a loop around his back.

"Be careful," Imogen said.

John smiled as he looked for solid footing past the edge of the boulders. Finding only loose rock, he stepped farther out, testing his weight carefully. The ground gave way, sending a section of small rock cascading down the mountain. He steadied himself with the rope and reached out again, finding some purchase on the ground he'd just cleared of surface rock.

He pulled himself back and looked at Ben. "I need your spear," he said.

Ben handed over the freshly cut sapling.

John used the butt of the spear to knock the loose rock free, causing a constant clatter of minor avalanches down the mountain face as he slowly, cautiously, and painstakingly made his way across the scree field to the boulder.

Ben found himself holding his breath as John neared his goal. Suddenly his footing gave way and he slipped onto unstable ground. He tried to use the spear to steady himself, but when he put his weight on it, it slid out from underneath him, dislodging another section of rock. He let the hastily crafted weapon fall lest he go with it, but to no avail. Despite his desperate attempt to find purchase, there was none to be had. The ground beneath him shifted and moved, taking him with it as it broke away and began to slide.

He scrambled to his feet, and though wildly unsteady, he managed to remain upright long enough to grab hold of the rope tied around his waist. Using it as an anchor, he ran in stumbling and haphazard fashion across the top of the flowing avalanche toward the boulders, crashing hard into the rock face. By the time he shook off the pain, the avalanche had run its course, taking a section of the scree field with it and leaving an area with more stable and solid footing across a wide swath.

Hound pulled him up and he sat down, taking a moment to collect himself.

"Are you hurt?" Imogen asked.

John shook his head without looking up. "Nothing that won't mend."

"Looks like you cleared the way," Ben said.

"Yeah, you're right," Frank said. "I bet I can get across now."

John untied the rope and handed it to Frank.

Frank dropped his pack and stepped carefully, steadying himself with his left hand against the upslope, placing his feet slowly and tentatively. The ground was solid. Though wet and slick in spots, the loose stone had fallen away, leaving much better purchase. Before long, Frank reached the rock, a stout boulder nearly four feet tall, anchored to the earth as if it were part of the bedrock. He tied the rope off, creating a taut line for the rest of them to hold on to as they traveled across.

Imogen went next, then Hound carrying Frank's pack. Both made it safely without mishap.

"How are we going to untie the rope at this end?" Ben asked.

"I'll do it," John said.

"You sure you're up to it?" Cyril asked. "You took quite a hit."

John nodded, rubbing his shoulder.

"All right," Cyril said. "You're next, Ben."

He nodded, hesitating for a moment before taking the rope in hand and moving into position.

"You ready, Homer?"

"Do I have a choice?"

He put Homer to his left, placing a hand on his back to steady him. "Stay with me."

"Where else would I go?"

Ben gave his dog a sidelong look and reached out with his foot, testing the ground before committing his weight. Homer was more tentative, like a dog being called into the water who wasn't sure he wanted to get wet. Ben waited for him to make the leap. After several moments of indecision, Homer scrambled out past the edge of the boulders, staying right beside Ben's leg as he slowly moved away from safety and out into the expanse.

"It's okay, just stay close to me," Ben said.

"I couldn't get any closer unless I was sitting on your head," Homer said.

Ben chuckled, taking another step. As he shifted his weight forward, the ground suddenly gave way, sweeping his legs out from under him. He slid beneath the rope, holding on for his life, putting tension on the line and sliding several feet down the mountain before the rope arrested his descent.

He reached frantically for Homer but just missed him as he slid past.

"Homer!" Ben shouted, watching his best friend slide away from him. He thought about letting go and looked plaintively to his grandfather for help that he knew wouldn't be forthcoming.

"No, Ben," Cyril snapped. "Hang on."

He looked back to Homer, now stumbling toward the section of slope that had already been stripped of rock by the avalanche. He watched helplessly as a kind of fear he'd never known gripped him. Homer gained speed, though he maintained his footing, now sledding down the mountain on his front paws and his butt. He raced past the rough patch that used to be the path and continued toward the level ground below.

Ben felt pain and panic welling up in his chest and realized that he was holding his breath. The helplessness was nearly complete. He had no power. He could do nothing to help his friend—all he could do was watch and hope.

He hung there by one hand, his eyes fixed on Homer as the dog neared the bottom of the slope. When he began to tumble the last fifty feet or so, Ben felt his heart fall. The idea of losing Homer was more horrible than almost any other thing he could imagine. His dog had been there all his life—a constant companion with unquestionable loyalty. The prospect of his death took Ben to a place beyond sanity.

When Homer reached the pile of rubble and debris littering the forest floor, Ben watched him come to a rest and lie still. He reached out to him with his mind, but there was only silence. His world began collapsing in on him.

"Ben, you have to make it to the rock," Cyril said.

He ignored his grandfather, his eyes fixed on the still form lying so far below, each interminable moment building on the next. Homer didn't move ... and his voice was silent in Ben's mind.

"Ben!" Cyril snapped, drawing Ben's attention reluctantly away from Homer. "You have to get to the rock. Focus! Bring your mind back to the task at hand and put aside your worries. They can't do you or Homer any good."

"But he's not moving," Ben said, his voice breaking and a lump welling up in his throat that threatened to dissolve what little composure he had left.

"Homer's tough," Cyril said. "And you can't do anything to help him from where you are. Get to the rock."

Ben didn't move, still hanging by one hand, still watching for any sign of movement so far below.

"Ben, I want you to use the detachment exercise that I taught you," Cyril said. "Step outside yourself and look at the situation from the position of a disinterested observer. Do it now."

It felt like a betrayal, like he was forsaking Homer, to tear his focus away from him, but he did it anyway, imagining that he was standing aside and watching from a safe, uninvolved place.

He saw himself in his mind's eye, hanging by one hand, the jaws of death reaching for him. Only then did he realize just how precarious his situation was. If he fell, the outcome wouldn't be good. From the perspective of the detached witness, it was blindingly obvious that he couldn't do anything, couldn't know anything for certain until he was able to reach Homer. That thought snapped him back to reality and gave him the strength to resist the onslaught of emotion tearing through him.

He set his feelings aside and focused on the task at hand, pulling himself back up and regaining his feet before carefully but quickly traversing the distance to the rock.

"You okay?" Imogen asked.

Ben shook his head tightly. "I have to get down there," he said as he peered at the cluster of boulders that was their next step on the way back to the trail. He held his hand out to Rufus and said, "Anchor me."

Hound took his wrist, his grip much firmer than the footing beneath Ben's feet. He stepped out past the rock and pushed at the ground with his boot, dislodging a section of scree and creating a minor landslide. Unsatisfied with the result, he reached farther and kicked still more free. After his fourth attempt, a large swath of rock fell away, clattering and tumbling as it went.

Ben nodded to himself, looking down the mountain a hundred feet to the backstop of rock below. Under other circumstances he would have hesitated, taking a more cautious approach.

"Ben, wait," Imogen said.

"No," he said, sitting down and easing himself out onto the slope. He slid on his butt with his feet out in front of him, gaining speed quickly, a cluster of pebbles joining him in his rapid descent until he hit the boulders he was aiming for. He quickly got to his feet and started to look for the next step to the path ... unfortunately, there wasn't one, at least not one that would get him there intact.

They would need to use the rope to descend close enough to the path to slide the rest of the way, and even then, they risked tumbling to their doom.

"Come on," he shouted to the others before climbing up the rocks to see if he could get a look at Homer. The lump in his throat began to swell anew when he saw that his dog still wasn't moving.

Again, he reached out with his mind and heard only silence in return.

Hound came clattering down next, followed by Imogen and Frank. The three of them made it with a minimum of bruising, though all three were clearly sore from the slide.

Ben looked up at his grandfather. "We'll need the rope!" he shouted.

John took a firm grip on the rope before carefully working his way down the edge of the boulder. When it pulled taut, he used it to steady himself as he walked out over the treacherous landscape. As he moved along the arc described by the rope's length, he gained speed until he was running, passing the apex of the arc and continuing on to the section of slope that Ben had freed of loose rock before letting go and sliding the rest of the way.

Then Cyril untied the rope and slid down to join them.

Ben snatched up the rope as it cascaded down the hill, then hurried to the other side of the rocky outcropping, searching for a suitable place to tie off. He wasted no time in finding one, slipping over the edge and onto the unstable ground. He hadn't gone ten feet when the scree began to slide. He lost purchase and found himself hanging by a thread again. When the slide had run its course, he continued to the end of the rope.

"Ben, wait," Cyril said.

He let go, sliding the rest of the way to the trail ... but he didn't stop there. His inertia took him over the edge while he frantically sought a firm handhold. He found one a few feet past the path, arresting his fall and giving him a moment to search for another handhold.

It took a minute, but he managed to climb back to the trail just as Cyril reached it, stopping himself with far more control than Ben had.

Cyril hugged his grandson without a word, then held him out at arm's length and eyed him sternly. "Being reckless won't help Homer."

"I have to get to him," Ben said, looking down at his dog. "I have to know. If he's alive, he needs my help."

"I know, but it won't serve Homer to get yourself killed. Right now, we need to help everyone else get to the path without going over."

Ben tore his gaze away from Homer and nodded, anxious to be on his way.

"We're ready," Cyril called up to Imogen, who was dangling from the end of the rope. She let go, sliding toward them, but not so quickly that they couldn't easily stop her when she reached the path.

Hound and Frank came next.

John untied the rope and let it fall.

Cyril looked up at him, then handed the rope to Hound. "Tie this around your waist and leave equal lengths on either side," he said. "Frank, Imogen, you take one side, Ben and I will take the other. Rufus, your job is to keep John from going over."

The plan worked, though somewhat haphazardly. Both men went over, but both were stopped by the rope. As Ben and the others struggled to arrest their fall, he wondered if maybe Hound should have been on an end instead of in the middle, given his strength and weight.

With everyone safely on the path, Ben started scanning for a way down to the bottom, but he could see no direct path that didn't involve a sure death.

"Could I borrow your monocular, John?"

The Highwayman handed over the little telescope.

Ben held his breath as he looked at his dog, searching for any sign of life. He wasn't sure, but he thought he saw him breathing. Even with the monocular, the distance was too great to be certain.

"We can get down there if we go through the trees beyond the scree field," he said, slipping past the others and starting out without discussion.

"What are you talking about?" Frank said. "Your stupid dog is dead, just let him go."

Ben whirled, rage and pain flooding into him as he lashed out at Frank, hitting him squarely on the nose, blood spraying across his face. Frank stumbled backward, stunned by the blow, then fell on his butt. Caught up in his rage and loss, Ben was moving toward his brother when Hound intervened, stepping past Frank and stopping Ben with a raised hand and a stern look.

"What the hell did you do that for?" Frank sputtered.

"If you ever talk about my dog like that again, I'll break every bone in your goddamned face."

"He's just a dog," Frank said, as he tenderly felt his bleeding nose.

"He's a better person than you'll ever be," Ben said, turning on his heel and heading toward the trees.

"Ben, wait," Cyril said.

Chapter 10

Somewhere in the back of his mind, he knew he was being unfair and reckless but he couldn't bring himself to care. All that mattered was Homer. He walked briskly, scanning the landscape for a safe way down. Once he reached the forested slope at the edge of the scree field, the ground became more solid and stable. He was just about to go over the edge when Cyril grabbed him by the arm and spun him around.

"Don't hit your brother," he said, anger flashing in his eyes.

"Tell him to stop insulting Homer."

"An insult does not warrant an assault."

"Sometimes maybe it should."

Cyril took a deep breath and looked down. "You're afraid and you're letting your fear cloud your judgment. You have to learn to master your fear."

"What I have to do is get to Homer."

Just then the rest of his family and friends reached them, Frank glaring at him past a swollen and possibly broken nose.

"I understand that," Cyril said. "But you have to be smart about it. There's a stalker down there somewhere. You can't face it alone."

"Oh God," Ben said, new fear flooding into his belly. "Homer's helpless against that thing."

"And so are you," Cyril said. "Do you think Homer would want you to die trying to save him?"

"No, but that won't stop me from trying," Ben said, turning away and sliding down the hill to a tree twenty feet below.

"Damn it, Ben," Cyril said, "slow down and wait for the rest of us!"

Ben ignored him.

"I'll wait here," Frank said.

"You'll be waiting a long time," Hound said. "Once we're down there, we won't be climbing back up here."

Frank's frown deepened. "Stupid dog," he muttered under his breath.

Cyril looked to John. He nodded and went over the edge. Ben was already two trees ahead of him and looking for another to arrest his descent. The calm voice of reason tugged at him, urging him to be careful, to pay attention to his surroundings, to think. He ignored that too.

It didn't take long to reach relatively level ground. Once there, he turned and started trotting through the forest. The trees were sparse enough to move through quickly, though he found that he needed to choose his path carefully because the ground was layered with uneven stones concealed by pine needles and forest debris.

He reached the mound of newly fallen rock and began to scramble up the side, sliding back a step for every two he took but finally reaching the top. He stopped short when he saw Homer, still and silent. After a torturous moment of indecision, his need to know doing battle with his fear of knowing, he raced to Homer's side. He was beaten up and bloody, but he was breathing.

Relief washed over Ben like a cool breeze on a hot day, taking his fear with it. He dropped to his knees and gently, tentatively pet Homer's head.

"Can you hear me?" he said. There was no response.

He carefully began to probe for injuries, first across the dog's head, then his body and finally his legs. He realized only after he'd finished that he'd been holding his breath to the point where his lungs were burning. With a gasp, his composure broke and he laid his head on the ground and wept.

"Please wake up," he whispered.

"Look out!" John shouted.

Ben's head snapped up.

The stalker was slowly and quietly slinking toward him across the debris field, his sword still driven to the hilt into its eye and out the back of its head. Suddenly, it snarled and leapt into a sprint.

The fear returned, though this time it was mixed with a sense of righteous anger. Ben scrambled to his feet, bringing a grapefruit-sized rock with him. No sooner had he set his stance than the stalker was on him, leaping toward his throat with a frenzied need to kill.

Ben brought the rock up and jammed it into the stalker's open mouth, wedging it between its teeth even as the thing crashed into him and knocked him onto his back. The uneven, rocky ground gouged him in a dozen places, but his attention was firmly fixed on the unnatural creature trying to end his life.

When the beast tried to pull back and dislodge the rock, Ben wrapped his free arm around its head right below the blade of his sword, holding it close so he could keep the rock in place. The stalker flailed against him, scratching and kicking, clawing into his flesh in a frantic effort to free itself from his grip, but he held on.

John was there a moment later, taking hold of the sword hilt and pulling the blade sideways with a heave, slicing through the creature's head and stilling its desperate struggle to kill Ben. As it went limp, the darkness that seemed to accompany it faded like smoke on a breeze.

The top half of the beast's head had been nearly severed. Black blood and slimy brain matter poured out of the gaping wound.

Ben rolled the thing off him, scrambling away from it, his heart pounding in his chest.

A moment later, the foul taste of the stalker's blood, rotten and fetid, flooded into his senses, and he vomited the contents of his stomach onto the rock. He rolled over onto his side and curled into a ball, waves of nausea and revulsion coursing through him. He heaved again, but his belly was empty.

"You okay?" John asked, still sitting on the ground, staring at the stalker's corpse.

Ben tried to speak, but succumbed to another round of dry heaves, his whole body wracked by convulsions.

Cyril scrambled to his side, rolling his grandson toward him and searching for injuries. When he saw Ben's face, he snatched the canteen from his bag and washed away the unclean, black blood.

Ben sputtered, his latest attempt to vomit transforming into a fit of coughing. He couldn't imagine feeling any more miserable—until Homer whined. He violently shoved his own discomfort aside and rolled to his hands and knees, crawling to his dog.

Homer whimpered again as his eyes came open. When he saw Ben, he said, "You smell bad."

Ben curled up next to him. "Deal with it."

Homer laid his chin on Ben's hand.

"Are you hurt?" Cyril asked, kneeling next to Ben.

"No," he croaked, "but I feel sick."

"My feet hurt," Homer said.

"I'll bet," Ben replied without opening his eyes.

The others finally arrived, coming up around them, Hound scanning for any further danger, Imogen going to Ben's side, and Frank sitting down on a rock, shaking his head.

"Let's get you cleaned up," Imogen said. "Sit up and take off that shirt … it smells awful."

He reluctantly obeyed, slowly sitting up and stripping off his shirt. He felt much better once the stench of the stalker's blood was off of him. Cyril handed him a wet towel and Ben went to work cleaning himself, taking extra care with the scratches left by the stalker's claws all across his chest. Most were superficial but a few oozed blood. Imogen carefully bandaged the wounds.

Once he was clean and wearing his spare shirt, he gently picked Homer up and carried him away from the carnage, sliding down the side of the debris field and scanning the forest.

"We need to find a place to camp," he said.

"We still have hours of light left," Frank said. "We should get the hell away from here in case the Dragon Guard come back."

Ben shook his head. "Homer isn't ready to travel yet."

Frank clenched his jaw.

Cyril looked at Ben and sighed, inspecting one of Homer's paws and nodding to himself. Then he turned to John and said, "Any suggestions?"

"Should be a stream not too far from here."

"Lead the way."

Homer grew heavier as they walked and the energy flowing through Ben from the fight began to ebb, but he didn't complain.

They reached the stream, burbling and rippling over its rocky course on its way to the Lake of the Woods. Ben gently laid Homer down. Then he went to the stream and washed his face and head again, this time far more thoroughly.

Satisfied that all of the stalker's blood was gone, he dug Homer's bowl out of his pack and filled it with water.

Homer gratefully drank his fill and then rolled over on his side, closing his eyes again. Ben went to work inspecting his wounds and cleaning them with a wet cloth. Given all that Homer had been though, it was a wonder that he'd fared as well as he had. He was bruised from head to paw, and he had a number of superficial lacerations that elicited a whine when Ben gently probed them, but no bones were broken.

After he'd finished tending to Homer, Ben lay back in the mossy grass and looked at the sky, so blue and calm.

"Are we going to talk about what happened?" Cyril asked, sitting nearby.

Ben sat up, nodding to his grandfather.

"You were reckless. If John hadn't been there, that stalker would have killed you."

"And if I hadn't gotten there as quickly as I did, it would have killed Homer."

"Perhaps," Cyril said, falling silent for a moment as he watched the water flow past them. "Our enemy is dangerous and determined. None of us can stand against them alone—not you, not me. To survive, we need to be able to rely on each other."

Ben looked at the grass, pulling a few blades up and letting them fall away in the breeze. Now that he'd had a moment to think about it, without the cloud of intense emotion obscuring his reason, he saw his many mistakes.

"I know. Truth is, Homer's hurt because of me. The rock slide was my idea. I put him in this situation." He stared off into the forest, a dozen "what-ifs" parading through his mind.

"What's done is done," Cyril said. "No sense beating yourself up over it. Also, I'm not sure the outcome would've been better if we'd tried a different strategy."

Ben nodded to himself, scanning the faces of his friends and family. When he settled on Frank, a pang of guilt tugged at his conscience—his brother's nose was swollen and red. Ben winced and said, "I'm sorry I hit you. I let my emotions get the better of me and I shouldn't have."

Frank nodded, muttering something under his breath. Ben ignored it. He hadn't expected Frank to accept his apology graciously.

"At least we got your sword back," John said, handing over the blade, now slightly etched by the blood of the stalker.

Ben took it, performing a cursory inspection before returning it to his scabbard.

"Thank you for saving my life."

"Anytime," John said.

"As I understand it, stalkers are territorial," Hound said. "Hopefully, that means there aren't any more nearby."

Everyone nodded agreement.

Ben lay down next to Homer and closed his eyes, quickly drifting off to sleep as the excitement of the day took its toll.

He woke some time later with a wave of nausea and prickly heat washing over him. He rolled onto his side and tried to vomit again, then broke out in a cold sweat.

Cyril came to his side, laying a hand on his forehead.

"You have a fever," he said, worry creasing his face.

"Hate to break it to you, but I'm not feeling all that great either," Hound said, his face pale and glistening with sweat.

"Are the stalkers poisonous?" Imogen asked.

"I'm not sure that poison is the right word for it," Cyril said, his hand on his chin, his brow furrowed.

"Then what is the right word?" Hound asked.

"Infection," Cyril said. "The stalkers are unclean in more ways than one. I suspect that wounds caused by them are tainted with the same darkness that animates them."

"So what are we going to do?" Imogen asked.

"All we can do is keep their wounds clean and let them rest," Cyril said.

"What if that's not enough?" she whispered, looking at Ben with worry.

"Hopefully, Chen will be able to help," Cyril muttered.

"Master Chen?" Imogen asked, with a hint of confusion.

Cyril nodded.

"He was around a lot when I was a kid," she said. "Why does he live way up in the forest now?"

"Isolation. After ..." Cyril's voice trailed off, a look of profound sadness coming over his face. He snapped back to himself a moment later. "He wanted to be left alone to meditate."

"Are you sure he's even still alive?" Imogen asked. "He was pretty old."

"I certainly hope he's still alive. But if he isn't, his cabin will still be there. We'll be safe there, for a while at least."

"How can you be so sure?" Frank asked.

"It's well hidden. I doubt the Dragon Guard could find it even if they knew where it was."

"What about a stalker?" Frank asked.

Cyril shrugged, shaking his head.

"Great," Frank muttered.

Ben was listening through the floating detachment of near sleep. He remembered the name, but he couldn't put a face to it. His grandfather had spoken of Chen on a few occasions, always with respect and affection. He wondered if the man could actually help. The thought evaporated as he slipped into sleep.

He woke suddenly, sitting up with a gasp, his heart hammering in his chest. The forest was dark and shrouded in mist, moonlight illuminating it with an eerie silver light—not enough to see by, but just enough to cast a thousand threatening shadows. He looked around, surreal panic welling up in his gut.

He was alone.

He struggled to stand up, but his legs wouldn't work.

One of the shadows began to move, red eyes in the night fixed on him. He looked around frantically. There was no stream, no mountain, nothing but trees and the pair of eyes coming for him. His heart swelled in his throat, each thunderous beat threatening to burst within his chest.

Terror and panic shoved aside all reason. The eyes were getting closer. They moved through the wispy fog, not quickly but inexorably, as if the thing looking at him knew there was no escape, knew that Ben was paralyzed, held to that spot by his own fear.

Helplessness filled him, and the eyes seemed to laugh with malice, savoring his plight. Then it bolted toward him, a shadow without form.

He woke screaming, sweat beading on his forehead, his heart slamming in his chest. It took him a few moments to realize that it had been a dream. The warm sun on his face helped bring him back to reality.

Cyril and Imogen were at his side a moment later.

"It's okay, just breathe," Cyril said.

"It was just a bad dream," Imogen added.

He shook his head, unable to form words, still struggling to calm his heart and slow his breathing.

Homer whined sympathetically.

It took nearly a minute before he had collected his wits enough to process what had just happened.

"I've never had a dream like that before," he said, still trembling. "It was so dark and so real."

Cyril pursed his lips and glanced down at the bandages tied around his chest.

Ben closed his eyes and lay back on the thick grass. "It's the stalker's magic, isn't it?" he asked without opening his eyes.

Hound came awake a moment later, scrambling to his feet and whipping Bertha out in one fluid, unconscious movement. His head darted back and forth, searching for a target. He blinked and swallowed hard, trembling just as violently as Ben had in the moments after he woke.

"You too?" Cyril asked.

Hound took a deep breath and sat down, nodding.

"I don't have nightmares," he said. "Even with all the shit I've done, I usually sleep like a baby."

"What did you see?" Ben asked, sitting up, a tremor in his voice.

"Eyes in the night."

Ben felt a chill race over his entire body, every hair standing on end.

"Is that what you saw too?" Cyril asked.

He nodded, swallowing the lump rising in his throat.

"Lie back down," Cyril said. "Let me take a look at those scratches."

Ben did as instructed, closing his eyes and trying to banish the pair of eyes he could still see on the insides of his eyelids. His mind was distracted by a sharp stab of pain when Cyril lifted the bandage up.

"Oh God," Imogen whispered, her hand going to her mouth.

Ben looked down at his chest. The scratches were black and festering, angry red swelling surrounding each of the deeper gouges. He laid his head back and closed his eyes.

"We need to clean and disinfect these wounds," Cyril said. "Hound, lie down and let me take a look."

Rufus sighed, nodding in resignation. He winced when Cyril pulled back the bandage, revealing the same unnatural infection.

"That's gonna leave a mark," he said.

"Another battle scar is the least of your worries," Cyril said. "John, do you think you can find a beehive nearby?"

"If there's one to be found," he said.

"I need honey," Cyril said. "It's a natural antibiotic. With any luck, it'll slow the infection, or at least the natural part of it."

"And what about the unnatural part?" Hound asked.

"We have to get to Chen. He'll be able to help."

"How can you be sure?" Ben asked.

"Because he's our only hope."

John picked up his bow and quiver but left his pack.

"Frank, why don't you go with him," Cyril said. "Two sets of eyes are better than one."

Frank looked like he was about to protest but thought better of it.

Cyril opened his pack and handed Imogen a bowl. "Fresh water, please."

She nodded, going to the stream.

"Any chance you have some whiskey?" Cyril asked Hound.

"Am I really that predictable?" he said, pointing to his pack. "Side pocket."

Cyril retrieved a metal flask tightly bound with leather.

"How strong is it?"

Hound opened one eye reprovingly. "What do you think?"

"Good," Cyril said with a chuckle.

"Take care of the kid first."

Ben focused on the pain while his grandfather and Imogen worked on him. It was cold and had an invasive quality to it that made Ben queasy, but that was better than the memory of the eyes in the night. When his thoughts turned to the dream, fear threatened to undo his reason.

After they'd finished tending to Ben, Cyril and Imogen cleaned Hound's wounds and changed his dressing.

Ben lay still, listening to the burbling brook. When sleep started to claim him again, he sat up abruptly, willing himself to remain awake.

"You should rest," Cyril said.

Ben shook his head as he got to his feet. He went to the stream to splash water on his face.

Suddenly, an angry shout drew everyone's attention. A long wailing howl filtered through the trees and then Frank came running toward them, waving his hands wildly. He reached the camp, still flailing against some unseen enemy, a number of angry welts marking his face and arms. He stopped, turning in a full circle before fixing Cyril with an angry glare.

"This is your fault," he said, before going to the water and carefully washing his face and arms.

Ten minutes later, John came out of the woods, a cloth wrapped around his face and head. He was carrying a chunk of beehive on a piece of bark.

He looked at Frank and shook his head. "Told you to wait."

"I thought they were gone," Frank snapped.

"They weren't."

"Ya think?" Frank said.

"Who says there ain't no justice?" Homer said.

Ben stifled a laugh and sat down by his dog, gently patting his head.

"How're you feeling?" he asked.

"My feet hurt."

"I know. Can you walk?"

"Yeah, but I'd rather not."

Ben lay back down. His nausea had subsided but he still felt sick—somehow hollow and cold. It was unlike any illness he'd ever experienced, but it was starting to feel less debilitating. His wounds hurt, but not so much that he couldn't manage. If Homer had been in better shape, he would have suggested that they press on.

"Nash has probably reached the barracks at Lake of the Woods by now," he said.

Cyril nodded. "The question is how quickly can she gather her forces and come after us?"

"She was pretty pissed off," Hound said. "If I had to guess, I'd say she'll come for us tonight."

"I doubt she could cover the distance before dark," John said.

"No, but she can get close and hit us first thing," Hound said.

John nodded, appraising the trail scrawled across the scree field above.

"Maybe we should find someplace where she can't see us from up there," he said.

"Now that you mention it, we are a bit too exposed for my taste," Hound said, getting to his feet with a grimace and gathering his pack.

"Why don't you all sit tight for a bit," John said. "I'll scout ahead."

Cyril nodded, working honey out of the honeycomb.

Hound sat back down without argument.

John set out along the steam, vanishing silently into the woods a few moments later.

Ben looked up at the blue sky, so calm and serene.

"We can never go home," he said to no one in particular.

"My home has always been wherever my family is," Cyril said. "But no, we can't go back to the shop, or to K Falls for that matter."

"Then where will we go?"

"I have a friend up north in the Deschutes Territory," Cyril said. "He'll give us safe harbor."

"You've never mentioned him before," Ben said, sitting up.

"No, I haven't."

"More secrets?" Frank said, shaking his head. "What else aren't you telling us?"

"A great many things, I suspect," Cyril said, holding Frank's eyes with his own.

"Don't you think it's time to share? Especially about magic. We're being hunted by magical creatures, after all."

"Nothing I could tell you about magic would be of any practical value against the stalkers. Best to avoid them whenever possible."

"Yeah, I figured that out all on my own," Frank said. "But if we can't avoid them, it'd be nice to have some magic to fight them with."

"Honestly, we'd do better with tech," Cyril said. "It's more predictable and doesn't carry as high a price."

"What do you mean by that?"

"Magic isn't free. It isn't a solution to all of your problems. And more often than not, the price is far higher than what you get in return."

"See, that's what I'm talking about," Frank said. "You know things about magic that you've never told us. How? And why have you kept it from us?"

"How? I've lived much longer than you," Cyril said with a shrug. "As far as keeping things from you … perhaps I have, but not for the reasons that you might imagine."

"Then why?" Frank said.

"To protect you," Cyril said. "Magic has an allure that's very dangerous, especially to young people. The kind of magic that comes easily always comes with a high price, but that cost usually doesn't become apparent until after the fact. Unfortunately, youth is impatient, often rushing headlong into danger out of ignorance or a misguided belief in immortality. The end result is an attraction to bargaining magic."

Cyril stopped talking and stared off into the forest, his eyes losing focus.

"Oh, come on, you did it again," Frank said. "What's 'bargaining magic'?"

Cyril seemed to consider the question for a long time before nodding to himself, taking a deep breath and sighing with resignation.

"Magic falls loosely into two categories—bargaining and manifestation. Bargaining magic involves beseeching entities from other realms for aid and assistance. A number of dangers are inherent in it, since the entities are motivated by needs and desires beyond our comprehension. They're often dishonest and manipulative. Great care and even greater knowledge is necessary when dealing with these beings in order to achieve the outcome you desire. Otherwise, you're likely to unleash forces into our world that don't belong here—forces that can easily consume you, or worse, transform you into something else."

Ben sat up frowning. "Is that where the stalkers came from?"

"I suspect so," Cyril said.

"What if we could get these beings to help us?" Frank asked.

"And how would you go about doing that?" Cyril asked.

"I don't know, that's why I'm asking you."

"Let's say we knew a spell to enlist the aid of some being or other—and that we had a dragon artifact sufficient to allow us to pierce the veil between our world and theirs. What would you offer in exchange for their help?"

"Whatever it took," Frank said.

"Exactly," Cyril said. "Often the price they demand is life—yours or another's. Who would you sacrifice?"

Frank fell silent, looking at the ground.

"Worse, once you've made contact with one of these beings, they know who you are. They will reach out to you again, sometimes when you least expect it, and sometimes with horrifying demands."

Homer whined softly, almost plaintively.

"What about 'manifestation magic'?" Ben asked.

"Manifestation requires payment up front in the form of years of practice, meditation, and mental discipline. Manifestation doesn't require a price to be paid for the desired outcome. Instead, the one wielding this type of magic must align their mind with the mind of reality, for lack of a better term, and, through vivid imagination and an indomitable will, inject their desired outcome into the very fabric of creation."

Ben frowned, growing realization welling up within him.

Just then, John materialized out of the forest. "I've found us a place for the night," he said. "It's about half a mile upstream."

Chapter 11

Ben leaned his head back against the boulder and closed his eyes, savoring the feel of the cool breeze on his face. The half mile walk had left him spent and exhausted, though he suspected his injuries had far more to do with his failing vitality than the stroll through the woods.

John had found a good campsite a few dozen feet from the stream. Large boulders formed an enclosed area with three narrow paths leading into the interior space. The rocks both hid them and provided some measure of protection against attack, though Ben knew it wouldn't be enough if the Dragon Guard found them.

Cyril arranged some smaller stones into a fire pit and sent John and Imogen to gather wood.

"Do you think that's wise?" Frank asked. "They might see the smoke."

"They already know we're out here. Besides, I doubt they're close enough to see anything."

"I hope you're right," Frank muttered.

Ben was tired, but he dared not sleep. When he felt himself begin to nod off, he snapped himself awake, scooted a few feet away from the rock he'd been leaning against and crossed his legs in the meditation position that his grandfather had taught him many years ago.

Cyril had told him that the first step to meditation was learning how to sit still. At first, Ben thought there would be nothing to it. He figured he'd be able to master the practice in an afternoon. Several years later, after countless hours of diligent work, it had finally become second nature. Now, the meditation pose was the most comfortable position he could imagine.

Every time he settled down to meditate, he was reminded of the long struggle he'd endured to accomplish the seemingly simple ability to sit still. Frank had mocked him, which in hindsight may have been what motivated him to keep working at it for so long, even after it seemed like such a thing was entirely impossible.

Now, when he sat down to meditate, his body settled into a state of complete rest and relaxation, all tension melting away in a matter of moments. Sometimes he felt like sitting still and calming his mind was even more restful than sleep. Today, he was hoping that would be the case, because he feared sleep and the nightmares it was certain to bring.

After a few moments of slow breathing, after his body had become still, freeing his mind from all of the distractions of sensation, he turned his focus to his coin, bringing the image into his mind and holding it with vivid clarity until he lost all sense of time and self.

Cyril had taught him that the item he focused on was less important than achieving that state of mind where his consciousness seemed to become one with the subject of his meditation. He had only managed to achieve that goal about three months ago.

The pride in Cyril's eyes when Ben had told him of his accomplishment was nearly as rewarding as the state of mind itself. When he managed to succeed, and that still required some effort on his part, he always came away from his meditation feeling calm and centered, as if all was right with the world, even when his reason told him that it wasn't.

He sorely needed that feeling right now.

When he returned to self-awareness and opened his eyes, the sky had turned deep blue and the brighter stars were beginning to peek through the fading veil of sunlight.

Cyril smiled, spooning some stew into a bowl from the small pot sitting next to the glowing embers of the fire.

While he ate, Ben turned Cyril's explanation of magic over in his mind, pondering all of the implications. He'd spent years practicing meditation, honing his will to the point where he could silence his mind and focus on a single thought. He couldn't help but wonder if Cyril had taught him the practice for a reason—and that thought sent chills up his spine and ignited his curiosity all at once.

"What kind of things can manifestation magic do?" Ben asked.

Homer yawned and rolled over on his side, licking his lips a few times before closing his eyes and settling in to sleep.

Cyril smiled, shrugging. "That's hard to say. Given sufficient imagination and will, I suspect most anything can be brought into reality."

Frank sat up, his curiosity piqued. "Can you turn a person into a frog?" he asked.

Cyril chuckled, shaking his head. "I doubt it, though I can't say for certain. Manifestation doesn't violate the laws of nature. Instead, it brings about the desired outcome through the natural order, often appearing to be a coincidence. As I understand it, there is no flash or fanfare when you successfully manifest a desire. In fact, it's hard to point to a result and say that it was brought about by magic at all since it looks to have just happened in the ordinary way."

"That sounds kind of boring," Frank said.

"Which is why I've withheld my limited knowledge of magic from you."

"What do you mean?"

"You're young enough that the work and effort required to use manifestation is more than you're willing to do. The next natural step would be for you to convince yourself that you're special, that you can use bargaining magic without consequences. Young people seem to be able to exempt themselves from danger in their own mind with alarming proficiency, especially when the source of danger is so mysteriously alluring."

Frank frowned. "There must be beings that are willing to help. I mean, they can't all be bad."

"Oh, they're not," Cyril said. "But the good ones are very reluctant to intervene in our realm for fear of subverting our free will. As a result, it is exceedingly rare that one will even answer when called."

Frank frowned again, staring into the fire for a while before speaking again.

"It almost seems like more trouble than it's worth."

"For the most part, it is," Cyril said. "Hence my suggestion that we seek out tech rather than magic to fight our enemies."

"I hope you're not suggesting we head up into the valley," Hound said.

"No," Cyril said, "there's too much disease and too many scavengers living in the ruins."

"Then where else are we going to find tech?" Frank asked.

"I'm hoping Chen can help us with that. If not, we'll have to seek out the resistance in Rogue City."

"What makes you think they still exist?" Frank said. "They lost the war. Those that didn't die probably scattered."

"Anywhere you find oppression and evil, you'll find people who choose to resist," Cyril said. "Locating them might be problematic though."

"Yeah, I don't imagine they put a sign on their door," Frank said.

Cyril chuckled, shaking his head. "We'll find them hiding in plain sight."

"What does that even mean?" Frank said.

"It's getting late," Cyril said. "Set your questions aside for now and try to get some rest."

Frank frowned but held his tongue.

The sky and the fire slowly went dark, plunging the forest into blackness. Ben leaned against the boulder, struggling against gravity to keep his eyelids open and failing. The first few times he started to nod off he was able to snap himself out of it, but sleep eventually claimed him.

He opened his eyes again and found himself in the forest, alone in the dark. And then he saw the eyes—tortured eyes, filled with pain and rage and malice. They watched him from the darkness, still and focused, unblinking. Ben knew deep down that he was dreaming, but he couldn't bring himself to wake up.

For the past several years, he had always known when he was dreaming. Occasionally, he was even able to exercise his free will within the dream instead of being at the surreal mercy of dreamland illogic. And he could always wake himself if the dream was going badly.

This was different.

He was rooted to the ground, unable to stand up or even feel his legs. The eyes in the dark were fixed on him like a raptor's gaze, unwavering and intent. He could feel the desperate need behind those eyes to either possess him or consume him, he couldn't decide which. Either way, he wanted out, he wanted to wake up, but he couldn't. It was as helpless a feeling as he had ever experienced.

Then the eyes shifted away from him, looking intently toward another point in the darkness. Ben felt both confusion and relief as his eyes followed the enemy's gaze.

Rufus Hound was standing in the forest, frozen in place, his feet literally rooted to the ground as if his legs were tree trunks. Somewhere in the back of his mind, Ben knew that reality didn't work that way, but at the surface, in the moment, it seemed like the most natural thing in the world that Hound would be half tree.

The eyes started to move, slowly at first, savoring the rising fear now radiating from Rufus. He gave a piercing battle cry, and Bertha appeared in his hands as he brought her up to his shoulder and fired. The report echoed into the darkness, a tongue of flame exploding from the barrel. The eyes kept coming. He fired again, then again and again, unloading his weapon at the approaching menace, but to no avail. The eyes kept coming.

In the space of a single heartbeat, the eyes leapt forward, changing from a slow, stalking approach to a bounding sprint rushing headlong toward Hound. Ben watched in helpless wonder and terror as the creature flashed into view under the silvery light of the moon. It was indistinct and shadowy. Ben couldn't tell where the night ended and the creature began. All he knew for sure was that it was big and it moved with power and terrible purpose—and that it was evil in a way that couldn't even exist in the real world.

It hit Hound in the chest and vanished inside of him. Rufus howled with rage and fear—a howl that transformed into the keening wail of something inhuman, something that should not be.

Hound shook, trembling, his head thrown back, his eyes clenched shut, his mouth open wider than should be possible, every muscle in his body straining in a desperate struggle against the dream-beast. He stood there for a long time, looking as if he was soundlessly screaming to the heavens for help. Suddenly, the tension broke and he hunched his shoulders forward, hanging his head for a moment before he started laughing—not human laughter, not the laughter of mirth, but the laughter of triumph.

Then he slowly looked over at Ben, his glowing red, virulently evil eyes boring into him. Ben snapped awake with a gasp, scrambling to his feet and drawing his sword all in one frantic attempt to escape the surge of fear coursing through him. His head whipped this way and that, taking in the camp and his family and friends, most still sleeping, blissfully ignorant of the danger in their midst.

Homer was growling, his teeth bared at Hound, who stood staring at Ben with a vacant expression and dull red eyes. He took a step forward, not easily or naturally, his legs flopping and jerking, uncoordinated like a puppet made to walk by a child that had never played with such a toy before. He bared his teeth in an inhuman snarl, staring at Ben with singular determination.

He took another step, nearly toppling over from a gross lack of coordination, stopping to right himself before attempting another step. Hound's face contorted, his mouth opening in an effort to scream but no sound came out. As his face spasmed, he stopped midstep.

Ben watched in alarm, growing understanding threatening to unravel his tenuous grasp on sanity. Hound's face relaxed and the eyes again fixed on Ben. He took another step, this time just slightly more coordinated than the last.

Homer barked, rousing Cyril and John in the same moment, followed by Imogen and Frank. John rolled easily to his feet, bow in hand and an arrow nocked.

Cyril took in the scene with a glance. Seeing Hound take another jerky, forced and awkward step toward Ben, he snatched up the stew pot sitting near the fire, filled with water to soak for the night, and hurled the contents at Hound's face. Water splashed over him, stunning him, not from force but from shock and surprise. He fell backward, stumbling to catch himself but failing, landing hard and struggling to gain enough breath to sputter through the rivulets of water dripping out of his hair.

After a moment, he shook his head, coming fully awake, wiping his face. "What the hell just happened?" he asked weakly.

Cyril took a moment to light his lamp before kneeling in front of Hound and looking into his eyes. "I believe you were possessed," he said quietly.

Hound looked around, frowning at the fact that he was several feet from his bedroll.

"I remember eyes and then darkness and struggle," he said, rubbing his face again. "But it was more than darkness, it was nothingness, utter emptiness."

"I saw it too," Ben said, almost afraid to give voice to his nightmare lest it be made real.

"The darkness?" Cyril asked.

"No, the eyes. I was watching them watch me, but then they looked away and I saw Hound in my dream. The eyes took him and I woke to find him coming toward me."

Cyril sat back heavily and closed his eyes.

"Are you trying to say that you both had the same dream?" Frank asked.

Hound nodded. "I didn't see Ben, but everything else was just like he said."

"It would seem that the stalkers are far more dangerous than we thought," Cyril said.

"Wait, are you saying the stalker that we killed is haunting their dreams?" Frank asked. "That's just crazy. The thing is dead."

"The wolf that it animated is dead," Cyril said. "Apparently, the being itself is not."

Frank huffed. "That's just not even possible."

"I think you'll find that when dealing with magic, there's no such thing as *impossible*."

"What are we going to do?" Imogen asked.

Ben was wondering the very same thing. He could meditate to rest his body, but he still needed sleep. Sooner or later, he would have to face his enemy again. If Hound couldn't resist it, how could he?

"Tie me to a tree and take my weapons," Hound said.

"He's right," Ben said. "Me too."

Cyril sighed, nodding in resignation.

Ben didn't sleep much for the rest of the night. When he started to drift off, he willed himself awake. When he failed at that, the discomfort of his bindings and the tree against his back woke him instead. He was grateful when the sky began to show signs of dawn, but not half as grateful as he was that the eyes hadn't visited him again.

Chapter 12

Ben trudged through the forest, each step a contest between his will and his exhaustion. He wasn't paying much attention to anything except his own fatigue but he knew that Hound was in similar shape.

They had broken camp at dawn and followed the stream, which ran roughly parallel to the trail cut into the forested hillside above. They planned on rejoining the trail when they reached Four Mile Lake.

When Frank came to an abrupt stop in front of him, Ben stumbled into his brother's pack, his awareness returning to the world around him rather than fixed on his internal struggle to place one foot in front of the other.

He looked around and saw that everyone else was frozen in place, scanning the trees for something—what he did not know.

"What is it?" he asked Homer.

"There's something out there, but the wind isn't right for me to smell it."

His mind focused anew, bringing him fully into the moment as he searched the wilderness for any hint of threat. A twig broke. His eyes snapped on target, all of his senses straining to detect the source of the noise. The brush moved, and a deer stepped out into a clearing, tentatively looking about.

Ben relaxed, feeling more than a little kinship with the animal, knowing how it felt to be prey. When the deer noticed them, it bounded into the forest, vanishing as quickly as it had appeared. Speed and stealth were its greatest defenses. Ben idly wondered what his were.

He knew from firsthand experience that facing a stalker was far more dangerous than he'd ever imagined. When he was willing to face the truth, he had to admit that the stalker may have already won. His injury, just a few scratches, might be his undoing—or worse, it might lead to the loss of his free will and allow the stalker to use his body to harm those that he loved.

That possibility terrified him more than any other. It was a violation so complete that it seemed worse than death. He vowed to himself that he would choose to end himself rather than let the stalker use him. As he considered suicide, he thought he heard laughter from somewhere very far away.

"We should keep moving," John said.

The day passed in a haze of weariness. Ben's mind and will were reduced to a singular function … taking the next step. His head hung and his attention narrowed to the ground immediately before him. When the sun slid behind the forested hills, relief washed over him at the thought of rest, followed by trepidation at the thought of sleep—a sleep that he knew he wouldn't be able to resist.

They reached the lake as the last light of day was fading into twinkling black. It was long, stretching for miles, but not very wide. Hundreds of fallen trees were crowded against the nearest bank, a few pushed up on shore but most were floating in a haphazard and random arrangement that blanketed the water for a hundred feet.

Ben dropped his pack and sat down heavily, taking a few moments to simply breathe the cool evening air.

Hound dropped his pack and flopped to the ground as well. "I'm stronger than this," he muttered.

"Let me take a look at your wound," Imogen said.

"I couldn't stop you if I wanted to."

"How are you holding up?" Cyril asked Ben, kneeling in front of him and peering into his eyes.

"I'm spent," he said.

"My feet hurt," Homer said, lying down on his side.

Ben gently stroked his fur.

"Have you felt any more influence from the stalker?" Cyril asked.

"I don't know. Maybe."

"How so?"

"I thought I heard laughter when ..."

"When what?" Cyril pressed.

"When I decided that I would rather kill myself than let that thing use me to kill you."

Cyril closed his eyes and bowed his head.

Then he turned to Hound and said, "What about you?"

"I can see its eyes every time I close mine."

"Does it feel like the product of imagination or influence?"

Hound took a moment to consider the question before shaking his head. "Hard to say. Probably a bit of both."

"Let's find someplace out of sight to make camp," John said. "That thicket looks promising."

"Is that the trail?" Frank asked, pointing through the growing darkness toward the west side of the lake.

Before anyone could answer, Imogen stood quickly, pointing into the trees. "What's that?" she asked.

Flickering blue light peeked through the forest. Ben's heart sank as he struggled to get to his feet.

"We have to move," Cyril said, helping Hound up.

They reached the thicket on the east side of the lake a minute before the Dragon Guard came into full view, blue flame burning from the barrels of their rifles like torches, casting eerie light across the still water. Nash was second in a line of six. Ben breathed an inaudible sigh of relief when he didn't see a stalker or tracking dogs with them.

The Guard stopped to make camp on the far side, much too close for Ben's comfort.

"We have to be quiet," Cyril whispered. "Sound carries across water. Also, we can't make any light."

"This is crazy," Frank said. "We can't stay here."

"Where would you have us go?" Cyril asked. "Rufus and your brother need rest. Besides, they might hear us if we try to move through the forest in the dark."

"Might be an opportunity," Hound said.

"What are you talking about?" Frank said.

"We could ambush them."

"You can hardly walk, let alone fight," Frank said.

"He's got you there," Cyril said. "Best to avoid detection."

"Yeah, that way they can get ahead of us and set a trap," Frank said a bit too loudly.

"Quiet!" Cyril whispered harshly. "Our best option is to stay put and be quiet."

Ben sat down to meditate while Cyril prepared a cold meal. It took longer than usual to settle into the calm and restful state where physical sensation faded into the background and his mind was free to turn inward, but eventually he succeeded. All tension drained away, leaving his body to rest—a rest that he sorely needed.

Focusing his mind was something else. Thoughts and fears crowded into his consciousness. What-if scenarios that started out badly and ended even worse wormed their way into his mind. In spite of his best efforts to focus, his fears repeatedly hijacked his consciousness and ran away with it.

When Cyril gently shook him back to the real world, he felt a sense of relief, followed by a terrible feeling of being trapped within his own body and mind with something dark and altogether beyond him.

A sliver of the moon was high overhead, casting just enough silvery light to throw the forest into a jumble of threatening shadows. Ben could barely make out Cyril's face in the dim light.

"Eat," he whispered, sitting down in front of his grandson as he handed him a bowl of dried fruit and jerky.

Ben took the food, nodding his thanks.

"Do you remember what I taught you about lucid dreaming?" Cyril asked, his voice so low that Ben had to strain to hear him over the gentle breeze blowing through the forest.

He thought about it for a moment, nodding. It had been many years, but the lessons came back to him effortlessly.

"Good," Cyril said. "Tonight, I want you to focus on the eyes in the dark before you go to sleep. Visualize yourself in that dream as vividly as you can, except this time see yourself having complete control over events. In that place, the world is yours to command as you will. The stalker is uninvited, an intruder in a realm where your will has total dominion."

"Do you really think that'll work?" Ben asked. "I mean, the stalker has magic and I don't."

Cyril chuckled softly to himself and then fell silent for a moment. Ben waited for his grandfather to order his thoughts.

"That's not entirely true. We all have magic within us to one degree or another. Most of us just don't believe it enough to do anything with it. Admittedly, in the waking world your power to cause change is limited to ordinary action, but in the dream state, your power is limited only by your imagination and your will."

Ben thought about the dream and the eyes in the dark. They seemed to be in control, seeming to savor his fear and helplessness, while he was frozen in place, defenseless.

"It feels like the stalker is so much more powerful than me. I'm not sure I can face it and survive."

"Uncertainty is to be expected," Cyril said. "When you see the eyes, I want you to think about your coin, see it in your hand. Then, make it float into the air."

Ben frowned in confusion as he tried to understand his grandfather's intent.

"Lucid dreaming can be instigated by using a trigger," Cyril said. "If you're able to deliberately will something to happen that's impossible in waking reality, then you'll know you're dreaming. At that point, you are in control. The stalker may resist, it may fight back, it may even be able to exert some measure of influence over your dream, but ultimately, the battle is taking place within your subconscious mind."

"You'd still better tie me up."

"I know," Cyril said with a note of sadness.

It was uncomfortable, but Ben was so tired that he knew he would have little trouble falling asleep. Cyril set a guard rotation, a precaution that Ben was grateful for. The last thing he wanted was to harm his family or friends.

As he drifted off, he focused on the eyes in the dark, seeing them in his mind's eye as vividly as he could—too vividly for comfort.

He wasn't sure when it happened, but at some point he realized that he was asleep … and dreaming. The forest was bathed in silvery moonlight. Wispy streamers of smoke-like fog blanketing the ground obscured his sight past a few dozen feet. The eyes were staring at him through the haze.

Fear gripped him, and he felt paralyzed. He looked down and saw that his feet were rooted to the ground, each of his legs a tree trunk with gnarled old roots burrowing deep into the dirt. He looked back at the eyes, panic beginning to well up in his belly, rising into his throat and threatening to undo all vestiges of reason.

He looked around wildly, searching for any source of help or escape when his eyes landed on Hound not ten feet away from him. Rufus didn't seem to be aware of anything but the eyes in the dark. The sight of the big mercenary, his legs also rooted to the ground like a pair of trees, brought Ben to his senses.

In that moment, he realized he was dreaming.

A snarl from the eyes sent a shiver of fear through him, but he focused his will, and the tree trunks abruptly transformed back into his legs. With a thought, he placed himself between Hound and the eyes.

An inhuman wail tore through the still night. Fear coursed through Ben, but he mastered it and held his ground, facing the beast with a growing sense of resolve. The eyes began to draw closer, the glowing intensity of their hatred shining like flowing lava.

Ben imagined a sword and it appeared in his hand.

The eyes laughed—a barking, gibbering madness tinged with rage as they began to circle, slowly at first, then with such impossible speed that they were suddenly on the other side of Hound. Ben tried to intervene, virtually disappearing from where he stood and appearing between Hound and the stalker, but it was faster, darting forward, a red streak in the dark plunging into Hound's chest.

Ben willed himself awake, freeing himself of the surreal dreamworld, gasping for air in a desperate attempt to calm his pounding heart.

"It has him," he whispered harshly into the night.

Hound began to struggle against his bindings, thrashing and flailing with unbridled fury. Failing to free himself, he tipped his head back and howled. A moment later John splashed a cup of water into his face, snapping him out of the stalker's dream-possession and leaving him confused and sputtering.

"You're awake," John whispered urgently. "The stalker's gone. You're safe."

Hound took several deep breaths and forcibly calmed himself, nodding in the dim light of the approaching dawn.

"They'll be coming for us," Cyril said, hastily packing his bedroll. "We have to move. Now."

John cut Hound and Ben loose, then swiftly packed his bedroll and helped Imogen gather her things.

Loud noises wafted across the water on the early morning air, strident, angry shouting in urgent, demanding tones. Nash was making her Dragon Guard ready.

Ben didn't waste any time. His legs were still tired and his head was a bit foggy from waking so suddenly, but he was eager to be on the move nonetheless.

"We'll head out along the lakeshore, fifty feet or so inside the wood line," Cyril said.

"Won't they be coming that way?" Frank asked.

"Possibly," Cyril said. "Hopefully, they'll opt for speed and take the trail along the other bank."

"What if they don't?"

"We fight."

"Maybe we should head off into the forest."

"No," Cyril said, shaking his head. "We need to stay close to the trail or risk getting lost."

"Maybe lost isn't such a bad thing right now," Frank said.

"It won't be long before they call another stalker to the hunt," Cyril said. "Speed is our best option."

Frank snorted, shaking his head.

Cyril ignored him, looking to the rest for confirmation that they were ready to travel. Satisfied, he said, "Lead the way, John."

The Highwayman set out without a word. Even with only the dim light of a deep blue sky, he was able to pick a trail through the brush that offered little resistance and left little sign of passage.

Ben's mind turned to the eyes as he walked. He'd managed to command his dream and he'd faced the stalker with some success. It was encouraging and terrifying in equal measure. He resolved to work on mastering his dreams. Before, the idea had seemed like a fanciful novelty—a neat trick he could use for self-amusement. Quite suddenly, it had become a matter of life and death.

"I smell someone coming," Homer said.

Ben froze, listening for any hint of the Dragon Guard, but heard none.

"They're coming," he said.

"I don't hear anything," Frank said.

Cyril looked to Ben for confirmation, for certainty. After a glance at his face, Cyril nodded.

"We need to hide," he said.

John pointed to a fallen log that had landed on a large rock, creating a space underneath that was well concealed by dying pine boughs. Within a few minutes, they were all crowded into the small space, straining to hear the approaching enemy.

Ben saw a flicker of blue light through the branches before he heard the Dragon Guard. He tapped his grandfather's shoulder and pointed toward the light. Cyril nodded, easing quietly toward the boulder.

The Dragon Guard moved deliberately, stopping every dozen steps or so to look and listen. Farther off, maybe another hundred feet away, another flicker of blue light peeked through the forest. A second Dragon Guard. Ben looked to Cyril and he nodded confirmation. The men were searching in a line perpendicular to the lakeshore.

The first man drew closer, alert and cautious. Ben found himself holding his breath as the Guard stopped not twenty feet away, his head slowly scanning the gloaming forest.

A twig broke as someone shifted position. The Dragon Guard looked quickly in their direction, frozen in place, straining to listen for another hint of his quarry's location. Then he began to move again, carefully placing each step to avoid making any noise himself.

Cyril eased out from under the tree, keeping close to the boulder, listening for the Dragon Guard's movements and stepping in unison with him. The soldier, armored in black, dragon-fire rifle held at the ready, stopped not ten feet from the fallen tree, searching for some hint of their presence.

A noise caught his attention, a stone hitting the ground. The Dragon Guard turned toward the distraction, his body tense as he strained to detect his prey.

Cyril came up behind him quickly, his left hand covering the man's mouth and jerking his head back as he drove his sword into the back of the man's calf, eliciting a muffled cry of pain and dropping the man to his knees in an instant. Cyril's blade came free a moment later and spun around in his hand seemingly of its own volition, now held point down. He quickly but calmly placed the point just inside the Dragon Guard's armored collar along the right side of his neck and drove the blade to the hilt down into his chest cavity.

The man stiffened and then went limp. Cyril waited for several seconds, looking and listening for any sign that the enemy had been alerted before drawing the crimson blade from the warm corpse and easing the man to the ground.

Not for the first time, Ben wondered about his grandfather's past. He was the most kindly, loving and wise man that Ben had ever known, and yet he'd demonstrated a willingness and ability to kill that could only be the product of a violent history.

Cyril knelt next to the dead man and hastily wiped his sword clean before quietly sheathing it. Then he motioned to the others to quietly come out.

With a gesture, he drew John and Frank to him so he could whisper ever so quietly, "Carry him to the lake."

Frank started to protest, but Cyril stopped him with a hand on his shoulder and a stern look.

He clenched his jaw and did as he was told.

As they neared the logjam lining the shore, Cyril picked up a fallen branch about eight feet long. Without a word, he slipped it between two logs and wedged them apart, motioning with his head to John and Frank. They rolled the body into the opening, then Cyril used his branch to shove the corpse into the inky water beneath. Imogen handed him the Dragon Guard's rifle.

"Wait!" Frank whispered urgently, as Cyril slid the weapon into the water. Within moments the logs floated back into place, creating an unbroken cover of timber and erasing all evidence of the dead Dragon Guard.

"I could have used that," Frank whispered harshly.

Cyril shook his head and put a finger over his lips before turning to John and nodding for him to lead the way. They moved as quietly as they could without sacrificing too much speed. Half an hour later, when the trail was in view at the north end of the lake, they heard a shout from far behind them.

"Sounds like they found something," Hound said. "I'll bet she's even angrier this morning."

"I'm not sure that's possible," Ben said.

"That's just 'cuz you don't have much experience with women," Hound said.

"We need to hurry," Cyril said. "Our best defense now is speed and the distance it'll buy us."

Chapter 13

John set a steady pace that quickly became grueling for Ben. Though he hurt and was struggling to keep up, he didn't complain. In the back of his mind he knew that the consequences of being caught were far worse than any fatigue or discomfort he was feeling. When they reached the trail, the ground became more even, allowing for faster travel.

Ben soon fell into the rhythm of placing one foot in front of the other. If he'd been well rested, he suspected he could have easily slipped into a meditative state as his focus narrowed to the relentless monotony of trudging through the forest. As it was, he needed all of his will and determination just to keep going.

After several hours, they came to a point where the trail wound up the side of a bluff that offered a commanding view of the forest that they had just passed through.

Hound stopped, sitting heavily and leaning against his pack, still strapped to his shoulders. "I hate to be the one to whine, but I need to rest for a few minutes or I'm going to fall over."

Cyril nodded reluctantly and Ben sat down too, leaning back and closing his eyes, savoring the feel of the cool breeze on his sweat-slicked skin. He was spent as well, but entirely unwilling to admit it.

"How are you feeling?" he asked Homer.

His dog grumbled as he licked his paw.

"I know how you feel," Ben said.

"I see them," John said, looking through his monocular.

"How close?" Cyril asked.

"Less than an hour and moving fast."

Hound sighed, regaining his feet with a bit of a struggle. Ben followed suit, only slightly refreshed by the brief respite.

"We should get off the trail," Frank said.

"Not just yet," Cyril said. "We're far enough ahead for now. Eventually, we'll need to take refuge in the forest. For now, we'll make better time on the trail."

Frank didn't seem convinced but he held his tongue.

Again they set out at a painful and exhausting pace. It wasn't long before Ben's world narrowed down to the next step. Through the fog of pain, a noise began to intrude, drawing his attention. The trail had come to one of the many forks of the Rogue River, turning to run along the top of a bluff overlooking the rushing waters a hundred feet below.

"The air smells good here," Homer said.

Ben smiled as he took a deep breath. The rushing water combined with the fragrance of pine needles created an invigorating and calming scent. On another day he would have been content to relax and spend an hour just enjoying the serenity of the wild. But not today.

Not long after they reached the bluff, they heard the strident voice of Nash somewhere behind them. Ben couldn't make out what she said, but he suspected she was commanding her soldiers to move faster.

"We need to hide," Frank said urgently.

The only reply he received was heavy breathing as all of the others struggled to stay ahead of their pursuers. When they came around a corner and saw the remnants of a fallen bridge, everyone stopped.

"Great! Now what?" Frank snapped.

"We find a way across," Cyril said, heading for the abutment. Everyone followed, standing with him at the edge and looking up and down the river.

"I told you we should have left the trail sooner," Frank said. "Now we're screwed."

"Perhaps," Cyril said, then turned to John. "May I see your monocular?" He brought it to his eye and peered downstream. "There," he said, handing the telescope back to John and setting out along the bluff without explanation.

Ben dutifully followed.

"We should go into the forest," Frank said. "He's going to get us killed."

Everyone ignored him, perhaps more out of fatigue than anything else. Frank reluctantly brought up the rear, muttering under his breath.

The river had cut a deep and narrow ravine through the forest, carving a gorge a hundred feet deep and at least as wide from bluff to bluff. Cyril led them to a place where the steep cliff gave way to a shallow draw worn into the bluff by a small stream. Below was a deep pool of calm water fed by a ten-foot waterfall that interrupted the flow of the river. On the opposite bluff was a fallen tree, its roots still tenuously hanging on to the dirt and rocks, its top submerged in the water, the entire thing upside down and leaning against the cliff like a ladder.

"There," Cyril said, pointing at the tree.

"What do you mean 'There'?" Frank said.

"That's our way across," Cyril said, heading down the draw toward the water.

"What about Homer?" Ben asked.

Cyril stopped, looking back at his grandson and shrugging.

"We'll have to carry him up," he said, turning back toward the water and descending cautiously.

"This is crazy!" Frank snapped.

"Quiet," John said, pointing to the abutment of the bridge not a half mile behind them.

Nash was standing with her fists on her hips, glowering at the fallen bridge. Six Dragon Guard stood with her, scanning the surrounding area for any sign of passage. It didn't take long for one to find a trail. Moments later another shouted, pointing in their direction.

"They've found us," Ben said, scrambling down the draw.

"You know I don't like water," Homer said.

"It's better than fire," Ben said.

Homer grumbled, but followed closely.

When Ben reached the point where the stream flowed into the pool below, Cyril handed him a blanket. "We have to jump and swim for it," he said. "Once you're across, use this to make a sling for Homer. We'll help you carry him to the top."

Before Ben could respond, Cyril jumped into the water. Ben looked at Homer, who was peering dubiously over the edge and virtually radiating hesitation, then he looked back at the string of Dragon Guard moving quickly toward them.

"Sorry," he said, pushing Homer off the edge and then jumping in himself.

The water was icy cold, shocking him into breathlessness. He kicked, struggling to return to the surface with the sodden weight of his pack and clothes. It seemed like forever before he broke through, gasping from the cold and a need for air. Homer was ahead of him, swimming toward the fallen tree.

The water splashed behind him as Hound leapt in, followed by Frank, Imogen, and finally John. Ben felt the cold sapping his already flagging strength as he struggled to reach the tree, energy draining out of him with each labored stroke.

He slipped under, the weight of his pack dragging him down. He kicked hard, his legs burning despite the frigid water. He broke free of the water's icy grip and took a gulp of air before slipping under again. This time, as he flailed for his life, his foot hit bottom, solid as stone. He shoved against it and came free again.

Cyril extended a branch to him. Ben was lost in panic but his flailing arm found the limb and he glommed on to it more out of instinct than thought, gripping the lifeline with white and frozen knuckles. Cyril pulled him to the bank and helped him climb out of the water and into the branches of the tree.

Water drained out of his clothes and pack, lightening him with each passing moment. The cool breeze almost felt warm compared to the river. Some measure of feeling began to return to his hands. He turned his attention to his friends and family.

Homer was clinging to the tree with his teeth. Cyril was holding on to the tree with one hand while extending the branch to Hound with the other. Frank was splashing and flailing but managed to stay above water. John was dragging Imogen across by her pack, ensuring that her head remained above water.

Frank reached the tree only moments after Hound, using the mercenary as a stepping stone to propel himself out of the water and into the relative safety of the tree. He clambered past Ben, ignoring his brother in a frantic effort to escape the water. Ben let him pass, instead putting all of his effort into trying to get Homer into the blanket sling.

Hound resurfaced and frantically grasped for the tree. With Cyril's help, he managed to pull himself from the water and into the branches. Imogen and John were next.

A shout from the bluff cut through the roar of the nearby waterfall, drawing Ben's attention. Six Dragon Guard stood atop the cliff aiming their rifles.

Another shout echoed into the canyon, followed by fire, orange and hot roaring across the expanse, illuminating the water with hellish red light. Flame hit the top of the tree, igniting the pine boughs with a whoosh. Sudden heat washed over Ben, clashing with the intense cold. Rather than alleviate the chill, it only served to magnify the burning sensation he felt over every inch of his body.

"Ready!" an angry voice shouted over the torrent.

Ben looked up and saw the tree aflame where it met the cliff top—their escape route was cut off. His eyes flickered to the Dragon Guard as they adjusted their aim downward. He prepared to hurl himself back into the deadly safety of the water, the only refuge from the flame about to rain down on them. Suddenly, a great cracking noise filled the air, seeming to reverberate through his entire body.

The tree broke free, its top plunging deep under the surface, dragging Ben with it. He struggled against the entangling branches, but was helplessly caught up, drawn under and held down. His lungs burned from lack of air even as his skin burned from the icy water.

The tree carried him downstream like a force of nature, bigger and more powerful than anything he could muster, even if he'd been well rested and healthy.

He focused on holding his breath, refusing to surrender one moment before death claimed him, but certain that the reaper was coming nonetheless. And then he broke the surface just long enough to take another breath before the tree pulled him under again. The water flowed swiftly, pulling him with it. He didn't resist, saving every scrap of energy for the task of holding on and holding his breath.

He came up again as the tree stabilized in the water. Even through his sputtering, gasping struggle to fill his lungs, he saw Frank trying to stay afloat. He'd fallen into the river several feet away from the tree. Ben let go of the trunk, grabbing the end of a branch and letting the current carry him toward his brother. He reached him just as Frank slipped under again. Ben frantically grabbed his pack and held on for all he was worth. It felt like his grip was slipping, that his strength was nearly spent, but he managed to pull Frank to the surface, using the water current to guide his brother toward the tree.

As the branches came within reach, Frank flailed until he found purchase, grabbing on to a limb and pulling himself to the trunk. Ben held on as the tree accelerated into the flow of the river. Worry for family and friends filled the back of his mind, but he had no time for it. All of his will and strength went into holding on.

Orange fire filled the air behind them, falling harmlessly into the water. A curse echoed into the canyon, muffled by the roar of the river.

Ben took a deep breath and looked around, wondering if everyone had made it, but all he could see was Homer holding on to a branch with his teeth and Frank, one arm looped over the trunk and holding on for his life.

Weak with exhaustion, his hands numb with cold, Ben focused on maintaining his grip. He knew with perfect certainty that he would drown if he let go. Only the buoyancy of the tree stood between him and an icy death. All that mattered was that he did not let go.

After several minutes, a shout roused him back to other concerns. He looked up and saw Cyril straddling the tree trunk and reaching out to him with a branch. Ben was afraid that he might slip if he let go, but he took the chance, reaching for the limb with one hand and taking hold with all of his limited remaining strength.

Cyril pulled him closer, drawing him into the tangle of branches where even if he did let go, he would be carried forward with the fallen tree. With one last pull, his grandfather managed to haul him up onto the trunk, helping him get wedged between several branches sticking up out of the water.

"Everyone else?" he asked weakly.

"Alive," Cyril said with almost as much exhaustion as Ben felt.

He didn't know how long they floated, sometimes at a frightening pace, down the river before the banks widened and the water slowed. He didn't have the strength to resist when John pulled him off the log and dragged him to the bank.

When he came to his senses, he was lying on the ground near a roaring fire, wrapped in blankets with Homer curled up against him. He had just enough energy to do a headcount. Satisfied that everyone had survived, he drifted off to sleep.

His first thought upon waking was of the eyes. They hadn't come. But then, he'd been so totally exhausted that he didn't remember having any dreams at all. He disentangled himself from the blanket, noting the discomfort of wet clothing clinging to his skin and feeling a chill in spite of the fire.

"Ah, good, you're awake," Cyril said, going to a makeshift clothesline strung up nearby and retrieving Ben's spare clothes. "Here, change into these."

Ben nodded wearily and started to undress. The warmth of the fire against his face and chest clashed with the chill of the cool evening air against his back. Within a few minutes he was wearing dry clothes and felt much better for it. The sky was just losing its blue. He tried to remember what time they'd come to the river, but his head was still a bit foggy.

Cyril handed him a bowl of hot stew. Ben smiled in thanks and dug in, savoring the warmth of each bite, but still wondering where they were— particularly in relation to the Dragon Guard. After he'd eaten, he took a look at everyone else. They looked just as cold and spent as he felt. Hound was asleep, as was Frank. Imogen poked at the embers with a stick, her eyes very far away. John stood with his back to the fire, watching the nearby river.

"Won't they see our fire?"

Cyril nodded without looking up.

Ben frowned, taking a moment to work through his grandfather's thinking before questioning him. It didn't take more than a moment to understand that they wouldn't have survived the night without warmth. Certain death now versus potential death later—bad choices and worse choices.

"How much distance did we gain by floating the river?"

"Enough for now," Cyril said. "Tomorrow is another matter. Rest, we'll be on the move at the first hint of dawn."

"How are you doing?" Ben asked Homer, gently stroking his side.

"The fire feels good. It makes me sleepy."

Ben scratched his ears and lay down, curling up in his blanket and drifting off to sleep. He woke to find himself in the dreamworld again, the eyes stalking him in the night. It was nearly identical to the previous attacks, except this time he knew immediately that he was dreaming. With a thought, his coin appeared in his outstretched palm, then floated effortlessly into the air.

He moved toward the eyes, putting himself in position to guard Hound, who was rooted to the ground and entirely oblivious of everything save the eyes. Rather than fight, Ben willed the fog to dissipate. It vanished so quickly that even he was a bit surprised. Still, the eyes watched him, snarling in the dark.

As they started to move toward him, he willed the night to become day, transforming his dreamscape into a bright sunny afternoon in the woods. It happened so quickly and so suddenly that Ben was again surprised by his omnipotence in this place. The stalker shrieked in pain and then vanished. Ben marveled at the ease of it. With a thought, he sent Hound back into sleep, his presence in the dream fading away as if he'd been willed from existence. Ben sat down and took a moment to consider the power that he had in this unreal realm. It was everything he ever imagined that magic could be, and yet he knew that it wasn't magic at all. With that thought, he slipped from dream into sleep.

He woke to find Cyril shaking his shoulder. The forest was black as pitch. The fire had burned down to coals, heat still radiating from the pit but the light was all but extinguished.

"Dawn is coming."

Ben nodded, rubbing his face and yawning, taking a few moments to clear the sleep from his mind before he got up and began packing his things, gathering his dry clothes from the line.

Light was just beginning to dim the stars when they set out along the riverbank.

Chapter 14

The sun had risen just to the tops of the trees and the morning air was still cool and damp. Ben realized after a time that he felt much stronger. He was more alert and able to take in some of the serene natural beauty of the wilderness. It struck him as an odd dichotomy that the world could be facing such a powerful force of darkness and evil, yet here, in this place, there was no evidence of it at all. Nature entirely ignored the plight of man.

He wished that he could ignore it as well, but that was no longer an option. The Dragon Guard had demonstrated how relentless they were. If he was to survive, if his family and friends were to survive, they either had to run away and hide somewhere outside the grasp of the wyrm ... or they had to slay the dragon.

He nearly chuckled at the thought. As a child, he'd read stories about the knight in shining armor courageously standing up for all that was good and decent in the world in the face of unspeakable evil, bravely entering the dragon's lair and facing his nemesis in mortal combat. It seemed so much more believable on the pages of a story. His new reality was something altogether different.

He simply didn't have the power to succeed against such formidable enemies. If he was being honest with himself, he didn't have the courage either. The idea of fighting the Dragon Guard made him shrink with fear. Standing against the dragon, a creature of magic and terrible strength, was preposterous at best.

And yet, others had done just that. The resistance had defeated four of the five dragons. Admittedly, they'd had the help of one of those dragons—if the stories were to be believed anyway. Ben wondered at the courage of those people, known today only by the titles they'd used to protect their true identities. What drove a person to risk everything for such a slim chance at something better?

Searching his own soul, he found himself wanting by comparison.

"Just because you're afraid doesn't mean you shouldn't stand up to a bully," Homer said, bringing Ben out of his self-reflection.

"Maybe it does when the bully is a hundred times bigger than me," Ben replied.

"You know what they say ... 'It's not the size of the dog in the fight, it's the size of the fight in the dog.'"

"Really?"

"Just saying."

"And what would you do against the wyrm?"

"Bite him on the ankle. Probably the only place I could reach."

Ben chuckled, his spirits buoyed by the ridiculousness of being lectured on the merits of courage by his talking dog.

"What's so funny?" Frank asked.

"I was just imagining the absurdity of fighting the dragon."

"Why the hell would you want to do that?"

"It's not that I want to," Ben said, shaking his head. "It's just that, well, someone has to or he'll win. Every year, the wyrm grows bigger and more powerful. Eventually, the whole world will fall to him."

"So? That won't happen for a long time," Frank said. "We just need to go somewhere that the dragon doesn't control."

Ben sighed. "But what about everybody else?"

"What about them?" Frank said, looking at Ben like he was crazy. "If they want to live, they'll run too."

"Not everyone has that luxury," Imogen said, a tremor of fear and sadness in her voice.

Frank just shook his head.

Ben put his hand on her shoulder, drawing her attention. "We'll get him back," he whispered.

She forced a smile.

"You seem to be feeling better today," she said.

Ben nodded. "I think the stalker is gone. Last night, I was able to gain control over my dream. I think I banished it."

"I feel better today, too," Hound said. "I don't remember much of my nightmare, except it suddenly got light and the eyes went away."

Ben smiled to himself. It felt good to have the power he needed to be safe from his enemy—even if that power was just a dream.

They stopped at a narrowing of the river as it plunged into a cataract where it cut a swath between two rising bluffs. The roar was deafening and the spray of the torrent chilled the air.

"Looks like we have to leave the river," Cyril said, turning to John. "Any idea where we are in relation to the trail?"

"Some ... I think," he said, looking into the trees and picking a direction with a hint of uncertainty before heading out.

They stopped to rest and eat lunch in a clearing bathed in sunlight. Ben was tired from the walk, but his exhaustion of the past few days was quickly fading. After lunch, he carefully peeled away his bandage and inspected his wounds. They still hurt, but the signs of infection and the angry, unnatural blackness was all but gone.

Cyril sat down next to him.

"Let me take a look."

He inspected the wounds and nodded approvingly. "Looks like the honey has eliminated the infection. More importantly, the magical taint left by your injury seems to be gone as well."

Ben hesitated for a moment before deciding to recount his experiences in the dreamworld.

His grandfather listened intently, silencing Frank with a gesture when he tried to scoff at Ben's story.

"You did well," Cyril said with a proud smile when Ben had finished. "Lucid dreaming is difficult to master. Likely more so with the presence of another's will in your dream."

"I'm a bit disturbed that we were having the same dream," Hound said. Ben nodded. "Me too."

"Do you really believe any of that?" Frank said. "I mean seriously, you were both just having a fever dream."

"You weren't there, Frank. It felt a lot more real than any dream I've ever had before."

"Same here," Hound said, a haunted look in his eyes. "Maybe, when we have a chance to stop for a while, you can teach me how to control my dreams too. I hate the idea of being helpless in a fight no matter where the battlefield is."

Ben smiled at him, nodding agreement.

Cyril looked at John and said, "So where do you think we are?"

"I'm pretty sure the Red Blanket River runs along the other side of that ridge," he said, pointing roughly north.

"So that puts the trail over there, then," Cyril said, gesturing east.

John nodded.

"That ridge looks pretty rugged."

"Yeah, but the Dragon Guard will be looking for us on the trail or along the river. We should probably avoid both," John said.

Cyril grimaced slightly at the steep climb ahead.

It wasn't long before Ben's legs were burning. Each step required deliberate effort, but each step also carried him closer to the ridgeline and the descent that would follow.

By midafternoon, they were resting at the top, looking through the trees at the flat-topped caldera of Mount Mazama in the distance. Snow still clung to its slopes, glistening brightly in the sunlight.

"Chen's place is down there," Cyril said, pointing into the forest. "We should be able to make it there by dusk."

"And then what?" Frank asked. "The Dragon Guard aren't going to give up looking for us."

"No, but they won't find us there," Cyril said with a knowing smile.

"What's that supposed to mean?"

"You'll see," he said. "We should get moving."

The descent was nearly as tiring as the climb had been, but for different reasons. Ben found himself moving with far greater caution. Coming up, a wrong step just meant that it would take a few more steps to reach the ridgeline. Going down, a wrong step could be disastrous. They moved from tree to tree, using the sturdy trunks to arrest gravity's pull.

By the time they reached the valley cut through the forest by the Red Blanket, everyone was once again exhausted. While they rested near the fast-moving stream, Ben found himself wondering what had happened to Zack, a pang of guilt assailing his conscience at the thought. Objectively, he knew there was nothing they could have done to free him from the Dragon Guard—they had barely escaped as it was. But still, he felt bad for his friend, even if his plight was mostly his own doing. He wondered if he would ever see him again.

"How much farther is it?" Frank asked.

"Maybe another hour," Cyril said. "It's hard to say from here. I'll need to get my bearings."

They set out again following the stream, Cyril stopping every so often to look for landmarks. Ben was just starting to worry that Cyril might be lost, when his grandfather stopped and smiled broadly, looking at a distinctive rock formation rising up through the trees on the far bank.

"We close?" Hound asked.

"We are," Cyril said. "Let's get across the river."

This one was far smaller, and much more shallow than the previous river. Ben didn't relish the idea of another soaking in a frigid mountain runoff, so he was grateful when they found a tree that had fallen across the water, providing a natural bridge.

Cyril led them over the river and up the far bank into a boulder field that had been overgrown by the forest. Giant rocks, some the size of houses, competed with the scattered trees for dominance of the hillside. It took a few minutes of searching before Cyril set out with renewed confidence.

He led them to a cliff that rose twenty feet straight up before continuing to slope sharply toward the next ridgeline. A few minutes later, they came to a large crack in the cliff, hidden by a thicket of trees. Cyril lit his lantern before leading them into the narrow cave entrance.

"I thought you said he lives in the forest," Frank said.

"He does," Cyril responded without slowing.

The opening took them into the earth for twenty feet before it turned and sloped up sharply, a series of time-worn stairs cut into the stone. The stairs led to a landing of sorts, more a wide spot in the cave than anything else. Standing in the center of the small room was a stone marker with a complicated rune carved into the face of it. Cyril gestured for everyone to stop as he approached the marker, lantern held high and one hand outstretched.

He muttered something under his breath and laid his hand on the stone, a knowing smile spreading across his face.

"All right, everybody cross to the other side of the chamber."

He kept his hand on the marker until he had crossed the threshold, then spoke a few more words before removing it.

"Where to now?" Frank asked, looking at the walls surrounding them. "And what was that all about? That thing looks like a dragon marker."

"It does, doesn't it?" Cyril said, going to a place in the wall and searching momentarily before reaching into a crack and taking hold of something within. A grinding noise, deep inside the bedrock surrounding them, reverberated through the chamber. Cyril laid his hand on the wall and pushed gently. A giant stone, balanced perfectly on some unseen fulcrum, turned aside, revealing another passageway.

"How the hell?" Frank asked, marveling at the size of the stone that Cyril had just moved with a gentle push.

"Go on."

After they filed through, Cyril pushed the stone door back into place. A grinding click confirmed that it was once again secure. Another few minutes of travel through a series of stone corridors, some cut, but most natural, brought them to the light of day.

They emerged into a verdant meadow surrounded by trees, which were in turn surrounded by cliff walls. The entire area was a hundred feet across at its narrowest point and looked like it might be two hundred feet long.

A little man with a completely bald head and a long white beard sat in the center of the meadow. He was perfectly still save for his easy and precisely rhythmic breathing. As they filed out, his eyes opened—sharp, intelligent eyes, filled with wisdom and compassion.

He smiled with mischief and came to his feet with fluid grace. He moved far more easily than Ben would have thought possible for a man of his age.

"I've been expecting you," he said, his eyes landing on Cyril. His voice was small and gentle—almost tentative, as if he hadn't spoken in a long time.

"It's good to see you," Cyril said, going to his friend and giving him a big hug.

Chen chuckled gleefully. "The years have been kind to you."

"You as well," Cyril said. "Your grotto is as serene as ever."

Chen smiled wistfully, looking around at the cliff-enclosed sanctuary.

"I've been well protected here ... I get very few visitors, which has been a blessing, though I do occasionally get lonely."

"I wish our visit was under other circumstances."

Chen nodded sadly. "So the battle has been joined again."

Cyril nodded solemnly, turning to his companions.

"The wyrm's minions have taken my daughter's son," he said, presenting Imogen.

Chen smiled at her sadly, taking her hands in his. "I hope that I can offer you some measure of kindness while you take rest here. Trust that your son is well and will soon be reunited with you."

"Thank you," she said, bowing her head.

"These are my grandsons ... Benjamin and Franklin."

Chen bowed to Ben, smiling warmly. "You have your mother's eyes, and her fierce spirit, I think." He looked down at the dog by Ben's feet, cocking his head to one side, his ready smile turning to a look of wonder. He glanced at Cyril briefly before kneeling in front of Homer and gently putting his forehead against the dog's. He muttered a few words in Chinese—words that carried a tone of great reverence. Homer wagged his tail and Chen laughed, coming to his feet easily and facing Frank.

He regarded him for several moments, his face becoming stern, before he grasped him by the back of the neck and pulled him close to whisper in his ear. Frank went slightly pale, pulling back from Chen with a look of fear.

Chen turned to Hound.

"Rufus Hound, at your service."

Ben couldn't help but smile at the sight of the big mercenary extending a measure of respect to Chen that Ben wouldn't have thought possible.

"You are a true friend to risk so much in a fight that is not yours."

Hound shrugged. "I like to fight."

Chen smiled and patted Hound on the shoulder, turning to John next. "John Durt."

"The Highwayman," Chen said, nodding with appreciation. "Your reputation is well deserved, I trust."

"I've never lost a person in my care," John said.

"I can't imagine a truer measure of competence for a man in your line of work."

Chen stepped back and appraised the group. After a moment, his eyes fell on Cyril. "Come, you are tired and in need of a hot meal."

He didn't wait for a response before turning and strolling off at a measured pace across the meadow to a well-manicured trail. The entire grotto was lush with green. A wide variety of trees grew in intervals that were almost naturally wild, yet provided each particular tree with just enough space for it to receive ample light.

The trail passed into another clearing. Raised garden beds interspersed with gravel walkways ran perpendicular to the path. The rich, black soil was mulched with pine needles and leaves. No crops were growing at the moment, but it was early in the year.

The trail intersected another just under the next stand of trees. Chen walked like a man of practiced patience—a man who had come to accept that all things happen in their time, regardless of desire.

"I like this place," Homer said.

"Me too. It's so peaceful and secluded."

"It smells good, too."

Ben smiled gently, and then more broadly as they rounded a corner and found a simple house built in a sheltered corner of the grotto. It was clean and well cared for. Plants were poking out of the soil in a dozen boxes and pots, their flowers not yet in bloom but making ready to fill the space with color.

Off to the side was a large table with benches on either side. A roof on six posts stood overhead. A pile of neatly stacked garden pots, boxes and tools was off to one side and an outdoor hearth burned with a low fire against the cliff wall.

"Please sit," Chen said, motioning to the table as he made his way to the fire. After checking his kettle and nodding to himself with genuine delight, he retrieved a tray of cups and brought them to the table, very deliberately placing one cup before each of his guests before returning to the fire for the kettle.

He poured hot spicy tea, admonishing each of them to refrain from drinking with a look that quickly turned from stern to mirthful, as if he were privy to a cosmic joke that they could only guess at. After all of the tea was poured and Chen took his place at the table, he lifted his cup. When everyone had followed suit he bowed solemnly.

"May this tea nourish our bodies as the light nourishes our souls," he whispered. Then he took a sip, savoring the moment as if it was the sole focus of his entire being.

Ben sipped the tea and felt the warmth wash into him. Sweetness and spice danced on his palate and he couldn't help but smile at the delight of it.

"This is wonderful," Imogen said.

"Thank you, my dear," Chen said with a humble bow. "It's my own special recipe. Enjoy. I will prepare dinner, and then we can talk."

Chen went to a nearby barrel and pulled a string of still wiggling trout from the water. He took them to a small table next to the fire and cleaned them, seasoning them each before laying them on the coals to cook in their own scales. It wasn't long before he brought a platter of fish to the table.

He didn't offer any other fare, but Ben felt like it was a feast. The trout was done to perfection, cooked in its own natural oils. Chen seemed to take an equal measure of joy from the delicate fish and from his guests' appreciation of his cooking. After the meal, he cleared the table and poured everyone another cup of tea, then he sat down and nodded to Cyril.

What followed was a careful recounting of everything that had happened since Enzo had taken Imogen's baby. Cyril told most of the story, occasionally stopping to clarify a point or to defer to one of his companions for a more full explanation when it was warranted. Chen listened attentively, his complete focus never wavering for an instant.

Cyril showed respect to Chen in the way a student respects a master—the way Ben respected his grandfather. He puzzled at the relationship the two men had. It was a deep and trusting friendship ... the kind of trust that can only be earned through shared hardship. Once again, Ben found himself wondering about his grandfather's past.

Once the telling of the story culminated with their arrival at the grotto, Chen nodded soberly and fell silent. After several moments, he went to the fire for the tea kettle, filling each of their cups again without a word.

Ben scanned his companions' faces. All of them were waiting for Chen to speak, some more patiently than others ... all save Frank. He looked afraid, uncharacteristically unconfident. Usually when he met new people, he was the very picture of charm, putting on a mask of humor and self-assurance that Ben had often wished he could match. But here, now, he was afraid. It seemed odd, given that Ben felt safer in this grotto than he had since Enzo had arrived with his henchmen at their shop.

"What do you think of Chen?" he asked Homer.

"His soul is clear white," Homer said, as if the meaning of such a statement was self-evident.

Before Ben could question his dog further, Chen sighed deeply, smiling to himself sadly.

"You are welcome to stay here for as long as you wish, though I suspect you will not tarry." He turned to Ben and held him with his very old and wise eyes. "You have done well besting the stalker in your dream, but you are still in danger."

Hound tensed.

"I thought it was gone," Ben said, alarm in his voice.

Chen shook his head. "It remains, awaiting a moment of weakness when it can strike without warning."

Ben closed his eyes, fear rekindling in his belly and washing away all sense of safety.

"You are wise to fear this enemy," Chen said. "It is not of this world. It lusts after form and life—two things that it can only find in the body of another. Fortunately, I can send it back to the dark place from whence it came, if you are willing."

Ben and Hound nodded in unison.

Chen nodded approvingly. "You will feel pain, possibly even great pain, but it must be endured if you are to be free of this taint."

"Whatever you got to do," Hound said. "I can take it."

"I trust that you can," Chen said. "For tonight, I will give you each a tonic that will help you sleep without interference."

"Thank you," Ben said. "I could really use a good night's sleep."

"And you shall have it," Chen said, coming to his feet. "Please, enjoy the tea and the fire. I must gather a few things from the grotto." He strolled away into the trees, picking up a small basket along the way.

Chapter 15

Ben couldn't help but smile as he watched the man vanish into the growing darkness.

"I like him."

"I thought you would," Cyril said.

"Why haven't we ever visited him before?"

"He values his solitude," Cyril said. "I didn't want to disturb him."

"But you seem like such old friends."

"We are. He's one of the best friends I've ever had."

"I remember him," Imogen said quietly. "I must have been very young, but he seems familiar somehow."

Cyril took his daughter's hand. "He held you the day that you were born. He was around a lot for the first few years of your life. You two were fast friends before you could even speak."

"Why would anyone want to live out here all alone?" Frank muttered.

"His work," Cyril said.

"What work?" Frank asked, looking around incredulously.

Cyril just shook his head sadly. "I don't think I could explain it to you if I tried. Besides, it's not my place to speak of it."

"He said that I have my mother's eyes," Ben said.

Cyril nodded sadly, his eyes becoming distant.

"How did she die?" Ben asked.

Imogen looked down at the table.

Cyril closed his eyes, and slowly shook his head.

"Perhaps another time," he said softly, swallowing hard and walking away from the table.

Frank looked at Imogen. "Do you know?" he asked.

She winced, nodding tightly.

"And you haven't told us?" he pressed.

"I swore not to," she whispered. "I'm sorry … I just can't. It's not my place."

Frank snorted. "Yeah, there's a lot of that going around today." He left the table muttering under his breath.

Ben remained silent, pondering the possible reasons his grandfather might have for keeping such information from him and Frank. Try as he might, it just didn't make sense, and yet, he knew instinctively that there was a reason, and a good one. Cyril wouldn't withhold such intimate details of their lives without cause.

As the light of day faded, Cyril returned to the sheltered table and lit his lantern. Chen returned a few moments later, his basket partially filled with a variety of different plants. He retrieved a cooking pot from his one-room house and went to work at the fire, brewing a temporary antidote to the stalker's taint.

As Chen worked, Cyril looked around, a hint of alarm ghosting across his face.

"Where's your brother?" he asked Ben.

"He got mad and wandered off."

Cyril started to get up, but Chen stopped him with a wave of his hand.

"The boy can do little harm," he said, stripping the leaves from a stem and dropping them into the pot. "Give him time to work through his frustration."

Cyril nodded reluctantly as he sat back down.

"Where will we go from here?" Ben asked his grandfather.

Cyril hesitated for a moment. Ben suspected that he was deciding how much to reveal rather than considering their prospects. Ben waited. He didn't like being kept in the dark any more than Frank did, but he trusted his grandfather without question. Part of that trust was accepting his careful control of information.

Finally, Cyril said, "We'll head west along the Red Blanket. It'll take us to old Highway 62. From there we'll go south to Shady Cove and then we'll go west through the forest."

"Why not just take the highway into Rogue City?" Imogen asked. "Wouldn't that be faster?"

"It would, but it would also be far more dangerous," Cyril said. "The Dragon Guard know we went north. It's a good bet they'll be looking for us to come back into town along the highway."

"So we circle around to the old interstate and approach from the west," John said.

Cyril nodded. "That's our best chance of getting into town without being spotted."

"Do you have a plan to get my baby back?" Imogen asked.

"I have a few ideas, but I won't know for sure until we get closer. We need to know where your son is being held before we can devise a plan."

She nodded tightly, tension and fear etched into her face.

Ben reached across the table and took her hand, offering a reassuring squeeze. She tried to smile.

"The tonic will take a few minutes to brew," Chen said, returning to the table. "Tomorrow, I will prepare the cure for your unnatural affliction. You will both be incapacitated for at least a day, most likely two."

"Don't much like the sound of that," Hound said.

"You will like the reality of it much less, I fear," Chen said. "But it is the only way within my knowledge to defeat your enemy."

"How does that work, anyway?" Hound said. "The thing just scratched me. How can it invade my dreams and take over my body from a scratch?"

"A stalker requires a host to exist in this world," Chen said. "When it injured you, it left behind a remnant of its dark essence. Had the wolf lived, the stalker would still cling to that host, but now the only link it has to this world resides within the two of you."

"I think I liked it better when it was flesh and blood," Hound said. "I can shoot a wolf."

Ben nodded agreement. It was a terrifying prospect to face an enemy that had power without form, though it had also led him to a greater understanding of his own mind and will—not insignificant achievements.

"Magic is often insidious," Chen said. "Particularly magic that calls on beings from realms other than our own." He returned to the simmering pot and poured the liquid into two cups, handing one to Ben and the other to Hound.

Both looked at the contents dubiously.

"Smells terrible," Hound said.

"It will taste even worse, but it will help you sleep without dreaming," Chen said, motioning for them to drink.

Ben nearly gagged. It was an awful, bitter-tasting brew, but he managed to choke it down.

Hound drained his cup in a gulp and then looked at it like he was considering taking revenge on it. But then he shrugged to himself and said, "I've had rotgut that tasted worse."

"You two should go to bed," Chen said. "It won't be long before sleep claims you."

Ben felt a wave of relaxation flow over him a moment later.

"I see what you mean," he said, going to his pack and retrieving his bedroll. He laid his head on the pillow, and just a few moments later woke to the sound of singing birds and a pale blue sky. After stretching and rubbing the sleep from his eyes, he got up and went to the table, willing the fogginess from his mind.

"Wow, I slept hard."

Hound sat up with a start, looking around briefly before he lay back down.

"I don't even remember falling asleep," he said, covering his eyes with his forearm.

"Me neither," Ben said, smiling his thanks to Chen.

Everyone else was already up and eating breakfast.

Chen served Ben and Hound bowls of oatmeal with nuts and berries along with cups of his wonderful spicy tea. Ben felt his grogginess lift as he ate.

"Mind if I go for a walk?" he asked when he had finished his breakfast.

"Of course not," Chen said. "Just don't attempt to leave the grotto without assistance. The wards are unforgiving."

"More magic that nobody will tell us about, huh?" Frank said.

"I just told you about it," Chen said matter-of-factly.

Ben left the table with Homer at his heels. The air was crisp and invigorating. The sky was clear and blue and serene. He walked for a few minutes before he came to a natural spring that bubbled up out of the ground into a shallow pool before running off toward the cliff. He idly wondered how it got out of the grotto, but dismissed the thought as he knelt down and splashed the frigid water on his face, gasping from the shock of it.

Fully awake and alert, he sat down in the plush grass and cleared his mind, settling into the comfort of his meditation quickly and easily. Far from being a distraction, the gentle burbling of the spring and the song of the birds lulled him into a state of non-thought that left him feeling calm and centered. After a time, he returned to outward awareness and found Chen seated nearby, sitting in the exact same position. The old man opened his eyes and smiled with an expression of knowing, as if he understood exactly how profoundly rewarding meditation was.

"Your grandfather has taught you well," he said.

Ben nodded. "He's always been there for me—always giving his knowledge freely and generously." Ben hesitated. "And yet, there are things he won't tell me." It wasn't a question, but he held Chen's gaze as if it were.

Chen didn't flinch or waver. "Do you doubt his intentions?"

"No," Ben said, shaking he head. "Never."

"Do you doubt his wisdom?"

Ben frowned, shaking his head again.

Chen smiled knowingly, rising and patting Ben on the shoulder in passing, leaving him to think about his many questions.

"Some things are better left unknown," Homer said.

"Do you know what my grandfather is hiding from us?"

Homer didn't answer, instead rolling over and wiggling into the grass, grumbling with pleasure.

"Easy for you to say," Ben muttered, coming to his feet and leaving his dog to happily rub his back against the ground. Homer kept growling and snorting as Ben walked away chuckling.

When he returned to the house, he found Chen and Cyril sipping tea and talking in low tones. Everyone else was absent.

"Ah, there you are," Cyril said, motioning for him to take a seat at the table. Ben obeyed without a word. Cyril pursed his lips, sighing resignedly as he regarded his grandson.

"I know you have questions. The truth is, you deserve answers … and I fear that I'll have little choice but to provide them all too soon. For now, I ask that you be patient. And know that I trust you. I've kept things from you to protect you, not because I don't believe that I can confide in you."

"That's what frightens me," Ben said. "Over the past few days, you've shown a side of yourself that I always suspected was there, but could never be certain of. Now … well, I'm not sure I want to know."

"What's coming will test you in ways you can't imagine," Cyril said. "No matter what happens, know that I believe in you. I always have."

Ben thought he saw a twinge of guilt in his grandfather's eyes, yet one more unsettling piece of evidence that the world he once knew had come to an end. Worse, Ben had a sinking sense that Cyril had some expectation of him. Of all the ways that he could fail in life, he was most afraid of disappointing his grandfather. He only hoped that he was adequate to whatever would be asked of him—but he feared that he wasn't. He fell silent, carefully considering his next words.

"You've trained me how to fight ... how to kill. You've trained me how to focus my mind, how to bring my will to bear on a single thought. You didn't do this by accident or on a whim. You've been preparing me for something my whole life."

Cyril looked down and took Ben's hand without a word. A few moments passed before a silent tear fell to the table. Ben felt a jolt of adrenaline in his stomach.

"I'm so sorry," Cyril whispered. "I wish I hadn't failed. I wish I could have found another way."

Just then, Frank and Rufus came out of the forest, heading for the table.

Cyril sniffed and wiped his face as he turned away, composing himself quickly.

"Ah, good," Chen said, drawing their attention. "Now that both of you are here, I'm ready to begin whenever you are."

"I was afraid you were going to say that," Hound said, with a crooked smile. "So how's this going to work?" He took a seat at the table and folded his hands as if he meant to give Chen his undivided attention.

"You and Ben will both remove your shirts and bandages. Each of you will lie down in the grass. Then I will tie your hands and feet to a set of stakes."

"Don't much like the sound of that," Hound said.

"Me neither," said Ben.

"A necessary precaution," Chen said with a helpless shrug. "During the process, the stalker will attempt to possess you. And it must for this to work—it must come to the surface before it can be banished."

"Sounds fun," Hound said flatly. "Then what?"

"I will apply a poultice to your wounds. You will drift into a place between sleep and waking for a time. As the medicine does its work, the stalker will realize that its taint is being drawn out of you. It will exert its will in a desperate attempt to remain in this world. That is when I will strip it from you and drive it from our realm."

"We'll get back to that last part in a minute," Hound said, eyeing Chen suspiciously. "Why can't we just let the medicine pull the taint out and be done with it?"

"The poultice will only remove the physical remnants of the infection. Magic is required to remove the rest."

"So you're going to use magic to get rid of it," Hound said. "I thought you needed part of a dragon to do that."

"Indeed," Chen said, pulling a small amulet from under his shirt.

Frank leaned forward with a start. "Is that a dragon bone?"

"Yes," Chen said, holding Frank's eyes with his own.

"How?" Frank asked. "Where did you get it?"

Ben frowned in confusion as he examined the circular piece of bone hanging from a sturdy leather thong threaded through a hole at its center. The medallion was an inch in diameter and not more than a quarter-inch thick. Intricate runes were carved into every part of its surface.

"This is very old," Chen said, holding it up and examining it as if for the first time, a look of wonder in his eyes. "It was given to me by my father as he lay on his deathbed."

"But ... how's that even possible?" Frank asked. "Dragonfall was only seventy-five years ago."

"You assume, like most people, that this is the first time the dragons tried to conquer our world."

"Wait ... you mean they've been here before?" Hound asked.

"Of course," Chen said. "Where did you think all of the stories of dragons and magic came from? They brought war to our world at least once before, very long ago. A great civilization fought them and prevailed, but at a terrible cost. Humanity fell into darkness and ignorance for millennia."

Ben's mind reeled as all of the implications and possibilities raced around in his head, jumbled and confused. If the dragons had come to earth before, they could come again. Even if they were defeated, they would be back.

Chen seemed to read his thoughts, offering him a helpless, yet sympathetic shrug.

"We can't win," Ben whispered.

"Sure we can," Chen said. "We did before and we will again."

"But eventually, sooner or later, they'll conquer the world."

"Perhaps, but the future is not set. They will attack. They will wage their war of conquest and tyranny, just as countless human governments have done over the ages. And ultimately they will fail, just as every government that has risen under the banner of evil has fallen, just as the dragons fell into myth and legend. Evil can only prevail in the short term. Over time, it always fails."

"Lot of good that does us," Frank said, his eyes never leaving the amulet until Chen slipped it back inside his shirt.

"Shall we begin?" Chen asked, looking to Ben and Hound for their assent.

Both nodded with a half measure of certainty.

Chapter 16

The grass was cool but comfortable enough. The ropes tied around his wrists and ankles weren't. Ben tried to ignore the pain, taking solace in the familiar blue of the sky. Homer lay down next to him, whining softly.

"It'll be okay," Ben said.

Homer didn't respond except by whining again. Chen patted him on the head as he knelt down between Ben and Rufus, carefully cleaning their wounds, then disinfecting them with alcohol. Once he was satisfied that they were thoroughly clean, he went to his hearth and stirred the pot of ingredients that he'd been cooking for most of the day.

The sun was warm, diminishing the chill of the air and drying their wounds. After a while, Chen returned with a pot of foul-smelling brew in one hand and a basket in the other. He began with Hound, applying a thick coating of a dark green paste to his chest.

"Holy shit, that smells bad," Hound said, turning his head aside.

Ben nearly vomited when the first wave of stench hit his nostrils, turning away as well and focusing his mind on other things in an effort to escape the unpleasantness of the moment. His efforts were met with limited success.

When Chen applied the poultice to Ben's chest, it burned painfully. He clenched his teeth and renewed his efforts to detach from the pain.

Imogen brought Chen a pot of hot water. He dropped two thick cloths into it, allowing them to soak for a few moments. After wringing out the hot towels, he laid one over the poultice on Hound's chest and carefully pressed it into place. Then he repeated the procedure on Ben.

The heat increased. Sweat began to bead on Ben's forehead.

Imogen left and returned with a bowl of cold water and a cloth. She alternated between the two of them, gently pressing the cloth against their foreheads to help ease the fever rising within each.

A prickly wave of heat flowed from the poultice into Ben's entire body followed quickly by sweat beading up and running down the sides of his chest. He started to feel trapped and helpless. Try as he might, he simply couldn't pull his mind away from the heat. When Chen had first applied the poultice, Ben had assumed that the temperature would naturally cool, but it didn't. Instead it just got hotter.

His mind wandered into delirium, only occasionally returning to reality to hear Imogen's soothing words and feel the bite of the rope around his wrists as he struggled to free himself.

He found himself back in the forest, facing the eyes in the night, rooted to the ground and helpless. Fear pressed in on him, surrounding and suffocating him with its insistent embrace.

The eyes began to move, slowly at first, and then so quickly that he could do nothing but watch them come, streaking through the fog. As the stalker crashed into him, the dreamscape vanished and he plunged into an icy darkness. It was so cold, so utterly devoid of light and so wrong that he tried to scream with unbridled panic, but no sound came.

It was as if he'd lost all form, all sense, save the awareness that he was alone in the cold dark. A fragment of a thought intruded into his misery, and it dawned on him that this was the true nature of the stalker's realm and existence. In spite of his terror, Ben felt a pang of sympathy for the horrible creature. Even though it had hunted him and nearly killed him, he wouldn't wish this existence on any being. It was little wonder that the stalkers would do anything to have form, to live in a world with light and warmth.

Then he heard laughter laced with incalculable malice … and the truth of the stalker's intent became clear. It meant to banish him to this realm forever, trading places with his soul as it possessed his body. The horror of it was almost more than Ben could bear.

He struggled to free himself, the cold despair seeping into every recess of his being, overtaking his mind, will, and soul until he felt utterly lost and cut off from all hope. He clung to memories of his life, to thoughts of Cyril and Homer, to places where he felt warm and safe, but even those were little comfort in the face of such utter dissolution.

And then there was a glimmer of light, somewhere very far away. He willed himself toward it, but then it was gone. Brief hope fell into renewed despair. He tried to wail, but without form, he had no power to act. The loneliness was utterly complete.

The light flashed again. And again, he yearned to reach out to it, to hold on to something, anything that could free him from this terrible realm, but he was impotent. His will mattered for nothing here. All he could do was experience the crushing cold and aloneness.

Terror rose within what was left of him, filling him with the thought that he might be trapped, doomed to experience this place of despair for all time, unable even to die. The thought filled him with a kind of panic that assaulted his sanity. Visceral fear invaded his psyche, overpowering his reason, shoving aside all remnants of hope and leaving him facing a horror that he had never even imagined could exist.

The light flashed again. He resisted the urge to hope in the belief that it was false, just a mirage created to shatter his sanity when it was cruelly ripped away from him. And it was. The void consumed him again. All sense of time faded, leaving only eternal darkness and unmitigated despair.

A shriek of primal rage brought him back to some sense of himself. Light flashed again, this time much brighter, followed by another plunge into the void. And then light flashed again, followed by a frantic, desperate struggle as the stalker fought to remain free of this place.

He felt its furious desperation as it tried to claw its way back into Ben's reality. One final flash of light and he felt his entire being yanked from the depths of despair and darkness as if someone had reached into black water and pulled him to the surface. The light faded with his awareness … and then there was nothing save the solace of oblivion.

Imogen tightened her grip on Cyril's hand as a tear slipped down her cheek. Ben's howl of fear and pain filled the grotto. When he went limp, Hound renewed his unconscious fight against his bindings, wailing against some unseen torment.

Chen sat between them, legs crossed, eyes closed, one hand on each of them. He chanted in Chinese, repeating the same series of words over and over again. While his body was relaxed and his breathing was in time to his chanting, his face revealed deep struggle and concentration.

"I don't know if I can watch this," Imogen whispered.

"You don't have to," Cyril said. "There's nothing you can do now."

She shook her head slowly, her eyes never leaving Ben. "No, I have to stay," she said quietly.

"Is this what magic looks like?" Frank asked, a mixture of wonder and fear in his eyes.

"Sometimes," Cyril answered. "As I said, bargaining magic always comes with a high price."

"Who's Chen bargaining with?"

"He's not. He's using manifestation magic to undo a bargain struck by another. And the stalker is resisting."

"Will they survive?" Frank asked.

Cyril nodded without looking away from Ben, worry etched into his face.

Homer came to Cyril and nosed his hand, looking up at him as if beseeching him to do something. Cyril scratched the dog's head. "There's nothing I can do," he whispered sadly.

Suddenly, both men cried out in unison, their bodies tensing as they arched their backs with only their heads and heels on the ground. They froze in that position for several moments, shaking under the strain, before collapsing and falling still and silent.

Imogen shot to her feet, taking several steps toward Ben, holding her breath and putting a hand over her mouth, tears flowing freely. When Ben started breathing again, she crumpled to her knees and wept.

Chen stopped chanting and opened his eyes, rising wearily to his feet.

"The taint is gone," he said. "Untie them and wrap them in blankets. They will sleep for many hours."

He walked away to his house, a bit unsteadily, and vanished within. Cyril went to Ben and gently removed the bindings, wincing at the angry welts on his wrists. Imogen brought his bedroll and laid it down next to him while Cyril untied Hound.

After they'd rolled them both into their blankets and made them as comfortable as they could, Cyril looked around aimlessly and wandered away into the trees without a word. Imogen sat in the grass nearby and cried quietly. John brought her a cup of water and tried to comfort her, but she gently rebuffed him.

He sighed quietly and went into the trees as well.

Frank followed him. "Wait up," he said.

John slowed his pace until Frank caught up.

"Does she know?" Frank asked.

John shrugged, not bothering to look at him.

"I mean, it's pretty obvious."

"I'm sure she has other things on her mind right now," John said.

"And that doesn't bother you?"

He shrugged again. "In time, all things will be set right."

"What's that supposed to mean?"

"You wouldn't believe me if I told you."

"Try me."

John regarded him for a moment and shook his head. "Some things are better left unspoken."

"What the hell is it with everybody? Everyone has a secret except me."

John looked at him sidelong for a moment, a bemused half smile on his face.

"What?"

John chuckled mirthlessly. "Nothing. Nothing at all."

They walked for a minute through the trees in silence.

Finally, Frank said, "That was something else. Ben didn't even sound human for a while there."

"It was disturbing."

"You're a master of understatement," Frank said. "What do you think of Chen?"

John fell silent for several steps. "He has a way about him. Can't help but respect the man."

"And he has a dragon bone," Frank whispered, looking around.

"You picked up on that too?" John said, his sarcasm lost on Frank.

They walked on in silence until Frank stopped John with a hand on his upper arm.

"Don't you think we could use that? I mean, given what we're up against, we need it more than he does."

John looked down at Frank's hand until Frank let go of him.

"What are you suggesting?"

"Well, nothing really," he said a bit defensively. "It'd just be nice to have some magic of our own, you know, to help us get Imogen's baby back."

John nodded soberly, turning back to the trail and walking away without a word.

Frank watched him go, his hand coming to his chin and his eyes searching the forest in thought.

Imogen sat at the table sipping tea while she watched Ben and Rufus sleep. Both men breathed deeply and rhythmically. Homer lay near Ben's head, watching him intently, as if willing him to wake.

Chen came to the table, startling her.

"I didn't hear you," she said softly, quickly regaining her composure.

"My apologies. I didn't mean to frighten you."

He poured himself a cup of tea, offering to warm her cup as well before taking a seat across from her.

"Will they be okay?" she asked.

He looked at them for several moments before nodding.

"The infection and the stalker are gone, but they've been through an ordeal that will haunt them, maybe for the rest of their lives. I cannot predict how they will react to such an experience."

"This is all my fault," she whispered, wiping a tear from her cheek.

Chen waited for her to look at him.

"You know that it's not."

"But it is," she insisted. "If I hadn't married Enzo, none of this would be happening."

"Your father said that Enzo enlisted the aid of a priest to charm you. Is this not true?"

She nodded.

"Then this is not your doing. You could have no more resisted the priest's magic than Ben or Rufus could have resisted the stalker's."

"But ... I left my family for a man that I don't even like, let alone love. I let him steal my baby, and then I led him to my father's home. And now ..." She gestured helplessly toward Ben.

"Listen to me," Chen said, taking her hand and drawing her attention back to him. "You are a victim of the wyrm, just as they are. Blame and guilt rest solely on the enemy and his minions. Do not volunteer to carry that burden for them."

"I just feel so helpless," she whispered, shaking her head and looking down at the table.

"How else should you feel?" Chen asked. "Your will has been usurped by black magic. You've been violated by a man who isn't capable of love. Your child has been stolen and for all of that you're being hunted by servants of the greatest force of evil to walk this world in many thousands of years. And none of that is your doing. You bear no blame for the things that have befallen you or your family."

"But they're doing all of this for me," she said. "Ben almost died because of me. And my father is determined to rescue my baby no matter the cost. I don't even think I could stop him if I wanted to."

Chen chuckled softly, shaking his head. "You couldn't. Your father is fiercely loyal to his family and friends. He will reunite you with your child or he will die in the attempt."

"That's what I'm afraid of," she said, new tears on her cheeks. "I'm terrified that I'm going to get them all killed."

"Don't underestimate your father. He's a resourceful man. Your enemy doesn't fully understand who they face."

She fell silent for a while before looking up at Chen intently.

"I don't remember much from my childhood, but I do remember that people respected my father, revered him even. And then my mother and my sister were killed. After that, we took Ben and Frank and we ran." She fell silent again, finally working up the nerve to ask the question. "Who is my father? Who was he then?"

Chen smiled sadly. "That is not for me to say. Trust that all will be revealed in time."

"I figured you'd say something like that."

He shrugged. "Who he was and who he is are one and the same. To know his heart is to know him."

She sighed heavily, rubbing the remnants of tears from her face. "I just wish there was something I could do."

"There is," Chen said, removing the dragon-bone amulet from his shirt and lifting it from around his neck. "I want you to have this." He held it out to her.

Imogen's eyes went wide and she leaned back, shaking her head. "No, I wouldn't know what to do with it. Besides, it's yours, a gift from your father … you should keep it."

"I have no further need of it," Chen said, leaning across the table and taking her hand. He pressed the amulet into her palm and gently curled her fingers around the ancient artifact. "It will serve you well in the coming days."

"I don't even know how to use it," she said, looking at the small charm with equal measures of awe and fear.

"Your father taught you meditation, did he not?"

"Yes, but I haven't practiced for years."

"I suggest you renew your efforts," Chen said. "Focus your mind on your child. See him alive and well and in your care. Do this every day. Keep this thought in your mind. Obsess on it. Focus on it to the exclusion of all else. This is the essence of manifestation magic. See the result you desire in full and complete detail as if it had already come to pass. The amulet will transmute your will into reality."

She frowned deeply, her eyes never wavering from the dragon bone. "That's really all there is to it? Magic, I mean?"

Chen chuckled, shaking his head. "Oh no, my dear. There is much more to magic than just that. But that is a start, and a good one. It will put you on the right path. Resist the temptation to beseech the aid of beings and entities from other realms. Now that you bear the amulet, you will occasionally see things that others cannot. Beings will attempt to bargain with you from time to time. Ignore them. Keep your mind focused on your son. Avoid speculation and worry, for these can be made manifest as well if you allow your mind to dwell upon them."

"It sounds like this can be dangerous."

"Indeed it can," Chen said. "If you find your mind wandering astray, remember the love you have for your son. Love is the greatest power of all, the very essence of creation. Hold that love in your heart and mind, and the darkness will vanish like the night falls to the dawn."

"Why me? Why not give this to my father?"

Chen smiled, shaking his head. "Your father doesn't need it. And he doesn't have the kind of love you do for your son. That is your true power."

"You could keep it and come with us," she said, holding it out to him.

"No," he whispered, shaking his head. "My fight is over."

"What do you mean?"

"I will pass from this world soon."

"But, why?"

"My time here is nearly at an end," he said with a shrug.

"No ... you've been so kind to us. Are you sick? Can we help you?"

He chuckled. "No, my dear, I am quite healthy."

"I don't understand."

"Nor would I expect you to, but perhaps, with diligent attention to your meditation, someday you will."

Sounds of someone approaching through the trees drew their attention. Chen leaned forward urgently.

"Quickly, put the amulet away. Tell no one of it save your father." He held her eyes with a sternness that he had not shown before. "Your nephew Frank must never learn that you have it."

Her eyes went wide and she nodded tightly, slipping the leather thong around her neck and dropping the amulet inside her shirt.

Frank came out of the trees a few moments later, casually scanning the scene, his eyes landing on Chen briefly before he smiled at Imogen.

"How are they?" he asked, gesturing toward Ben and Rufus.

"Still sleeping," Imogen said.

"I doubt they'll wake until morning," Chen said, taking up his kettle. "Tea?"

Frank sat down next to Imogen, nodding to Chen.

Chapter 17

Ben woke under the stars. His mouth felt like it was full of cotton and his head hurt behind his eyes. When he stirred, Homer sprang to his feet, spun in a circle and licked Ben's face. He groaned but scratched Homer's ears nonetheless.

"How long was I out?"

"All day and most of the night," Homer said, lying down next to him, tail wagging.

"Did it work?"

"Chen said it did."

Ben rolled over on his back and felt his chest. The scratches were still tender but the wrongness that had permeated his wounds was gone. More importantly, he didn't remember any dreams. Then his experience in whatever dark and cold realm the stalkers came from hit him like a falling tree.

All of the fear and despair he'd felt came rushing back, threatening to overwhelm his sanity. Homer nosed him, whining softly. "You're safe," he said.

Ben focused on his breathing, trying to slow his racing heart. He felt a profound sense of gratitude to be here in this world. Even with all of its hardships and problems, it was infinitely better than the alternative. And yet, a deep and abiding dread filled him at the thought of such a horrible place even existing. For all of the beauty and light in the world, Ben would know for the rest of his life that there was a place of total hopelessness somewhere out there—a place that he never wanted to return to.

He took a moment to relax his body while he looked up at the stars. One of those points of light was the home of the dragons. They could get here, but Ben couldn't bring himself to imagine a circumstance where people could go there. And even if people could take the war to the dragons' home, he doubted humanity would be able to do much of anything against them. It seemed like such an insurmountable challenge. The dragons had all of the advantages.

"Not all," Homer said.

"What do you mean?"

"Dragons can't love."

Ben smiled in the dark. It was a small comfort, but it was enough for the moment. He spent a few minutes thinking about their situation and their enemy. As he pondered the state of his life, and faced all of the challenges arrayed against him, he was surprised to find that he wasn't nearly as afraid as he had been just one day before. Then he realized why—his time in the stalker's realm had shown him that there were greater things to fear than death or injury or failure.

But also, his experience had provided him with a kind of certainty that he'd never known before. If the dragons were willing to call on such creatures, to bring them into this world and unleash them on defenseless people for the purpose of terrorizing innocent communities into capitulating to their rule—if that was what was in the heart of the wyrm, then Ben resolved to cut it out of the beast's chest.

He had no idea how he would accomplish such a thing. Just one day ago, it had seemed like a laughably impossible task. But now, with his new understanding of the enemy, the difficulty and danger of slaying the dragon was dwarfed by the absolute necessity of it.

As the first inkling of dawn began chasing the stars away, Ben felt a greater sense of purpose than ever before. Then he remembered his grandfather's tearful apology, and it occurred to him that perhaps this had been his purpose all along.

When Chen emerged from his house, Ben got up and went to the table.

"Good morning," Chen said.

Ben nodded to him. Then after several moments, he said, "Thank you, Chen. I don't even want to think about what would have happened if you hadn't saved me."

"You are very welcome," the little man said, stirring the bed of coals and setting the kettle next to the fire before coming to the table.

"Did you know? What it would be like, I mean?"

Chen shook his head slowly, his eyes never leaving Ben's.

"I didn't know a place like that could exist," Ben whispered. He swallowed hard and looked at the table, marshaling his courage before looking up again. "Was that hell?"

Chen shrugged. "Perhaps, but if it is, that is only one of many."

Ben closed his eyes in dismay. One such realm was bad enough. The thought of other places like that was more than he wanted to contemplate.

"How many different realms are there?"

"A great many," Chen said. "Perhaps an infinite number."

"Are they all so horrible?"

"No ... of course not. This world is proof positive that there is also light."

Hound woke in a flurry, wrestling his blankets to get free, scrambling to his feet in a crouch, ready for an attack.

"Rufus!" Ben said. "You're safe ... it's over."

Hound stopped, looked around at the serene setting in the growing light of dawn, took a slow deep breath and ran his hand through his hair. He opened his mouth to speak, then stopped and started looking for his shirt.

"How are you feeling?" Cyril asked, as he sat down next to Ben.

"Better," he said, glancing at his grandfather and then looking away quickly. He wanted to confront him about his past, and about his plans for the future, but he wanted to have that conversation in private.

"I'm glad to hear it," Cyril said. "You both had us worried."

"I can tell you one thing," Hound said, easing himself onto the bench across from Cyril. "Next time I run into one of those damn things, I'm going to feed it a grenade or two—no hesitation, no bullshit."

"Had I known that they were as dangerous as they proved to be, I would have urged greater caution," Cyril said. "Do you remember anything from the banishing?"

Ben and Hound nodded, their eyes haunted and distant.

Cyril looked to Chen.

"Try to avoid thinking of your ordeal," Chen said.

"Easy for you to say," Hound said. "You weren't there." He paused to look at Cyril, shaking his head in dismay. "I don't scare easily, but that place ate what courage I had for lunch. I think I'd do just about anything to keep from going back there."

"Your feelings are understandable," Cyril said. "We aren't meant to live in such a place."

As the rest of the group came to the table, Chen poured tea and then began preparing breakfast.

Ben considered his newly decided, self-appointed purpose while he ate.

He was going to kill the dragon.

A part of him still laughed mockingly at the thought, but another part of him was resigned to the task, determined to find a way.

He would need weapons—and magic. But mostly he would need information. The how of it would be dictated by the true nature of the dragon, his vulnerabilities and his strengths. Ben knew that he was woefully ignorant of so many things—things that he would need to learn before he could achieve his goal. Worse still, many of those pieces of the puzzle would be carefully guarded secrets.

Then there was the need for help. He couldn't accomplish such a thing by himself. As always, his first and most important ally was Homer.

"Would you think I was crazy if I tried to kill the dragon?"

"Yeah, but I'd help anyway."

Ben smiled to himself before draining his teacup.

"So what are we going to do now?" Frank asked.

Ben felt a twinge of relief. He'd been weighing the idea of blurting out his newfound purpose, but the thought of saying it out loud made him uneasy.

"We'll be on our way tomorrow," Cyril said.

"We still need weapons," Frank said, holding up his hatchet. "This isn't going to cut it."

"Probably not," Cyril said, hesitating for several moments before nodding to himself. "I have a cache of weapons hidden west of Rogue City."

"What?" Frank said. "Why is this the first we're hearing of it?"

Cyril shrugged offhandedly. "Wouldn't have done any good to tell you."

Frank huffed, shaking his head. "I'm tired of being kept in the dark. We need to know everything you know or we can't help you anymore."

Cyril smiled at his grandson sadly. "If you wish to go your own way, I won't stop you. I will miss you though."

"What are you talking about? I'm staying with you. We just need you to stop keeping secrets."

"*We* or *you*?"

Everyone else fell deathly silent.

"Ever since this whole thing started, you've been holding back," Frank said, his anger dissolving as he donned a mask of sadness. "We're family. Why don't you trust us?"

Cyril leaned forward intently, holding Frank with his eyes until the young man started to fidget.

"We are at war. The most valuable commodity in war is information. If I told you we were headed for a weapons cache and you were captured by the Dragon Guard, they would torture you until you revealed our destination. Then, they would be waiting for us when we arrived. But ... if I withhold that information, then you can't betray our purpose to the enemy."

Frank listened with his mouth agape, shaking his head ever so slightly.

"What the hell are you talking about? We're just trying to get Imogen's kid back. After that, we run."

"Well, let's just focus on rescuing Imogen's son for now," Cyril said. "After that we'll have better information and we can make a more informed decision." He held up his hand to stop Frank from speaking. "But, you need to understand that our success depends on treating this endeavor as a military operation, because that's essentially what it is. We intend to gather information about the enemy and then use that information to exploit their weaknesses, attack their position, rescue my grandson and retreat with minimal casualties on our side."

Frank put his hands up helplessly. "All right, that sounds like a military thing when you put it that way. Can you at least tell us what kind of weapons you have stashed away?"

"A few blades, a few guns, some grenades," Cyril said.

Hound smiled, leaning in with interest.

"Why hide them in the first place?" Frank asked.

Cyril chuckled. "What else would I do with them? We've lived in a peaceful little community for years, and I didn't want a bunch of weapons lying around for my two very curious grandsons to find and play with."

Frank opened his mouth to say something, then closed it again, frowning deeply.

"Take the day to rest and make ready to leave at first light," Cyril said to the group. "Now, if you'll excuse me, I think I'll go for a walk."

"Sounds like a splendid idea," Chen said.

After the two men were out of earshot, Hound smiled broadly and said, "I have to say, I do like the idea of more guns ... and grenades."

John nodded.

"I'm so tired of his secrets," Frank said. "We have to band together and force him to tell us everything. Our lives might depend on it."

"Force him?" Ben asked, chuckling. "How're you going to do that?"

"He's got a point," Hound said. "Besides, I get why he's playing things close to the vest. Can't say I blame him."

"But—"

"I won't go against him," Imogen said, cutting Frank off with a stern look.

"Me neither," Ben said.

"Looks like you've been outvoted," Hound said.

John nodded again.

"Don't you want to know the truth?" Frank blustered.

"What truth are you talking about?" Hound asked.

"I don't know!" Frank said. "That's the point."

When he was met with silence, he huffed and walked away into the woods.

Cyril and Chen walked through the trees in silence for a while until they reached a meadow and stepped out into the early morning sunshine. Chen stopped to close his eyes and lift his face to the light.

"You aren't going to come with us," Cyril said.

"No, my path leads elsewhere."

"I both expected and feared that you'd say that."

"You will need my help to escape the enemy," Chen said.

"What do you mean?"

"They search the forest for you. I will lead them away to the east so you can flee to the west."

"What are you saying, Chen? They'll almost certainly have a stalker working with them and you're not as spry as you used to be."

"No," Chen said, smiling wistfully. "But I'm still more nimble than I look."

"They'll catch you."

"Yes, they will."

Cyril blinked, deflating sadly as realization settled on him.

"Are you sure?"

"I've seen it. My time in this world is nearly at an end."

Cyril shook his head in dismay. "There must be another way."

Chen put his hand on Cyril's shoulder. "As always, there are many paths. I choose to walk the one that will serve the greater good."

"How will your death serve the greater good?"

Chen looked up at the sky, pointing to the bird circling high above them.

"It arrived this morning," he said. "It marks our position. Even here, the wyrm's minions will find us. I will delay them and buy you the time you need to escape."

"You can't just throw your life away. Not for us, not for anyone."

"I've already lived my life. I'm old. My time in this world will come to an end very soon, whether I choose to help you or not."

"I don't want you to die," Cyril whispered.

"Do not despair … I will pass into the light, for I have seen that as well."

"You succeeded?" Cyril asked, startled.

"Oh yes. It took many years and required far more discipline and dedication than I ever thought it would, but I have glimpsed the light ... and it's more beautiful than words can convey. Very soon, I will return home."

Cyril looked down at the ground. "I'll miss you," he said quietly.

"Have faith. In time, we will be reunited," Chen said.

"I hope you're right."

"I am," Chen said with a knowing smile. "How much will you reveal to them?"

Cyril frowned deeply, shaking his head. "As little as possible. I don't dare tell Frank the truth. He's my grandson and I love him, but I don't trust him. I can't."

"No, you can't. Ben is another matter."

Cyril smiled with genuine affection that turned quickly to sadness. "I just hope he doesn't hate me when he realizes what I've been preparing him for his whole life."

"He won't hate you," Chen said. "He has a well-trained mind. I'm sure, at least on some level, he is already aware of his destiny. As the harshness of reality sets in, he will come to understand the necessity of your decisions."

"I hope you're right. I've wanted to tell him the truth for some time now, but I just can't bring myself to do it ... I don't want to strip away his innocence. And, if I'm brutally honest with myself, I don't want to face his judgment. Truth is, he has every right to hate me. I hate myself for what I've done."

"Nonsense. All four of us swore a magical oath to give our all to this cause. You couldn't have done otherwise, even if you'd wanted to."

"I had no idea just how costly that oath would be," Cyril said.

"Far less costly than the alternative," Chen said. "Only one remains."

"That doesn't make it any easier to live with."

"Perhaps not, but the magnitude of the evil that humanity faces can't be defeated with half measures. Only a complete and unwavering commitment will see us through to the light."

"I know," Cyril whispered. "I guess I was just hoping that someone else would step forward and finish what we started. It's already cost us so much."

Chen nodded sadly, motioning for them to continue walking.

Chapter 18

"I think we're being watched," John said, pointing out the bird when Cyril and Chen returned.

Both men nodded.

"We should probably leave now," Cyril said, "if you two are strong enough to travel."

"I'm good," Hound said.

"Me too," said Ben.

Everyone gathered their belongings, then Chen led them to the gate, staff in hand. He opened the secret door and laid his hand on the marker, whispering a few words under his breath.

Several moments later, they filed out of the cave and were met by the screech of a hawk, mingled with something unnatural, filtering through the trees. It was answered in the distance by the scream of a bobcat.

"I don't like cats," Homer said. "Especially when they're as big as me."

"I know how you feel," Ben said.

"This way, quickly," Chen said, leading them down to the bank of the Red Blanket.

"Where are you taking us?" Frank asked.

"Away from the stalkers," Chen said without looking back or slowing.

They followed the river at a brisk pace, crossing several small streams that added to the river's flow. At every break in the thick trees, Ben searched the sky for the hawk. It was always there, circling high overhead, marking their position for the enemy.

With each sighting, he felt the urge to move faster. Every time the stalker-hawk shrieked, fear surged into his gut. Early in the afternoon, the bobcat screamed. It was close. Too close to escape.

Hound stopped, dropping his pack and adjusting the rounds in his shotgun, choosing to lead with two of his grenades.

"There's a clearing up ahead," Cyril said, pointing to a meadow surrounded on three sides by a bend in the river. "We'll make our stand there."

Ben felt his heart hammering in his chest as he dropped his pack and drew his sword. He glanced at everyone else and saw a mixture of resolve and fear. Cyril stood ready, sword in hand. John had positioned himself between the enemy and Imogen, arrow nocked and ready. Frank was sheet-white and trembling. He looked around nervously, his eyes flicking to every sound emanating from the forest.

Hound stood in the middle of the meadow, his jaw set, a tight grin on his face.

Chen came to Ben's side and put a hand on his shoulder. "Let your training guide you," he said. "Free yourself of thoughts and worry. Allow your quiet mind to have free rein."

Ben frowned at the old man, puzzling over his words. Then the bobcat screamed again.

"Come get some!" Hound shouted.

A moment later, the cat, just two feet tall at the shoulder, bounded into the meadow. It was fast, hitting the ground once and springing toward them. Hound's grenade hit just behind it, exploding with enough concussive force to send the stalker end over end through the air toward them. It hit close, not ten feet away. Hound ejected his second grenade and fired a slug before the possessed bobcat could recover, tearing a gaping hole in its side. It screamed in fury as it scrambled to its feet.

He fired again, this time peppering its face with shot and blowing it over onto its back. He advanced quickly, racking another round and firing immediately, hitting the cat in the throat. The force of the blast ripped its head nearly off and the beast went still.

The hawk shrieked overhead.

"Come on down here, you bitch," Hound shouted into the air. "Bertha's hungry."

"Nicely done," Cyril said, handing Rufus the grenade round he'd ejected. "You might need this."

He slipped the shell into his pocket with a nod of thanks.

"We should go," Chen said. "The Dragon Guard will be coming with all possible speed."

"They're never going to stop, are they?" Imogen asked, a tremor in her voice.

"Not until they think we're dead," Cyril said.

"Or we kill them all," Hound added, reloading his shotgun.

"This is a nightmare," Frank said. "Chen's right, let's get out of here."

They set out along the river as it widened and the flow increased. They had walked for less than an hour when the sound of horses brought them to a halt.

After taking a moment to listen, Chen turned and started out again. "Come, we haven't much time."

"Time for what?" Frank asked.

Chen didn't answer.

The hoofbeats of too many horses drew closer and then passed them, moving ahead along a parallel path to the river.

"We should double back," Frank said.

"No, your best chance is the boathouse," Chen said without breaking stride.

"More water?" Homer said.

"We might not have a choice," Ben said, glancing at the swiftly moving river.

"You want us to take a boat?" Frank said, hurrying to catch up when no one else stopped.

"I do," Chen said. "The Red Blanket is your best chance for escape."

"Won't the Dragon Guard get there before us?" Hound asked. "They are ahead of us after all."

"The trail leading to the ford from the road is a narrow switchback," Chen said. "They'll have to slow considerably to negotiate it safely."

"Hope you're right," Hound said.

As the terrain leveled out, the river became even wider, its flow easing from a frothy torrent into a gentle ripple. A small house stood along its bank, the mossy roof fallen in and the timbers rotting under the weight of neglect. An old aluminum boat lay upside down on the porch.

A little-used trail wound out of the forest to the edge of the river at a wide, shallow point and continued on into the forest on the far side. Ben couldn't tell how far the enemy was from the sound of their approach—all he knew for certain was that they were coming.

Chen stopped in the middle of the clearing, smiling calmly to himself, his eyes distant. "It's just as I have seen," he said quietly to himself.

A shout through the trees drew their attention.

"You must go," Chen said. "The river will carry you to safety. Return to shore when you hear the river's roar."

John and Rufus shared a look and then went for the boat. It was light but sturdy, easily large enough to carry all of them.

"Grab those oars," Hound said to Frank, pointing to the porch.

"Come with us," Cyril said, turning Chen away from the approaching enemy.

He shook his head resolutely.

"You don't have to do this," Cyril said. "We can all escape."

"You're wrong, my friend."

"Please come with us," Imogen said.

He smiled kindly at her with a sense of calmness, even serenity, about him. "With a glimpse of the one true light comes a new understanding of reality, a knowing of things to come. I could flee with you now, but such a choice would lead to your death. I have seen every path open to me and this is the most honorable. This path reveres life and free will—the creator's two great gifts to us all. I have been awaiting this moment for some time."

"You *want* to die?" Ben asked.

"Death is ultimately an illusion … as is life. We are all nothing more than a drop of ocean spray cast into the air for a brief moment. Eventually, we all fall back into the vast ocean of light and become one with God again. Having seen the beauty and bliss that awaits, I yearn to return home."

"I don't want you to go," Cyril said, holding back tears.

Chen hugged him. "And yet, I must," he said, pointing toward the approaching enemy. "And so must you."

Cyril clenched his jaw, the sadness in his eyes transforming into anger and resolve. "I will finish what we started … or die trying."

Dragon Guard on horseback came into view, just a few hundred feet away.

"Try to make it the former, old friend," Chen said, turning toward the approaching enemy and taking a stand in the middle of the meadow.

"Come on," Hound called out from the river's edge.

Cyril put his hand on Chen's shoulder for a moment before turning away and heading for the boat. Ben followed with a sense of loss already welling up within him. He had only known Chen for a few days, but in that time he'd come to respect him more than any man he knew save his grandfather. He found himself lamenting the loss of a thousand conversations that he would never have with the wise old monk.

The thought hit him like a blow to the head. He stopped in his tracks to look back. Chen stood easily, awaiting his enemy, holding only his staff as a weapon. As certainty settled on him, Ben's head snapped back to his grandfather and a thousand questions were answered, all in a rush. The puzzle of his past filled in and he understood his purpose—he understood what his grandfather had been grooming him for his entire life. He almost laughed when he realized that it was the very same purpose that he had set for himself this very day.

"Take them alive!" Nash shouted over the din of hoofbeats.

Chen stood serenely, awaiting his doom.

"Ben!" Cyril snapped, drawing his attention away from the coming threat.

All thoughts of purpose and destiny faded as the very real danger coming for him focused his mind on the present moment. He raced for the boat. Everyone else was already aboard, even Homer. Ben shoved the boat out into the water and clambered over the side, John pulling him in as Hound shoved away from the bank with an oar.

With a growing sense of helplessness and anger, Ben turned to watch as the Dragon Guard approached Chen. Nash remained mounted, watching her squad of six advance on him. Chen waited calmly until the first got close enough. Then with a thrust of his staff and a shout that reverberated through the forest, he spooked the man's horse, causing it to rear and throw him to the ground.

Two of the remaining five drew their dragon-fire rifles, tongues of blue flame sprouting from the barrels as they brought them to bear.

"Hold!" Nash snapped. "I want him alive."

Three dismounted while the first to fall groaned in pain and the other two extinguished their fire and returned their rifles to their backs. Three big men clad in armor and armed with swords advanced on Chen.

Armed with only a staff, he stood his ground with a stillness and a certainty that Ben knew he couldn't match.

The first Dragon Guard pointed his sword at Chen. "Lay down your weapon."

Chen moved with fluid grace and startling speed, slapping the man's blade aside with one end of his staff, bringing the other end around and striking him on the side of the neck just below his helm and above his armored collar. He fell to the forest floor and went still.

Before the other two could react, Chen brought his staff back and drove the butt of it into the throat of the man to his right, dropping him to the ground, bright red blood frothing and sputtering from his mouth.

The third advanced, charging with a battle cry. Chen became still, waiting for the moment to strike. When the Dragon Guard got close enough, Chen spun, ducking under and aside from the charge, whipping his staff around by one end, catching the man in the back of the legs, and knocking him face first onto the ground. Chen moved quickly, taking two steps toward the man and driving the butt of his staff into the back of his neck. Ben could hear bone breaking.

Nash cursed loudly and ordered the other two Dragon Guard to engage. As they were dismounting, Chen casually strolled over to the man writhing on the ground and hit him across the temple, knocking his helm off and stunning him further. A second blow finished him.

The two remaining men converged on Chen, both with swords drawn. He jabbed the first in the upper arm as he raised his sword. The man screamed, dropping his blade. Chen brought the other end of his staff into the groin of the second man, doubling him over before spinning around and catching the first across the side of the neck, sending him to the ground, still and lifeless.

The last Dragon Guard standing backed away from Chen's advance, but not nearly fast enough. The staff came around again, catching the man at the knee, sweeping his legs and dropping him to the ground. A final blow to the man's throat ended his life.

"You'll burn for this," Nash said, her rifle coming over her shoulder, flame igniting as she brought it to bear on Chen.

What happened next challenged Ben's sanity.

Chen sat down cross-legged, eyes closed, cradling his staff across his lap.

Fire sprayed from the barrel of Nash's weapon, surging across the forest floor like an orange wave, engulfing Chen in a conflagration that would have sent any other man screaming and struggling for one last breath. Chen sat still, calm as a mountain lake on a summer's day. The fire roared and raged around him, burning him with it, but still he did not move.

A bowstring twanged behind Ben, but he couldn't take his eyes off Chen, now fully engulfed in flame, a pillar of fire amidst a field of crackling orange.

Nash screamed as John's arrow drove into her leg. "Bitch," he muttered, as the scene of horror floated out of view, the flow of the river carrying them away from their hunter.

Cyril sat with his face in his hands and wept. Imogen sat by his side, trying to console him even as tears streamed down her cheeks.

Ben might have cried as well, had it not been for the burning anger in his gut.

"Hang on," Hound said as the banks narrowed and the river gained speed. Within a few moments, all thoughts of sadness and mourning were set aside in favor of guiding the boat down the rapidly flowing river.

Spray soaked them. Even in the warm sun, they were shivering with cold as air and water conspired to rob them of their body heat. Ben wasn't sure how long they'd floated, struggling to keep the boat in the middle of the rapidly flowing white water, but he was greatly relieved when the river widened once again and they slowed.

His relief didn't last long. When they rounded the next bend, the sound of a torrent roared at them.

"Head for the bank!" Cyril shouted.

Hound and Durt rowed with all their strength, but the river pulled them on.

"Head for the rocks," Cyril yelled, pointing toward a number of boulders near the bank.

Moments later, the boat crashed into the rocks, turning sideways and sliding toward the cataract.

"Jump!" Cyril shouted, shoving Frank overboard toward the river's edge.

Ben didn't hesitate, grabbing Homer and flipping overboard into the icy water. He came up, kicking for the bank and quickly found, much to his relief, that he could reach bottom. Imogen came up nearby, sputtering and gasping for breath. He grabbed her by the wrist and hauled her closer until she could get her feet underneath her.

John was the last to jump, only seconds before the boat was dragged away by the current, vanishing into the torrent. Ben sat heavily, water draining out of his pack and clothes. Homer shook his fur dry a few feet away.

"Ahh," Ben said, holding his hands up to ward against the spray.

"I told you I don't like the water," Homer said, sniffing the air.

"At this point, I think I agree with you," Ben said, wiping his face.

"There's a clearing over there," Cyril said. "Let's get into the sun and get dried out a bit."

They strung a line and hung up their spare clothes, taking an hour to eat lunch and regain their strength. It was somber and quiet, all of them turning their thoughts inward and mourning the loss of Chen ... all except Frank.

"Do you think we got away?" he asked nervously.

"For now," Cyril said without looking up.

"I don't see the hawk," Frank said, scanning the sky.

"Nash will probably fall back and regroup," Hound said. "But I'm pretty sure she won't give up."

"No, she won't," Cyril said.

Ben wanted to talk to his grandfather about his new understanding of the world, and about his family's history, but he thought better of it, his glance turning to Frank. He didn't trust his brother, not with important things anyway, and this was the most important thing in the world. He could only imagine what Frank would do with the knowledge of their grandfather's role in the war against the wyrm.

The more he thought about it the more certain he became.

Cyril was the Wizard. Chen had been the Monk.

Two of the four who had led the fight against the dragons. Heroes of humanity.

The magnitude of the danger they faced began to sink in. Up until today, Ben thought they'd just crossed a Dragon Guard Commander and were the targets of a petty vendetta driven by her embarrassment at their escape. Now he understood the full scope of the forces arrayed against them.

If the Dragon Guard knew the truth of who they were hunting, they would bring to bear all of the power at their disposal. Eventually, the dragon himself would come. As was the case with most important answers, this one only served to create a thousand new questions—questions that Ben didn't dare voice except in the most guarded of whispers.

His mind turned to the stories he'd heard about the war. There had been four leaders of the resistance: the Wizard, the Dragon Rider, the Monk, and the Dragon Slayer. All four had managed to conceal their identities, an impressive feat in and of itself. All four had fought and prevailed against the dragons for years until the last dragon defeated them. After that final battle, they vanished from sight, presumed dead and gone.

Ben had been three years old when the war ended and the dragon proclaimed victory. That was the year his father and mother had died. An uneasy feeling began to turn in his stomach.

"Do you remember my mother?" he asked Homer.

"No," he answered sleepily, lazing in the bright sunlight.

"I think I know the truth about my past."

Homer grumbled, rolling to his feet and going to Ben, nosing him on the chin. "Keep it to yourself. It's not safe to talk about it."

"I know," Ben said, scratching his dog's head. "But it's also not safe to remain ignorant. I have questions that need answers."

"When the time is right, Cyril will tell you what you need to know."

"Like how it is that you can talk," Ben said.

Homer grumbled again and flopped over on the mossy riverbank. "The sun feels good."

Ben looked at him and shook his head.

Chapter 19

"We have to go back," Frank said nervously.

Everyone looked at him like he'd lost his mind.

"Chen had a dragon-bone amulet," he said. "We need it."

Cyril looked down, shaking his head sadly.

"It's too dangerous," Imogen said.

"Not half as dangerous as trying to fight these people without weapons or magic of our own," Frank said. "Besides, Chen killed most of the Dragon Guard and John wounded Nash. She's probably on her way back to the Lake of the Woods right now."

When nobody tried to argue, Frank got to his feet and hoisted his pack.

"Let's go, right now, while we have the chance."

No one moved to get up.

"Are you kidding me? We can't pass up this opportunity. We have to have that amulet."

"And what would you do with it?" Cyril asked without looking up.

"Magic," Frank said with exasperation.

"You know nothing of the powers that you wish to wield," Cyril said. "You would only harm yourself or those around you."

"This is unbelievable," Frank said. "We need an edge. Even without the amulet, there are weapons back there—swords and those fire rifles the Dragon Guard use."

"The blades might be of use, but they aren't worth the lost time or the risk," Cyril said. "As for the rifles, I doubt they would function in our hands, or worse, they may do us harm for attempting to use them."

"What are you talking about?" Frank said. "They're just guns … and we need guns."

"No, they're not just guns," Cyril said. "They're almost certainly enchanted, and that means you wouldn't be able to use them."

"How do you know?" Frank said. "Is this just one more thing you're holding back?"

Cyril sighed but made no effort to argue.

"Okay. Rufus and I will go while you wait here," Frank said.

"Think so, do ya?" Hound said, looking at Frank with a mirthless grin.

"Come on. You know better than anyone that we need more guns."

"I do, but not those guns. If Cyril says they're dangerous, I believe him."

"Why? Why do you all follow him so blindly? He's made the wrong decisions at every turn. If you'd just listened to me, we'd be in Rogue City by now and Imogen would have her baby back."

"Or we'd be dead," John said.

"Just drop it, Frank," Ben said.

"Or what? You gonna hit me again?"

It was Ben's turn to sigh. "I said I was sorry."

"Sorry doesn't fix my nose," Frank said. "You owe me. Come with me. We can go get that amulet and their weapons."

"It's not going to happen, Frank. We're headed west."

"If your apology meant anything, you'd take my side," Frank said.

Ben stood up and strapped on his pack, looked Frank in the eye and turned away from him, heading west along the river.

"One of these days, you're going to need my help," Frank said. "We'll see how you like it then."

"Now can I pee on his leg?" Homer asked.

"Tempting, but no," Ben said.

They followed the river for several hours, Frank bringing up the rear, muttering curses and occasionally shouting them. Everyone tried to ignore him, which only antagonized him further.

"He's going to be a problem," Homer said.

"I know."

"Maybe we should have let him go back on his own."

"He wouldn't have," Ben said. "He needs an audience … and people to lean on."

"Goddamn it!" Frank finally shouted. "We have to turn back. We can't just leave magic behind us."

Everyone stopped.

Cyril looked around for a moment, checking the sun in the sky as it slid west.

"We'll rest here for a few minutes," he said. Then he walked over to Frank and said quietly, "Don't you think they'll be waiting for us there?"

"Who? Nash was injured and her men are all dead."

"The men we saw were killed, but there may have been more," Cyril said, holding his hand up to stop Frank from objecting. "But I'm far more concerned about the bird. It hasn't been following us since we escaped, but it's still out there somewhere. If I had to guess, I'd say it was waiting for us to come back for Chen."

Frank frowned, shaking his head as he worked through Cyril's warning. "Doesn't matter," he said. "It's just a bird. Rufus could blow it out of the sky."

Ben watched his brother and grandfather argue.

"Maybe I should encourage him to go look for that amulet," he said to Homer. "At least that would give me a chance to talk with my grandfather without fear of him overhearing us."

"He wouldn't find it," Homer said. "But that might be fun, too."

"What do you mean?"

"Chen gave it to Imogen while you were out," Homer said.

"What?"

"He told her to keep it a secret."

Ben started laughing.

When Frank and Cyril stopped arguing and looked at him, he realized they could hear him and decided to use his strange behavior to his advantage, striding up to Frank like he meant to hit him again.

"I'm tired of your whining," Ben said loudly. "If you want to talk, then tell us how you got us out of jail."

"I told you—"

"No, you didn't. If your story were true, the Dragon Guard wouldn't be hunting us. If you bailed us out like you said, according to their rules, they wouldn't be the least bit interested in us. So tell me, how did you get us out?"

Frank glowered at him, shaking his head. "That really hurts, Ben. You're my own brother, and you don't even trust me." He touched his nose tenderly and made his way around him, heading west along the river.

"There's something there," Homer said.

"No doubt about it," Ben replied, sharing a sad look with his grandfather as Cyril put a hand on his shoulder.

"Whatever the reason for their initial interest, they have greater reason for hunting us now," Cyril said quietly.

"I know," Ben said, holding his grandfather with a deliberate look. "Frank's right about one thing—you've held back important information. Sometime soon, we're going to have to talk about that."

Cyril looked down sheepishly. "When it's safe, we will," he said.

Ben nodded, heading out to catch up with Frank.

After several hours of walking, John stopped to check the position of the sun. They'd followed the river as it turned northwest. Now it was bending around due west.

"We'd make better time on the road," he said, pointing through the trees up the rise to the north. "It runs along the Red Blanket into Prospect where it meets up with the old highway."

"You think its safe?" Cyril asked.

"I wouldn't go that far," John said, "but it's faster."

"What do you know about Prospect?"

"Abandoned ... about a year ago."

"Well, I guess it's in our path."

John nodded, turning toward the road. Ben was silently grateful for the even ground of hard-packed dirt. The road was overgrown with grass but the foxtails were still too green to be a nuisance. More importantly, he saw no evidence of recent passage.

Homer grumbled when a gentle rain began to fall. Ben tossed up his hood and trudged on. They saw little in the way of wildlife, mostly birds and squirrels—nothing large enough to be a threat. Ben suspected that the stalkers had chased off most of the larger animals ... he didn't blame them for leaving.

The day wore on and his boots and pants got progressively wetter and heavier. Worse still, his coat started to soak through. He didn't complain out loud, but he did wish for a break in the weather, something that didn't look to be forthcoming given the monochromatic grey of the sky. The rain wasn't heavy, but it was steady and unrelenting. By the time they saw an old rusty sign for the city of Prospect, he was cold, wet, and miserable—his coat entirely inadequate to the weather.

"Maybe we can find a place with a roof for the night," Hound said.

John had stopped, staring at the dilapidated buildings that had once made up the tiny town. At its height, Ben guessed that the place had been home to a thousand people.

Now the buildings were broken down and overgrown, moss clinging to the parts that were shaded by trees. Several of the houses had collapsed in on themselves.

"Doesn't look like anybody's been here for a long time," Imogen said.

"Doesn't mean they haven't," John said, not making any move toward town.

"Let's find someplace dry," Frank said. "One of the houses is bound to have a roof."

"We should be cautious," Cyril said.

"Of what?" Frank asked.

"Scavengers … stalkers … bandits. Take your pick."

"Is that smoke?" Ben asked, pointing toward the north end of town.

John squinted into the rain, nodding after a moment.

"Are you sure?" Frank asked. "Looks like a cloud to me."

"It's not," John said. "Someone lives here."

"All the better," Frank said. "Maybe we'll find a hot meal."

"Wishful thinking," Hound said. "Odds are better that we'll end up being the meal if we aren't careful."

"Oh God," Imogen said. "They wouldn't really eat us, would they?"

"Maybe not literally," Hound said, with a half grin.

"Better to avoid them," John said. "People who live in places like this tend to be desperate."

"Where else are we going to stay?" Frank asked. "We don't have much light left, and I'd rather not sleep in the rain."

"Let's find a place at the south end of town and try to avoid notice," Cyril said. "With any luck, we'll be on our way before they know we're here."

John scanned the ruined town again, turning off the road and heading toward the backyards of the line of houses running along the south side of the road. He picked his path carefully, stopping often to watch and listen for any sign of a threat, but the houses were all vacant, cold and broken. The road ran east to west for several hundred yards before turning north toward the hazy streamer of smoke rising in the distance.

"I don't think anyone lives on this end of town," John said, "and a few of these houses look intact enough to keep us dry for the night."

"Pick one and let's get out of this rain," Hound said.

John pointed to a house they had passed a few moments before. "Roof's intact," he said, walking back the way they'd come.

The old fence surrounding the backyard was broken in several places, the boards having come loose and fallen into the tall grass, allowing easy access. John slipped through and carefully approached the back door, stopping for nearly a minute, listening intently. Satisfied, he motioned for the rest of them to remain quiet while he opened the door. When the hinges creaked, he winced and came to a standstill. He waited for several moments before stepping inside.

"Do you hear anything?" Ben asked Homer.

"Nothing but John and the creaky floorboards."

Ben deliberately released the tension in his shoulders. Something felt off about the place—the entire town just didn't seem right.

A few minutes later, John returned, moving less cautiously than he had when entering.

"Empty," he said.

They filed inside. The place smelled of mold and rot. The air was stale and cold, but it was dry. A few of the windows were broken, but most remained intact and dirty enough that they were difficult to see through. John led them into the living room.

Old chairs and a couch surrounded a low table, all set on a moldering rug atop the hardwood floors. Tracks of a raccoon or some other small mammal led upstairs, but there was no indication that people had been there in a very long time.

"Looks like they left in a hurry," Imogen said, leaning in close to examine a number of framed pictures on the wall.

"Stalkers'll do that for ya," Hound said.

John drew the heavy curtains shut across the front windows. "We should be careful about light," he said.

"Let's get some wood for a fire," Frank said. "We could probably burn that table."

"Not tonight," Cyril said. "The smoke might alert the town's inhabitants."

"Oh, come on," Frank said. "It's almost dark. Nobody's going to see the smoke at night. We'll keep it small."

"No, Frank," Cyril said. "It's too dangerous."

"But my clothes are soaked and I'm tired of being cold. We need a fire."

"Not tonight. Hang your clothes on a line and wrap up in your bedroll. You'll be warm enough."

Frank clenched his jaw and shook his head, glaring at Cyril, but when nobody else sided with him, he did as he was told.

Ben drew first watch. He sat listening to the sound of rain on the roof, expecting something bad to happen. The darkness inside the house was nearly complete, but the only thing he heard was the sound of the rain. When his watch ended, he was grateful to wake Hound and curl up in his blankets.

Chapter 20

Ben woke to a commotion sometime during the night and saw light flickering across the walls of the room. He could hear Frank and Cyril whispering intensely.

"I told you no fire," Cyril said.

"It was my watch," Frank said. "I was cold … and I'm tired of you telling me what to do."

"You jeopardize us all."

"Bullshit," Frank said, his voice rising. "Go back to sleep, old man."

Hound and John woke up as well.

They all froze at the sound of footsteps upstairs. Not those of a man, but of a barefoot child running across the floor.

"What was that?" Imogen whispered.

No one responded, everyone holding still, straining to hear whatever came next.

Laughter echoed down the staircase, a child playing.

"I thought you checked upstairs," Frank said to John.

"I did," John said, pulling on his boots.

"Sounds like you missed a kid," Frank said, turning toward the stairs.

"That's no child," Cyril said, stopping Frank with a hand on his arm and a warning in his eyes.

Frank took in Cyril's expression with a glance and looked back to the staircase. Footsteps started down the stairs, boards creaking under bare little feet, slowly, tentatively, as if a child were sneaking up on someone in a game of hide-and-seek. Then, in the space of one step, the sound changed into heavy boots bounding down toward them. All eyes were on the landing. Three rushed steps later, the sound transformed into a howl of such inhuman anguish that Ben felt his blood freeze in his veins.

A shadowy apparition hurtled down the stairs, indistinct in form and inky black. It crashed into the wall at the landing, its entire smoky substance exploding like a hurled ball of tar, but then coming back together just as quickly and coalescing into something that could not be. A creature of darkness. It had no eyes or mouth, no claws or fangs, but it radiated malice and fear. The wall where it had hit was scorched and smoldering.

While all eyes were on the beast, the front door burst open with such force that the top hinge broke free, the door slamming against the wall with a crash and coming to rest at a sickly angle. The thing in the landing spun in a ball of blackness, tentacles whipping out a few feet every now and then, leaving black scars on the surfaces they touched.

Ben felt visceral fear well up within him with such intensity and gibbering madness that he nearly lost all sense of himself and bolted for the door.

Imogen screamed.

Standing in the threshold of the front door was another beast, this one seven feet tall and looking for all the world like Satan himself. Reddish-black skin, chiseled muscles, horns sprouting from his forehead, a barbed tail, and hateful glowing red eyes.

"Hold!" Cyril shouted.

Frank cried out in terror and ran. Somewhere in the distance, Ben heard the back door burst open as Frank fled into the night. Then he realized that he was up and holding his sword, facing the twin beasts with Homer growling at his side.

"Be gone!" Cyril shouted. "You have no power in this world!"

Both beasts roared in rage. The spinning blob of darkness darted across the room toward Ben. He swept aside, bringing his blade up and through the thing, but there was nothing there. The apparition passed him, tentacles whipping overhead as he ducked away. It hit the wall with a loud thud, vanishing with a shriek, leaving a black stain.

Then the devil stepped into the room.

Hound brought up his shotgun and unleashed a round. The blast passed straight through the creature without so much as a scratch. Wind blew into the room, extinguishing the fire in a gust, plunging the room into darkness.

Footsteps rushed in next. Ben heard angry shouts, as if women were barking curses at him. A voice from outside chanted guttural, menacing words in a language that he couldn't understand. Imogen screamed again, her cry cut short by a sickening thud.

The devil roared, deafening and filled with rage. And then it was gone. The room fell into silence for a brief moment. Ben was left bewildered and stunned by the sudden and entirely incomprehensible events.

Cyril lit his lamp and held it high, scanning the room, a look of pure horror and dread on his face.

It was only then that Ben realized that Imogen was gone.

"Hound, go get Frank," Cyril said.

Rufus stood wild-eyed, shotgun in hand, face pale white. "What the hell just happened?" he asked.

"We were attacked with magic," Cyril said, coming to face the big mercenary. "I need you to go find Frank before he gets himself killed. Bring him back here and wait for us."

Hound nodded but didn't move.

"Go, now!" Cyril demanded, pointing at the back door, only turning to John after Hound was in motion. "Do you have your wits?"

"No more than usual," John said, a tremor in his voice, but steady enough. "Where's Imogen?"

"Taken," Cyril said, turning to Ben and checking him with a look. When Ben nodded readiness, he was rewarded with a brief but sincere look of pride. He realized in that moment that just a few days earlier he might have bolted with his brother. His trial with the stalker had stretched the limits of his fear and left him with more courage than he ever thought he might be able to muster.

"Bring your weapons, leave everything else," Cyril said, heading for the door.

Ben followed, sword still drawn. Questions swirled in his mind, but he pushed them aside in favor of action. John was a step behind him.

"Head for the smoke," Cyril said.

John took the lead, not bothering with stealth, moving into the center of the road, arrow nocked, head swiveling this way and that. They moved at a trot, turning north on the main road through town. It wasn't long before they saw a glow in the distance. The drizzle had stopped, but the sky was still black with heavy clouds. The light in the distance had the character of fire, orange and flickering.

John took them to the edge of the road and into the front yards of the houses lining the street, using the bushes and trees for cover as they approached the light. He stopped behind a low hedge, going to a knee and peering over at the scene beyond.

Set well off the road, in the middle of a grassy field was a church surrounded by at least a dozen large lamps set atop posts in a circle. The building was simple, rectangular, and pure white as if it had been painted yesterday. It was fifty feet long and half as wide, two stories tall with a steeple on the end closest to the road.

The devil stood on the front porch, his appearance all the more terrifying in the light.

"How is that even possible?" Ben whispered.

"Listen to me, both of you," Cyril said. "Those are apparitions. They have no substance, but they can play tricks on your mind. You have to resist the urge to fear them. That is their power."

"If you say so," John said.

"What's our plan?" Ben asked.

"We don't have time for anything but a frontal assault," Cyril said. "Rush the building, ignore the apparitions and kill everyone inside except Imogen."

"Subtle, I like it," John said, leading them to the end of the hedge. He looked back to see if they were ready.

When Cyril nodded, they all bolted for the church.

The devil didn't seem to see them, standing stock-still as if a statue. Even so, John and Ben hesitated to approach the thing. It looked as real as anything Ben had ever seen and far more terrifying. Cyril ran up the stairs onto the porch and slammed into the door with his shoulder. It was locked. A chorus of women shouting curses erupted from within. He wedged his sword into the crack between the double doors and levered one until the wood broke around the lock. Then he stepped back and kicked with all his might. The door slammed open and he rushed inside followed by Ben and John, both giving the immobile devil a wide berth.

Ben felt like he'd stepped into madness itself. The inside of the church was one large room with a high arched ceiling. A dozen tall stained-glass windows lined the walls, six to a side with an oil lamp burning beneath each, casting dim, shadowy light into the chamber. The far wall held a large crucifix … all vestiges of the godliness that had once adorned this hall ended there.

Where the pulpit had once stood was a statue of a beast so grotesque and unnatural that it hurt Ben's eyes to look at it. The thing was ten feet tall and made of charred wood and bleached bones cobbled together into a monster with three arms and a wide maw gaping in rage at the world.

At the feet of this monstrosity was a circle drawn on the floor with what Ben could only guess was dung. The stench of death and offal filled the place. At five points around the circle, braziers burned some foul incense, sputtering black smoke into the already fetid air.

Within the circle was an altar formed from bones piled up and wired together with animal sinew and intestine. Imogen lay semiconscious on the altar, an angry welt on her cheek. A man stripped bare to the waist, wearing only what appeared to be a long skirt made of black leather stood before her, facing the beastly statue. Angry scars of crudely cut dragon runes stood out across his back and shoulders. He held his arms up and out, a long dagger in his right hand, as he chanted in the same tongue that Ben had heard at the house.

All of this horror assaulted Ben in the first moment that he stepped inside the pure-white church. The next moment, chaos erupted as three women dressed in tattered, dingy dresses charged them with horrible fury, all three wielding long knives.

Cyril didn't even flinch, almost as if he knew what to expect. He advanced toward the first woman, sword at the ready. She hurled herself at him with reckless abandon, neither fear nor strategy driving her attack, but instead something else, something like desperation. Cyril stepped to the side away from her knife hand and thrust quickly into her ribs, withdrawing his blade an instant later and turning toward the man standing over his daughter, ignoring the woman as she slumped to the floor with a groan of pain.

The man's chanting came to a crescendo as he raised the knife in both hands over Imogen, standing on his toes in preparation for his strike. An arrow sank into his shoulder, turning him and driving him forward with a grunt. Only then did he seem to notice the commotion behind him.

Imogen came fully awake in a panic, shoving against the man who'd fallen on top of her, driving him away and toppling herself off the altar and onto the floor.

One of the women crashed into John. He managed to get a hand on her wrist before she could plunge the blade into his chest, but the force of her charge drove him against the wall. He hit hard, his head leaving a dent in the plaster.

The third woman charged Ben. He let her come, a feeling of calm settling on him in spite of the danger swirling around him. He gave himself over to his training, meeting her downward thrust by slipping to the side and sweeping up with his blade, cleanly severing her knife hand at the wrist. She shrieked in pain as he spun and kicked her in the back, sending her crashing into the wall near the door. The building shook with the force of her impact and she fell still.

He turned in time to see the other woman raising her blade over John's unconscious body, but knew he would be too late to help him. Homer darted in and bit the woman in the leg, shaking and growling for just long enough to make her cry out in pain, before letting go and scurrying out of reach.

Ben raced to John's side and kicked the woman in the belly with all possible force, curling her up like a bug and sending her crashing against the wall. She too fell still.

A roar of pure malice tore into the night directly behind Ben, freezing him to the spot for a moment. He turned and came face-to-face with the devil, a giant battle-axe in its hand. It raised the blade and brought it down at him. Despite Cyril's warnings, Ben simply couldn't make himself stand his ground against the beast. He flinched backward, falling to the floor in horror as the thing came for him, bringing the axe down on him with terrible force and speed. He rolled to the side, doubt flooding into him as the sound of splintering wood erupted behind him.

The man in the circle turned his full attention on Cyril while Ben scrambled to his feet, turning once again to face the devil … but the thing vanished, transforming into black smoke in the space of a heartbeat.

A moment later, two men in black plate armor, armed with broadswords and shields appeared between Cyril and the man in the circle. It was only then that Ben saw the deformity of the man. His face was hideously misshapen, as if one side were made of wax, heated to the point of melting and then allowed to harden once again. His eyes shone with madness and pain. Festering boils stood out on the side of his neck. His stringy black hair was patchy … it looked like large chunks had been pulled out all over his head.

Cyril ignored the two plate-clad men, walking between them even as they swept their blades through him with absolutely no effect. The hideous man snarled a curse at him, raising his hand and barking words in some unclean language. Smoky blackness flowed from his outstretched palm, hitting Cyril and stopping him in his tracks. He struggled to move, but the darkness held him fast.

With a sneer, the man pulled a revolver from his waistband and slowly raised it. Ben didn't have time to think, he barely had time to act. In the back of his mind, he wondered how the man could behave so calmly with an arrow jutting out of his shoulder. He raced toward him, ignoring the two apparitions that moved to intercept him, hoping beyond hope that his grandfather was right about them. Their blades passed through him without a scratch only a moment before he released his sword, throwing it overhanded at the man in the circle.

He had practiced the technique countless times before, just as he'd practiced every other technique he'd been taught, but he'd never thrown at a live target. The blade flew end-over-end, its dull tech metal glinting in the lamplight until it struck the man just below the shoulder, taking his arm off above the elbow a breath before he could pull the trigger. The severed limb fell to the floor with a sick thump, the pistol clattering out of the hand's grip, a round firing harmlessly into the far wall.

The man shrieked with a mixture of pain and perverse glee as he turned to his altar, allowing his own blood to flow into the stack of bones and gristle, all the while chanting with triumphant exaltation.

Ben stood in stunned horror as the statue began to come to life.

Imogen regained her senses and her feet, drawing her knife and rushing at the man, only to bounce off some unseen force as if there were a wall of impenetrable glass surrounding him.

The magic holding Cyril vanished when the man turned his full attention to his new incantation, his voice rising higher and louder with each verse of his terrible spell.

"Run!" Cyril shouted at Imogen.

She turned just in time to see the statue come to life, solid and deadly. It raised its fanged maw to the ceiling and roared with such force that the walls shook. Imogen rolled out of the way a moment before it brought one if its three arms down like a club, smashing floorboards with the force of the blow.

When she came up, she yanked the dragon-bone amulet from around her neck, met her father's eyes and threw it to him. Ben watched his grandfather catch it with his free hand. Cyril went perfectly still for just a moment before pronouncing a single word with terrible, reverberating force. Ben felt a shockwave wash over him, setting his hair on end with a feeling of power and warmth. The man in the circle flinched and yelped. The animated statue was driven back long enough for Imogen to race past her father to safety.

Then Cyril began chanting, his words now light and airy, filled with hope and promise. A look of horror came over the man in the circle as Cyril sheathed his sword and motioned to the ground with an open palm. A circle of light appeared around him, as if projected on the floor from some higher plane. A swirl of faintly glowing motes of light surrounded him as well, filling the space inside the circle.

"You have no place in this world!" he shouted, motioning to the ground again as if slamming his hand onto a table. The circle of light expanded by double. The man shrieked in horror, turning to run, but then stopping at the edge of his circle as if caught between two equally terrifying options.

"Return to the foul realm from whence you came!" Cyril commanded, thrusting his hand at the ground again. Again the circle of light expanded, this time overlapping the enemy's circle. The dung that had been used to draw the outline burned away in an instant when the light flowed over it, thick black smoke rising into the air.

The moment the circle was broken, the animated statue turned on the man who'd summoned it, taking him up with all three arms and clamping its fanged maw on to his hip. The man screamed in terror. The statue seemed to struggle for a moment, its whole head shivering with the effort, the dying man's screams turning from fear to agony. Then it bit through the hipbone, pulling one of the man's legs free and hurling it into a stained-glass window with enough force to shatter it.

The beast lifted the man overhead and deliberately clamped its jaws on to his head and one shoulder, again struggling to bite through him, but succeeding in a matter of moments. When the hideous man died, the creature lost cohesion and fell to the floor in a jumbled mass of bones, charred branches and stones amidst its summoner's remains.

Cyril turned in a circle, searching for any other enemy. Seeing only the two women that Ben had subdued, both slumped unconscious against the walls of the defiled church, he released his magic and retrieved his grandson's sword and the man's revolver without a word, tipping over three of the oil lamps on his way to the door.

"Get John," he said to Ben as he went to Imogen and looked her in the eye, asking without words after her well-being, wincing at the angry welt on her cheek. She nodded tightly.

Ben picked the Highwayman up and carried him out of the building a safe distance before laying him gently on the ground and checking his breathing and pulse. Cyril knelt next to him, placing his hands on his head while closing his eyes for several moments.

"He'll have a headache, but he'll be all right with some rest."

They watched the flames build within the church. Once it was fully engulfed, Cyril turned to Imogen and handed her the amulet.

"No," she said, "you should have it."

"Chen gave it to you for a reason," Cyril said, pressing it into her hand. "Keep it safe and keep it secret. Frank can never know you have it."

She nodded reluctantly, retying the thong and putting it around her neck, hidden under her shirt.

"You're the Wizard," Ben said.

"I am," Cyril said, turning to face him, apprehension etched into his face.

Ben was quiet for several moments, holding his grandfather's eyes before he nodded firmly.

"We have to kill the dragon."

Cyril's eyes went glassy with tears. He blinked several times before hugging Ben fiercely.

"Yes, we do."

Chapter 21

John leaned on Imogen while they walked back toward the house. The burning church filled the night sky with an eerie orange glow behind them.

"Are you sure you can travel?" she asked him.

"No choice," he said. "The fire will attract stalkers."

"I hadn't thought of that," she muttered.

Ben walked with his grandfather in silence, questions swirling in his mind. He trusted John, but the secret he now shared wasn't his to tell so he kept it to himself, all the while making a list of things he wanted to ask when the time was right.

"Here," Cyril said, handing Ben the revolver. "It has five rounds."

Ben took the weapon, nodding seriously. "You've never taught be how to use a gun."

"I'm sure Hound can give you a few pointers."

Ben tucked his new weapon into his belt at the small of his back. The sound of footsteps coming up the road met his ears.

"Smells like Frank," Homer said.

"We saw the fire and came as quickly as we could," Frank said. "What happened?"

Cyril walked past him without meeting his eyes.

Frank watched him walk by, his arms out to the sides, his hands held up helplessly. "What?"

"Not now, Frank," Ben said, without stopping.

"I just wanted to help," he called after them.

"Give them some space," Hound said, stopping Frank from hurrying after them.

Dawn was just beginning to lighten the sky when they arrived at the house. Ben frowned at the walls where he'd seen the apparition leave scorch marks. They were unmarred. He found it a bit unnerving that magic could make him see things that weren't there, adding that to his long list of questions.

They built a fire and cooked a hot breakfast before setting out for the road. It was a cold morning, but the heavy grey clouds didn't rain on them. Ben was almost as happy as Homer about that fact. They walked on until dusk, taking frequent breaks to give John the time he needed to recuperate.

"We should hold up here," Cyril said. "I don't want to camp too close to the road, and we don't have much light left today."

"How about the level ground at the base of that hill?" John said, pointing at a small rise several hundred feet into the forest.

"Good enough," Cyril said, following John into the trees.

They didn't build a fire and tried to remain quiet, which wasn't difficult given their fatigue from the ordeal at the church and from walking all day. During the day's travels Ben found his thoughts turning back to Chen. By the time they made camp, he didn't feel much like talking. He laid his bedroll out and stared at the stars as they winked into view overhead.

He woke to John gently shaking his shoulder.

"Your watch."

Ben took a deep breath and sat up, rubbing sleep from his eyes. The forest was dark, lit only by what starlight could penetrate the canopy. He wrapped a blanket around his shoulders and sat with his back against a tree. For quite a while, the only noise he could hear was the distant ripple of the river and the breeze moving through the trees. It was almost like a lullaby, threatening to put him back to sleep.

Then a shot rang out in the distance, followed by shouting and the scream of a cougar. Ben sat up straight and still, straining to listen. A cry of pain. Then another. More gunshots were followed by another inhuman scream. Still more shots and a chorus of shouting. All very distant. Too far to pose an immediate threat, but close enough that everyone else was awake and holding stock-still.

"What the hell was that?" Frank whispered.

"Sounds like a stalker-cat versus a posse," Hound said.

"Who do you think won?" Frank whispered again.

"No one," Cyril said. "Try to go back to sleep. I'll take the next watch."

Ben struggled to return to sleep, but managed eventually, waking with the light of dawn and a sense of relief. He gave silent thanks for whoever had tangled with the stalker in the night and offered a prayer for their wounded. He found himself torn when he considered the plight of any survivors. If his experiences had taught him anything, it was that there were indeed some things worse than death.

He noticed that Imogen was taking a few minutes to meditate, legs crossed and back straight just the way Cyril had taught them. He couldn't help but think that the amulet had something to do with her renewed interest in their childhood lessons.

After a cold breakfast, they started out again under grey and heavy clouds, returning to the old highway. Frank was quiet and brooding. Ben couldn't decide if that was a good thing or not. He knew his brother well enough to know that he was still angry. Ben just hoped that his unhappiness wouldn't translate into anything stupid. When Frank got like this, Ben was always on his guard for some form of retaliation or other. When they were kids, Frank's antics were usually petty and mostly harmless, but now, with all that they faced, his petulance could easily become a problem.

Ben brought up the rear to keep an eye on him. While they walked, he considered the future, both immediate and long-term. He had faith and unshakable trust in his grandfather. His newly confirmed suspicions about Cyril's past led him to believe that they would be successful in rescuing his nephew. After that, Ben would need a plan if he was to carry out his purpose.

That was the point where his mind got hung up on reality. The dragon was a beast of magic and legend, powerful beyond measure, surrounded by loyal servants and guardians. In the light of a new day, his goal seemed entirely out of reach, even with his grandfather's guidance and wisdom.

Then he thought of his ordeal with the stalker. He remembered the cold dark with a shiver. If he could come back from that with his sanity still intact, he could find a way to defeat the dragon—unless, of course, his sanity wasn't intact and his plan was pure delusion.

Ben shook himself out of such thoughts. He needed to believe that he was still master of his own free will. The alternative led to madness.

"Keep us parallel to the road about a hundred feet inside the forest," Cyril said.

John looked back, nodding.

Frank huffed, shaking his head and muttering, "We'd make better time on the road."

Nobody bothered to reply.

Close to noon, John stopped not far from the point where a long bridge spanned a broad canyon that looked like it had once been filled with water. Now a narrow river flowed quickly along a deep channel cut in the middle of the canyon. The bridge was in disrepair, several sections having broken and fallen away, but it looked passable on foot.

John scanned the far side with his monocular, patiently watching for any sign of danger.

"What do you think?" Cyril asked.

"I don't like it."

"Why not?" Frank asked, frowning. "Seems sturdy enough."

"I don't doubt the bridge," John said. "But the far side is lined with boulder falls on both sides ... lots of cover for an ambush."

"Who's going to ambush us?" Frank said.

"Don't know."

"I don't see an alternative," Cyril said. "The terrain is too treacherous to navigate along the other side of the canyon."

John nodded, his eyes never leaving the far side of the bridge.

Ben looked at Homer and said, "Do you smell anything?"

"No, but the wind is blowing the wrong way," Homer said.

They waited for half an hour, all eyes on the far abutment, before finally deciding that it was safe to cross. The road was broken and cracked, weeds growing out of the spider web of fractures in the surface. There was little evidence of recent passage, but that only meant that anyone who'd come this way was traveling on foot.

When he stepped onto the bridge, Ben found himself wondering at the rusting metal rods woven into the stone, forming an eerie skeleton where the flesh of the bridge had fallen away into dust. The raging river a hundred feet below seemed to warn him not to come too near the large holes lest more of the surface give way and cast him in.

They reached the far side, cautiously approaching the boulders, steep embankments rising away as if the road had been cut through a hill that once stood where they now walked.

A man stepped out from behind the nearest boulder.

Hound brought his shotgun up, Durt his bow.

The man held out empty hands, though he had a pistol on his belt.

"Go easy," he said. "You might want to look around before you do something you'll regret." He was tall and lean, wearing a broad-brimmed hat and a long leather riding coat.

"Lower your weapons," Cyril said, scanning the tops of the embankments on either side. A dozen men or more had weapons trained on them, all waiting for an excuse to fire.

John lessened the tension on his bow but kept the arrow nocked. Hound kept his aim steady on the man.

"We're not looking for any trouble, friend," Hound said. "We just want to be on our way."

"Trouble is, you're headed towards my town. Worse still, you're coming from Prospect and I know for a fact that it's haunted."

Cyril gently laid a hand on Hound's shotgun, beseeching him with a look to lower the weapon. Hound complied but kept Bertha at the ready. Cyril stepped forward, hands out at his sides.

"We've just come through Prospect, and we had a run-in with a few very dark characters. They're all dead now, so they shouldn't cause you any more trouble."

The man cocked his head, frowning with curiosity. "Tell me, how exactly, did you go about killing a ghost? 'Cuz like I said, I've seen 'em with my own eyes."

"Those weren't ghosts," Cyril said. "They were summonings. A man with a pile of dragon dung called them into this world to do his bidding. He's the one we killed."

The man seemed to consider Cyril's words, but didn't look entirely convinced. "We'll just set that aside for a moment while you tell me what your business in my town is."

"Like my friend said, we're just passing through. We aren't looking for trouble."

"If your account's true, seems trouble found you anyway. Who's to say it won't follow you?"

Cyril shrugged helplessly. "Trouble finds us all from time to time."

"Can't argue with that. We've been plagued by stalkers for weeks. They roam the wilds to the north, only venturing into town at night. How is it that you've managed to travel through their territory unscathed?"

"Oh, we haven't been unscathed," Cyril said. "We've encountered three and killed two."

"And the third?"

"We lost sight of it two days ago."

"Probably the one we killed last night," the man said, rubbing his chin.

"I doubt it," Cyril said. "We heard your fight—sounded like a cat. The one we saw was a hawk."

"Never heard of a bird turning dark."

"First one I've seen."

The man looked from face to face, scrutinizing each of them. He seemed to consider their request but finally shook his head slowly.

"I just can't let you in," he said. "We're getting pressure from Rogue City from the south and these damned stalkers from the north. I just don't see the upside to letting a bunch of armed strangers into my town."

"I understand your concern," Cyril said. "And I sympathize with your plight. Would you be willing to escort us through town and send us on our way?"

"Not armed like that," he said, gesturing toward Bertha. "Besides, if we left right now, we'd get to town just before dark."

Another man came out from behind the nearest boulder and went to the first man, whispering something to him urgently.

He looked up, scanning them for a moment before his eyes fell on John. "My man tells me that you're a Highwayman."

"I am—name's John Durt."

"I've heard of you," the man said. "Tell you what, you let me hold your weapons and I'll put you up for the night at the jailhouse."

"Don't much like the sound of that," Hound said.

"Best I can do," he said. "People depend on me to keep them safe and I don't know you."

"Did you hear what that other man said?" Ben asked Homer.

"No, the wind's still wrong."

"Stay alert. If things look like they're going south, I want you to run and hide."

"What else would I do?" Homer said.

Cyril looked back at them. Ben could tell in a glance that his grandfather knew something was wrong. He scanned the area again and decided that they were hopelessly outnumbered and outgunned. They'd walked into a trap and the only way out was through it.

"We accept," Cyril said with his best salesman's smile. "Provided that I have your word that our weapons will be returned to us."

"Of course," the man said. "It's a dangerous world. I wouldn't put a man out into the wilds without the means to defend himself. Truth is, you seem like good folks, but a man can't be too careful these days."

"He's lying," Frank whispered, just barely loud enough for Ben to hear.

The man motioned to someone behind the boulders and a man came out carrying a large bag.

"Put your weapons in here and we'll be on our way."

Cyril nodded agreeably, unbuckling his belt and handing it to the man with the bag. He turned to the rest of them, his eyes deadly serious. Frank was about to say something when he saw his grandfather's look and stopped. Ben was relieved when Frank unbuckled his belt without protest.

Hound bit his lip, shaking his head, but he unloaded Bertha and slipped her into the bag along with his pistol.

"You take real good care of her," he said with a hint of menace.

Ben unbuckled his sword belt, taking care to leave the revolver tucked into his pants where it was.

"I don't think my bow will fit," John said.

"The arrows will do."

John nodded, removing his quiver.

Once all of their weapons were removed, save the few they'd managed to hide, the man smiled.

"Well, all right then," he said, motioning to his people. Three men came out from behind cover and took up positions behind them. One had a bow, another a crossbow, and the third carried a rifle.

"My name's Carlyle," he said.

"Sheriff Carlyle?" John asked.

"That's right."

"Word is, you're a fair man," John said.

"I try to be," Carlyle said. "Some days that's harder than others."

He set a brisk pace, fast enough that nobody was interested in talking until they stopped for lunch.

"How many stalkers have you killed?" Cyril asked.

"Pretty close to a dozen," Carlyle said. "The first one showed up about a year ago, then every few months until recently. Now they attack every few days. The dragon's people offered to protect us, for a price of course."

"The price is higher than you might imagine," Cyril said.

"How do you mean?"

"The dragon's the one creating the stalkers, or his people are anyway. When a community comes under attack, his Dragon Guard ride in and offer protection."

Carlyle shared a worried look with one of his men. "You sure about that?"

"That's how it happened in K Falls," Cyril said. "Night after night, the stalkers terrorized people until the Dragon Guard came and offered to defend us. Once we invited them in, they took over. They run the whole town now."

"That's where you live?" the man who'd whispered to Carlyle on the bridge asked.

"It was," Cyril said. "We're hoping to find someplace a bit more friendly to settle down."

Carlyle nodded thoughtfully, taking his last bite of lunch and gathering his things. "We should be on our way."

Chapter 22

While they walked, Carlyle drew Cyril away from the rest of them.

"You're sure the dragon's people and the stalkers are working together?"

"As sure as a man can be," Cyril said. "It's how the wyrm expands his territory, and it sounds like your town is next."

They walked in silence for a while before Carlyle sighed, shaking his head in dismay. "How do you fight something like that? Those stalkers are wicked and deadly. People are afraid, and I don't blame them. Sooner or later, they're going to demand the protection of the Dragon Guard."

Cyril nodded. "Tyrants always come under the guise of a protector."

"Now that you say it out loud, I'm surprised I didn't realize it sooner," Carlyle said. "When you think about it, it's almost a perfect plan."

"I don't know about perfect, but it seems to be working for them."

Cyril walked silently with the man, who seemed to be struggling to accept what he'd just learned.

Ben glanced back at the three men bringing up the rear. All three carried their weapons at the ready like they were guarding prisoners.

Frank came up alongside Ben and gave him a worried look. Ben responded in kind. Even with so much contention between them, they were brothers and could read each other's expressions at a glance. In this case at least, Ben knew that he could count on Frank to work with him for their mutual survival.

For the moment, there was nothing to do except play along with the charade. He only hoped that things wouldn't get too far out of control before they could make their move.

By late afternoon, they'd arrived in Shady Cove, a small community along one of the many forks of the Rogue River. A makeshift wall of timbers surrounded the town with a guard tower built up next to the gate. The man in the tower waved to Carlyle and barked orders to open the gate.

Carlyle's second, the man with the bag of weapons, trotted ahead, slipping inside before the gate was fully open. Ben could see him talking urgently with the men standing watch, but could only wonder what they might be saying. A furtive glance in their direction by one of the guards told him that it wasn't anything good.

Another two armed men took up position behind them as they were escorted into town. The few people on the streets looked at them with a mixture of wariness and sympathy. Carlyle sent most of them on their way with a stern look. The jailhouse wasn't much, but it was solidly built of stone and steel. When

Carlyle led them inside, Ben started to worry that they were walking to their doom.

"Bolt!" he said to Homer.

He didn't hesitate, racing off between the buildings.

"Hey!" one of the men shouted. "The dog just ran off."

"He doesn't like being inside," Ben said with a shrug. "He won't hurt anyone."

"Probably ought to send someone to round him up just the same," Carlyle said, nodding to one of his men before turning back to Cyril. "Might be a bit cramped, but you'll be safe," he said, gesturing to the large holding cell that occupied a third of the single-room building.

The second man rested his hand on the pistol at his hip. Ben looked to Cyril. He just smiled graciously at Carlyle.

"Thank you for your hospitality," he said, strolling into the cell like it was a room at an inn. After they'd filed in, the second man closed the door quickly and started laughing.

"That was easier than I thought," he said, pulling out a flyer with their pictures on it ... a reward of a thousand silver drakes was being offered for each of them.

Cyril turned to the sheriff, his demeanor deadly serious. "Have you betrayed us?" he asked calmly with an undercurrent of menace.

Carlyle looked down, seemingly torn. "I'm not sure yet," he said. "The Dragon Guard have posted quite a reward for you, but after thinking on your words today, I don't know if I want to collect."

"What are you saying, Sheriff?" the second man asked, clearly shocked. "They're worth six thousand drakes. How can we pass that up?"

"Money's worth less than a clear conscience," Carlyle said. "Stow their weapons in the locker. I need to think."

The second man hesitated, but complied after a moment, securing the bag of weapons in a steel locker—one of several lining the wall opposite the cell.

"You do that, Sheriff," the second man said. "While you're at it, think about what the Dragon Guard will do to our town if they find out we let these prisoners go."

Carlyle held his eyes for several moments before nodding. "Go on, make preparations for the night guard. I'll be along shortly."

After the man left, Carlyle approached the cell, stopping well out of arm's reach.

"I didn't want to do this," he said, "but I'm not sure I have much choice now. Two Dragon Guard representatives arrived from Rogue City a couple of days ago. My deputy is probably headed to talk with them right now. And he's right about the consequences if I let you go."

"Did the wanted poster say what we'd done?" Cyril asked.

"No, just names, pictures, and some pretty big numbers."

"My daughter's husband gave their firstborn baby to the priest," Cyril said. "She left him and came home to me. When he came for her, we fought back. That's our crime."

Carlyle frowned, shaking his head in dismay. "Doesn't sound like much of a crime to me."

"No, not at first anyway," Cyril said. "I think they're more upset about the eight or ten Dragon Guard we killed trying to get away from them."

Carlyle blinked a few times, going very still. "That's a lot of blood."

"Not nearly as much as I'm willing to spill to protect my family," Cyril said. "Mark my words, Sheriff, if you choose to serve the dragon, then you're choosing to serve evil."

"Like I said, I need to think," he said, walking out the door, leaving them alone in the cell.

"What the hell are we going to do now?" Frank asked. "If the Dragon Guard are here, we're screwed."

"I can't argue with that," Cyril said, taking a seat on one of the benches lining the walls.

Ben sat down next to him and leaned in close. "I still have that revolver," he whispered.

"I know, but that would draw too much attention. Keep it hidden for now, but be ready if things get violent."

"What are you talking about?" Frank asked.

"Give me a minute, Frank," Cyril said. "I need to think this through."

"What's there to think about? We have to get out of here."

"I agree, but we'll have a far better chance with Carlyle's help, if he decides to give it. If we make our move now, it'll force his hand."

"So what? We just wait for someone else to decide our fate?" Frank said.

"Sometimes doing nothing is the best strategy," Cyril said.

"I might agree with that in principle," Hound said. "Don't much like the feel of it in practice."

"Carlyle has the reputation of an honorable man," John said.

"It might be better for him if we escape without his help," Imogen said.

"Who cares about him?" Frank said. "We have to think about ourselves."

"And once we're out?" Cyril said. "How many of these people would you kill to escape?"

Frank started to say something but thought better of it, instead turning in a huff and running his hands through his curly black hair.

The door opened and the deputy entered with two Dragon Guard on his heels, both dressed in riding leathers and crimson cloaks. One was marked with the single rune scar while the other was scarred on both cheeks.

"Just like I said," the deputy whispered.

The lead Dragon Guard held up the wanted poster to compare pictures, nodding appreciatively to himself.

"The six of you have caused quite a stir," he said. "The prices you command make me wonder at your value."

Cyril didn't bother to get up or even meet the man's eye.

Hound stepped up to the bars and folded his arms across his chest, offering nothing more than a shrug.

"Come now, the priest himself has taken an interest in you. That simply doesn't happen. Perhaps if you help me understand, I can make your transport to Rogue City more comfortable."

"This is all a mistake," Frank said. "We're just travelers who look like the wrong people."

The lead man looked at his companion and then laughed, his demeanor turning deadly serious a moment later. "First, you will address me as Dominus. Second, if you lie to me again, I will personally cut out your tongue. Do you understand?"

Cyril was up, placing a hand on Frank's shoulder in an instant.

"There's no need for that, Dominus," he said. "As you said, the priest has taken an interest in us. Honestly, I don't know why that is, but then I don't know your ways very well either. It may be that he wants to talk to us, which would require that my grandson keep his tongue."

The Dragon Guard narrowed his eyes at Cyril, cocking his head to one side, before turning on his heel and heading for the door.

"So when will I get the reward?" the deputy asked, following behind in a rush.

Cyril stepped over and took Imogen's hand, closing his eyes for a moment and then watching the door intently. It closed but didn't quite latch. He let go of his daughter's hand with a grin and a wink. She looked from him to the door.

Cyril turned to Ben and said, "Call Homer. He might be able to bring us that key ring." He pointed to a peg on the far wall.

"You think his dog is going to break us out of here?" Frank asked incredulously.

"Pretty sure of it," Cyril said.

Ben stepped up onto the bench and looked out the window. After a few minutes, he saw Homer peek around the corner of a nearby building.

"The door's unlatched," he said to him. "Come inside the building ... and be careful that nobody sees you."

"The guy they sent after me couldn't find his ass with both hands," Homer said, nearly vanishing into the rapidly growing shadows.

A minute later he nosed his way into the building.

"Bring me the keys," Ben said aloud, just for appearances, pointing at the ring.

Homer trotted over, reached up with both front paws on the wall and took the key ring in his mouth.

"I don't believe it," Frank said.

"Told you he wasn't stupid," Ben said.

"We could leave your brother here," Homer said.

Ben just chuckled as he knelt down and took the keys, giving Homer a scratch behind the ear. They were out of their cell a few moments later and had their weapons soon after that.

"Did you see any way out of town?" Ben asked Homer.

"Just the two gates, but there are a few places along the walls with gaps big enough that I could squeeze through."

"Could we?"

"I doubt it."

Hound took a moment to check the other cabinets. The first contained blankets and pillows. The second held uniforms. The third was locked, but opened with one of the keys. He smiled broadly at the contents, holding up a box of shotgun shells.

"Is that a rifle?" Frank asked.

"Yeah, but I doubt it'll do you any good," Hound said, pulling out a weapon made of plastic and tech metal. It looked like a typical rifle, except the muzzle had a hole no bigger than the diameter of a push pin.

"Why not?" Frank said, taking the weapon.

"No power cartridge," Hound said, pointing to a rectangular opening along the underside of the weapon just in front of the trigger guard.

"What is it?"

"Gauss rifle," Hound said. "If we had power for it, it would definitely be worth taking, but as it is that thing's just a club." He pulled out another small box, nodding to himself. "These might come in handy though."

"What are they?" Frank asked, clearly disappointed by the uselessness of the powerful weapon he held.

"Pistol bullets," Hound said, stowing them in his bag with the shotgun shells. "I suspect they fit the guns the sheriff and his deputy carry."

A cat screamed in the distance. Everyone froze, straining to listen. Shouts filled the small town, followed by the sounds of men running to take up defensive positions.

"Never thought I'd be glad to hear that," Cyril said. "Let's go. Stay to the shadows and keep Bertha quiet unless it's absolutely necessary."

"You really going to carry that around?" Ben asked Frank.

"Well yeah, you never know if we might come across the ... what was it that it needs to work?" he asked, turning to Hound.

"Gauss rifle power-cell," Hound said. "And I can pretty much guarantee you won't find one."

"I'll take my chances," Frank said.

"I thought you might. Just remember, if we get into a fight, that hatchet is a better weapon than a tech rifle without power."

Cyril cracked the door and peeked out, waiting a moment before opening it just enough to stick his head out. He looked back and nodded, leading them out into the night, stopping at the corner of the building and scanning the shadows for any hint of threat before racing across the alley behind the jail and in between two houses.

The stalker screamed again. Shots rang out, followed by more shouting.

Cyril headed for the wall at the edge of town. At each road or alley, he stopped in the shadows, watching carefully for several moments before running across into the cover of darkness again. Many of the houses had lamps hanging beside the doors, all burning brightly as if they served to ward against evil. The doors remained locked and the shades were all drawn. All the townspeople who weren't manning the walls were huddled inside their homes.

"There's someone up ahead," Homer said to Ben.

Ben tapped Cyril on the shoulder and motioned toward the wall. They came to a halt, remaining in the alley, waiting and listening.

Two men walked by, each holding a lantern high, both nervously looking up at the wall as if they expected a beast to come over at any moment.

From the direction of the north gate where they'd entered the town, Ben heard someone scream in pain. Then more gunshots added to the tension in the air. The two men on patrol hurried off toward the sounds.

"We'll move along the wall looking for a way out," Cyril whispered. "If we don't find one before we reach the south gate, we'll have to fight our way through."

"I've got one grenade round left," Hound said. "I could just blow a hole in the wall."

"Let's save that option for now," Cyril said. "I don't want them to notice we're gone and we might need that round later."

Hound nodded in the dark.

When they reached the timber wall, they moved cautiously and quietly, slowing when they approached a guard tower occupied by a single man whose attention was directed entirely outside the town.

Once past the light of the tower's lamp, they moved more quickly, searching without luck for a break in the wall. There were a few gaps wide enough to reach through, but none large enough to accommodate a man.

When they neared the corner of the wall and another tower, an alarm bell began to ring. One of the two men in the tower quickly raised his lamp, throwing light onto the perimeter road.

"Stop!" he shouted.

"The prisoners have escaped," the second man yelled.

Both brought their weapons to bear, a tech bow and a crossbow.

"Run," Cyril said, racing in between the nearest houses and out of view of the tower. Reaching the alley behind the row of houses, he turned north into town, heading back the way they'd come.

"Where are you going?" Frank whispered harshly.

"Shut up and follow me," Cyril said over his shoulder without slowing. He raced up the narrow alley without concern for stealth until he reached the guard tower that they'd already passed under. He turned into the gap between two houses and crept up to the threshold of the tower's light, peering out of the shadows at the guard.

The man was now alternately scanning both inside and outside the town.

"Get the rope ready," Cyril whispered. "Don't move until I give the signal."

He poked his head out, looking both ways before withdrawing quickly. Sounds of men approaching reached them followed by a scream of pain and terror. All eyes turned up toward the top of the tower. A mountain lion had the man by the throat, shaking the life out of him before tossing his corpse to the road and turning its malevolent black eyes down toward the town.

"Come," said a voice from behind them. They all whirled to see two Dragon Guard several streets away looking straight at them. The lead man beckoned to the stalker. "These are your prey."

The stalker screamed and leapt onto the roof of one of the houses right next to them.

"Run toward the posse," Cyril said, slipping out into the relatively well-lit street and running, hands up and open, toward the dozen men coming their way. An arrow whizzed overhead, driving deeply into the stalker but with no effect.

"Ignore the prisoners!" Carlyle shouted. "Kill the stalker!"

Cyril and the others ran toward the wall and out of the way, giving the townsfolk a better line of sight on the stalker. Shots cracked overhead and bowstrings snapped. The stalker roared in rage but wasn't deterred by the onslaught of arrows and bullets.

When Ben reached the wall with the rest of his friends and family, he turned back and watched as the stalker leapt to the ground and began to approach, snarling with malice and anticipation.

The Dragon Guard reached the road behind the stalker a moment later.

"Hold," the Dominus shouted.

The stalker stopped, looking back at him with a tortured whimper.

The Dominus fixed his gaze on Cyril and commanded, "Lay down your weapons and surrender."

Ben looked from the Dragon Guard to the townsfolk. Carlyle locked eyes with Cyril.

"The Dragon Guard sent the stalkers," Carlyle said. "Take them!"

"Your whole town will burn for this," the Dominus said.

"Yeah, but you'll die first," Hound said, raising Bertha and firing his last grenade round at the stalker-cat, hitting it in the head. The explosion sent blood and meat splattering across the road, killing the stalker and leaving little more than a bloody stump where its head and neck used to be.

John loosed an arrow at the Dragon Guard, hitting the lesser-ranked man in the chest and dropping him to his knees, the riding leathers he wore providing nowhere near the protection of their customary black battle armor.

"What are you doing, Sheriff?" his deputy said in horror.

"Protecting Shady Cove," Carlyle said.

The Dominus ran off in between the houses, fleeing for his life.

"After him," Carlyle barked.

Most of his men complied, but the deputy and two others turned on Carlyle.

"No, we need them," the deputy said. "We can still collect the reward and we can beg the Dragon Guard for protection."

"You idiot," Carlyle snapped. "Didn't you see the man command the stalker. They sent them to scare us into submission."

"You're wrong," the deputy said, his hand moving slowly toward his pistol. "You're not fit to be sheriff."

Carlyle's eyes went flat and hard. "This job isn't about money or power. It's about doing right by the people."

"Not any more," the deputy said, going for his gun. He didn't manage to clear the weapon from its holster before Carlyle pulled and shot him through the chest, bringing his pistol to bear on the other two men a heartbeat later.

"Lay down your weapons or die."

Both hesitated until the deputy fell face first into the dirt.

The sound of Rufus racking another round into Bertha got their attention.

"I suggest you do as the man says," Cyril said.

Both men laid down arms and stepped back slowly, looking from Carlyle to Hound.

"You know the way to the jailhouse," Carlyle said to his two former posse members.

"And us?" Cyril asked.

Carlyle looked at them and sighed. "Frankly, I'd like you to get the hell out of my town."

"Walk us to the gate and we'll be on our way, Sheriff."

"Good enough."

Chapter 23

"I still don't see why he wanted that gauss rifle back," Frank said. "It didn't even work."

"Maybe 'cuz it was his," Hound said.

Frank huffed, shaking his head.

They'd walked down the road for an hour or so before turning into the forest, heading west for another hour before stopping to make a cold and dark camp.

Dawn brought a deep blue sky filled with fluffy white clouds. Ben couldn't help but marvel at the beauty of it. The air was clear and fresh and the forest was filled with bright green shoots and new leaves.

After a cold breakfast, they set out cross-country due west. The terrain was anything but forgiving—steep rises leading to sharp ridgelines and even steeper descents into valleys cut by trickling streams all running toward the Rogue River. Fortunately, the forest was thick enough that there were plenty of trees they could use to aid in their ascent and slow their descent, but not so thick that it hindered travel.

Occasionally, they came across old roads cut through the forest centuries ago and mostly neglected over recent decades. Only the absence of mature trees and the presence of tall grass marked their locations.

While they made slow progress, they began to feel a sense of safety in their relative isolation. Tracking them through the rugged forest would require a stalker or dogs or a very skilled outdoorsman. Even if the Dominus had survived Carlyle and his posse, it was inconceivable that he could have reached Rogue City, rounded up soldiers and returned to lead a search overnight. It would be at least a day before the Dragon Guard would find their trail and even longer before they'd get close enough to pose a threat.

"Where are we going to go after we get Imogen's baby back?" Frank asked when they stopped at a stream to rest and eat lunch.

"I have a friend up north, in the Deschutes Territory," Cyril said. "He'll take us in until we can decide what comes next." He glanced at Ben with an unspoken admonition to remain silent.

"You know the dragon will be moving north soon enough," Frank said.

Cyril nodded. "By the time he's ready to take another territory, we'll have moved on."

"But where?" Frank asked.

"Not sure," Cyril said. "We need better information about the spread of the wyrm's minions before we decide."

Frank pursed his lips, clearly not satisfied with the answer but apparently willing to accept that Cyril didn't have any more to offer.

"Are you going to tell me what happened back in Prospect?" he asked instead.

Cyril held him with a glare until Frank looked down.

"You'd know what happened if you hadn't run off," Cyril said. "We were attacked by some very bad people. They took Imogen, so we killed them."

Frank started to say something but stopped when he saw Cyril's expression.

"I couldn't help it," he finally muttered.

"We should get moving," Cyril said.

By late afternoon, Ben was tired and his legs felt like rubber. The up and down from one ridgeline to the next was taking a toll on him. He wondered at his grandfather's ability to maintain such a grueling pace given his age, but Cyril seemed to be the least exhausted of them all ... except maybe Homer.

When they had reached yet another ridge, John stopped them with an urgent gesture, pointing down toward an old forest road. They could see a trap containing a very agitated coyote. Not far off was a man and a horse-drawn cart with an empty cage in the back.

Everyone took cover, watching and listening.

"Well now," the man said to the coyote, "looks like my luck is your misfortune. The priest will pay well for you and you'll be back out in the wilds in no time." He worked at pulling two ramps out of the back of his wagon while he talked to the animal. "The bad news is, you won't quite be yourself after he's done with you." He slid the empty cage down to the road and pushed it out of the way with some effort.

"Let's see about getting you loaded," he said, climbing onto the wagon and unwinding a rope from a hand winch mounted to the front of the wagon's bed. The coyote snarled and snapped at him when he hooked the line to the cage.

"You're a feisty one," he said, chuckling but taking care to keep his hands out of reach. He climbed back into the wagon and slowly dragged the cage to the ramps and then up into the bed. Once it was loaded, he tied it down and nodded approval.

"You're not a cat, but then they're far less agreeable when caged."

Sunlight fell on the man's cheek—it was scarred with a rune, the mark of the Dragon Guard, but this man wasn't dressed in any type of uniform. Instead, he wore clothes one might expect of a hunter or trapper. Only the scar gave him away.

He went to the empty cage and baited the trap, sprung it once and then set it again.

"Let's get you back to Rogue City," he said, climbing into the driver's seat and urging his horse into motion.

John nocked an arrow, but Cyril slowly shook his head, motioning for quiet while the man with the coyote rode away. After several minutes, he stood up and surveyed the forest with a frown.

"Is that where the stalkers come from?" Imogen asked.

"Seems that way," Cyril said.

"So why didn't we kill him?" Frank asked. "And how do they turn a coyote into a stalker?"

"Better to leave as little trace of our passage as possible," Cyril said. "As for the how, I have my suspicions, but I couldn't say for sure."

He headed down to the road, stopping to look at the trap for several moments before reaching inside and pulling the trigger, causing the door to fall on an empty cage.

"Shouldn't we destroy it?" Frank asked.

"No, a sprung trap isn't out of the ordinary—a destroyed one is," Cyril said. "Our best defense right now is to pass unnoticed."

When night began to fall a few hours later, they found a secluded meadow to make camp.

"How much farther?" Frank asked.

"A day, maybe two, depending on the terrain."

"Wasn't the Deschutes Territory hit in the initial attack?" Ben asked.

"It was, but the population in that area was far lower than in other places," Cyril said. "They've been able to clear out the dead and rebuild, or so I've heard."

"I still don't understand how the dragons managed to wipe out most of the world overnight," Frank said.

Cyril's eyes lost focus for a few moments before he snapped back to the present and nodded to his grandson.

"I've never really talked about it, avoided it, in fact," Cyril said. "I guess you're old enough to hear the story." He paused to collect his thoughts. "You boys remember your history lessons?"

They both nodded, though Ben had to wonder which lesson his grandfather was referring to.

"I've never been much of a student," Hound said. "So I wouldn't mind a refresher."

Cyril nodded with a grin. "After the old governments ran out of other people's money and went broke, the world devolved into chaos for a while. People were desperate for security, any kind of security. The corporations were only too happy to provide it. They began to take geographic areas under their direct control, forming their own militaries and police forces to establish order. And people were happy to have it … at first, anyway.

"The thing about corporations is they understand basic economics, unlike politicians and bureaucrats. The corporate masters know that an economy runs on productivity and nothing else, not consumption and certainly not debt. Unfortunately, they always tend to lose sight of the human component—people become numbers, units of production, all expected to add to the bottom line. While that kind of thinking does lead to a higher standard of living for most, it fails to take into account that some people simply can't be as productive as others, whether due to age, illness, or disability.

"Some corporations solved that problem with pretty draconian measures. It was a dark period of history called the 'purge.' That led people to revolt against their corporate masters. Rather than lose their power, the corporations agreed to reforms, and the continental conglomerates were formed. Six super corporations were charged with managing the resources of each major land mass, and make no mistake, they considered people to be a resource, both to be protected and exploited.

"Over time, the world stabilized. The six conglomerates formalized trade relations and agreed to reduce their military capabilities. One of the consequences of this was a dramatic reduction in nuclear weapons worldwide. Each conglomerate kept a few dozen nukes, but they were all carefully controlled. Unfortunately, some genius came along and invented the neural-pulse bomb, and since it was a brand-new weapon of mass destruction, it wasn't controlled by the trade agreements. Before you knew it, the world was in another arms race.

"And the timing couldn't have been worse."

"Wait," Frank said. "How does a neural-pulse bomb work. I mean, I've heard of them before, but I never understood how they killed so many people."

Cyril nodded. "When a nuclear weapon detonates, it creates an electromagnetic pulse capable of disrupting electrical systems. It didn't take long to discover that the effect could be duplicated with conventional weapons. The neural-pulse bomb was the next evolution of that idea. It emits an electromagnetic pulse that disrupts the electrical activity in the nervous systems of mammals. The effect doesn't last long, just a few minutes, but we can't survive even that long without a heartbeat. By that time, everybody in the area of effect is dead."

"I'm usually a big fan of weapons," Hound said, "but that one makes my blood run cold."

"Tragically," Cyril continued, "when the dragons came, the corporate conglomerates were busy building up enormous stockpiles of these weapons, complete with stealth delivery systems. Worse, nobody saw Dragonfall for what it was. The eggs hatched and the dragons went into hiding until they could grow in size, magic, and influence. Over a few dozen years, they secretly gathered followers, promising them magic and power, systematically infiltrating higher and higher levels in the corporate structures until they were ready to strike.

"That was the day the world ended—the day your grandmother died," Cyril said, looking to Ben and Frank in turn. "Now, get some rest, tomorrow's going to be another hard day."

And it was. They walked up and down for most of the day, from one ridge to the next, until Cyril stopped atop a bald, rocky bluff and surveyed the forest stretching out before them.

"There," he said, pointing toward a valley two ridgelines over. "We'll reach my cache tomorrow."

"Glad to hear it," John said, pointing toward the sky. "Looks like the bird is back."

All eyes turned upward and found a hawk circling high overhead, directly above them.

"We'll keep an eye on it," Cyril said, "see if it follows us."

They made camp that night under the trees next to a burbling stream. When they set out the following morning, Ben searched the sky, feeling a twinge of fear when he saw the hawk overhead.

"What do you think they'll send at us next?" Hound asked.

"A lot more than before," Cyril said, anxiety ghosting across his face.

More than anything else, Ben was disconcerted by his grandfather's worry. It took a lot to get to him, but something clearly had, more so than all they had already been through.

"What do they have besides the Dragon Guard and stalkers?" Frank asked.

"A dragon," Cyril said, with a deadly serious look.

"But he's nowhere near here," Frank said.

"Dragons can fly," Cyril said. "We need to move."

He set a brisk pace, driving all of them harder than Ben would have thought possible. He started to wonder at his stamina, when a thought occurred to him that drove out all other considerations.

The dragon's egg.

The story of the resistance told of a single unhatched egg—the source of the Wizard's power. He'd seen Cyril use the bone amulet, seen the power he could command with a trinket made from a long-dead dragon. He could only imagine what his grandfather might be capable of with a living dragon egg.

While they trudged up a steep incline, understanding of the true nature of their plight flooded into Ben as if he'd been struck by lightning. He stopped dead in his tracks, his mind abuzz with fear and possibility.

Cyril was taking them to the egg—the centerpiece of his weapons cache, a source of power unequaled in all the world. And the potential doom of humanity.

If the egg hatched, there would be two dragons, almost certainly a breeding pair.

"What's wrong?" Frank asked when he saw Ben's dumbstruck expression.

Ben struggled to shake off the implications of his sudden understanding, shaking his head and willing himself to continue toward the ridgeline.

If the dragon knew that the egg was back in play, that the Wizard was at work in the world again, he would stop at nothing to recover his potential mate. That was what Cyril really feared. Ben looked up, marking the position of the bird with renewed concern. The Dragon Guard was coming, and there was no telling what they might bring with them.

"You look like you saw a ghost," Frank said.

"Just contemplating our enemy," Ben said, setting out again. He knew the look on Frank's face. His brother was a lot of things, but he wasn't stupid. Ben chided himself. He would have to become a better liar, in word and deed, if he was going to keep Frank from discovering their family secret.

Nearing the top of the ridge, he pondered what Frank might do with the knowledge, how he might leverage it. He knew one thing for certain … if Frank discovered that Cyril was the Wizard, that he possessed the dragon's egg, he would want the egg for himself above all other things. Enough even to cut ties with his family and strike out on his own.

The end of that particular set of bad decisions would be Frank's capture or death and the wyrm's ultimate victory—an outcome that Ben vowed to himself to prevent, no matter the cost.

He stopped at the top of the ridge, leaning against a tree to catch his breath while the consequences of his silent vow penetrated to the core of his being.

He might have to kill his brother.

He'd thought about it before, but never more seriously than typical brothers in a fight. He'd even said it, but never with the full force of intention or with any real consideration for the implications of such a thing. He tried to imagine carrying through with it and was immediately assailed by his conscience, by an internal rebellion of such magnitude that he realized in an instant that he simply didn't have it in him.

Frank was untrustworthy, infuriating, and totally self-centered, but he was also his brother, his family. How could he ever bring himself to turn on family? And yet …

How could he not? If the world truly did hang in the balance, if Frank's monumental selfishness might lead to a future of darkness and slavery, tyranny and domination, how could Ben put his own feelings ahead of that?

He looked over at Frank and shoved the dilemma from his mind. Not because he'd arrived at anything resembling a decision, but because it was simply too painful to consider.

"There are some things all of you should know about the place I'm taking you," Cyril said, his eyes never leaving the forested valley below. A few broken-out rooftops could be seen through the trees and the remnants of an old wooden fence marked a line along one side of the creek.

"Such as?" Hound said when Cyril didn't continue.

"It's haunted."

"I don't believe in ghosts," Frank said.

"You should," Cyril said, looking at him with a deadly serious expression. "All of the stories of magic, of haunting, of strange and unnatural creatures—all of them have a basis in reality. Some have been embellished, but the sources of all those stories are real. This is no different.

"This place has been called many things over the centuries. It's a natural electromagnetic vortex that warps space and time. Before the dragons arrived, it was harmless enough, little more than a curiosity, but now it contains some unique dangers and properties. My theory is that the veil between worlds is naturally thin here, and the dragon's presence makes it permeable.

"You'll see things that don't make sense. You may be faced with apparitions. It's important that you don't look at them. If they notice that you can see them, they will act. I believe that many of the entities called ghosts exist in our midst all the time, but we can't see them. It's only in places like this, places where the veil is thin, that they become visible. Our perception of their existence gives them power to manipulate us through that perception."

"So what should we do?" Imogen asked.

"Honestly, it would be better if you all waited here," Cyril said.

"Not a chance," Frank said.

John pointed toward the bird still orbiting overhead.

"We probably should stay together," Hound said. "Just tell us how to handle these ghosts and we'll be fine."

"Ignore them," Cyril said. "Pretend they aren't there. Don't let your eyes linger on them, don't react to their behavior, don't heed their words or howls."

"Howls?" Ben asked.

"They'll make all manner of noise to frighten you—some of which are truly terrifying."

"Why on earth would you hide your weapons here?" Frank asked.

"What better place than one with built-in supernatural guard dogs?" Cyril said.

Ben suspected he had other reasons.

"Everyone down," John said, ducking behind a tree.

The sound of horses coming up the road reached them shortly before four men came around a bend. They were all armed with blades and one carried a bow.

"The bird is overhead," one said.

"They should be around here somewhere," another said.

"Bounty hunters," John whispered. He motioned toward the one with the bow. "I know that one."

"Quietly back up," Cyril whispered.

They crept backward, putting the top of the ridge between them and their hunters.

"So what now?" Frank asked.

"We wait."

"For what? The Dragon Guard?" Frank said. "If these guys got here this quickly, the wyrm's people aren't far behind."

"He's got a point," Hound said.

Cyril looked up at the hawk and frowned.

"Frank, you and John and Hound go up to the ridge and watch them, but stay out of sight," Cyril said. "If they head this way, come back without alerting them to our presence."

Ben was grateful that Frank didn't argue.

Once they'd reached the ridge, Cyril leaned in to whisper to Imogen and Ben. "Have you ever seen a small bird harass a hawk?"

They both nodded with confusion.

Cyril smiled, taking Imogen's hand and motioning for Ben to take her other hand.

"Close your eyes for a moment, take a deep breath and clear your mind," he said softly. "Let go of your thoughts and picture a hawk. Picture three or four small birds hitting it in the back of the head, tearing out its feathers, harassing it mercilessly. Hold that thought in your mind, picture it vividly."

Ben did as instructed. He'd seen it many times before, a big bird soaring on the wind with two or three smaller birds taking turns diving at the back of its head, and usually driving it off. He pictured it in his mind, holding the image with as much clarity as he could muster.

"Good, now let go of the image and open your eyes."

When they both complied, he smiled and pointed at some moss hanging from a tree.

"Do you remember what that is called?"

Both looked at him with more confusion, shaking their heads.

"No matter, I just needed you to truly let go of your thought. A spell is never actually cast until you release the thought form you've created into the world."

"What are you saying?" Imogen asked.

"We just cast a spell," Cyril said. "Now we wait for reality to obey."

He looked up at the hawk and smiled when he saw a pack of crows headed toward it.

"How can we even be sure that we did that?" Ben asked.

Cyril shrugged. "Does it matter?"

The crows cawed raucously, gaining altitude on the larger bird before tipping over and diving at the back of its head, hitting it with enough force that it started to evade, shrieking in anger, even trying to roll and claw at them a few times, but the crows were far more aerobatic, avoiding it easily and resuming the attack. The hawk tried to remain overhead, but as it started to lose feathers, it turned to flee. The crows pursued, harassing it relentlessly.

"Magic always works best when it's used in congruence with the natural order," Cyril said. "Crows are prone to attack larger birds … it's in their nature and there are plenty of them living in these trees, so they seemed like the natural choice."

"Could you have driven it off in another way?"

"*We* could have, but it would have required more time and will," Cyril said.

John returned quietly. "They left," he said. "Looked like they were following the bird."

"Excellent," Cyril said. "Let's give them some time and then we'll go retrieve my cache."

Chapter 24

They waited atop the ridge for several minutes, watching and listening for any sign of the bounty hunters. Satisfied that they were gone, Cyril motioned for John to lead the way. They slowly descended, stopping frequently to check for danger, but the narrow valley seemed to be completely devoid of life.

They headed for an old road that had been cut into the embankment of a shallow creek that ran between a cluster of old buildings—several houses, a few outbuildings, and a small garage. All of them looked as though they'd been abandoned decades ago.

When they reached the road, they stopped, listening intently for approaching riders. The place had an eerie silence about it, as if fog had settled over new-fallen snow on a dead-calm night … except it was the middle of the day and the blue sky was filled with cottony white clouds.

"Take a firm grip on your courage," Cyril said, looking to each in turn to punctuate his words before heading for the cluster of buildings.

Everything looked normal enough, yet Ben's skin tingled with dread. He found himself checking his sword in its scabbard.

"This place is wrong," Homer said.

"Stay close."

"I don't think I can get any closer," Homer said, trembling as he leaned against Ben's leg.

A door slammed, then slowly creaked open.

"Where did that come from?" Frank whispered harshly.

John pointed toward one of the houses while Rufus pointed to another in a different direction.

"Ignore it," Cyril said, seeming to orient himself, and then frowning.

"What's wrong?" Imogen asked.

"The houses are out of place," Cyril muttered.

"What the hell does that mean?" Frank asked.

"It means that things have moved," Cyril said.

Ben saw something in the trees. He fixed his attention and waited, straining to hear footsteps. A figure in a dingy white dress flitted between the trees and vanished behind one of the houses.

"I just saw a woman."

"Ignore her," Cyril said.

"Does anyone else see that?" Hound said, pointing toward a bank of heavy fog rolling slowly down the valley toward them.

"Yep," John said.

Imogen nudged Cyril. "There's a little girl over there watching us."

"Don't look at her!" he whispered.

Ben couldn't help looking her way, but he managed to keep his head still, peering out of the corner of his eye. She was standing between two trees not forty feet away, looking straight at them. She looked normal enough, except that she was barefoot and wore only a simple nightgown. Her hair was stringy black and unkempt.

When the fog reached them, the little girl vanished along with all of the houses. The temperature fell several degrees, damp air soaking into them.

"Stay together," Cyril said. "This way."

Ben could just make out his grandfather's silhouette through the thick fog for a moment before he vanished as well.

"Follow my voice," Cyril said, sounding very far away. Ben moved toward him cautiously, his heart pounding in his chest. The fog cleared around them and Ben found himself alone with Homer pressed up against his leg.

The little girl stood not ten feet away looking straight at him.

"Will you help me, mister? I got lost in the woods and I can't find my mommy."

Ben froze, not daring to look at her, struggling to resist acknowledging her presence, and yet knowing that he would ultimately fail.

"Over here," Cyril said.

Ben hurried away from the girl, heading back into the fog toward his grandfather's voice. From behind him he could hear her calling to him, her voice fading into the heavy fog, "Please, mister, don't leave me here."

His conscience nagged at him to turn back and help her. What if she was real? What if he was leaving a little girl all alone in the forest? He stopped, torn between reason and conscience.

Before he could make a decision, Cyril appeared out of the white air and took him by the elbow.

"Ignore her," he said intently. "She's not real."

Ben nodded tightly, taking a deep breath to steady himself. Another break in the fog and he saw that everyone else was waiting on the porch of one of the houses. Cyril led him there quickly before the fog closed in around them again.

"Stay close together," he said, opening the door slowly. The rusty hinges protested loudly. Cyril waited for a moment at the threshold. The house was dark and dank, the air within musty and stale.

"Come on," he said, leading them into the living room. It looked as though it had been abandoned quickly. Pictures still hung on the walls, the glass stained by years of neglect. Furniture was arranged around the hearth. The air smelled of mold.

Cyril took a moment to light his lamp, casting a flickering light that did little to diminish the unwelcoming feel of the place. A hallway leading to the back rooms and a doorway opening into the kitchen branched off the living room. Cyril chose the hall, moving cautiously.

The front door slammed shut behind them with such force that one of the pictures fell off the wall and shattered. Ben froze, scanning the room without moving his head. Even Hound looked scared, which did little to bolster Ben's courage.

"I thought you said they couldn't do anything but scare us," Rufus said.

"Apparently I was wrong," Cyril said.

"Great," Rufus said, unslinging Bertha.

"Don't go blasting away at ghosts."

"Could be there's more than ghosts here."

"Point taken," Cyril said, leading them halfway down the hall before stopping.

"What's wrong?" Imogen asked.

"Wrong house," Cyril said. "Back the way we came."

They reached the living room and the door slammed open again, rattling more pictures from the wall, their glass panes shattering when they hit the floor. The little girl stood in the doorway, her head down, her face obscured by her black stringy hair. She swayed from side to side, breathing shallowly and quickly, enough to make a living person hyperventilate.

They all stopped, involuntarily staring at her.

"I knew you could see me," she said, her voice no longer that of a little girl. She looked up at them. Her face was gaunt and cracked, as if the skin had been pulled tight and dried in place. Her eyes were gone, leaving only empty sockets filled with impossible blackness. Her smile was sweet and innocent, but began to transform as her mouth opened wide.

"Close your eyes!" Cyril shouted.

Ben heard him but he simply could not pull his attention away from the terrifying spectacle before him.

The girl's face grew into a skull, eyes shining with blackness that seemed to dampen the light where she looked. Her mouth filled with rows of sickly yellow teeth filed to needle points. Her flesh fell away and then her body with it as her skull grew impossibly large and rushed at them, washing through them, insubstantial as air, yet filling Ben with a paralyzing terror.

The only reference he had for the experience was his time in the stalker's realm—and that saved him. He was able to remain rooted in place, holding his sanity tightly with every scrap of his will. Homer lay prone beside him, eyes buried beneath his paws while he whimpered. He was the only one to heed Cyril's warning.

Imogen screamed, then bolted down the hallway. John stood stock-still, trembling but unable to take action. Frank shouted an obscenity and fled into the kitchen. Hound held his ground, bringing Bertha to bear on the now-empty doorway, but holding his fire.

A child laughed in the distance, the sound muffled by fog.

"What the hell just happened?" Hound finally said.

Cyril opened his eyes and pursed his lips after a quick headcount.

"You just saw a ghost." He looked at John and then at Ben. Ben nodded that he was in command of his faculties. Cyril offered him a quick smile and went to John, slapping him across the face. The Highwayman shook his head, coming to his senses and searching for an enemy he could fight.

"How?" was all he could muster.

"There are forces at work here that are far beyond normal understanding," Cyril said.

"Where's Imogen?" John asked, his own fear suddenly displaced with worry for her.

"She ran down the hallway," Ben said. "Frank went into the kitchen."

John headed for the hallway, but Cyril stopped him with a hand on his arm.

"Slow down, we'll go together."

Hound went to the kitchen door and peered through. "Looks like Frank went out the back door," he said. "I'll go get him."

"When you find him, take him up the hill out of the fog," Cyril said. "Wait for us just over the ridge where we hid from the bounty hunters."

Hound nodded, heading into the kitchen.

"How're you doing?" Ben asked Homer.

"Ghosts shouldn't be as scary as they are."

Ben knelt down and pet him for a moment before following Cyril and John.

The doors of the bedrooms and the bathroom were all standing open. They found Imogen huddled in a corner of the last room. She was trembling and crying, her forehead pressed against her knees as she rocked back and forth.

Cyril went to her, approaching slowly, laying a hand on her head and whispering a few reassuring words under his breath. She looked up, confusion in her eyes.

"What happened?"

"Ghosts," he said. "You're safe now."

"This was her room," Ben said, looking at a dust-covered frame atop an old dresser. The picture it held showed the girl standing in a grassy yard, the green ground dappled with sunlight. She was laughing and playing, wearing a brightly colored dress. Then in the next moment, her visage changed and she was looking straight out of the frame at him with black, empty eye sockets.

"Holy shit," he said, leaping back, trembling anew. "How's that even possible?"

Cyril laid the frame down on its face and put a hand on Ben's shoulder.

"The veil is thin here. The rules of reality as you understand them don't apply."

Ben swallowed hard and nodded, even though he couldn't bring himself to comprehend, much less accept what he'd just seen.

"Let's go," Cyril said, leading them out of the house and onto the porch. Ben felt as if he'd stepped into another world. The fog was gone, but it was night. He struggled to reconcile what he knew with what he was seeing. They'd entered the house in midafternoon, and they'd only been inside for a few minutes, yet the forest was dark as pitch. He stepped off the porch and looked at the sky. There were no stars and no moon, though he knew that the moon should be high in the sky at this point in its cycle.

He turned to Cyril, beseeching him for an explanation with a look, but got only a helpless shrug in return.

"I think the next house is that way," he said, holding his lamp before him like a talisman.

They moved together in a tight cluster, nobody wanting to get separated from the group. Ben saw movement out of the corner of his eye. Before he knew it, his head snapped toward the potential threat. A creature stood just outside the range of Cyril's lantern. It looked almost human, but stood just under three feet tall. It had a wrinkled face, pockmarked and dotted with warts and moles where it wasn't covered with a bushy beard. Malevolent green peered out from under thick eyebrows. It smiled at Ben, revealing sharp canines as it tossed a rock into the air and caught it before hurling it at Ben with surprising force.

He tried to dodge out of the way, but the rock struck him on the shoulder hard enough to leave a mark. The thing laughed with malicious glee and then raced into the darkness more quickly than Ben would have thought possible.

"That wasn't a ghost," Ben said, drawing his sword.

"No, it wasn't," Cyril said, without slowing.

They reached the next house and Cyril stopped on the porch, shaking his head. "Doesn't make sense," he muttered.

"I can't argue with that," Ben said.

Cyril pulled the door open and raised his lamp, casting light into the main room and shaking his head again. "Layout's all wrong."

A rock shattered the window next to them. All eyes turned to see the creature in the woods smile maliciously at them and then vanish into the darkness.

"What is that thing?" Imogen asked.

"Something from another realm that slipped through the veil," Cyril said. "Don't bother with it unless it gets close."

He led them to the third house, nodding to himself when they reached the porch. "This looks right," he said, pulling open the creaking door.

Light filtered out of the forest in the distance, like dozens of torches casting their illumination through lingering mist. Figures moved in the trees, some of them shaped like men, others shaped in such hideous forms that Ben found himself hoping he would never have to see them up close.

"Inside, quickly," Cyril said.

A chorus of howls erupted from the night, some trailing off into shrieks of rage and pain, others transforming into gibbering laughter laced with madness.

After everyone had filed inside, Cyril quietly closed the door. The house was in similar condition to the others, dilapidated and falling to ruin. All of the furniture was decaying and smelled of rot. Cyril paused for only a moment before heading to the hallway leading into the back of the house. He stopped at the second door and frowned at the broken lock, leaning in to examine it more closely.

"What's wrong?" Ben asked.

"I put this lock here," Cyril said. "It's been broken from the inside."

Ben and Imogen shared a look when Cyril drew his sword and used it to open the door, revealing the landing of a staircase. As he cautiously peered around the corner, his frown deepened.

Laughter from somewhere outside filtered through the walls. Ben scanned the hallway in both directions for movement but saw nothing. Cyril started down the stairs.

Ben followed, taking note of footprints in the heavy dust coating the steps. The prints were small, almost childlike, except that the feet that made them wore heavy boots.

Cyril stopped at the bottom landing and carefully surveyed the shadows, his sword at the ready. After several moments, he moved slowly into the basement, stopping a short way in and raising his lamp.

His light illuminated a pentagram carved into the concrete, an intricate rune etched inside each point. The pentagon within the star contained twin circles, the outermost touching all five sides, the innermost just a few inches away. Myriad arcane symbols were carved into the space between them.

"What is this?" Imogen asked.

"Black magic," Cyril said. "Don't step on it."

After a few more moments of examination, Cyril pulled his attention away from it and went to one of the walls, running his hand over the blocks, tracing a line of mortar.

"Here," he whispered. "Ben, come hold the light. John, watch the stairs. Imogen, watch the pentagram."

"For what?" she asked, her eyes going slightly wider.

"Anything unusual," he said, handing the lamp to Ben, sheathing his sword and drawing a knife.

He started scraping away at the mortar. His work was slow at first, but after he'd dislodged a few chunks, the rest began to fall away more quickly. He pulled a block out and set it aside, motioning for Ben to hold the light higher.

There was a space behind the wall.

The next block came free quickly. It wasn't long before Cyril had opened a passage large enough for a man to squeeze through. He took the lamp from Ben and leaned inside, filling the space beyond with light and plunging the room they occupied into darkness.

Footsteps behind them drew their attention, small feet coming impossibly fast down the stairs. John shouted in the dark and then fell, scrambling to regain his feet. Cyril pulled his lamp back into the room, drawing his sword as he whirled. Ben already had his blade out and at the ready, but he wasn't quick enough.

The little creature darted across the room and stabbed Ben in the leg with a long knife, then retreated into the pentagram. His green eyes glinted with hate and his smile was more a threat than an expression of mirth.

"My master will take your world," he said, dodging slightly to one side, catching John's arrow out of the air.

Ben slumped to one knee, pain flooding into him. Bright red blood flowed from his wound onto the floor. He felt as though his life were being drawn out with it, as if the arcane symbols of the pentagram were pulling the vital fluid out of him. Red quickly filled all of the grooves in the ritualistic circle.

The little creature began speaking in some language that Ben had never heard before.

"Hurry," Cyril snapped. "Get Ben through the gap in the wall." From the tone of his voice, Ben knew that his grandfather recognized the words being spoken.

John and Imogen worked together to pull him into the small space. Homer followed with Cyril right behind him.

"Oh God, this is really bad," Imogen said, trying to stop the bleeding. John handed her a cloth and his belt. Ben felt cold.

"Focus on my voice," Homer said. "I'm right here with you, you just have to stay awake."

"All right," Ben said, his eyes falling shut, coldness flowing into him.

Hateful laughter echoed into the room.

Ben opened his eyes and saw Cyril kneeling over him, one hand on Imogen's shoulder, the other on his wound. Warmth began to flow into his leg.

"Stay awake," Homer said, nosing his face.

Ben struggled to keep his eyes open.

More laughter.

Cyril ignored it as he went to the back of the room.

Ben raised his head slightly, trying to watch his grandfather. He saw Cyril touch a panel on the wall, and after a moment, he heard a low whirring sound. The panel lit up, casting a dim rainbow of light over him. He looked toward the laughter and saw something that made no sense.

There was a gap in the space within the pentagram, a tear in the world. It looked like a rip, the edges glowing slightly red, the space within entirely black. While Ben watched, the space within became more distinct. A room came into view. Walls of stone, a flickering candle, a door made of stout timbers bound with heavy black metal—the place looked medieval.

"What the hell?" he muttered, pointing weakly at the figure stepping through the portal.

It was a human man, pale as a ghost with ice-blue eyes and shock-white hair. He wore black armor with spikes on the shoulders and elbows, and he carried a staff with a large talon bound to the top. He surveyed the scene, then smiled at Ben with calculated malice.

Imogen yelled a warning a moment after he raised his staff and pointed it at John. Darkness flowed out of the talon. Streamers as black as night, wispy yet solid, struck John in the chest and flowed into him. His eyes went black and he stood calmly, turning to face the man.

"Command me, Master," John said, his voice devoid of emotion, numb and dead.

The man spoke in a language that was entirely alien.

John nodded and drew his knife, turning toward Ben.

Through his delirium, Ben found himself reaching for the pistol tucked into his belt.

"What are you doing?" Imogen snapped at John.

He ignored her, raising his knife slowly over Ben's chest.

Ben pointed the gun at the man and focused on steadying his hand.

The man smiled, raising his staff and speaking a few words. A shimmering field of darkness appeared in the air as if he had erected a magical shield. He stood behind it, his eyes shining with confidence.

Ben fired. The bullet passed through the shield and tore into the man's shoulder, bright red blood spraying across the room.

The man shrieked in pain and rage, turning to look at Ben with a mixture of murderous rage and uncertain disbelief.

Ben pulled the trigger again. Another sharp crack reverberated through the basement, this time missing completely.

The man shouted a command to his diminutive minion and they fled up the stairs.

John blinked, frowning at the knife in his hand. "What happened?"

"Magic," Cyril said. "Get him up."

Ben struggled to maintain consciousness as they carried him into a room unlike any he'd ever seen before. The ceiling was lit through some power other than flame and the walls were fashioned of metal, dull grey and smooth. Shelves and tables were filled with a variety of strange devices and objects.

"Lay him here," Cyril said tersely, holding what looked like a large bird egg over him.

As Ben tried to focus on it, he thought he saw scales covering its surface. Somewhere in the distance, Homer whined and then Ben felt a great warmth flood into him … followed by oblivion.

Chapter 25

He woke slowly, his mind thick with confusion. His mouth was dry and sticky, his eyes wouldn't open. He groaned.

"He's awake," Imogen said from somewhere very far away.

"You're safe," Homer said. "Take it easy—go slow."

"What happened?" he asked.

"You got stabbed," Homer said. "That little runt that threw a rock at you stuck you in the leg with a knife."

Memory of the event returned in a flood, bringing more questions. He worked his eyes and managed to open one and then the other. The grit of dried tears felt crusty and old on his eyelashes. The ceiling was lit uniformly, casting a cold white light into the room. He closed his eyes again, warding them against the brightness.

Imogen brought him some water, which he drank eagerly, sputtering a bit for his enthusiasm. Pain stabbed into his leg and he gasped, taking a moment to lie still and assess the extent of his injuries. After the intensity diminished, he opened his eyes again and let them adjust to the light, looking around the room and trying to make sense of where he was.

"What is this place?" he asked.

"That's not important right now," Imogen said. "We're safe. Here, drink this."

After downing the sweet syrupy liquid, he felt warmth flow into his chest followed by a wave of sleepiness that claimed him in a matter of minutes.

The last thing he heard was Homer telling him to rest.

When he woke again, he was more alert and clearheaded. He didn't try to move. Instead, he opened his eyes and allowed them to adjust to the light before turning his head from side to side. To one side was a large door on giant metal hinges, locked from the inside with a series of bolts three inches thick. Turning his head the other way, he saw Cyril lying on a cot next to him, unconscious and bleeding slightly from a wound on his leg.

Ben rolled onto his side, fear and worry overcoming caution. The pain in his leg was greatly diminished.

"Go easy," Imogen said. "You've had a rough couple of nights."

"What happened?" he asked, reaching for Cyril.

"Stop!" Imogen said. "He said we're not to touch him until he wakes."

Ben blinked the sleep and confusion away, sitting up carefully.

"Don't overdo it," Homer said.

Ben frowned, examining his leg. His wound was mostly scarred over, still tender and red, but far more healed than should have been possible. He looked back to Cyril and saw that he bore a similar wound on his leg, his bandage red with blood. He lay on his back with both hands resting on an egg in the middle of his chest. Ben leaned in, looking at the egg more closely. It was six inches long and half as wide. While the surface was pearly white, it was covered with scales like those of a snake.

He sat back, questions and suspicions swirling in his head. "What happened?" he asked again. "Tell me everything."

Imogen nodded, pulling a chair up next to him.

"Lie down," she said.

He eased himself back to the cot and looked at her pointedly.

"Your grandfather is the Wizard ... but you already knew that," she said. "You were injured by the servant of the man who came through the portal, the one you shot." She smiled, laying a hand on his shoulder. "And it was a good thing too. Dad said he would probably have killed us all if you hadn't driven him off."

Ben gestured toward Cyril. "What happened to him?"

She shook her head, frowning with worry and confusion.

"He used magic to take your wound onto himself so he could stop the blood loss. He said it was the only way to save you."

"How is that possible?" Ben asked, looking over at his grandfather with renewed concern, and respect.

Imogen shrugged. "I don't really know. He didn't tell me much more about magic than he told you. I've always known that he was the Wizard, ever since I was a child, but he swore me to secrecy." She stopped, frowning more deeply. "I think he put a spell on me so I wouldn't tell anyone. I've wanted to tell you several times, but I always seem to forget. It's strange."

"Will he be all right?"

"He said he'll be fine. It'll just take another day or so for him to heal. How's your leg?"

"Sore."

"He said it would be. He also said you should drink this." She held up a bottle filled with bluish liquid.

"What is it?"

"He called it tech medicine. Once he stanched the bleeding, your heart started to give out. After it stopped for the second time, he said that this was the only thing that could save you. You woke up, so it must be helping."

"It is helping you," Homer said, "but it's doing something else too."

"I have so many questions," Ben whispered, looking over at Cyril.

"Me too," Imogen said.

"What about Frank and Rufus?" Ben asked, suddenly realizing that they weren't in the room.

"We don't know. We haven't opened the door since we carried you in here, and your grandfather made it very clear that we have to stay here until he wakes."

Ben noticed John lying asleep, his face pale and beaded with sweat. "What happened to him?"

"That man who came through the portal—Dad called him a 'warlock'— he used some kind of black magic to take control of John. He came down with a fever a few hours later." She looked over at him, worry etched into her face. "I'm hoping my father can help him once he wakes up."

Ben gave her hand a squeeze, drawing her attention back to him. "I'm sure he'll be fine."

"I hope so," she said. "We've been friends since I was seven years old. In fact, I met John the day we moved to K Falls." She sighed, shaking her head sadly. "If I hadn't been such a fool, none of this would have happened."

"What do you mean? This isn't your fault."

"But it is. I have terrible taste in men. John has always been there, he's loyal and honest and good, but I wanted excitement and adventure, so I've kept him at arm's length. I've been so unfair to him, and now he's lying there dying, for all I know. And it's all my fault."

"No ... it's the warlock's fault or it's the dragon's fault, but it's not your fault. John's here because he cares about you and he wants to protect you. He chose to be here and he did so for pretty good reasons. So don't blame yourself."

"But I do," she said, wiping a tear from her cheek. "All of this, you, my father, John, my baby. It's all my fault. If I hadn't let Enzo—"

"Stop it!" Ben said. "Women fall for assholes all the time. At least you have an excuse. You were charmed."

"Doesn't make it any easier."

"No, but it does make it not your fault. We have enough to worry about without carrying burdens that aren't ours to bear."

She nodded, handing him the bottle of medicine.

"We'll get through this, Big Sister, I promise."

She smiled. "Drink up."

He took a swig of the syrup, draining the bottle, and then drifted off to sleep again. He woke feeling much better but still took his time assessing the state of his injuries before sitting up. His leg was still slightly sore, but he thought it would support him, though certainly not comfortably.

Cyril was still asleep with the egg on his chest under both of his hands. His wound had stopped bleeding. John was wrapped in a bundle of blankets, his face pale and sweaty, his teeth chattering with each wave of chill.

"Go easy," Imogen said.

Ben nodded, gently probing the scar on his leg and shaking his head in wonder. The wound had been deep. Now it was just a tender scar.

"How long has it been?"

"Three days."

"My wound—"

"Magic and tech," Imogen said, shrugging.

"John doesn't look so good."

"No, and I'm worried about him. I don't know what to do."

"Did you try magic?" Ben asked.

She frowned and shook her head, then looked at Ben more seriously. "Chen gave you that amulet for a reason."

"Will you help me?"

"Sure, if you'll help me up."

Ben and Imogen sat on the floor next to John and held hands, each laying their free hand on John's chest.

"Are you sure about this?" Homer asked. "I mean, you don't really know what you're doing."

"We're just going to visualize John getting well."

"I think you should wait for Cyril to wake up," Homer said.

"We have to try."

"So what do we do now?" Imogen asked.

"I think it's just like chasing off that hawk. We create in our minds what we want to happen and then let it go."

They shared a look, closed their eyes, took a deep breath and let it out. Calmness came over them both, flowing from them into the room. As they both inhaled for the second time, a wave of translucent, shadowy black energy exploded from John, blowing both Ben and Imogen across the floor, stunning them senseless for a few minutes.

When Ben regained consciousness, a nagging sense of urgency tugged at his awareness, but he couldn't remember why. He hurt all over—but more than that, he felt a foul, unclean violation of his entire body, as if every vein, every bone, every muscle had just been subjected to a deluge of spiritual filth. He lay face down, his head throbbing with each pounding heartbeat.

A feeling of unease began to come over him. Disquiet gave way to growing inadequacy and unworthiness. A profound sense of judgment settled on him and began to take root, undermining his confidence, causing him to question his very right to exist.

"What the hell are you doing?" Homer said, barking out loud to punctuate his question.

Ben shook his head, his awareness coming back to the moment, the overwhelming feelings of guilt and failure receding somewhat but still nagging at the edge of his thoughts. He got to his hands and knees and looked around for Imogen. She was curled into a ball, weeping uncontrollably.

"I lost my baby … I lost my baby," she whimpered through her tears, each ragged breath spent on speaking the words "I lost my baby."

Ben went to her, shoving his own despair farther away, focusing on the present moment, clearing his mind of all concerns save for the well-being of his friends and family. Somewhere in the depths of his mind, he knew instinctually that deep personal attachments have power.

Nothing fortifies the will like a strong emotion.

"Imogen!" he said, rolling her up to a sitting position so he could look her in the eye.

She kept repeating "I lost my baby."

Ben brushed the hair from her face and shook her gently but her eyes remained far away and fixed. Her hysteria was nearly complete. He slapped her.

She blinked, muttering, "I lost my baby."

"Imogen. Come back to me," he said, taking her by the chin and turning her head so she was forced to look into his eyes.

She blinked again but then wailed, low and long as if she'd just remembered something too terrible to face.

"I lost my baby."

Ben slapped her again. She slumped to the floor and groaned, lying still for a while before curling into a ball again.

Ben waited for nearly an hour, listening intently to her breathing and watching over her.

"What happened?" she mumbled, sitting up as if from a long sleep.

"I don't know," Ben said. "I got blown across the room and then felt this crushing despair, like I didn't deserve to live. It was awful."

"I felt the same thing," she said, shuddering. "What about John?"

"Doesn't look like anything's changed," Ben said. "Whatever's got him is clearly beyond us. He'll have to hold on until Cyril wakes up. Thankfully, whatever hit us didn't seem to have any effect on him."

Ben helped Imogen to a chair and then sat down on his cot. He felt unclean, as if the inside of his body had been very deliberately soiled.

"What just happened?" he asked Homer.

"You played with magic that you didn't understand."

"Yeah, I know. Aside from that, what did you see?"

"A wave of blackness knocked you on your ass."

"A lot of help you are."

"I was being helpful before you played with forces of darkness beyond your comprehension—you know, when I told you not to. Now I'm just mocking you."

Ben looked at him and sighed, lying back down and closing his eyes. He could still feel the aftermath of the darkness within him. His mind kept wandering to ugly and dangerous thoughts. Sleep came after a struggle and he woke with a pent-up scream in his lungs, sitting quickly, searching frantically, coming aware a moment before releasing his fear in a wail of terror. He let the air out slowly, focusing on his breathing, willing his pounding heart to calm. He frowned when he realized that he couldn't even remember what he'd been dreaming about.

Chapter 26

When he woke the following morning, Cyril was smiling at him.

"You're awake," Ben said, sitting up quickly. Pressure built in his head, followed by pain and dizziness. He steadied himself, taking a moment to assess his new symptoms.

"Easy," Cyril said, putting a hand on Ben's shoulder. "How's your wound?"

"Nearly healed. How's yours?"

"On the mend," Cyril said.

Ben looked over to John. His fever seemed to have broken and he was sleeping soundly.

"How did you heal him?" Ben asked.

"I didn't … you did, sort of," Cyril said. "His fever has broken, but there's still some residual taint within him that I can't seem to root out. Something is blocking me."

"You mean what we did actually worked?"

"It did, to a point, though you utterly failed to protect yourselves—one of the many lessons about magic that you must learn. A consecrated circle will protect you from most beings from other realms, as well as their conjurings. You should always prepare a circle before you have any dealings with such forces."

"So now will you answer my questions about magic?"

"I will, but perhaps I should start by telling you about my past."

Imogen sat down next to Ben on the cot and nodded for her father to continue.

"My father found the dragon's egg shortly after Dragonfall. The dragons encase their eggs in rock, transport them into our solar system through some unknown power and then hurl them at the planet as meteorites. This egg hit a space station first, which shattered its casing. It fell to earth along with thousands of rock fragments. As a result, it didn't penetrate deeply enough into the crust to receive the heat it needed to hatch.

"When my father first found it, he thought it was merely a curiosity. Years later, when rumors of dragons began to circulate, he looked at it more closely and became convinced that he had a dragon's egg. When strange things began to happen in proximity to the egg, he knew he needed to find somewhere safe to hide it. He searched for a piece of property with a long history of haunting or unusual activity. That's how he found this place.

Cyril smiled gently at Ben. "He died the year your mother was born, leaving me the title to this property and a letter about the egg with a stern admonishment to keep it secret. I treated it like a curiosity as well, but kept it to myself nonetheless. I noticed that when I was around it, I could do things more easily, I was more creative … and luckier, so I started spending more time here, just to experiment and learn. I discovered that I had the most influence if I was physically touching the egg, but I could still use its power if it was within a few dozen feet. Also, I learned to sense its presence.

"Will seemed to be the key … a fact later confirmed in no uncertain terms by Sephiroth."

Ben started to ask a question but Cyril silenced him with a raised hand.

"I'll get there, but yes, Sephiroth was the rebel dragon. He was the real leader of our revolt. Now, back to magic.

"Will is the key. To manifest an outcome, your will must be sufficient to overcome reality's inertia in order to cause the desired change. To bargain with beings from other realms, you must have the will to resist being swayed from your purpose by their offers and charms."

He stopped and looked up at the ceiling, as if looking through to the broken-down house above.

"I was here with your mother, Ben—she was just a year old when it happened. It was so quick and so final. All at once, right in the middle of the afternoon, the world died. They detonated several large nukes in high orbit over every continent. The resulting electromagnetic pulses destroyed most electronics and shorted the grid. There were a fair number of people who had home power plants, but the system still ran on a grid so everything stopped when the power stopped.

"But that didn't really matter because the second wave hit thirty minutes later. All the neural-pulse bombs owned by all six of the corporate conglomerates were launched simultaneously, while at the same time, all global defense systems were disabled. Their plan was nothing if not thorough. Every significant population center in the world died in the space of five minutes.

"Your grandmother died that day, Ben," Cyril said. "She was working and had to be in the city. One flash of finely tuned electromagnetic energy and she was gone.

"I hunkered down for years after that. Even though this area hadn't been hit, people forgot how to be civilized for a while. I learned how to fight during that time and I raised Laura as best I could.

"I always came back to the egg. The more I focused my will on it, the more easily magic came to me. I knew that I possessed the single most-prized object on the entire planet.

"Laura was nine when the dragons made themselves known. Four came forth and set fire to the countryside, showing any who dared to look what they really were. They claimed responsibility for the bombings—gloating about how easily they had conquered our world.

"That was the day the resistance was born. I started a cell with a few of the people who lived in the Rogue River Valley. We began preparing—for what we didn't really know. But then one of the dragons moved into a military base under one of the smaller mountains in the Cascade Range, just north of here.

"We started organizing raids on the wyrm's minions with some success. Then the dragon came against us. He wasn't very big—they're only the size of a bird when they hatch and this one had grown to be no bigger than a horse.

"I was in position to take a shot on a priest we'd been wanting to kill, while the rest of my men were waiting to steal a supply wagon during the ensuing confusion. The dragon came out of the night sky right on top of them before I could take my shot. I was a hundred yards away, helpless to do anything save listen to their screams turn into the crackle of burning flesh. His fire burned them crisp in a matter of seconds. Then he landed in the middle of their charred and twisted remains, shattering them into pieces and scattering the parts haphazardly around him.

"He roared in triumph.

"I froze, not daring to move. Right then and there, I learned the true meaning of the phrase 'alpha predator.' As I watched, praying that he wouldn't see me, another dragon came out of nowhere, hitting the first and tearing into one wing with his talons. As the dragons began fighting, a woman leapt off the second one, rolled to her feet and immediately started shooting at the first.

"When the priest came out to join the fight, I took my shot and killed him. The first dragon fled, with the second giving chase.

"That was the day I met your mother, Imogen. She was the crazy woman riding the dragon. Sarah. She was several years older than I was but I was smitten in a glance. She was more than beautiful, she had a certainty of purpose about her that entirely overpowered my common sense.

"She invited me to join Sephiroth against the other dragons. Before I could answer, the rebel dragon returned and immediately detected the egg. With a bit of persuading by Sarah, I agreed to join them. Looking back, I'm quite sure that Sephiroth would have killed me and taken the egg if I'd refused."

"I thought he was good," Ben said.

"He was a dragon," Cyril said. "We are a lesser species. And although Sephiroth was the runt of the litter, smaller and weaker than the rest, he was also smarter. He decided that the only way he would ever win against his brothers would be to enlist humans against them. He recruited us, mostly because Sarah had raised him and he trusted her. She had found him as a sickly hatchling and nursed him to health and then to strength.

"He let me keep the egg, but only after I swore to keep it secret. I suspect he had plans to hatch it the moment the last of his brothers was dead." Cyril held the egg up in the palm of his hand. "This is almost certainly a female. If it hatches, humanity will probably never reclaim this world."

"Why don't you destroy it?" Imogen asked.

"I don't know how," Cyril said with a helpless shrug. "I tried all kinds of things … all except heat, anyway. Besides, I think we're going to need the egg before this is over. Now, where was I?

"Ah, I fell in love with Sarah and joined the resistance. We met the Dragon Slayer and the Monk in that first year. Along with Sephiroth, the four of us formed the core leadership of the entire rebellion, and we managed to kill three dragons and countless of their slaves and servants. At one point we had several sizable fighting units at our command and some pretty impressive tech, most of which was useless against the dragons.

"Ultimately, we were undone by a man talking when he should have kept his mouth shut. Someone gave up our base of operations—a large underground military facility built by the NACC under Mount Shasta. We had taken it as our base and used it successfully for years without detection. It helped that it was a hub for several underground roads running off in five directions with various facilities and exit points along them.

"When the dragon attacked, Chen and I and the Dragon Slayer were just returning from a meet with a weapons dealer who turned out to be a no-show. We were close enough that we could see the whole thing but too far away to do anything about it.

"The dragon landed at the entrance, ripped the door open and started breathing fire. He'd take a long, deep breath and then roar fire for a minute or more into the bunker. The three of us stood there, helplessly watching for almost an hour while the dragon transformed our home into a raging inferno. Long after we knew that everyone inside was dead, Sephiroth launched from the entrance, his scales glistening red with heat. He flew into the sky with the wyrm in pursuit.

"Stalkers, Dragon Guard, and several priests came out of the surrounding forest and assembled near the entrance.

"We watched as Sephiroth was overtaken by his brother. The wyrm tore his throat out, roaring in triumph and flying away with the corpse clutched in his talons.

"Then, we watched as a small army of soldiers and dragon-conjured monsters went into our home. None of our people came out of that hole alive. Your mother died that day, Imogen. Thankfully, your sister had brought you here for a few days.

"So, first it killed my mother and now it's taken my baby," she said, nodding to herself.

"The Dragon Slayer lost his wife and three sons that day. Watching our home and our families be so completely destroyed broke our spirit. We disbanded, right then and there. The Monk went into seclusion at a magical sanctuary we'd built. I moved to Ashland in the hopes of giving my daughters a chance at a normal life. The Dragon Slayer went north into the Deschutes Territory.

"We agreed that we wouldn't contact each other unless it was important, and we haven't, until now." Cyril shook his head sadly. "I led death right up to Chen's front door, and I'm afraid I might be doing the same thing to the Dragon Slayer."

"The letter you had me send at Rocky Point … it was to him, the Dragon Slayer."

Cyril nodded.

"What will he do?"

"That depends entirely on what he can do."

Ben knew better than to press an answer like that.

"Why don't you ever call him by his real name?" Ben asked.

"To protect him. We all took titles to use in the field. In a way, those titles became our persona and reputation, often gaining us support with a mere mention. Also, they helped keep our true identities secret.

"The Dragon Guard caught up with us a few years later in Ashland. That was the day your mother and father died, Ben."

He looked up sharply, cold rage slowly filling him up. He knew that his parents had been murdered, but he didn't know that it was at the hands of the wyrm's people. Rather than trust himself to speak, he nodded for Cyril to continue.

"I took the three of you and fled, eventually ending up in K Falls. It didn't take long to realize that you were special, Ben. If the egg was anywhere near you, you would make things move with your mind, much to your delight and my concern, so I installed this bunker and hid the egg here.

"Raising the three of you, I made an effort to teach you a number of basic skills. Some, like meditation and visualization, will help you wield magic, others like hand-to-hand and bladed combat will keep you alive in a fight."

Cyril paused and looked at the floor, looking back up at Ben with a twinge of guilt.

"That blue serum you've been drinking is going to do more to you than just heal your leg."

Ben frowned. He hadn't given it a second thought.

"You'd lost so much blood that your heart was shutting down," Cyril said. "It was the only thing I had that would keep you alive ... so I used it."

"What?" Ben asked. "That blue juice?"

Cyril nodded seriously. "The conglomerates spent years trying to build an artificially intelligent computer, but it was always just a little farther off. They did, however, manage to create a cognitive-and-sensory-augmentation computer implant with a neural interface."

"I don't know what that means," Ben said, putting his forehead in his hands. "My head hurts."

"That's because a computer is being built inside your brain."

He looked up, frowning with alarm.

"The serum also regenerates tissue and manufactures blood cells, which is what I needed—to get blood into your veins."

"So, what does this computer do? Is it going to take over?"

"I'm not entirely sure," Cyril said with a guilty shrug. "We took it from an abandoned NACC weapons lab. It was labeled: Combat Agent Augmentation Implant. A few specifications were given, but not enough information was available to risk using under less desperate circumstances."

"Well ... it did heal my leg pretty quickly."

"Just be aware of how you're feeling," Cyril said. "Take note of any changes."

"Right now, my head hurts."

"In that case, you should lie down and get some rest."

Ben nodded, lying back on the cot, his head full of swirling ideas, questions, and pain. He didn't sleep, instead, drifting into a detached, weightless state. It felt as if all of his memories were suddenly called up one by one, impossibly quickly, in perfect chronological order. He had no concept of time, only that his entire life was just filtered through in profoundly intimate detail.

He sat up with a gasp as if he had been suddenly released from paralysis. His head hurt even more.

"You okay?" Cyril asked, leaning over to look into his eyes.

"I just saw my whole life, everything I've ever done, all in a rush. I thought I was dying."

"You're all right. Lie back down."

Ben closed his eyes against the image of the ceiling spinning. He focused on his breathing, stifling an urge to vomit. The pain in his head intensified gradually over several minutes. At its peak, Ben could do little more than breathe. He lay on his back trembling, his eyes fixed on the ceiling, his mind fixed on the burning agony in the center of his head.

And then it was gone.

All of the pain, the disorientation and the nausea vanished. It felt like a cool breeze washed over him. He sat up, concentrating on the spot in his head where it had hurt so much, but the pain was no longer there.

"What's happening?" Cyril asked.

"Lots of pain and then it was gone. Now … I'm not sure."

He got up, pacing absentmindedly until he realized that his wound didn't protest in the least.

"John should be strong enough to travel by tomorrow," Cyril said. "I just hope Frank and Rufus didn't get into too much trouble on their own." He opened a compartment on one wall and removed a sword and handed it to Imogen. "It's identical to ours—balanced like the one I taught you with."

She smiled her thanks and drew the blade, testing the weight.

"It feels fast," she said.

"And very sharp."

"Good," she said, carefully returning it to its scabbard.

"I have a few other weapons, including a sword for Frank, a good old-fashioned brush gun and a tech pistol with some smart ammo. I also have a few grenades and some explosives … but more importantly, I have this."

He held up a simple dull-black ring with a single black cube not an eighth of an inch to a side set into it like a gemstone. Smiling at their confusion, he slipped the ring on his finger and the cube floated into the air. A moment later it vanished in a streak. Ben searched for it without success.

"What's it do?" Imogen asked.

"It's a surveillance drone," he said, motioning to the nearby wall.

A screen of light appeared, showing an image of the three of them. After orienting himself, Ben pointed to the drone, which was wedged into a corner of the ceiling. Then it came free and floated into the middle of the room, the image on the screen shifting as it moved.

"It can fly anywhere I tell it to," Cyril said, "and relay images and audio back to the holo-screen projected by the control ring."

"I didn't know magic could do something like that," Ben said.

"Oh, it's not magic," Cyril said. "This is all tech, which brings me to an important point. The dragon can see electronics and electricity in general and he doesn't like it at all. If he's anywhere nearby, you must shut down all electricity or you'll draw him right to you."

"That ring is one of the most magical things I've ever seen," Ben said.

"And yet it's just an advanced piece of equipment used by the NACC military. Lot of good it did them. Now, remember the part about electricity. The priests can see it a long way off as well, so be careful with tech."

"What about this implant growing in my head?"

"I'm hoping your body will provide adequate shielding."

Ben blinked a few times as the potential consequences of the implant started to become known.

"When will I know?"

Cyril shook his head helplessly.

Ben shrugged. "So far it's healed me, given me a headache, and thoroughly invaded my privacy. I guess I'll just have to wait and see what happens next."

Chapter 27

While Ben lay resting, he quite suddenly heard a voice in his head, a loud booming, drown-out-everything-else kind of voice.

"Hello, I am your newly installed combat augmentation implant—"

"Stop!" Ben shouted at the top of his lungs.

Quiet descended over the room, all eyes on him. Ben took a moment to savor the silence.

"Whoever you are, you're talking too loud," Ben thought, enunciating the words in his mind.

"Oh, my apologies, is this better?" the voice said at a much more reasonable volume.

"Yes, that's much better."

"What's happening?" Cyril asked.

"The implant is talking to me," Ben said, closing his eyes and relaxing into his cot.

"I'm afraid there's been some mistake," the augment said. "After a review of your memories, I see no indication that you are an NACC combat agent."

"That's because I'm not. The NACC is dead and gone. You're leftover tech—salvage."

"Why would you implant me if you're not an NACC combat agent? This package is specifically designed to work in conjunction with combat-agent body armor, weapons and other cyber upgrades. Without those components, your combat effectiveness will be less than 17% of optimum."

"I needed to heal. You helped me heal."

"Unlikely. There are many more suitable treatments for your injuries. Using me to mend a wound would be a gross waste of resources."

"Well, you were all we had, so here we are."

"I can't establish a link with the network. This bunker is blocking my transmission."

"Good, don't ever broadcast without my permission."

"I'm supposed to uplink to the network to complete my installation process. How can I do that without establishing a link to the network?"

"You can't. In fact, don't. Don't connect with any electronic device without my express instruction."

"This is highly unusual. You're not an agent. Technically, you don't even have clearance to know that I exist. Also, your memory record is quite odd. Until I can verify your clearance and establish a complete neural link, you will be denied access to many of my capabilities."

"Capabilities? Like what?"

"You don't have clearance to know that."

"Of course I don't. So what can you do for me?"

"Clarify."

"What capabilities do I have access to and what do they do?"

"Full record of all sensory perceptions with complete retrieval. Receive on all radio frequencies. Health optimization and tissue regeneration. Historical database with large selection of works on all topics. Needless to say, some of those documents are classified."

"Do you have to do what I tell you to?"

"Normally, yes, without question. But, since you're not authorized to receive this technology, I'm not really sure. I think I'll decide on a case-by-case basis."

"Great. Can you take control of me?"

"No, that would defeat my purpose."

"Tell me about your purpose."

"I exist to provide sensory, cognitive, and combat augmentation to my host. If I could control you, then you'd just be a soft and fragile robot without human intuition, creativity, or empathy."

Ben paused, screwing up his face while he thought.

"Am I your host?"

"Yes, but you are not authorized to be my host."

"And yet, I *am* your host."

"Yes."

"Do you have to obey your host?"

"Yes, but you are not authorized to be my host."

Ben chuckled to himself.

"Can you hear him, Homer?"

"No, thank God. You seem distracted ... and annoyed."

"Who's Homer?" the augment asked.

"My dog."

"Dog's can't talk."

"Stop ... just stop. Be quiet for a while."

Ben waited, expecting a response, but his mind was silent.

"So now you have two voices in your head," Homer said.

Ben opened his eyes and found Cyril sitting across from him, looking at him intently.

"Are you back?"

"I think so," Ben said. "What happened?"

"You went into a trance and I couldn't wake you. Your turn."

Ben described the conversation with the augment, realizing several moments in that he was repeating every word verbatim. His recall was crisp and precise. By the time he finished, Cyril was leaning slightly forward, listening intently.

"The healing works and the recall obviously works. I suggest you try to access the historical archive."

At the suggestion, his augment said, "What would you like to know?"

"Tell me about the purge."

Images and footage of mass killings flickered through his mind. He picked one and looked more closely, reading about an atrocity committed more than a century ago as if the article lay on a table before him.

"The archive works," he said without opening his eyes.

Cyril launched his drone and floated it up near the ceiling.

"Active NACC device detected."

"What just happened?" Ben asked the augment.

"I gained access to the drone and then restricted your access to receiving its feed only."

"Looks like the radio works," Ben said. "I can see what the drone sees. This is going to take some getting used to."

"Can the augment shield your EM output?"

Ben directed his attention to the machine within and waited for an answer to the question.

"Yes, but doing so would limit your combat effectiveness."

"I don't care. Reduce my EM output as much as possible at all times."

"Understood."

"And he might actually obey," Ben said, rubbing his temples.

"I'm sorry about this," Cyril said. "This implant might help you, but it's also going to change you. Just make sure you're the one making the decisions."

Ben nodded, deciding to change the subject.

"I want to know more about magic."

"Magic doesn't exist," the augment said.

"Stop talking and listen," Ben said.

"Like what?" Cyril asked.

"You tell me," Ben said. "What do I need to know?"

Cyril took a deep breath and sighed, shaking his head.

"Far too much, I'm afraid," he said. "But I'll make an effort to be more clear, now that the truth is out.

"There are perhaps as many ways to use magic as you can imagine, but it mostly falls into a number of broad categories. Basic manifestation causes objects or events to come into the caster's life in the normal way. I've used this type of magic to the most profound effect, through simple little things that gave me access or information or advantage. This is the easiest type of magic to use and the most difficult to misuse.

"Manifestation can also be used to create more spectacular effects, but only with great preparation. Once a spell has been prepared, for all intents and purposes, the desired result of the spell can be bottled up awaiting the command to become real. This type of magic is necessarily practiced in conjunction with other types of magic."

"How did you cast the circle of light in the church?" Ben asked. "Was that a prepared spell?"

"It was. In fact, I've had that spell prepared and waiting to be cast for decades. Truth is, I wasn't even sure it would work anymore."

"I'm glad it did," Ben said.

"Me too. It was one of the spells Sephiroth taught me. I guess I just never had as much faith in him as Sarah did."

"She was the Dragon Rider," Ben said, a bit tentatively.

Cyril nodded. "Yes. She and Sephiroth wrote a book of magic—the Dragon's Codex. I used several of the techniques in that book to create my 'Halo' spell." He chuckled. "I created it, so I got to name it."

"So how do you create a spell?"

"That's pretty complicated. Before you can even try, you need a patron—a being from another realm capable of delivering the results you desire. For a white wizard, the only choice is your guardian angel. All other choices are black magic.

"Once you've successfully summoned your guardian angel and he has agreed to help you, then you can begin the process of preparing a spell."

"Isn't that bargaining magic? Calling on other beings?"

"No, you don't bargain with your guardian angel, you beseech him for aid," Cyril said. "He will help you to a point, and in a limited number of ways—ways that he will explain in detail once you manage to summon him."

"How do you do that?"

"That's even more complicated, and it takes months, if not years, to accomplish. For your part, focus your efforts on basic manifestation. That practice will prepare you well for more advanced forms of magic later on."

"Where is the Dragon Codex?"

"Gone … with Sarah and everyone else," Cyril said. "It was inside the bunker when the wyrm burned us out."

"Do you think it could have survived?" Ben asked, leaning forward.

Cyril thought about it for a few moments, shaking his head and shrugging.

"It's hard to say. The bunker was pretty deep and very well secured, but the fire was devastating. Besides, the place is full of stalkers now. I wouldn't want to go looking for it."

"But it's a book of magic," Ben said. "Why wouldn't you want that?"

Cyril smiled at his grandson's enthusiasm.

"Magic is usually more costly than it's worth. Unless you stick to basic manifestation."

"But manifestation can't do everything that magic can do."

"No, far from it. Magic can do some spectacular things—things that defy explanation or understanding. Those types of spells are costly, and often less effective than a well-placed nudge or an unlatched door."

Ben frowned, looking down at the floor and finally shaking his head.

"No. There has to be more it can do for us. We need something to use against a dragon—an unlatched door isn't going to cut it."

"No, nor do I expect it to. Magic will serve when needed, but you shouldn't believe that it will do the work for you. It's just a tool, like tech or a hammer ... it can only do what you use it for. Magic, when mixed with ample imagination and sufficient will can do amazing things, but without you to give it life and purpose, it will do nothing at all."

"Do you have to touch the egg to use it?"

"No, but its more powerful when I do," Cyril said. "The truth is, you can use the egg just by being in proximity to it and I encourage you to try. You should begin working to hone your will and your imagination."

"How did you kill the other dragons?"

Cyril snorted, shaking his head. "In truth, we didn't. We just arranged the conditions and lured the dragons in—Sephiroth did the killing, all except for one, and that was a fluke. Still, that's the one that earned the Dragon Slayer his name."

"How did he do it?"

"He fell off a balcony and landed on the dragon's head, sword first, and a pretty special sword at that—the Dragon's Fang. Sephiroth had made it from one of his teeth, with a little help from Sarah and me. It was the sharpest, hardest, and most well-balanced sword I've ever held. Our swords are modeled after it. Anyway, the Dragon Slayer fell, stabbed the wyrm through the brain and killed him instantly."

Ben sighed.

"I know you want something that we can use," Cyril said. "The truth is, every battle is different. We won't know what his vulnerabilities are until we get closer. Until then, there's no sense planning for anything other than our next objective."

Ben nodded, looking unconvinced. "What happened to the dragon carcass?" he asked. "The one the Dragon Slayer killed."

"That's a good question," Cyril said. "One I wish I could answer. It was being transported to a bunker we'd set up for just such an occasion when the transport team was attacked and killed to a man. The carcass was gone when the follow-on team arrived."

Ben sat quietly for a moment, probing his mind for another question to ask.

"Why don't you rest now," Cyril said. "There will be time for more questions later."

Ben nodded, easing himself back onto his cot. He spent the remainder of the day resting his body but working his mind, questioning the augment on everything he could think of, pushing the limits of the machine's security and becoming more familiar with the capabilities he'd gained. Even lying flat on his back, it was an exhausting exercise.

Ultimately, he ended up where he'd begun, with the augment insisting that a network link was necessary before more implant capabilities became available.

John woke that evening and immediately pronounced himself fit to travel, though he had some difficulty getting to his feet. Cyril put him back to bed.

The following morning, they packed their gear. Cyril lit his lamp and shut down the bunker before opening the door a crack and peering out. After a few moments, he opened the door wide and stepped out, one hand holding his lamp high, the other inside his shoulder bag, resting on the egg.

He approached the basement room cautiously, stepping through the breech in the wall and scanning the room for threats before finally stopping to appraise the rift floating inside the pentagram. Ben couldn't take his eyes off the spectacle.

It was a tear in the world.

Like the fabric of reality had been ripped open. Beyond, was a room.

Before Ben could move, Cyril laid a hand on his shoulder.

"Don't step within the lines," he said, pointing to the grooves in the floor stained with Ben's own blood.

Cyril went back into the bunker and retrieved a bucket of supplies. Then he closed the door.

"Ben, Imogen, come and add your bioscans to the computer."

"Huh?"

Cyril instructed Ben to put his hand on a panel and look at a point on the wall. After a moment, a light flickered and turned green.

"Now you," he said to Imogen.

"What did we just do?" she asked after following his instructions.

"You two will be able to open the bunker now. Just don't come here unless it's a dire emergency."

He went to the door at the top of the staircase and locked it.

"Now, let's rebuild that wall," he said.

"With a hole in the world right there?" Ben asked.

"It's not going anywhere. We'll deal with it after we secure the bunker."

Cyril mixed mortar and put them to work. In less than an hour the wall was rebuilt.

"All right, now for the more interesting work," he said, releasing his drone and sending it slowly through the rift and into the room beyond.

The feed came up in Ben's mind almost instantly, but then went fuzzy for several seconds while it passed through the rift.

"This is highly irregular," the augment said.

"Quiet. Just show me what the drone sees."

The image became gradually clearer until it was sharp in Ben's mind. He saw a large stone room with a blood-soaked pentagram carved into the floor. The view spun, gradually revealing the other side of the rift. Ben could see a dead dragon, deliberately bled out into the pentagram.

"I'm not getting anything," Cyril said.

"I am," Ben said. "Bring it back."

After a moment of hesitation, Cyril nodded and the drone returned to his ring.

"What did you see?"

"A dead dragon. And this," Ben said, gesturing toward the pentagram.

"Dead dragon?"

"Yeah, like it'd been sacrificed to cast a spell."

Cyril stepped back, blinking a few times.

"What's wrong?" Imogen asked.

"That warlock is far more dangerous than I thought."

John pointed dubiously at the rift and asked, "Where is that, anyway?"

"Another version of right here," Cyril said. "If I had to guess, I'd say it's an earth that got conquered by dragons millennia ago."

"Shouldn't we go get some of the dragon blood or something?" Ben asked.

"No," Cyril said, shaking his head emphatically. "That's someone else's circle. There's no telling what might happen if you step inside it."

"I guess that's good to know," Ben said. "Still, I'd love to see what's on the other side. They might have magic we could use."

"I'm sure they do, but it's too dangerous. The drone might be seen if dragons are plentiful there, and the last thing we need is another dragon coming into our world. No, we have to close this rift."

"How do we do that?" Ben asked.

"In this case, I think we just have to undo the circle. I'll need a drop of your blood."

"My blood? What for?"

"You consecrated the circle for the Warlock," Cyril said, pointing to the dried blood on the floor. "With your blood, and some sanctified water, I believe I can dispel the protections provided by the circle. Without the underlying foundation spells for support, a complex and powerful spell like this rift will usually collapse on its own."

"Usually?"

"Magic isn't an exact science," Cyril said, holding up a needle.

Ben took it and pricked his finger, squeezing a drop of blood into the cup that Cyril offered.

After filling the cup with water and muttering over the mixture for several minutes, Cyril nodded to himself and got to his feet.

"Everyone upstairs," he said, hoisting his pack carefully to avoid spilling the contents of the cup. When they were all upstairs, Cyril handed Ben his pack and went back downstairs to the landing with the cup of enchanted water.

He took a moment to speak a few more words over it and then tossed it in a stream at the edge of the circle, racing upstairs quickly as soon as the liquid was away. When he reached the top of the stairs, he slammed the door and waited. A low hum built in the air, almost lower than a person could hear—more felt through the ground and the air. It built, filling the air with pressure and terrible expectation. Then it changed ... as if a belt had snapped, the even, rhythmic thrumming started to lose cohesion, becoming discordant.

A moment later, the entire house jolted, knocking Ben against the wall. As he caught his balance, cold flowed into him. A howl of maniacal torment erupted from the forest outside, wailing loud and long, finally trailing out and vanishing.

"Huh, I wondered why the haunting had gotten so severe," Cyril said. "I'll be right back." He went downstairs again, returning a minute later, nodding in satisfaction.

"It's closed, and I think the ghost is less apt to show herself now that it is. Let's get out of this immediate area just the same."

When they emerged from the house, it was morning on an overcast day. Dew dripped on them from the fir needles overhead as they wound their way out of the valley and up toward the ridge where Frank and Rufus were supposed to be waiting.

Ben frowned at the large number of new horse tracks on the road. He suspected they would find a cold and empty campground once they crested the hill. Cyril stopped just shy of the ridge and drew his tech gun, motioning for the others to follow suit. Ben drew. John nocked an arrow. Imogen drew.

They reached the top of the ridge and looked down into their former campsite, which looked to be the scene of a recent skirmish. The really fast dwarf that had stabbed Ben was sitting by the cold fire pit.

He smiled at them. "My master would like to negotiate," he said, picking his teeth with a bird bone.

Ben started to speak but Cyril silenced him with a sharp look. The little man's smile grew broader.

"Who is your master?" Cyril asked.

"You may call him 'Master.'"

"Doubtful," Cyril said. "What's he want?"

"The egg."

Cyril locked eyes with the little man.

After a moment, the dwarf's smile morphed into an expression of pain and fear. He broke eye contact with Cyril and ran away—very quickly.

"We'll see him again." Cyril said. Then he sighed and shook his head. "There are always unforeseen consequences with magic." He took a step toward Ben and faced him squarely. "I put the egg somewhere to keep it safe. One of the results of that decision was to create a rift that allowed a conquering warlock to invade our world."

"You didn't know—"

"Irrelevant. The result of an action is the reality you create. Intent is fantasy. Intent is want and dream. Let good intent guide you to be sure, but judge the outcome of your actions by the results that you achieve in the real world. A wizard must measure himself by the most demanding of masters—Reality. And the reality is, I brought a potent enemy into this world."

"So ..." Ben said, waiting for Cyril to give him his full, and somewhat upset, attention, "... let's use him against our enemy."

Cyril lost some of his emotion, deflating in the process. "That's often easier said than done. Truth is, we should be planning to repel an attack."

"You think he'll come so quickly?" Imogen asked.

"Perhaps quicker than you think," the dwarf yelled from behind a tree fifty feet away. Then he chuckled with delight. "Master has your friends. I was supposed to tell you that before."

"Shit," Cyril muttered.

"Indeed, Wizard," the dwarf yelled.

"You hear well," Cyril said without raising his voice.

"Better than you."

"Who does your master have?"

"One called Hound and another called Frank."

Cyril looked to Ben and Imogen. Both nodded support.

"Where?"

"Not far."

"We'll meet with him. Lead the way."

The dwarf raced off thirty feet into the forest, then stopped and looked back at them impatiently. Cyril walked toward him without hurrying in the least. When he got within ten feet, the dwarf raced off another thirty feet and stopped to wait.

"Are you training in a virtual-reality simulation?" the augment asked.

"No. Now be quiet. I'm busy."

Two hundred paces up the road, they came to the corpse of one of the bounty hunters. He'd been killed by a shotgun blast to the face several days prior and left to rot. Scavengers had already started picking at him.

They traveled up the road for a mile until they reached a steeply sloping embankment rising to a plateau that had been built up to form the foundation of a now-dilapidated house. The Warlock stood behind Frank and Rufus, who were both on their knees facing the top edge of the slope. Both wore gags and blindfolds, and their hands were bound behind their backs. A bounty hunter stood on either side of them.

"Hello!" the Warlock said, holding his open right hand up high.

Chapter 28

Cyril stopped a hundred feet away, unslinging his brush rifle and working the lever to check the round in the chamber. The dwarf raced back to his master.

"You have a charming little world here," the Warlock said, his voice carrying far better than it should have. "Only one dragon ... and a single unhatched egg. I'm new to your language, but I believe the word I'm looking for is *Ripe*."

Cyril released his drone, letting it float ten feet overhead.

Ben assessed his surroundings. When the drone feed became available, he pushed it into the background.

Cyril took aim with the brush rifle and fired. It was a clean shot, aimed directly at the center of the Warlock's chest, but when the bullet got close, within a few yards, it got hot—really hot. Most of it burned away to vapor, leaving only a small pellet of molten lead to penetrate the Warlock's shoulder.

He shuddered in pain at the burning within his flesh, staring with terrified eyes at Cyril. Then he drew a deep breath, tipped his head back and screamed with complete commitment, every part of his being caught up in the act.

Cyril slung the rifle and dropped his left hand into the shoulder bag containing the egg.

"Leave my people unharmed or die now," he said. His words seemed to reverberate through Ben.

The Warlock shrieked into the sky again and withdrew, taking his two bounty hunters and the dwarf with him, leaving Frank and Rufus bound and on their knees at the top of the rise.

"Hold still or you'll fall," Cyril yelled. "We'll be a few minutes getting up to you."

Ben watched the drone's view shift, rising higher into the sky, searching for the Warlock in the surrounding forest. The view changed, everything becoming shades of red, revealing the Warlock's outline in the distance through the trees, then the view returned to normal, except that now the Warlock was marked. The point of view shifted again, seeking a break in the trees and then got much closer.

The Warlock stood with one of his men before him, the tip of the dragon's talon resting against the man's chest. Streaks of blackness swirled around them both. The bounty hunter screamed as he took on the Warlock's wound, blood spilling from his shoulder while the hole in the Warlock's shoulder closed. The man fell to his knees, looking up helplessly at his master. The Warlock smiled as he watched the man whither and age, his life draining away in a matter of moments.

The Warlock tipped his head back and threw his chest out as the life energy of the man flowed into him.

"That's not good," Ben said.

"No," Cyril said, drawing his tech revolver and flipping the cylinder open to replace one of the rounds. A moment after he closed the chamber, Ben saw a bullet indicator light up in the corner of the drone feed.

Cyril aimed his revolver in the general direction of the Warlock and fired. It was louder than a normal bullet. The drone began tracking it immediately. The round rose at a steep angle into the sky until it reached the apex of its arc, where it opened a tiny pair of wings and began targeting the Warlock, tipping into a gentle controlled glide straight for the enemy, over a mile away.

For many seconds, the bullet simply floated through the air, descending toward its target, gaining speed with every passing second. It was quiet as the wind, making no noise at all until the last few hundred feet when it activated a booster rocket that propelled the seeker round into the Warlock's back with terrible force ... except, a light flared when the round got within a few feet, much like it had when Cyril shot him the first time. The round was deflected wide, hitting him in the same shoulder he'd just healed, but this time, the damage was far more severe.

The bullet exploded on impact, blasting his left arm off, sending it flailing through the air, spraying blood across the foliage as it flopped to the ground a dozen feet away. The Warlock was thrown to the ground, stunned by the blast. He rolled to the side, his hand going first to his head, then to his arm. Realizing he'd been dismembered, he screamed anew, struggling to get up, crying out in rage and pain and cursing his enemies. It took a few moments for him to compose himself enough to regain his feet, but he did. Blood dripped from the gore dangling from his shoulder.

He ignored it.

He leaned on his staff and scanned the sky, his eyes locking on the drone after a few moments of searching.

He barked an order at the last bounty hunter. The man retrieved the severed arm and brought it to him. He smiled at the drone as he laid the dragon's claw on the man's chest and drained his life to reattach his own arm. He bound it in a sling and looked very intently at the drone before turning toward Rogue City and moving into the forest.

"He'll be back," Cyril said.

"And I bet he'll be happy to see you," Ben said.

"I just hope I see him first. Now, let's go get your brother."

They headed up the driveway leading to the top of the plateau.

"What weapon was that anyway?" Ben asked.

"A seeker round—long-range, drone-guided—I don't have many, but he seemed worth the shot."

"Magic or tech?"

"All tech."

"If tech is so powerful, how did the dragons take over the world?"

"I already told you ... mostly subterfuge."

Ben looked sidelong at his grandfather, eliciting a wily smile. "Why not just use a gun like that one on them?"

"Tech doesn't work very well around a dragon. In fact, tech doesn't work very well around me either, if I make the effort.

"Magic can greatly increase the odds of a malfunction or a chemical-reaction failure or a material break or any of a thousand other things that can make a piece of technology fail. The more complex and delicate the technology is, the more vulnerable it is to magical interference. The highest of technology fails almost completely when in the presence of a wyrm."

"Why doesn't the egg kill your drone?"

"Because it's not a dragon yet, and I'm not making an effort to disrupt tech right now," Cyril said. "I have to focus on it—the dragon just does it with his presence."

"What about my augment?" Ben asked, a cold feeling seeping into his bones.

Cyril looked at him and shrugged before continuing the climb.

"Your fear is irrational—dragons don't exist," the augment said.

Ben ignored him, following Cyril.

Finally, they reached Frank and Hound and cut their bindings.

"Good to see you," Rufus said. "We were beginning to worry."

"What took you so long?" Frank asked.

John had walked the perimeter of the house. "Look at this," he said, from near the front door.

Ben went with Cyril. The body of a man had been cast aside, completely desiccated, drained of all vestige of life.

"Looks like one of the bounty hunters," John said.

"This Warlock is going to be a problem," Cyril said.

"So let's turn him against the wyrm," Ben said.

"How?"

Ben started to speak and then stopped, frowning to himself and shaking his head.

"For now, he's left us alone," Cyril said. "Let's use that time to get to Rogue City."

After a moment's hesitation, Ben agreed.

Both Frank and Hound were relieved to be free of their captors. They were beaten up, bruised and sore, especially where they'd been bound, but neither of them was seriously injured.

"So what happened?" Cyril asked.

"Really? I was just going to ask you the same thing ... but all right," Hound said. "I found Frank and we went to the camp like you said. Not long after, a guy comes out of the house with another little guy following him. We waited. Days pass. We argued about what to do, but decided to wait like you said. Then the guy came back with the bounty hunters and took us. I got one of them, but that albino bastard spelled us or something. Then they tied us up, and the guy said he was going to wait for you to come find us. Then you shot him and he ran away and here we are. Now you."

Cyril smiled, chuckling to himself for a moment.

"Ben got wounded by that guy's servant so we holed up in my bunker to let him heal."

"Boring," Hound said. "Ours is better."

"Undoubtedly ... we slept a lot."

"How's my face look?" Hound asked with a crooked smile. "Am I going to have any new scars?"

"There's one on your cheek that looks promising," Cyril said.

"Hot damn! Women love scars."

Imogen closed her eyes and shook her head.

"I don't know what the hell you're talking about," Frank said. "That guy was terrifying."

"Shake it off," Hound said. "If you let shit like that get to you, you'll never make it in this business."

"I'm not in this business, I just want to go home," Frank said.

Cyril pursed his lips and looked down sadly at Frank.

"Home is gone," he said, holding out the brush rifle. "Take this."

Frank looked a bit confused, but took the rifle nonetheless.

"I also have a sword for you," Cyril said, handing Frank the last of the tech swords, complete with belt and scabbard.

"I'll teach you how to use the blade. Rufus will show you how to use the rifle before we head out ... no argument."

Frank hesitated, looking at the rifle in one hand and the sword in the other.

"All right."

"Good. Strap on the blade. Rufus, give him a crash course in the rifle."

"You sure about this?" Ben asked as he and Cyril walked away from Frank and Rufus.

"One of the best ways to conceal is with distraction and half-truth," Cyril said. "He's got a piece of my weapons cache, and more importantly, a bigger piece than you, or so he thinks. That ought to keep him occupied for a while. I don't want him to become aware of the egg."

Ben went to the house and sat down on the last good step of a broken-down staircase leading up to the porch.

"Much of your sensory input is anomalous," the augment said.

Ben chuckled. "How so?"

"Your encounter with the individual you call the Warlock couldn't happen."

"Seemed like it happened to me," Ben said.

"The rift in time/space is impossible as well."

"Yep."

"This Warlock should not be able to drain the life from other people. Such technology does not exist. I would be aware of it."

"What if you're wrong?"

The augment didn't answer.

Ben cleared his mind and focused on his coin, conjuring a vision of it in his mind's eye, floating in empty space, slowly revolving on its axis. He held the vision for a long time, losing all sense of self in the process.

Chapter 29

He returned to full awareness when Frank fired a round from the large-bore, lever-action brush rifle that Cyril had given him. Ben didn't really prefer the weapon … it was large, heavy, and ponderous … though he certainly would have taken it if it had been offered. He was more concerned with Frank being armed with something so powerful.

"That won't attract attention," Ben muttered to himself.

"I bet it will," Homer said.

Ben scratched him on the head and got up, heading for the cluster of people around Frank.

"How am I supposed to know how to shoot a rifle unless I try it out?" he said, both hands out, the rifle in one of them.

"Ammunition is scarce," Cyril said. "And enemies are searching for us."

"I just wanted to see how she handles … and I love her. Thank you."

"Don't shoot again unless we're under attack," Cyril said, taking a few steps closer to Frank, forcing him to retreat by a step.

"I won't, I won't. Calm down," Frank said, backing farther away.

"Sorry," Hound said quietly.

Cyril looked to him and shook his head tightly.

"We have to be on our way. Everybody, gather your things."

Cyril used the drone to find a route through the forest that offered the least resistance. It took all of five minutes to evaluate the terrain, roads, traffic, and waterways, then plot a course leading to the outskirts of Rogue City.

Imogen intercepted Frank before he could interrupt Cyril with questions about the drone, explaining the device to Frank and Rufus as best she could.

Ben watched through his feed in amazement … a simple tech device that could take pictures and relay them back to another position. The strategic power such a thing gave a field commander, let alone a rebel, was staggering.

Cyril recalled the drone, placing it in a position a thousand feet directly overhead, scanning in all directions at once. He navigated through the forest with the aid of the drone-constructed map and the holo-projector in the ring.

By midday the hawk came into view, gliding in a circular orbit around their position.

Frank aimed his rifle at the bird. Hound stopped him from firing, taking hold of the weapon and staring Frank down with a withering glare.

"That bird means there are Dragon Guard nearby," Hound said. "You can't hit it, anyway."

"Maybe I can."

"Let me rephrase … that rifle won't send a bullet high enough into the air to reach that damn bird right now."

"Oh … how am I supposed to know that?"

"You know that, because I just told you."

"He is right about one thing," Cyril said. "We do have to deal with the bird."

John sat down, breathing heavily, still not fully recovered from his ordeal with the Warlock's darkness.

"Let's find a place to rest," Cyril said. "Maybe draw the bird closer in."

John nodded but made no move to get up until Cyril set out for a thicket of trees.

Ben watched the drone float higher into the air as it tracked the hawk's movement. When it was many hundreds of feet higher than the bird, it stopped and held position relative to Cyril.

From that altitude, a squad of Dragon Guard could be seen approaching from the east. Ben watched in amazement as the view narrowed in on the threat with breathtaking speed, providing a close-up view of the entire force in an instant. He could see Nash leading a wolf-stalker and a dozen men. Her second in command stopped to view the hawk through a telescope.

Ben schooled his fear. Nash was relentless, motivated by hate, and now she was very well prepared to hunt them down and kill them.

Cyril sighed, shaking his head.

"Nothing is ever easy," he muttered.

"We have to kill the hawk," Ben said.

"Won't matter," Cyril said. "The wolf will pick up our scent."

"So what do we do?" Imogen asked.

"We attack."

"What the hell are you talking about?" Frank asked.

Cyril ignored Frank and faced Ben.

"When your hand is forced, when you have no good options and few sane ones, when your enemy thinks they have you at a disadvantage … attack. Strike by surprise and strike hard. Then vanish if you can."

"This is insane," Frank said.

Cyril projected a screen with a view from high above. Their position was marked with color, as were those of the hawk and the approaching Dragon Guard.

"If we move here," Cyril said, pointing to a spot on the screen, "the hawk will follow. That will channel Nash into this valley, providing us with a perfect ambush point."

"She has twelve men and a stalker. What do you want to ambush her with?" Frank asked.

"Oh yeah, I didn't tell you about the explosives," Cyril said, holding up a tablet two inches long and half an inch wide. "This will take a pretty big bite out of her, if we set it right."

Frank looked at Cyril and shook his head in disbelief. "You never tell me anything."

"I just did."

"There are some moments that I wouldn't ever want to miss," Homer said.

Ben stifled a smile.

"So what do you have in mind?" Hound said.

"I want to fill this bag with rocks and set it on top of this ex-plus charge."

"Ex-plus?" Imogen asked.

"Very high explosive. About twelve times as powerful as TNT by weight."

"I don't know what TNT is either," she said.

"It explodes," Cyril said. "We can ambush Nash and her Dragon Guard with it—right here." He pointed to another spot on the screen. "Trouble is, this only works if most of us go this way to draw the bird, while one or two of us go plant the bomb."

"I'll go," Ben said. He was tired of being hunted and chased. He wanted to hit back.

"I should go," John said.

"Like hell," Imogen said. "You can barely walk."

The Highwayman seemed to deflate a bit.

"No," Ben said, tapping the side of his head. "I'll do it."

"All right," Cyril said. "Place this tablet in the sand along the streambed. Fill this bag with rocks ... the best are the size of a man's thumbnail. Put the bag on top of the ex-plus. That's all. I'll activate it when the enemy gets into position. Once you place it, follow the stream to the grasslands. We'll be waiting for you on the far side. Don't dally."

"Keep your drone watching me."

Cyril nodded, pausing for a moment before hugging him. "Be careful."

"I will be," Ben said, heading off into the forest with Homer at his side.

He set a fast pace, just a step or so slower than a jog, skirting trees and brush, clambering over fallen logs and running along clear paths. He relied on the drone feed to guide him toward his mark. It was starting to change the way he thought.

The feed also told him that the Dragon Guard were making good time, advancing almost as quickly as Ben, but not quite. He could move through the forest on his own with pretty good speed, and with the help of the drone to navigate, he reached his destination well ahead of the enemy.

He found a place in the narrow valley where the stream widened into a gravel bed two dozen feet across with water scarcely three inches deep flowing lazily over it. He raced fifty feet downstream and filled the bag three quarters full with small muddy rocks.

His first attempt to lift the bag met with failure. Bracing himself, he hoisted it up onto his shoulder and headed for the ambush spot. It was heavy. His legs started to lose strength, but he pushed on, driving himself forward by sheer stubbornness.

Reaching the shallow spot, he stopped, listening. Voices of men in the distance, cutting their way through the forest, wafted to him on the breeze, just barely detectable.

Ben checked the feed. Nash and her pet were still a ways off, but they would arrive within the hour. He took a breath, scanning the creek bed for just the right rock, smiling when he saw it. It was large and firmly embedded into the ground. The side facing the onrushing current was flat, and the water rose up in front of it just enough to cover the bag of stones.

He flopped the bag down on top of the rock and dug the ex-plus tablet out of his pocket, slipping it into the side seam of the bag before tying it off securely. Then he carefully placed it into the water, facing it upstream with the ex-plus tablet tucked into the crook between the streambed and the large stone.

He waited to ensure that the current wouldn't dislodge the bag. Then he took a moment to go upstream to look at it, satisfied that it was completely obscured by the water.

"They're getting close," Homer said. "I can smell one of them."

Ben nodded, heading off downstream toward the meeting point. He moved quickly, not bothering to cover his tracks, opting instead for speed. He had just reached the edge of the large grass field when an explosion echoed in the distance behind him.

In his hurry, he'd been ignoring the feed. Now he stopped to look.

Nine bodies were sprawled across the streambed. They'd been torn apart, killed in a moment of flying stones.

Ben stared at the image and felt a growing sense of guilt and complicity. He'd never killed before. And although he hadn't pulled the trigger, he'd placed the weapon. He'd taken part in the carnage he was seeing unfold several miles away—and it revolted him.

A shot rang out from the opposite direction. His feed changed to the hawk, now diving for the forest at a remarkable speed. The seeker round couldn't keep up on the way down, but it was there to strike when the hawk ran out of sky and had to level off. After closing on its target, the bullet accelerated for the last few hundred feet and exploded on impact, blasting the stalker into several pieces and casting them to the ground, still smoldering as they fell.

The feed shifted back to the scene behind him. Nash, her stalker, and three of her men were searching through the dead for survivors. Ben sat down and watched. She was angry, but also genuinely sad at the loss of her men. Her human response bothered him enough that he kept watching.

Eventually, she gathered her remaining men and set out toward Ben. At that point, the view shifted to him, standing in the forest looking up at the drone. He nodded and headed toward Cyril.

By the time he reached the others, it had started to rain and Ben found himself wishing once again that he had a better coat.

The rest of the day followed a carefully defined course that avoided an encounter with a bear and another with a Dragon Guard scout patrol that was headed toward Nash.

At the first glimpse of the city, Cyril turned east into the forest and up to the top of a spur. They emerged into a fifty-foot circular clearing filled with tall grass. A large house stood on the opposite side. It had glass doors and windows that gave way to a great room walled with a series of tall windows facing the valley below.

"Perfect," Cyril said. "Hold here."

He sent his drone inside the house and confirmed his suspicions that it was empty.

"We can't produce any light in view of the city or we'll be detected," Cyril said. "This is important."

"What are we going to do here, anyway?" Frank asked.

"Recon," Cyril said. "We need information before we plan our attack."

A glint caught Ben's eye and he looked down into the grass that was growing from a spider web of cracks in the vanishing pavement of the driveway. He stopped and looked more carefully, finally kneeling down and searching.

He found a coin, half covered over with moss. He rubbed it clean, then stopped, staring in disbelief—it was his coin, right down to the year. He stood up and pulled out his lucky coin. He held the two up together, first one side, then the other, inspecting both for any deviation.

"Hey, what'd you find?" Frank asked, his mouth going open when he saw the two coins Ben was holding.

"A coin," Ben said, still a bit enthralled with the unlikelihood of finding a coin exactly like his.

"Where? There might be more," Frank said.

Ben pointed to the spot he'd found it, then pocketed his lucky coin and handed the other one to Cyril with a question on his face.

Cyril examined it for a moment, smiling with pride and handing it back to Ben with a very deliberate wink.

"I don't see any more," Frank said. "Are you sure it was right here?"

"I'm sure," Ben said, following Cyril inside.

The house would have been spectacular in its time, with a beautiful view and perfect seclusion. Now it was just as neglected, decaying, and falling-down broken as all the other places that had been abandoned.

"We'll stay here for the night and leave at dawn," Cyril said. "Nash will have our trail by then."

"Maybe we should ambush her again," Frank said.

"It would be nice to have her off our heels," Hound agreed.

"That it would," Cyril said. "But she's still dangerous. Dragon-fire rifles and a stalker are not to be taken lightly. Perhaps another avenue of attack will present itself. For now, I'd like to keep some distance between us and Dominus Nash."

After they'd cleared out a large room on the side of the house facing away from town, everyone settled in to wait while Cyril used his drone to explore the central parts of Rogue City.

By evening, Ben was bored ... and he had access to the drone feed. He could only imagine how Frank and the others felt.

The drone had already made its rounds through the entire inner city's defenses, an impressive array of magic and guards and mechanisms, and then made its way into the temple, searching out the infant child—finding him in a royal nursery, inside the temple's inner sanctum. After all of the particulars were known, Cyril set the drone down atop another building and watched one particular door for hours.

Guards came and went. Cyril watched. Ben checked in on the feed now and then.

Finally, Frank couldn't stand it anymore. "I'm so bored!" he said. "Can't we just go get him already?"

"We need more information," Cyril said.

"We need to do something!" Frank said.

"Doing the wrong thing is far worse than doing nothing."

Frank opened his mouth and thought better of it, turning for the door instead. "I need some air."

Cyril resumed watching the activity at the wall around the inner city. He continued to focus his attention on one specific area—one door. Most of the buildings nearby were vacant, those few that were occupied housed drug addicts or fugitives. It was a dark, sparsely populated and mostly criminal area.

The only traffic in or out of the door was bought and paid for.

Ben snorted to himself, realizing that choosing to act against the dragon made him a criminal. The thought was laughable if the word had any meaning, but the reality was that he would be considered a criminal. And yet, he didn't think he would fit in with the people living in the darker, less well-kept parts of town.

Another lesson.

Criminal had two meanings. First, those who hurt other people or stole and damaged property. Second, those who threatened the established power structure. So be it.

"Let's go," he said to Homer, heading for the staircase leading to the second floor.

"Be careful," Cyril said.

"Yep," Ben said, testing each stair before putting weight on it. A few creaked, one even cracked, but none gave way. He stopped at the top and looked both ways, smiling when he saw the double door at one end of the hall. The floor was mostly stable, a section of it was moldered through, but there were plenty of sturdy boards to make it past.

Ben pushed the door open slowly, loud creaking reverberating down the hall. He took a deep breath and shoved it open all the way.

Save for a moldy bed and decaying furnishings, the room was empty. He went to the large closet and found several rows of rotting clothing along with two cabinets.

Ben tried to open the cabinets, but both were locked. He drew his blade and started to place the point.

"Perhaps I could offer a better solution," the augment said.

Ben stopped, standing up, half annoyed, half intrigued.

"Go on."

"These cabinets are protected with rudimentary encryption. I could open them for you."

"Great. Do it."

"I have so many questions," the augment said.

"Oh, for the love of God, you and me both. Either help me or shut the hell up."

After a momentary pause, Ben felt a taxing of his new cognitive abilities. The two cabinets whirred and then opened.

"Huh," he said. "Not bad."

"If I just understood … more … perhaps I could be of greater help."

Ben paused, considering his response for a moment. "Okay. There's an evil, magical dragon that's hunting us and I intend to kill it."

"I opened the cabinets," the augment said. "I hoped that you would act in good faith."

Ben sighed, pulling the door of the first cabinet open. Hanging there was a series of business suits, completely pristine and perfect. The second cabinet contained the same, with the exception of the last hanger. On it was a long, brown, leather riding coat with a matching broad-brim hat. It was just like new, as if it had been taken right off the production line and stored in this box.

Ben pulled the coat out and held it up.

"What are the odds?" he asked Homer.

"I'm not a betting man."

With a cocky smile and a flourish, he swept the coat around himself. It fell onto his shoulders like it was tailored for him, fitting perfectly. He checked the sleeves—perfect. He buttoned the coat—perfect, with just enough room for an undercoat.

He picked up the hat and smiled at it, carefully settling it on his head.

He laughed out loud, chuckling in his belly. The hat also fit like it was made for him.

He went back downstairs, wearing his new garments.

"What the hell?" Frank said. "Where'd you get that?"

Ben pointed toward the stairs.

"Just fancy clothes left. Be careful, the stairs and the floor aren't all there."

Frank hurried up to the stairs, cursing in pain when a board broke through and barked his shin. He took a moment to recover before reaching the second floor and heading for the master bedroom.

"All that's left are formal suits!" Frank hollered.

"That's what I said," Ben muttered.

Chapter 30

"Nice coat," Cyril said.

Ben was just about to reply when he saw John slump against the wall. He rushed to keep him on his feet.

"Bring him here," Cyril said, motioning to his bedroll.

He gave the Highwayman a serious look and said, "You have to tell me what's blocking my spell or I can't help you."

John looked around and nodded when Imogen was nowhere to be seen.

"I had my fortune read once," he said. "I don't want anyone to see what I saw."

"I can't see your fortune unless I try to … and I won't."

John thought about it for a few moments, finally looking up at Cyril and nodding.

Cyril put one hand on the egg and another on John's forehead, closing his eyes for a moment. Then he quickly, deftly, and precisely drew a circle on the floor with chalk. It contained a number of odd symbols and glyphs that Ben had never seen before, but his grandfather drew each like he knew exactly what they meant. He stepped inside and started muttering a mantra under his breath, faster and faster. After nearly a minute, the circle pulsed with a soft, white light.

He knelt at the edge of the circle and laid his hand on John's chest and then began speaking softly in some language that Ben had never heard before, his words filled with intent and unnamed meaning. A shadow suddenly sprang from John's flesh, exiting his body all at once and lashing out at Cyril. When the smoky blackness rushed at him, it crashed into a wall defined by the circle and vanished with a faint wail.

He smiled reassuringly at John and said, "You should get some rest." Then he took a minute to wipe away the chalk circle.

A moment later, Frank came back downstairs. "Nothing," he said, as he headed out of the room again. "Maybe there's something in the basement."

It wasn't long before Frank returned. "Not much down there either, just this old bag of tools."

"Dump it out and let's see what you got," Hound said.

Frank nodded, knelt down and emptied the bag on the floor. A hammer, pliers, wire cutters, several screw drivers, a utility knife, and a roll of tape spilled out.

"The pliers and wire cutters are keepers," Hound said.

"I'll keep it all … for now, anyway," Frank said, returning the tools to the bag.

After dinner, Ben went to bed early since he had last watch. When he woke to the light of day, he sat up quickly, looking around with a hint of confusion. Someone should have woken him. He went to Cyril and shook him awake.

"It's past dawn. Watch broke down. I just woke up."

Cyril took a deep breath and sat up, rubbing his face.

"Wake everyone for me?"

Ben nodded, going to Hound first. When he nudged Frank with his toe, something didn't feel right. He pulled the blanket back and discovered that his brother was gone. His rifle, sword, hatchet, and tools were all there, but he was gone.

"Shit," Ben said. "Frank's gone."

Cyril stopped preparing breakfast and looked up, shaking his head and cursing under his breath. He launched his drone and did a quick but very thorough search of the house and the immediate area.

"Why would he leave his weapons?" Imogen asked, frowning.

Ben stopped in his tracks when the thought hit him. He went to his pack with a sense of certainty. The coin he'd found the day before, the one he'd put into his pack, was gone.

"He took my coin," Ben said.

"He's in town, drinking and whoring," Hound said. "And the bastard didn't even invite me."

"You're probably right, but he's still putting us all in danger," Cyril said.

"Enzo is well connected in Rogue City," Imogen said. "He'll have people looking for us all over the place."

Cyril sent his drone into the sky.

"Oh ... this is interesting," he said, drawing everyone's attention with the tone of his voice. They all gathered around the screen as it focused.

The Warlock was standing in the middle of the road, a few hundred feet from the main gate to the inner city.

"What's he doing?" Imogen asked.

"Looks like he's challenging the priest," Cyril said.

The street around the Warlock cleared, but a few people got on nearby rooftops to watch. The main gate opened a crack and a single Dragon Guard strode out. He reached the Warlock and started speaking. The Warlock smiled as he tipped his staff forward, blackness flowing out of the dragon's claw and into the Dragon Guard. The man struggled for a moment, but then went calm. The darkness continued to flow. When the Dragon Guard went to one knee, the darkness stopped.

The Warlock looked up at the top of the wall and laughed, the Dragon Guard taking up a position to his right.

The gate opened wide and a dozen horses thundered forth carrying fully armored Dragon Guard armed with dragon-fire rifles. The Warlock stood his ground, shadow springing forth from his staff and forming a vague, filmy sphere of indistinct energy surrounding him.

The leading three riders fired, jets of orange flame streaking out before them and washing over the sphere protecting the Warlock. Fire raged over its surface. Laughter erupted from within.

The moment their fire ended, his began. He thrust the dragon's claw toward them and a cone of flame exploded, roaring, thrumming, and howling down the street, igniting everything in its path, filling the width of the street and extending for two hundred feet before him. The Dragon Guard fell, horses and riders burned black in a matter of seconds. When the flame was spent, the Warlock waved at the gatehouse. A volley of arrows came off the wall. He deflected them with his magic, laughing at them anew.

A small orange-red sphere streaked off the gate tower straight at him, reaching him in less than a second and exploding in a ball of fire, completely engulfing him before rising into the air in a black cloud of smoke.

The Warlock stood, unscathed, though somewhat smudged by the attack. He called out to the priest, taunting him.

The gate opened and fifty Dragon Guard began to advance. The Warlock smiled again, raising his staff and sending darkness at one on the leading edge. The man went to his knees, falling to the dirt and clutching at his throat, struggling against the magic coursing through him. After a moment, the man calmed and the darkness stopped flowing.

His comrades backed away from him while he regained his feet. The Warlock directed his darkness at another man on the opposite side of the advancing formation. The first man attacked the man nearest him, feinting high and then sweeping his feet out from under him. In the moment of stunned confusion that followed, the possessed Dragon Guard killed the other with a sword-thrust to the throat.

The second possessed man was up now, sword drawn. He stabbed one of his fellow Dragon Guard in the back of the knee, dropping him to the ground with a shriek of surprise and pain. The formation began to lose cohesion as Dragon Guard started to turn on each other.

The Warlock waded into the melee, using the dragon's claw on the end of his staff with deadly effect. He cut a swath through the Dragon Guard, facing only those that got in his way before vanishing into the keep.

"Well, I'm sure glad we pissed that guy off," Hound said.

Once the Dragon Guard killed the two possessed men, they managed to regain some semblance of order.

Flames erupted from the top of the gatehouse, drawing everyone's attention. The priest and the Warlock traded fire, each absorbing or deflecting the other's magic.

Suddenly, a mountain lion leapt off a wall, hurling itself at the Warlock. Both went tumbling to the floor, separating an instant later as if driven apart by some unseen force. When they came up facing each other, the Warlock sent darkness into the cougar. It took only a few seconds before the cat rolled over and began purring.

The Warlock pointed his staff and the cat leapt at the priest, landing on his chest and toppling him to the ground before tearing out his throat with one snap of his jaws. Blood gurgled forth while the priest died, the Warlock drawing what remained of his life force out of him, using the energy to heal a few minor injuries.

Dragon Guard arrived on both sides of him a few moments later. The Warlock bowed mockingly and jumped off the gatehouse, gliding easily to the ground on a shimmer of shadow, landing at a leisurely pace and vanishing into the alleys of the outer city while the Dragon Guard scrambled to organize a response. The cat left the inner keep as well, vanishing into the city, only an occasional shriek of terror to mark its passage.

Not long after, a detachment of Dragon Guard left the keep and fanned out into the city while the rest of the inner city closed and locked all of their doors and manned all of their battlements. The place was shut tight. A few minutes later, a number of birds left the towers, all flying east.

"The Warlock complicates things," Cyril said. "We should avoid him."

"Let's hope we can," Imogen said.

"What do you suppose he was after?" Hound asked, rubbing his broad chin.

"I think he was trying to call out the dragon," Cyril said.

"What?" Hound said.

"The dragon is coming here?" Imogen asked.

Cyril nodded. "He'll come in person to avenge one of his priests."

"Maybe we'll get lucky and the Warlock will kill the dragon," Ben said.

"Or the other way around," Cyril said. "At the moment, I have a grandson or two to worry about. Give me a few minutes." He sat down, cradling the egg in his lap, his eyes closed, his breathing regular and steady. After nearly half an hour, he opened his eyes and stretched his legs before getting to his feet.

"Frank's alive, but he's been taken. Looks like he's in a warehouse."

Imogen stood quickly. "Can you show me the city?"

Cyril projected a holo-screen and brought up an image of Rogue City.

"There, that area," Imogen said, pointing to a dark and largely abandoned part of town. The image focused.

"Enzo has a warehouse right around here."

The image focused again.

"This one ... see the men at the door?"

"All right," Cyril said, sending the drone toward the building. It moved quickly, arriving directly above the warehouse in a matter of minutes. He carefully searched for a broken window and floated inside. It was a large building, easily thirty feet tall. The room the drone entered was completely empty, save a few stacks of pallets in one corner.

It moved to the other end of the building and projected an image of Frank tied to a chair, blindfolded and gagged. A man was sitting in front of him, backward on a chair, talking to him even though he couldn't respond. Another man paced back and forth.

The drone moved closer, activating audio recording, remaining high in the rafters.

"Boss is sure taking his time with this one," the pacing man said.

"Probably letting him sweat," the seated man said. "He'll be here soon enough and we can get started. I for one, am looking forward to it. Aren't you?" he asked Frank, laughing loudly when he tried to respond around the gag.

Cyril scanned the interior for a nearby broken window and left the building, calling the drone back to him.

"Time to go," he said, gathering his things.

Imogen looked at John and asked, "How are you feeling?"

"Better ... thank you."

Ben was packed and outside waiting before anyone else was ready. Frank was a pain in the ass, but he was still his brother, and he was about to be tortured.

A few minutes later, they were on the move through the forest, circling the town so they could enter through the abandoned area and avoid the Dragon Guard patrols that were searching for the Warlock.

Chapter 31

They stayed a few hundred feet outside the markers. Cyril kept his drone a thousand feet overhead, watching in all directions at once. Ben found it disorienting, so he didn't watch, focusing instead on moving quickly.

"Stop," Cyril said, just loudly enough for everyone to hear him. "Dragon Guard, half a mile that way, looks like a routine patrol along the marker line."

After the patrol had passed, they continued on, coming to an abandoned house just outside the markers. At one time it had been white, with a picket fence. Now the wall around the front door was broken in and the roof had buckled, coming down onto the porch. The rest of it didn't look all that stable.

Cyril stopped for a moment to send his drone into town and plan his course. Within a few minutes, they were inside the markers and heading up a street between two rows of uninhabited houses, all falling down from neglect.

A dog barked at them from a backyard. They kept moving. Two more dogs came out of an alley and ran behind them, barking, but keeping their distance. Three more came out, followed by half a dozen more, all racing to catch up with the pack.

"This is a problem," Cyril said. "Face them. Don't let them circle us."

"One blast from Bertha and they'll scatter like mice."

"And the Dragon Guard searching for the Warlock will come straight here."

"Right," Hound said.

A pack of twenty dogs had gathered, all snarling and snapping but not advancing since everyone had stopped, facing them with weapons drawn.

Homer positioned himself directly behind Ben so he could look between his legs.

"That's a lot of dogs," he said.

"Yeah, I was just thinking the same thing."

A particularly large dog, bristling with aggression, stepped out of the crowd, barking at Ben, snarling and snapping as he inched closer, threatening to attack with every part of his being.

"Hold," Cyril said.

Ben ignored him. His mind was focused on the threat advancing toward him.

"That's the one," Homer said. "Kill him and the others will run away."

The alpha dog.

He locked eyes with the animal and leaned into a challenging posture, leading with the point of his sword. The alpha barked more viciously, charging forward, snapping at him. He brought the tip of his sword into place in a blink, catching the dog in the mouth and thrusting forward when the animal lunged. His blade drove out the back of its head, killing it instantly.

The others barked and yelped, a few whimpering, all of them losing confidence and backing away, barking more out of fear now than threat.

"God, I hated doing that," Ben said, cleaning his blade.

"Why?" Homer said. "Did you see how big he was? You know he wanted to eat your liver, right?"

Ben looked at Homer and shook his head.

"Come on," Cyril said, guiding them with the aid of his drone. He avoided a gang of thugs by taking them a few blocks out of their way, cursing under his breath when a street kid saw them and vanished into the underbrush along a nearby building.

"He's just a kid," Ben said.

"He works for someone," Cyril said. "We need to get indoors."

Several blocks at a jog, everyone looking over their shoulder, brought them to the last block of houses butting up against the warehouse district.

"Three blocks this way," Cyril said, staying close to the buildings as he led them toward Frank, everyone following in single file and making an effort to remain silent. A few blocks later, Cyril stopped beside a warehouse, motioning for everyone to remain still while he focused his drone.

Halfway down the two-hundred-foot-long building was a single door guarded by two men. Several horses were tied up nearby. The loading doors on either end were closed and locked. The door on the opposite side of the building was unattended.

Cyril sent the drone inside and found Frank, still tied to a chair, but without the gag and blindfold. Enzo sat facing him, leaning forward with a smile. Frank had been beaten, though not too severely.

"This will only get worse," Enzo said. "Just tell me where she is."

"I told you already, she's in a house near the whorehouse where you found me."

Enzo got up and hit him. He took a moment to adjust his leather glove before he backhanded Frank again and sat back down.

"If she had come into town, my people would have told me," Enzo said. "So, where is she?"

Frank's head lolled forward.

"You're trying my patience," Enzo said. "I can let my friend with the knives have a go at you if you'd like."

Frank shook his head.

"Where is she?"

Enzo grabbed him by the hair and jerked his head back so he could look him in the eye.

"Tell me where she is or I'll start cutting on you."

"All right ... all right," Frank said. "There's a house outside of town."

"Good ... where?"

"I might be able to find it on a map," Frank said.

Cyril closed the holo-screen and withdrew around the corner, well away from Enzo's men. Ben continued to watch the feed while one of Enzo's men went to a horse to find a map.

"We need to take those men quietly," Cyril said.

"I can take one," John said.

"Maybe we can distract the other one," Ben said.

"What did you have in mind?" Cyril asked.

"I'll go around the building and tap on the wall. Maybe he'll come to investigate."

"When he does?" Cyril asked.

"I'll take him down. Once he rounds the corner, you take the other one."

"All right, we'll give it a try," Cyril said.

Ben smiled and headed off toward the back of the building. He reached the far corner and peeked around. Both men were still at their post and both looked bored.

Ben stepped back and tapped the butt of his sword against the wall three times, waiting and watching the men through the drone feed.

Both looked his way, then at each other. They shrugged but did nothing. Ben tapped again. Both looked at each other again and then headed his way. He hadn't expected that. He ran to the back corner and waited. When the two guards reached the front corner, Ben tapped again. Both men drew knives and continued around the corner toward him, out of drone view, heading for the back of the building.

With Homer right beside him, Ben sprinted the length of the building and around the corner.

"Hurry, if we run, we can get behind the other building before they come back," he said in passing as he raced across. Cyril motioned for the rest of them to follow, maneuvering the drone into position to see the two guards.

He was the last across. "Don't change plans on the fly," he said to Ben. "It makes me nervous."

"Things happened," Ben said.

"They always do. Let's get to the back door," Cyril said, leading them along the wall, stopping to peek around the corner before continuing on. He studied the lock on the door for a few moments before quickly picking it, yet another skill that Ben didn't know his grandfather possessed. Then he sent the drone back inside the building to scout the positions of the people in the room.

There were four men plus Enzo and Frank. Two had knives. One had an axe and a knife. The last had a crossbow. Enzo was armed with a thin short sword. Frank was unconscious, his face looking even more severely beaten.

Cyril showed everyone the room on his holo-screen. John pointed at the man with the crossbow, nocking an arrow. Hound pointed at the man with the axe, hefting Frank's tomahawk with a wry smile. Cyril pointed out the two with knives and motioned to Ben and himself. Ben nodded.

Cyril checked one more time, lining everyone up to enter quickly before opening the door.

John was through in a blink, arrow up and away before anyone in the room had even registered their presence. He turned and moved along the wall toward the end of the room where Frank was being held, nocking another arrow.

Hound was through next, rushing into the large room with surprising speed and hurling the hatchet at the startled axe man with terrifying force. It whipped end over end, burying the entire blade into the man's chest. The thug toppled over backward and crashed to the ground.

Enzo and the other two drew and faced the oncoming threat. Ben was in next, running toward the men surrounding his brother. The nearest moved to engage. Ben pressed cautiously, waiting for the man to strike—a rushed and clumsy thrust with a long knife. Ben moved sideways, grabbing the man's wrist with his left hand, yanking his arm out straight and pulling him slightly off-balance, before cleanly driving his blade through the man's bicep in alignment with the muscle, pulling his blade straight out a second later.

The man screamed. Blood sprayed across his tunic and the floor as he flopped over, wailing in tortured agony. Ben stepped past him.

Cyril reached his man a moment later, feinting left, driving right, thrusting his sword into the man's heart and withdrawing it an instant later, passing the man without a second look on his way to Enzo.

When Enzo raised his blade to face him, Cyril swatted it aside like it was a minor annoyance, slapping his sword down onto Enzo's shoulder and drawing the edge up against his neck.

"On your knees or I'll bleed you where you stand."

Enzo looked around wildly, his eyes landing on Imogen. After seeing the look she gave him in return, he slowly went to his knees, his whole body trembling, a stifled whimper escaping him, followed by a flinch.

Cyril turned to Ben. "Untie your brother," he said.

"Hey, why didn't you kill this one?" Hound asked, rolling Ben's man onto his back with a boot.

Ben looked up from cutting Frank's bindings and shrugged.

"Did you think we were going to make nice with them?" Hound said. "Can't very well kill him now and that just complicates things." He rolled the man onto his stomach with his foot, causing him to scream again. Then he knelt down and tied the man's hands behind his back while he writhed in pain.

Frank was in and out of consciousness from the beating he'd taken, so Ben carried him to a pallet and gently laid him down while he prepared his bedroll.

Cyril tied Enzo to a chair, turning him away from Frank, then did what he could to magically speed his grandson's healing.

"He'll be out for a while," he said. "Time to get some answers."

He circled Enzo, who sat silently, fear shining in his eyes.

"Where's the child?" Cyril asked.

"In the nursery," Enzo said quickly, as if he was happy to have a question he could answer so easily.

"Can you get in?"

"Maybe," Enzo said, "but they aren't going to let me in without a good reason. Unless—"

Cyril waited, looking at him very deliberately before nodding.

"If I brought Imogen with me, that would be an explanation that the priest would believe."

"You scheming little rat," Imogen said, drawing her sword and leveling it at him. "I'll never trust you with anything ever again."

Cyril gently laid a finger on her blade, lowering it.

He turned to Enzo again. "What are their plans for the child?" he asked.

"Last I heard, they were going to take him to Denver," Enzo said.

"Denver?!" Imogen said. "Why?"

"I don't know, something about his lineage," Enzo said. "They said he was special."

Cyril sat down heavily in the chair opposite Enzo.

"I was afraid of something like that." He sighed, looking up at Imogen helplessly. "The priest knows that your son is my grandson."

Her eyes went wide and glassy, she dropped her sword, her hand came to her mouth while she shook her head back and forth, her eyes never leaving Cyril's, pleading with him to make reality something other than it was.

He shook his head sadly, going to her, but she shoved him away and walked off, one hand over her mouth, the other on her stomach as she struggled to control her sobbing. Cyril let his hands fall to his sides, closing his eyes while tears ran down his face.

"It'll be all right, Baby," Enzo said, "we can have another kid."

Cyril spun, leaping at him and drawing back to hit him with all his might … but he stopped when Enzo flinched away from the impending blow. He backed off and composed himself.

John quietly followed Imogen.

"So how are going to get inside?" Hound asked.

"The door on the back wall, in the bad part of town, not too far from here," Cyril said.

"All of us?"

Cyril winced, shaking his head.

"I'd leave Frank and Imogen here," Hound said. "He needs time to heal and she's too close to this."

"Think you can get her to stay here?" Ben asked, looking across the warehouse at Imogen, sitting with her back against a wall and her knees drawn up against her chest. John sat nearby, but not too close.

"Probably not," Cyril said.

"I'm telling you, it'll all be easier if you get her to go in with me," Enzo said.

Hound leaned into him, letting his face go slack and his eyes go dead. "You don't need to talk unless we tell you to talk." Hound nodded until Enzo started nodding in agreement.

Hound stood back up and looked at Cyril. "We still have two out front. Fortunately, they probably expected to hear some screaming from Frank."

"See if John will help you with them," Cyril said.

Hound nodded somberly, running a cloth over the tomahawk blade even though it was already entirely clean before heading off toward John and Imogen.

She returned, somewhat more composed. "How can you be sure?" she asked. "How does the priest know he's your grandson?"

"Dragons have a thing with blood," Cyril said. "The wyrm has tasted mine. His priests will know."

"Are you sure?"

Cyril took her into his arms and nodded. "I'm sure." He waited until she had finished crying, before holding her out at arm's length.

"Be thankful," he said. "If it was any other baby, the priests would have sacrificed him by now."

Her eyes grew wide.

"Oh God, how can that be?"

"Babies have a lot of life energy," Cyril said. "There's power there."

"Oh God," Imogen whispered.

"When the dragon arrives, he won't come alone," Cyril said. "A high priest will be with him. If we wait too long, the baby will probably be out of our reach. Time is limited."

Chapter 32

Hound eased the front door open and John loosed an arrow. A man grunted and then gurgled when he tried to wail. The other said "Huh?" as Hound rushed out onto the porch and threw the tomahawk—one soft thud preceded a heavy thud. They carried Enzo's guards into the building one at time, barring the door after they'd finished.

When they returned to the other end of the warehouse, Cyril said, "We have a few hours of daylight left. We should use that time to plan so we can go in at dark."

"Chesapeake? No," Hound said, holding up the bloody tomahawk.

"What?" Cyril said.

"I got two kills with this baby today," Hound said. "That's a sign. She needs a name."

Cyril opened his mouth, then closed it, tilting his head to the side for a moment.

"Uh … Francine? No, definitely not, I went with a Francine once. She was crazy. It was a lot of fun while it lasted, but it didn't end well. No matter … I'll come up with something. You were saying?"

"We need a plan," Cyril said. "I want to go in just after dusk."

He spent a few minutes detailing his strategy, using recorded video from his drone reconnaissance to lay out the entry, the path through the inner city to the temple, and the access to the nursery. He provided probable points of resistance, doors that would need to be picked or forced, guard locations and patrol routes.

Once again, Ben found that he was impressed with his grandfather. His hours of watching had yielded a sound plan with a high probability of success.

After Cyril had finished, Imogen said, "I'm not staying here."

"Come, let's talk about this," Cyril said, motioning for her to walk with him.

"There's nothing to talk about," she said, going with him nonetheless.

"What do you think we're going to do with this one?" Hound asked Ben, motioning to Enzo with his head.

"Hard to say. I've never seen my grandfather so angry."

"Me neither," Hound said. "Of course, if he had something interesting to say …"

"I don't know anything," Enzo said, pleadingly.

"Of course you do, you just don't know what it is yet," Hound said. "For example, how many guards watch over the nursery?"

"I don't know."

"Okay, is there a back way in or out of the inner city?"

Enzo hesitated.

Hound slapped him hard on the side of the head, laughing and pulling the chair close so he could look him in the eye.

"See, you do know something useful," he said.

"Did you have to hit me?"

"No, but I wanted to," Hound said.

"I know how you feel," John said.

"Me, too," Ben said, slapping him on the shoulder from behind, causing him to flinch and then shrink in on himself.

"About that back way in," Hound said, leaning toward him with a humorless grin.

Enzo winced. "They'll kill me."

"Who?" Hound said.

"The …" he said, stopping and shaking his head firmly. "I'll tell you where it is, but not who owns it."

"All right, we'll start with where," Hound said.

Enzo sat back, taking a deep breath and visibly relaxing.

"There's a bakery—"

"Bullshit!" Hound shouted, coming to his feet, launching forward at Enzo—fury, rage and wrath all bundled into the expression on his face and the bulging vein on the side of his head.

Enzo's eyes grew wide and his face went white. "I swear …"

Hound sat back down as quickly and fluidly as he'd lunged at Enzo, all of his anger and aggression gone in an instant. Enzo was trembling.

"So tell me about this bakery."

Enzo nodded quickly, gulping a breath before beginning. "It's in the block bordering the inner wall. There's a tunnel that goes under the wall to another bakery inside."

"Can you show me on a map?"

"Yes," Enzo said.

"Good," Hound said, looking at Ben.

"I don't have a map."

"Maybe Cyril can help after he's done smoothing Imogen," Hound said.

"Probably—" Ben said, holding his tongue when there was a knock at the door—three loud, deliberately spaced clangs.

He looked to Hound, who had already unslung Bertha and was moving toward the door. Cyril had his pistol out and was moving to a get a different angle on the door. John was moving toward Imogen while watching the door and nocking an arrow.

Ben suddenly realized that he was standing in the middle of the warehouse watching everyone else prepare for battle. He rushed forward, drawing his revolver, sighting down the wall toward the entrance.

Cyril nodded to Hound.

He approached the door carefully, pushing it open with Bertha. "Come in, quickly," he said, "hands open … where I can see them."

A woman entered. She was in her late twenties, had shoulder-length dirty-blond hair and hard facial features. She was fit—moving with a sinewy, almost catlike grace, as if balance and poise were just innately part of her.

John slipped out of the shadows and closed the door behind her, stepping back to be ready with his bow if necessary. Hound stood ten feet away with Bertha pointed at her chest.

"Start talking."

"I'm looking for a friend of Thomas Sinclair," she said.

"Hold," Cyril said, raising his hand. "Lower your weapons." He approached to within five steps of her and stopped. "He was my friend, once."

"He still is, I think," she said. "My name is Kathryn, but my friends call me Kat. We have transport ready for you."

Cyril chuckled to himself. "Efficient … and greatly appreciated, but we're not ready to go yet."

"I don't understand."

"We have business in Rogue City," Cyril said. "Perhaps it would be best to arrange a rendezvous."

"No chance," she said. "You were a bitch to track down. This guy, Enzo, was our only lead. If you hadn't gotten together with him, we'd still be sitting in the dark."

"Fair enough," Cyril said. "I hope to have our last errand wrapped up by dawn. Would you like to wait here? My daughter and my injured grandson will be staying as well."

"That might be acceptable," Kat said.

"Ah … so you have a commander in the shadows."

"Of course," she said. "Would you expect otherwise, given my employer?"

"Fair enough," Cyril said. "If all goes well, we'll be on our way at dusk. If your friends would like to come in or stay out, that's their choice—though I would prefer to remain undetected."

"Understood," she said, deliberately scanning the room and its occupants. "Your business is serious, I think," her eyes landing on Enzo, tied to a chair.

"Yes, very much so," Cyril said.

"Perhaps I should go get my friends," Kat said. "With your permission."

Cyril took a long breath, held it for a moment and let it out all at once, nodding.

She bowed her head to him respectfully and left at a full stride, stopping at the door for a moment to look both ways before slipping out of the warehouse.

"What the hell just happened?" Hound asked.

"I sent for help," Cyril said. "It just arrived."

"Help from who?"

"The Dragon Slayer," Cyril said. "She works for him."

Silence fell on the room for a moment. Then there was another knock at the door.

Hound answered it with Bertha in hand but lowered, a frown capable of stopping a charging bull on his face as he motioned for Kat and her two friends to enter. He closed the door behind them after a wary look this way and that.

"Annabelle and Adam Cook," Kat said.

"I'm Cyril Smith. This is my daughter, Imogen ... my grandson, Benjamin ... Rufus Hound ... John Durt. My grandson Frank is recovering from injuries over there in the corner."

Annabelle, tall and thin, blond and fair, green-eyed and freckled, stepped up to Cyril with supreme confidence and bowed her head, almost as if in homage.

"Please, call me Belle. My father speaks fondly of you. Kat tells me you have business to attend to before you're willing to leave."

"Yes, my infant grandson is being held hostage in the keep and I plan to rescue him."

She stepped back, smiled incredulously and shook her head. "You have got to be kidding."

"Not at all. Worse, the dragon will be here tomorrow."

"What!"

"His priest was killed. Birds went out."

"And you're still here? Are you mad?"

"Perhaps," Cyril said. "I am forever grateful to your father for sending you, but I can't ask you to mount an assault with me. Please, just give me a location where we can meet for transportation. If all goes well, we'll be ready to leave by dawn."

"If not?"

"There's always that," Cyril said. "Do you have siblings?"

"What's that have to do with anything?" Belle snapped.

"Your father was always a family man. I just hope he has lots of children."

"Oh ... sorry," Belle said. "I'm a bit overprotective of my sisters."

"Two?"

She nodded.

"Good," Cyril said. "He deserves to have a big family."

"Can we get back to what the hell you're planning?" Belle said.

"When the sun goes down, four of us are going to sneak into the temple and kidnap my grandson," Cyril said.

"You say that like it's an afternoon stroll," Belle said.

"I have a plan," Cyril said. "Just stay here and be patient."

"No, I'm coming with you," she said.

"No, you're not," both Adam and Kat said in unison.

"We got lucky finding them," Belle said. "We're not losing them now."

"You're not going on an assault against a wyrm fortress," Adam said.

"I'll go," Kat said. "Sounds like fun. You two stay here with their people. We'll go kick some wyrm ass and be back by morning."

"Kat, this is about more than that," Belle said.

"No, it's not," Kat said. "You should probably be ready to run when we get back."

"You're such a bitch," Belle said with a half smile.

"You two are making me hot," Hound said, smiling at both of them shamelessly.

"Married," Annabelle said, holding up her wedding band and pointing at Adam.

Hound nodded at Adam like he respected him for marrying a woman as attractive as Annabelle.

Adam took a step closer to his wife.

Kat just chuckled, shaking her head at Hound. "You're so totally out of your league." Then she shifted her gaze to John and smiled. "You, on the other hand, I see promise in you."

John stood very still, looking at her like she'd grown a horn out of her forehead and he was hoping that she might just go away. She laughed, turning back to the group.

Imogen frowned.

"Don't we have work to do?" Kat said.

"Wow ... bossy," Hound said. "Maybe I dodged a bullet."

"You might have to, if you keep that up," she said.

Cyril stepped into the circle of people, drawing their attention and commanding their silence with his.

After a moment, he said, "This is deadly business ... I plan on killing a number of the wyrm's people in the process of this raid. Successful or not, we will provoke the dragon." He turned to Annabelle. "Again, your father is gracious to have sent you, and again, I can't ask you or your friends to go into battle with me."

Kat held up her hand to forestall Annabelle's response, who shook her head with a humorless grin.

"First, I hate the dragon, maybe even more than you do, so the chance to kill some of his people and perhaps even light his house on fire sounds good to me. Second, you are my mission—I was assigned the task of returning you safely to my employer. It's pretty obvious that we're not going to talk you out of this, so someone has to go along and make sure you stay alive. That's me."

"If you insist," he said, "but you will follow my orders."

"Agreed," Kat said.

"Will you wait here?" Cyril asked Belle and Adam.

"We should go with you," Belle said.

"No, having too many people is a liability," Cyril said. "I need the two of you to stay here. Will you?"

"Yes, but we're coming for you if you're not back by dawn."

"If we're not back by dawn, you should run."

"He's right," Kat said.

"You're being overprotective," Belle said.

"That's what your father pays me for."

Chapter 33

Ben took a moment to check on Frank. He was unconscious and his face was bruised and swollen, but he was breathing steadily. That was good enough for now. He went to Cyril and found John, Rufus, and Kat with him. They were watching Cyril's screen while he went over the plan for getting inside yet again.

Ben had been through the plan so many times that he could see it when he closed his eyes, and without the aid of his implant—which had been pleasantly silent lately. After a final equipment check, Cyril led them outside. When Homer followed Ben, Kat stopped and cocked her head at him.

"You're bringing a dog?" she asked.

"Yes," Ben said, walking past her with Homer on his heels.

Homer growled on his way by her. "I don't like her," he said. "She smells too clean. Also, you can tell a lot about a person from their name."

"Be nice," Ben said. "She's on our side … for now, anyway."

Ben fell in beside Cyril, listening to Hound and Kat banter behind them while John remained silent. The last remnants of daylight had just faded and the stars were shining brightly. Ben thought he saw movement ahead.

"There's more than one of them," Homer said, sniffing into the breeze. "At least three."

Ben reached out and gently touched Cyril's arm, drawing his attention, and bringing them all to a halt. "There's someone hiding alongside the road up ahead."

Cyril launched his drone and switched to thermal vision, making it easy to pick out the four men hiding in a broken-down house. The image shifted back to normal as the drone floated closer.

"Ambush," Cyril whispered.

"Surely, they see us by now," Kat said. "Maybe we should just call them out."

"I'd like to cause as little commotion as possible," Cyril said. "We'll try and go around them." He reversed course, turning at the next cross street and hurrying for two blocks before turning back toward the inner wall. As they reached the next corner, they heard running and loud breathing.

Four men came around the corner and fanned out, all armed with makeshift weapons—an axe, a club, a staff, a knife.

Hound laughed, jacking a round into Bertha's chamber. The telltale sound of a shotgun being loaded stopped them in their tracks.

"Whoa … we don't want no trouble," the one with the knife said.

"All evidence to the contrary," Cyril said. "Drop your weapons and run away or we'll kill you."

The guy started trembling, still holding the knife.

"Three," Hound said.

They all looked a bit confused.

"Two," Hound said, firming up his aim at the man's chest.

The would-be mugger dropped the knife and ran, vanishing between two houses in a matter of seconds. The other three took a moment more to comply. When Hound turned his shotgun on the nearest, all of them let go of their weapons like they'd suddenly gotten hot, then turned and ran off in different directions.

"Damn," Cyril said. "We have to hurry."

They reached the staging house in about twenty minutes. Cyril had already searched it with the drone a number of times, but he did one last sweep before they approached.

John led, opening the broken back door quickly, causing a single loud squeak rather than any prolonged creaking. He left the door fully open and moved inside, arrow nocked. By the time everyone had slipped inside, John had returned.

"Clear," he said.

"Thank you," Cyril said, sitting at the kitchen table, which was still sturdy, if not a bit unkempt. The drone left through a broken window, a large holo-screen coming up as it circled overhead, switching to thermal for a moment and scanning the nearby blocks. A group of ten men was gathered in a house a few blocks away. Ben felt his breathing quicken at the sudden knowledge.

A deadly threat had been exposed.

He had to wonder how much the enemy knew. Were they beginning a search or were they planning an assault? As he asked the questions in his mind, the drone darted forward, arriving over the house a few seconds later, scanning for an entrance point. After a few minutes of searching, the drone discovered a broken dryer vent that allowed access. Once inside, Cyril maneuvered it quietly and carefully until it reached the main rooms occupied by the gang of thugs. He piloted the drone up onto a door frame and landed it, enabling audio recording.

"This is stupid!"

"The profit is worth the risk."

"Unless we get killed."

"Well, I won't, so it's worth it to me."

"How many men can we muster … total?"

"Thirty-four—nine with guns, the rest with blades."

"How long do you think they'll be there?"

"Hard to say … it looks like they're planning an operation against the inner city."

Cyril closed his holo-screen but kept the drone in place, recording and sending.

"We have to move to another location," he said. "They know where we are."

"How?" Kat asked.

"Doesn't matter," Cyril said. "They know ... they're coming. We have to be somewhere else when they get here."

That was when Ben noticed the dead man. He was lying haphazardly in the corner of the pantry, a chef's knife in his hand. Ben wasn't entirely certain why he went to him, but he found himself drawn toward him. He looked down at the decaying corpse, shrugged to himself and bent over to search. The kitchen knife was well made but it was no combat blade. He fished around in the man's pockets, coming up with another gold NACC coin ... exactly like his lucky coin.

He stood up quickly, blinking in wonderment at the coin in his hand. A mixture of unease and exhilaration swept through him. This was the second identical coin that he'd found since they'd retrieved the egg. His coin.

Magic. It hit him like a bag of hammers. His grandfather had already taught him a basic manifestation spell, and a pretty useful one at that. He finished searching the man and found a handful of bullets that wouldn't fit his pistol and a small folding knife of exceptional quality.

"Can anyone use these?" he said, shaking the half-full box of bullets after pocketing the knife and coin.

Hound leaned in to look, shaking his head.

Everyone else shrugged as well.

"Keep them," Cyril said. "A handful of bullets in a fire can cause quite a distraction."

Ben dumped them into a pouch and discarded the box.

"How about this?" he said, flipping the coin to his grandfather.

Cyril looked at it and then at Ben, who held up his lucky coin.

"You found another one?"

"On the dead man with the bullets," Ben said. "All this time, you've been teaching me magic without even telling me what you were doing."

Cyril smiled, chuckling to himself and nodding to Ben.

"You've been a good student," he said, flipping the coin back to Ben. "And it looks like it's paying off. Magic is powerful, but money is easier and far more widely accepted."

Useful magic indeed, thought Ben, as he pocketed the coin.

"Ready to go?" Cyril asked, looking around to a chorus of nodding heads.

They left in a quiet file, moving a block away from the inner wall, then turning and running three blocks before coming back toward it and a row of abandoned houses just across the street.

Cyril stopped them with hand signals, then sent his drone into a house to scan it before leading them inside. John and Rufus quickly and very thoroughly searched the house in a matter of seconds, just to make sure.

"This isn't an ideal location, relative to our target, but it'll have to do," Cyril said. "We'll wait for an hour or so ... let the muggers lose interest."

"Fun," Kat said. "Or, I could go and take them out."

"No," Cyril said. "I don't want to kill if we can help it."

"I won't ... I promise," she said, drawing a sleek-looking pistol. "This is a silenced, air-powered dart gun. It fires a high-speed projectile coated with a neurotoxin. It's semi-automatic, has a range of fifty feet, it's quiet as a whisper, and it will drop a full-grown man within two seconds and keep him out for two hours. The toxin is a family recipe."

"Seriously?" Hound said, with a big stupid grin.

"More than meets the eye, big boy," she said.

"Are you sure you can do this without killing anyone?" Cyril asked.

"I guarantee it," Kat said. "These guys are a bunch of amateurs. I shoot them, they go to sleep."

"You probably shouldn't go alone," Ben said.

"What? You and your dog?"

"You could do worse."

"No, I need to move quietly. A dog ... no."

"He'll be just fine," Ben said. "I'll be your backup. If all goes well, I won't do anything. If you need help, I'll be there."

"Those are the terms," Cyril said.

"Fair enough ... come along, dog boy," she said.

"You aren't trying to make any friends are you?" Ben said.

"Only with those that I might like to be friends with," she said, offering a smile to soften her words. "Stay close, do as I tell you, and don't get us killed."

"I'll follow your lead. That's the best I can offer."

"I'll take it," she said, smiling more broadly and slapping Ben on the shoulder. "You'll do just fine."

By three blocks from the house, Ben found himself preoccupied with wondering how Kat could be so stealthy and yet so graceful at the same time. She glided through the world, shifting into shadow as necessary, dragging Ben behind, ever aware of possible threats, and equally aware of places offering concealment.

He felt cumbersome by comparison, traveling through the night like a lumbering beast, huffing and shuffling. Within half a block, he surrendered to her guidance, judging her mastery of the night as far superior to his, and learning very quickly that he was not wrong.

She stopped a block from where the gang was holed up, sliding into a shadow that both concealed them and offered a good view of the target house.

Ben looked to the feed in his mind's eye. It showed a thermal image of the entire house and all ten of the inhabitants. Four men with rifles and pistols were perched in the second story windows, two at the front and two at the back. Two men with rifles and pistols stood guard on the front porch. A man with a shotgun stood just outside the back door. Three men sat at a table in the dining room.

He described the house to Kat in detail, specifying where every target was and what they were armed with.

"You sure?"

"Absolutely," he said.

"You might be more useful than you look," she said. "We'll move around to the back door and I'll take him first."

"I'm right behind you."

Ben felt his heart rate accelerate as they circled through the broken-down neighborhood to target the guard standing watch at the rear of the house.

Kat stopped at the corner of a neighboring house, peeked around, brought her pistol up and fired once. A few moments later, Ben heard a thud.

She gestured for him to wait, standing stock-still, listening intently.

"Are you sure this is wise?" the augment asked. "You are seriously outnumbered. Perhaps I could provide a better tactical option."

"Either help me, all the way, or be quiet," Ben said.

The augment didn't respond.

After nearly a minute, Kat peeked around the corner again, this time looking for the men in the window on the second floor.

She grabbed Ben's arm and dragged him around the corner, racing for the back porch, her eyes never leaving the empty window. He followed, as quietly as he could, all the while recognizing that he was inadequate in a dozen different ways, not the least of which was an inability to move through shadow without detection.

Kat searched the downed man in a matter of moments, handing Ben his shotgun—a sawed-off, double-barrel, pistol-grip, break-action weapon capable of firing a number of different rounds. Then she handed him a belt full of shells, at least a dozen, with a tailored leather holster for the weapon.

He wrapped the belt around his waist, ensuring that the shotgun didn't interfere with his sword and that both were easily hidden by his coat.

"Once the door opens, I'll try to take everyone, but if I can't, you'll have to take the ones I miss."

Ben felt a rush of fear … excitement … glory. He nodded, drawing his blade.

Kat opened the door, slowly, quietly, just an inch, then quickly stepped inside, stopping the door before it could hit the wall. She moved to the dining room, lithe and quiet. Ben followed, trying with all his might to be as silent as she was.

"Huh?" said one of the men as she slipped into the room, firing three times in rapid succession, taking all the men at the table in passing.

She motioned for Ben to hold position as she flitted across the room, opened the front door a crack and shot one of the guards. She waited for a moment until the second guard came to check on his partner and shot him as well, closing the door and heading for the second floor, motioning for Ben to remain where he was.

He waited while she went upstairs, listening intently. A thud, then another, then two more. She came back downstairs a few moments later.

"Come on," she said, motioning for Ben to help her move the bodies from the front and back porches into the house. It took a minute or so, but it reduced the likelihood of an alarm being sounded.

"Good," she said once they were finished, looking around the room like they'd just rearranged the furniture. "We should be getting back."

Within a few minutes, they were back at the house with the others.

"Well done, and quite impressive," Cyril said.

"Thank you," Kat said with a respectful nod.

"It's nearly time to make our assault on the keep," Cyril said. "I expect someone to be along shortly. When they bribe their way in, I'll arrange for the door to fail to latch." He gave Ben a wink. "We'll move quickly and assault the room, killing the two guards."

Like clockwork, a prostitute arrived at the door a few minutes later, flirting with the guards who were only too happy to take her bribe money. More importantly, they were also distracted by her charms, letting the door close without taking care to lock it. Cyril focused his will into the moment. The door didn't latch and the guards were too busy flirting with the prostitute to notice.

"Quickly," Cyril said, racing toward the wall. Rufus and John were right behind him. When Cyril reached the wall, he bounded up the three steps to the landing and rushed inside, catching two men very much by surprise. John reached the landing a moment later, sending an arrow into the room.

When Ben arrived, both men were dead and Cyril had already moved through the room and killed the guard standing outside the door to the inner city. He was dragging the body into the gate room.

He brought up a holo-screen and scanned the area, looking for any sign of detection. Finding none, he closed the screen and planted an ex-plus tablet in one corner of the room.

"Let's pile those bodies on top of the ex-plus," he said, motioning for Ben to help him.

Doors locked and keys stolen, they entered the inner city, moving toward the center of town ... the dragon temple. Cyril quietly guided them through the privileged and protected neighborhoods of Rogue City. He relied on his drone to avoid the seemingly random patrols that wandered the streets, playing cat and mouse with them on one occasion, going one way around a block while they went the other.

The few people they encountered seemed frightened by their weapons, often whispering among themselves. Cyril ignored them. Ben tried to but he knew full well that it would take just one report to the Dragon Guard and they'd be on the run.

As they neared the temple, the homes became bigger and more well-protected, with high walls and fences. The streets were lined with oil lamps flooding the area with light.

Cyril walked at a measured pace, one hand on the egg, eyes straight ahead.

"Walk like you're supposed to be here," he said without looking back.

Ben wasn't sure exactly what that meant but he did his best to be calm and at ease. He thought it odd that the few people looking out a window or those out for a late-night stroll seemed to take little or no notice of them, one even nodding hello in passing.

Cyril stopped when they reached the temple's outer fence, a ten-foot-tall, wrought-iron cage surrounding the grounds in a perfect circle. Surrounding the fence was a wide footpath, often patrolled by Dragon Guard.

The entire temple was ablaze with lamps burning brightly in the night. Every railing, every roof peak, spire and pinnacle was adorned with a lamp, and not a single one was dark.

Cyril pulled up the holo-screen and did a final scan. "Guards will be around in five minutes. Let's go."

They raced to the fence. John immediately wrapped a stout steel chain around a section of five bars, locking it into place with a fair amount of slack. Hound slid a crowbar into the links and wound it around a few times until he had tension on the bars. Then he heaved with all his strength, and the bars bent. He pulled again and they bent farther, enough for a man to slip through. He unwound the chain and stepped inside the fence, leaving the crowbar in favor of Bertha. John quietly laid the chain down on his way through.

One by one, they entered the temple grounds. Leading the others, Cyril headed toward a side door in the temple itself. After taking only five steps, he crashed into a magical barrier that knocked him flat on his back.

"What the hell was that?" Hound asked.

"I saw a flash," Homer said.

"Me too," said Ben, rushing to his grandfather's side.

Cyril took a moment to recover before he got to his feet and carefully raised his right hand toward the barrier. It lit up where he touched it, sparking and crackling. He withdrew his hand quickly, as if from a flame.

"This isn't good," he muttered, putting his hand on the egg and closing his eyes. After a minute or so, a plane of magical energy, red-orange in color, became visible. It surrounded the entire temple. He let go of his will a moment later and the shield slowly faded from sight.

"We have to abort," Cyril said. "I can't get through this circle. It feels like all of the priests in the temple cast a protection spell on it."

"But …" Ben said, unable to think of what to say next.

"We'll fall back and come up with a different plan," Cyril said. "For now, we have to go."

"Too late," said a voice from behind them, outside the bars of the fence. "Lay down your weapons and step through, please."

They turned as one and saw a man dressed in a deep crimson robe. His face had taken on some of the characteristics of a dragon—his eyes were catlike and his skin looked almost scaled. The black claws at the end of his fingers were small but sharp.

Four Dragon Guard and a stalker mountain lion were arrayed around him.

He held his arms out. "Surrender is really your only path to survival," he said, smugly.

"Get down," Cyril shouted, tossing something over the fence.

Ben went to a knee, and was thankful for it. The force of the blast nearly knocked him over and the ringing in his ears was deafening.

"I didn't like that," Homer said.

"Me neither."

Cyril put a hand on Ben's shoulder and pointed for him to get through the fence. He nodded, scanning the area and finding that the priest, his stalker pet and the Dragon Guard were all little more than paste on the road. Whatever his grandfather had thrown, it had been powerful.

Ben headed across the street, wishing he could find a shadow in the light of the temple.

"I still can't hear right," Homer said.

"Me neither, but it'll come back."

He stopped to wait for his friends, working his jaw to pop his ears, feeling a sharp stab of pain from each. Everyone else looked to be in similar shape, but all things considered, it was probably the best they could have hoped for.

Using hand signals, Cyril got them moving at a light run toward the door in the wall. By now the streets were full of people wondering about the explosion. Most didn't give them a second look. A few watched them run by with suspicion.

The alarm bell sounded and the inner-city guard began to mobilize, every available Dragon Guard arming up and taking to the streets to secure the temple.

Cyril stopped on a corner, breathing deeply. "We're clear to the door, but four Dragon Guard just arrived and they've seen the bodies we left behind."

He projected a holo-screen. The Dragon Guard were clearly agitated, calling for reinforcements.

"So we should probably hurry," Hound said. "Hit 'em hard and fast and be on our way."

While they considered their options, a cougar stalker came into view, taking up position at the door. Cyril panned the drone and saw a dozen more Dragon Guard just arriving, along with another two priests.

"That way is looking less and less promising," Cyril said. "Let's try your way, Rufus."

Hound nodded, pulling out a map and orienting himself before pointing out the location of the bakery.

"Good," Cyril said, heading out, his drone scouting the way for them. He was successful at avoiding the Dragon Guard that were now becoming more prevalent on the streets. The neighborhood gave way to a small market area with dozens of shops, their overpriced wares displayed behind windows.

They reached the bakery and checked to make sure it was empty of employees, then went around behind the building and found the back door.

Kat smiled at it and went to work, sliding a pick and a wrench into the keyhole and opening the lock in a matter of seconds.

Cyril nodded approvingly, going inside and motioning for the others to follow, before closing and locking the door behind them.

"All right, where?"

"Give me a minute," Hound said, looking around the room.

Cyril called up his holo-screen and sent the drone high, looking at the door through the wall. Images of two priests, a stalker, and a platoon of Dragon Guard appeared.

He chuckled and shook his head. "Sometimes it's just too easy," he said as he activated the ex-plus charge he'd set inside the wall.

A loud crack reverberated throughout the city followed a few dozen seconds later by the sound of rocks the size of a man's fist raining down on everything and everyone.

After a few moments, the cloud of smoke and dust drifted away, revealing a pile of rubble—all that remained of the gate room. The gap in the wall was fifty feet wide.

The Dragon Guard were simply gone, erased from the world in the blink of an eye.

"That'll certainly get their attention," Kat said, smiling. "I'm so glad I came along."

"Ah, here," Hound said, opening the door to the cellar.

Cyril lit his lamp, casting light down a steep staircase. As he descended, he tested each stair before committing his weight to it and found them to be far more sturdy than they looked.

Hound descended next, the others following close behind. After a few moments of searching, Rufus found what he was looking for. He shoved a crate aside and took a step back, motioning to a tunnel entrance.

"Excellent," Cyril said, peering inside. "Looks like we have to crawl for a ways and then it opens up a bit." He checked his gear and entered the tunnel, plunging the cellar into darkness.

A few moments later, light emanated from the tunnel.

"It's clear, come on down," Cyril said, holding his lamp high to illuminate the way.

Hound went last, taking a few moments and some grunting to move the crate back into place.

The five-foot-wide stone passage was arched just a few inches above Ben's head. He could stand without stooping, but it felt oppressive to have the ceiling so close.

The tunnel ran straight toward the wall. After a few minutes, Ben started to feel like he was walking through a tomb. It was crushingly quiet. Every footfall, every breath felt like a violation of the silence. By the time they reached the door on the other end, he was eager to see the sky again.

The second bakery was empty as well, a small thing that Ben found himself profoundly grateful for. They were able to leave without a trace, even taking a moment for Kat to lock the door so the owner would be none the wiser.

Chapter 34

The warehouse district was void of all activity. The explosion had spooked everyone, especially those who actually had something to hide. The Dragon Guard were all inside the inner wall protecting their own, leaving the streets clear. Cyril and his group passed through the area with relative ease, just a few dogs straggling behind them, but they weren't too aggressive.

When they neared the warehouse, the feral dogs stopped, yelping and then running away. Ben looked at Homer.

"I smell a stalker," he said, "and that blond bitch."

"Nash?" Ben asked, alarm surging into the pit of his belly.

"Yeah, the one that's been chasing us from the start."

"Stop!" Ben whispered urgently.

"What's wrong?" Cyril asked, motioning for everyone to wait.

Ben had to think for a moment to justify his concerns. "Why did the dogs suddenly back off?"

Cyril shrugged, considering it for a moment. "They did seem spooked."

He launched his drone and sent it up high, switching to thermal vision and scanning the area for several blocks. When his screen settled on the warehouse, he could see the images of more people than there should have been … along with the silhouette of a wolf.

"Quickly, into this building," Cyril said, rushing to the nearest warehouse.

Aside from a mountain of crates piled up at one end, the place was cold and empty. Cyril brought up his holo-screen and sent the drone into Enzo's warehouse for a closer look.

Imogen, Frank, Annabelle, and Adam were all tied up in the center of the room. Enzo was still tied to the chair, but was separate from everyone else. Frank was still unconscious, but that hadn't stopped them from dragging him out of bed, tying his hands behind his back and leaving him on the floor, his head cradled in Imogen's lap. Adam had a bruise across his cheek and a very black eye, but he looked more angry than hurt.

Three Dragon Guard had taken up positions around the room in easy range of the two doors and the group of hostages, rifles in hand and at the ready.

Nash sat in the chair opposite Enzo. Her wolf-stalker sat next to her, occasionally baring its teeth at Enzo when he was reluctant to answer a question. A young boy was on his knees on her other side, a collar around his neck. He looked thoroughly defeated.

"Shit," Cyril said, under his breath.

"Oh God, she's got Zack," Ben whispered.

"I'll be right back," Kat said.

"No," Cyril said.

"Annabelle is my charge."

Cyril held up both hands to forestall any further protest.

"We're going in, but carefully," Cyril said. "The Dragon Guard probably have orders to kill the hostages if we attack. Their armor will stop your darts cold, and that stalker will ignore them altogether while it rips your throat out."

"Very well, what's your plan then?" she asked, her fists on her hips.

"We hit them hard and fast from both sides in a coordinated attack," he said, pointing to the holo-screen. "I'll come through this door with John and offer to negotiate. The rest of you will circle around and prepare to come through the back door when I give the signal."

"That won't work," Homer said.

"Why not?"

"The wind is blowing this way."

Ben hesitated for a moment, trying to figure out what Homer was getting at.

"I feel you may require a psychological evaluation," the augment said. "Dogs can't talk."

"Be quiet," Ben said. "What are you talking about, Homer?"

"The stalker can smell better than I can. If you send people around the building, the wind will carry their scent to it in a matter of seconds."

"That won't work," Ben said to Cyril, pointing at the screen. "The stalker is a wolf. It has a great sense of smell, but the wild dogs ran off because they smelled it first. That means the wind is blowing our way. If we send people around the building, we'll lose surprise."

"Huh," Cyril said, nodding his head in agreement. "I can't fault your logic."

"But that means a single entry breach through the front door," Hound said. "Risky."

"Yes, but less risky than losing surprise," Cyril said.

"Or," Kat said, pointing at the holo-screen, "one of us goes around here, to the front of the building, and hits this Dragon Guard through the window the moment everything starts."

"What about his armor?" Hound asked.

"Won't matter if I shoot him in the face," Kat said.

"Fair enough," Hound said.

The holo-screen image shifted, scanning the ground-level windows in the warehouse along the side in question and finding a pane with a broken section large enough to make a precision shot through.

"All right," Cyril said. "Kat will take position and hit the guard on this corner. That's one."

"What's the signal?"

"I'm not sure yet," Cyril said with a smile and a shrug.

"I might get a shot through those broken second-story windows," John said. "If I get up on the building across the way."

"Take a look and come back with your assessment," Cyril said.

"That leaves one," Hound said. "I go through the door and take him with Bertha."

"That leaves Nash and her dog," Ben said.

"That's you and me," Cyril said.

"Oh, I got a new gun," Ben said, drawing the shotgun and pointing it at the ceiling.

Cyril cocked his head. John nodded approvingly. Kat just smiled.

"Nice piece," Hound said.

"Rufus, could you give him a few pointers, please."

"Happy to," he said, holding out his hand for the weapon.

Ben watched him unload it and work it like he understood it intuitively ... like he could use it as easily as he could use his right hand.

To his surprise, Rufus Hound turned out to be an excellent instructor. He patiently and thoroughly showed him how to use the shotgun in every way, examining all of the shells in his belt and reporting that he had ten shot shells, plus the two already in the chambers, and four slugs.

He showed Ben how to load the weapon, how to draw quickly, how to target broadly ... unless he was shooting a slug, in which case, accurate aiming was important. After Ben was confident that he'd learned everything he could about his new weapon, Hound had him work a few drills with it empty, just to get the feel of drawing and firing.

When they returned to the group, John had done his recon and had a target. Cyril went over the plan one last time.

The night air was cool, but Ben felt warm. Energy born of fear and exhilaration flowed through him. It was a good plan, but one shot from a dragon-fire rifle ... inside a building ... could be catastrophic. Timing was everything.

Kat and John split off, each moving to their respective positions.

Cyril, Ben, and Hound made their way to the warehouse, moving slowly and carefully, sacrificing time for stealth. Cyril knelt when he reached the door, pulling up a small, dim holo-screen and scanning for Kat and John. Finding both in place, he slowly turned the knob, pushing the door open just an inch or two, before looking up to Rufus and nodding.

Hound shoved the door open violently, rushing in and turning to his right, toward the lone Dragon Guard watching over the group of prisoners and the two doors, leveling Bertha and firing. The Dragon Guard staggered back. Hound fired again. The man's head peeled apart, spraying blood across the floor as he fell.

Ben followed Cyril into the room. A moment after the first shotgun blast, the Dragon Guard nearest the front wall slapped his neck, staggered a step forward and fell on his face. A moment after that, an arrow stopped mid-shaft in the forehead of the Dragon Guard opposite the first. The man slumped to his knees and fell over onto his side.

Nash leapt forward past Enzo, yanking Imogen to her feet by her hair and putting a blade to her throat, using her as a shield.

Cyril and Ben fanned out around the rest of the hostages, pointing their weapons at Nash.

"Zack, come this way," Ben said.

Zack looked at him, confusion, hope, and fear battling within his expression. He finally looked down and remained on his knees. Ben turned his attention to Nash and her pet.

"Stop circling me, boy, or I'll cut her throat."

The stalker barked, remaining beside her leg.

Ben stopped, leveling his shotgun at the stalker. It snarled and snapped, but held position right next to Nash.

"You've been quite the prey," she said, a sense of relief in her voice and expression, though the tension in her blade hand remained steady.

"What do you want?" Ben asked.

Nash looked at him like he was a simpleton, shaking her head.

"Prestige ... rank ... authority ... power," she said. "I want what everyone wants."

Ben felt a creeping sense of wrongness begin somewhere in the middle of his back and work its way up his spine and across his scalp. He realized in that moment that there were people in the world who were not like him in any way.

"Lay down your weapons and you'll be granted leniency," she said, changing the angle of the blade at Imogen's throat to punctuate her demand.

"Kill her and your only leverage is gone," Ben said while Cyril moved to get a better angle.

"Stop!" Nash said to Hound when he started to untie the prisoners. He stood up, smiling at her crookedly.

"You and me could have worked out so differently," he said, walking around the cluster of hostages. "You ..." he said, looking her up and down, "you're an Amazon. You got a body to die for." He raised his empty hands, shaking his head as he took a step closer. "We could've been good together."

"What?" Nash said, lowering the knife for a moment, bewildered by Hound's advances.

Kat shot her in the face three times in half a second.

Then the wolf came for her, snarling and snapping as it lunged. She fired ... one, two, five, eight, dart after dart, backing up as she shot. The stalker still came.

Ben leveled his shotgun at it, firing the first round quickly once he'd acquired a reasonable target, just like Hound had taught him. The shot peppered the beast, stopping it momentarily. He took a quick breath and careful aim before the stalker could renew its charge.

As the round exploded, thoughts of the effectiveness of the technique raced through Ben's mind. The first round stops, stuns and disorients the target, maybe even damaging it, giving a moment in the fog to take aim with the second round, firing true ... firing for effect.

The blast hit the wolf directly in the face, blowing it over backward. It skittered across the floor, scrambling to its feet. Ben dropped the shotgun as he drew his sword and rushed it before it could fully recover. He hit it across the back, then the neck, and finally through the width of the head. It fell into an expanding pool of blood.

He spun, scanning the warehouse, his sword trailing dark droplets across the cement floor. Nash lay still, unconscious.

Ben looked at her helpless body for a moment and then strode toward her, raising his blade.

"No!" Cyril shouted, rushing to his side. "No, Ben," he said, a hand on his arm. "If she is to be dispatched, I'll do it. I won't make an executioner out of you."

"But she's at the heart of everything," Ben said. "All of our problems are her fault."

"She certainly had a hand in it," Cyril said. "But she's just a lackey."

"What difference does that make? She did evil to us."

"Yes, she did," Cyril said. "And now we need to figure out what we're going to do next. Killing her has nothing to do with that."

Ben took a deep breath and let it out, centering himself and releasing his emotions. "No, but strategically, we can't afford to let her make a report to her commanders."

"That's fair," Cyril said. "We'll manage that when we come to it."

They went to work untying Imogen and the others and using the bindings to tie Nash's hands behind her back. Enzo craned his neck to see what was happening.

"That thing would have had me if you hadn't intervened," Kat said to Ben, putting a hand on his arm. "Thank you."

"You're welcome," Ben managed, his mouth going suddenly dry.

"Oh, man up, already," Homer said.

"Shut up."

Zack was on his knees, his head bowed low, trembling. Ben knelt down next to him. "Hey, it's me. You're safe."

Zack didn't move.

"Ben?" he whispered, still on his knees, his forehead to the floor.

"Yeah ... it's me, you're safe."

Slowly, tentatively, Zack looked up, as if he expected to get hit. When he saw Ben, he started crying and lunged into him, hugging him fiercely, sobbing and whimpering uncontrollably. Ben held him and let him cry, tears rolling down his own cheeks.

"You're safe," Ben whispered, not sure if he was lying or not.

Zack spent a few minutes in hysterics before falling unconscious. When he did, Ben carried him to the corner where they'd put Frank and wrapped him in blankets.

"I'm sorry about your friend," Cyril said.

Ben nodded, looking down, feeling a sense of guilt for bringing Zack into the situation ... then feeling a sense of anger at the dragon for creating the situation in the first place. He decided that anger at the dragon was more productive.

Once he'd laid Zack down and checked on Frank, he returned to the group. They could hear dogs barking in the distance.

"So what's the plan?"

"We were just discussing that," Cyril said. "Annabelle wants to cut and run."

She glared at him.

"But I want to make another attempt on the keep."

"Do you have a way through the shield?" Ben asked.

"Sort of," Cyril said. "It's complicated."

"It's insane," Belle said, looking at Cyril. "My father used to tell me stories about you—he said you always refused to do black magic. Why would you start now?"

"Desperation," he said softly. "I'm out of options."

Imogen sat quietly, tension virtually radiating from her as she clenched her hands together and held her breath.

"Black magic?" Ben asked.

"Technically … yes."

"Isn't that dangerous?"

"Certainly, but within acceptable limits if used correctly."

"What, exactly, are you planning to do?"

Cyril took a deep breath and held it for a moment before letting it out slowly.

"I'm going to beseech my Guardian Angel to bind the demon Magoth to my will and then command him to transfer my consciousness into Enzo's body."

Chapter 35

Ben stared in disbelief. He wasn't sure what left him more dumbfounded, the fact that his grandfather was considering such a thing, the fact that he obviously believed such a thing was possible, or the fact that he talked about it so matter-of-factly.

"As Enzo, I can gain access to the temple with ease and will be given relative freedom of movement. All that remains is finding the child and getting him out safely."

"Wait ... back up to the part where you bind the demon Magoth to your will," Ben said. "What the hell is that?"

Cyril shrugged. "Black magic, though done with the blessing and guidance of my Guardian Angel."

"Why doesn't *he* just help you?"

"He will, but within certain limits."

"So he won't just go get Imogen's baby, but he'll summon a demon for you and bind it to your will."

Cyril shrugged helplessly. "I didn't make up the rules."

"There has to be a better way," Ben said. "You've harped on the importance of relying on basic manifestation and now you're talking about a demonic summoning."

"I'm open to suggestions," Cyril said. "As long as that circle is protecting the temple, I'm out of options."

A dog barked nearby.

"They smell the blood," Homer said.

Ben glanced at the two doors—both closed and locked.

Cyril was looking at him when he looked back. He knew in a glance that his grandfather had made up his mind. Cold dread settled in the pit of his stomach.

"Please don't do this," Ben said.

Cyril brought up a holo-screen and displayed a picture of his infant grandson.

"That's you," Cyril said. "My grandson. My blood. He's helpless and he's defenseless and he needs me. I don't want to do this, but I don't have another option, not even a bad one. Either I do this or we leave and forsake our family."

Imogen sat quietly, looking at the holo-screen with tears streaming down her face, her hands clasped together between her knees.

Ben nodded, a sick feeling in his gut. He knew that he wouldn't be able to live with himself if they left without trying everything possible. But black magic …

A dog pawed at the door, snarling and growling, then jumping up, hard nails scratching against the lacquered wood. Another yipped, followed by a chorus of barks and yowls as the rest of the pack arrived.

"Fortify the doors," Cyril said. "Looks like we're staying here for a while."

The doors were stout and the bars were sturdy. The dogs wouldn't be getting in. Ben peered out the window, estimating forty or fifty dogs milling around in front of the warehouse with more in back.

"What's happening?" Zack asked, rubbing sleep from his eyes.

"We're surrounded by a pack of wild dogs," Ben said. "How are you feeling?"

"Are they going to get in?"

"No, but we're stuck here for now."

"Oh," Zack said with a shrug. "It's not so bad here as long as Dominus Nash is asleep. And I'm glad you killed her wolf—I hated that thing."

"I'll bet."

"Do you have anything to eat? She didn't feed me much."

"Of course," Ben said, going to his pack for some food.

Zack sat down with his back to the wall and ate until he was content. "Thank you," he said with a sigh. "I haven't been full in weeks."

"What happened to you?"

"They detained me. Nash said I had information that she needed to find you. I told her I didn't know anything, but she didn't believe me. She liked to slap me across the face, hard. If I flinched, she'd do it over and over again. A slap doesn't sound like much, but after a few dozen, it really starts to hurt.

"She asked me all kinds of questions about you ... and Cyril ... and Frank ... and Imogen. She wanted to know where you came from and how long you'd been in town. All kinds of stuff.

"I tried to hold out, but she started slapping me. After a while, I just couldn't take it anymore. I told her anything she wanted to know. I'm sorry."

"Oh God, Zack, you have nothing to apologize for," Ben said. "If anything, I got you into this. I'm so, so sorry you've had to go through this."

He smiled just slightly. "I always wanted to have an adventure. Never thought it would consist mostly of getting the shit slapped out of me by some Amazon bitch."

"It isn't over yet," Ben said, stifling a chuckle.

Zack looked over at Nash, asleep and bound in the corner.

"I want to kill her with my bare hands," he said, his voice dead calm.

"I know the feeling."

Zack frowned. "What's your grandfather doing?"

Cyril had tossed a rope over a rafter and was tying one end of it around the ankles of a dead Dragon Guard. He hoisted the body into the air, got the cooking pot out of his backpack, cut the man's throat, and started collecting blood.

"Black magic," Ben said, still in a state of disbelief.

"So he is the Wizard, then?"

Ben nodded.

"Nash was so certain—she seemed to think that I should have known."

"I didn't even know," Ben said.

"All this time," Zack said, shaking his head.

"Can't say I blame him. He's lost a lot—two wives and a daughter."

"Shit," Zack whispered.

Ben nodded, watching Cyril carefully pour blood in a circle on the far end of the warehouse. His grandfather would do literally anything for family, a vulnerability that the wyrm would certainly exploit if given the chance.

Imogen was sitting next to Frank, who was still unconscious but recovering from the beating he'd taken. She had her knees to her chest and was rocking back and forth. Ben sat down next to her.

"This is all my fault," she said.

"Stop that," Ben said. "We've been over this. You're the victim here."

"Yeah, but he's casting a spell that he'd never cast in a million years. He's using magic that he swore he'd never use, magic that he has always cautioned against. What if something happens to him?" She put a hand over her mouth.

"He's tougher than anyone I know and smarter too," Ben said. "If he says he can do this, then he can. We just have to trust him and support him."

Cyril stood up, scrutinizing his work, nodding to himself in satisfaction. It was a gruesome sight—a magic circle drawn in blood.

He went to the other end of the warehouse and dug around in his pack for a moment.

"Ben, come here," he said, "I have a job for you." He handed Ben a large piece of chalk. "You're going to draw this one."

"What do you mean?"

"You will all need to be inside a consecrated circle during the summoning," Cyril said. "A wizard can only consecrate one temporary circle at a time, so you'll have to do this one."

"Me? But I don't know how."

"That's why I'm going to teach you. Start by drawing the outer circle. You want it as circular as possible, and big, so get an idea where you're going to draw it first and put down some marks for the center, and several around the edges to use as a guide. Once you start your line you don't want to lift the chalk until you come full circle. Also, while you're drawing it, don't ever step outside of it until you have entirely completed it, and then take care to never step on the lines."

"Slow down," Ben said. "So I start by marking the outline of the circle I want to draw."

"Correct."

"All right," Ben said, surveying the warehouse floor and picking his center point. It took about thirty minutes for Ben to draw his first magic circle. While he worked, Cyril lectured and offered guidance and advice. Everyone else watched with varying degrees of skepticism.

"Good," Cyril said, evaluating each symbol carefully before nodding his approval, and glancing over at Frank, still sound asleep. "Now for the most important part. Sit with me."

Ben sat down on the cold floor. Cyril sat opposite him and handed him the egg. Ben took it reverently, his heart rate accelerating. It was just slightly warm to the touch.

"Cradle the egg in your lap and focus on the circle. See it in your mind's eye, see it laid down in light, shining down from your Guardian Angel."

Ben did as he was told, focusing his will and his imagination. After a few moments of clearly visualizing the circle of light, he felt an odd sensation, like grace brushed up against him. A knowing came over him—within the confines of this circle, no evil could befall him. He opened his eyes to find Cyril smiling at him proudly.

"It usually takes people much longer to see the image clearly enough to consecrate the circle, at least the first time. You've trained your mind well."

Ben smiled his thanks for the compliment.

"So I'm safe inside here."

"You are ... unless someone undoes your circle. In this case, I'll be dealing with incorporeal beings, so they can't physically interfere with it, but the Warlock, for example, could walk up and rub the chalk away on the outer edge with his boot and your circle would fail."

Cyril guided each member of the group over the chalk lines, taking great care to avoid even the tiniest smudge, carrying Frank and placing him gently on a bedroll that Ben laid out for him.

"What are you doing?" Enzo asked, looking around a bit wildly when Cyril tipped his chair back and started dragging him across the warehouse.

After positioning Enzo, Cyril came back to the rest of them. "What I'm about to do is dangerous. It might also cause you to reevaluate your understanding of reality. I suggest you look the other way, but I'm sure a few of you will ignore that suggestion.

"Whatever happens, you must stay inside the circle. If you leave the circle or if you break the circle, you will be at Magoth's mercy. Also, you must remain quiet. Do not talk. Any words you utter will be heard by the demon and he will use them to engage you, offering promises and enticements to draw you out.

"Once the spell is complete, my body will be in a trance state inside my circle. My awareness will be inside Enzo, so someone will have to come untie his body. One last thing," Cyril said, looking to each person in turn, "I've been training Ben since he was three to become the next Wizard. If anything happens to me, the egg goes to him, no matter what Frank says or does."

Ben swallowed hard, went to Cyril and gave him a hug. Cyril returned the hug and then held him at arm's length, patting him on the shoulder.

"If all goes well, we'll be on our way by dawn," Cyril said. "Remember, stay in the circle and stay quiet."

He gave them one last solemn look to drive home his warnings and then returned to the other end of the warehouse and his circle drawn in blood.

Chapter 36

Ben watched intently as Cyril sat down in the middle of his circle and began to meditate. After an hour, everyone else had lost interest and were taking advantage of the opportunity to rest.

Ben watched.

When Cyril stood and began speaking in an unknown language, everyone else sat up again—all except Frank and Nash who were still unconscious.

Cyril knelt to the east, speaking under his breath as he put his forehead to the floor. He stood, whispering another string of words before turning south and repeating the process, kneeling to each of the four cardinal directions before facing east again and sitting back down.

Eyes closed, legs folded with his feet on his thighs, he began to chant, speaking in the same alien language he'd used before, repeating the same sing-song mantra over and over again. Time seemed to slow. Ben felt the mantra reverberating in his chest, even though Cyril wasn't speaking loudly. Each time he repeated the string of unintelligible words, Ben felt a sense that something deep and ancient was stirring within him.

Cyril stopped abruptly and rose once again, standing with his arms out and his head back.

He shouted to the ceiling, crying out with an intensity of emotion that Ben had rarely seen his grandfather display. All at once, he collapsed, going to his knees and placing his forehead on the floor.

The air grew still and silent—expectant. Ben realized that he was holding his breath. Slowly, almost imperceptibly, an indistinct haze formed in front of Cyril. It had the quality of vapor but glowed slightly before it coalesced into the form of a man, dressed in a simple robe. He was slightly translucent and glowed with a soft white light, yet Ben sensed a solidity about him that seemed somehow more concrete than anything in the real world. He had a presence and calmness that suggested a kind of permanence that was beyond Ben's ability to fully comprehend.

"Why have you summoned me with blood?" His voice was strong and substantial, yet sounded very far away.

"Desperation," Cyril said, his head still bowed to the floor.

"Rise."

Cyril stood, bowing his head before his Guardian Angel, who reached out and laid a hand on his head.

"You're situation is desperate indeed, yet the solution you have chosen is more desperate still."

"I can see no alternative," Cyril said. "I beg for your counsel. Show me a better way."

The angel was silent for a few moments.

"I cannot see another path more likely to lead to the preservation of your grandson, and yet, this path is fraught with risk."

"I know," Cyril said.

"And still you would proceed?"

"Yes."

"Very well," the angel said, laying his hand on Cyril's head again.

After a moment, the angel became less distinct and then vanished altogether.

Cyril stripped off his shirt and went to work drawing a number of symbols on his chest in blood.

Ben felt a bit queasy.

Cyril didn't seem to be fazed in the least. He focused on the task at hand until his chest and face were covered with an elaborate series of runes.

With that requirement completed, he cut the side of his hand and let blood drizzle onto the floor before him, then smeared it around until it covered a spot large enough to stand on. He hesitated, closing his eyes and tilting his head back for a moment before stepping very deliberately onto the blood.

He began to chant, this time in an entirely different language, spitting harsh and angry words at the world in defiance and challenge. He stopped, waiting for a moment before repeating the chant, his face red with anger as he hurled the words into the universe like a curse.

When he stopped again, a faraway howl seemed to move through the entire warehouse. The temperature dropped and the lamplight dimmed. The shadows in the corners of the room appeared to take on substance.

Cyril repeated the chant.

The howl—angst, frustration, rage, madness all bound into a single long wail—started somewhere else and ended right in the middle of the warehouse as a creature of darkness and malice seemed to draw itself together from the shadows in the room. It continued to wail, a horrendous, terrifying noise that filled Ben with dread.

Frank began to stir. Ben looked at his brother with a start, suddenly realizing that he would certainly ask questions the moment he saw what was happening. He winced, taking a moment to think through his options, deciding to wait and watch since Frank didn't wake before the demon wail trailed off.

The dogs outside scattered, yelping in fear.

A creature of shadow floated in the middle of the room, facing Cyril. From his position, Ben couldn't see the demon's face.

"Come forth!" Magoth commanded, his voice deep and reverberating, yet raspy at the same time ... like fingernails on a chalkboard. Ben thought he might do anything the demon commanded just to make him shut up.

"You have no authority!" Cyril shouted back at Magoth. "You are a foul and condemned creature, damned to the hells for your treachery and betrayal, and you deserve every moment of suffering that you have been forced to endure. I denounce you and call you out into the light, you unworthy and wretched servant."

Magoth roared, a sound evoking paralyzing terror. Cyril stood fast, not flinching or wavering.

"You have been cast down," Cyril shouted. "You have no authority. You have no free will—it was stripped from you as part of your well-deserved punishment. You are bound by universal law to obey me, for I have the blessing of those that struck you down."

A series of gibbering, whining, and sobbing sounds emanated from the shadowy form of the demon.

"Please, Master, don't be so harsh," Magoth said, his voice no less discordant, but instead of authority, it conveyed a sense of utter subservience. "Come to me and I will give you all that you desire and more. The child will be in your arms in a matter of minutes."

"Your bargains will all be rejected, just as you have been rejected from the light. You will submit and serve me. I will do nothing for you."

"No!" Magoth howled. "Come to me now!"

"You will submit!" Cyril shouted. The air around him started to glow as his Guardian Angel came into view right behind him. The angel looked like a young Cyril, yet much larger, standing twelve feet tall.

Magoth collapsed into a barking, wailing, panicked struggle to flee, but he couldn't seem to break free of the invisible bonds that held him fast.

"Submit," the Guardian Angel said.

"I don't want to!" Magoth shouted.

"Submit!" the Guardian Angel said again as the entire room pulsed with a flash of brilliant white light.

Magoth fell to the floor, wailing in anguish, howling in agony, writhing in pain, his shadowy, indistinct form seeming to change shape as he suffered.

"Submit."

"Please, Master, just come to me, all will be well," he said, desperation dripping from his horrible voice.

"No, you will submit," Cyril said.

"You will submit," the Guardian Angel said.

Magoth howled again, rage made manifest in sound trailing off into nothing.

"I submit," he said, defeated. "What command would you have me fulfill?"

"I would have you transfer my conscious awareness and volition into the body of Enzo Gervais, placing his consciousness into a state of hibernation," Cyril said, pointing at a very wide-eyed Enzo, still tied to a chair and gagged to ensure that he wouldn't interfere with the summoning. "Once you have performed this task, you will return to the realm from whence you came."

Frank sat up and looked around.

Ben slapped a hand over his brother's mouth. He tried to resist, but Ben overpowered him quickly, wrapping him into a grappling hold. Imogen scrambled around in front of Frank so she could look him in the eye, but he kept struggling, craning his neck to see Cyril and his twelve-foot-tall Guardian Angel demanding the submission of a demon kneeling in the middle of the room.

Ben looked to Kat. She cocked her head, questioningly. He nodded emphatically. She shrugged, drew her pistol, and shot Frank in the leg. He stopped struggling a few seconds later. Ben laid him back down.

"Best demonic summoning ever," Homer said.

"That's not helpful," Ben said.

"Maybe not, but it's true."

The air grew colder still, breath becoming visible. Magoth began to undulate, his already indistinct form morphing continuously, never quite fully forming into anything before beginning to transform into something else.

Cyril sat down on the blood smear and closed his eyes. Shadow fell over the room, the light dimming even further, throwing the room into darkness, save for the area illuminated by the soft glow of Cyril's Guardian Angel.

The air got heavy. Then a muffled clap echoed throughout the warehouse.

"It is done," Magoth said.

"What's done?" Nash said, sitting up. "And what the hell is going on here?"

Magoth swirled around, parts of his body moving at different speeds as he turned to face Nash. Though his body was unformed and constantly changing, shadow moving as he moved, his face was a perfectly white porcelain mask, entirely androgynous and smiling hideously, floating where a face should have been. The mask was unchanging, even when he spoke.

"Come to me, I will free you."

Before Ben realized what was happening, Nash was up and sprinting toward Magoth. The demon didn't seem to notice any of the others even though he was only a few dozen feet away.

Ben reached for her but she crossed out of the circle before he could lay a hand on her, stopping short only a moment before he too would have passed out of the magical protection.

Nash made it three steps before Magoth exploded into a cloud of shadow that expanded to fill the center of the room in an instant. Then the demon flowed into Nash through her mouth, her nose, and her eyes, lifting her a foot off the ground while he took possession of her. An instant later the shadow was gone and the light returned. Nash easily broke her bindings and smiled at them, turning toward Cyril, whose consciousness was now in Enzo's body.

"Fool!" she said, tipping her head back and laughing with pure glee.

Ben could see from the horrified expression on Enzo's face that Cyril hadn't expected this.

"You will return to your realm," the Guardian Angel said.

"No, I won't," Magoth said. "You know the rules. As long as I have a willing host, I can stay—and Dominus Nash is so very willing."

The Guardian Angel pulsed with light, filling the room with dazzling brilliance.

Magoth leaned in to laugh at him very deliberately.

Ben got up quietly and walked over to the edge of the circle, motioning for everyone else to remain seated, even though both John and Rufus had weapons at the ready. Once he had an angle that wouldn't hit Cyril or Enzo, he pulled his revolver and aimed it at Nash. Since her armor would stop body shots, and Ben wasn't confident that he could make a headshot, he opted to fire at the backs of her legs.

The first round hit, dropping her to one knee. She cried out in surprise. Ben fired a second round, tearing again into the leg that he'd already hit. She whirled, the fury in her eyes seeming to reach out for him. The demon's anger felt palpable, almost tangible. Ben fired again, hitting Nash's metal breastplate and blowing her onto the floor.

A moment later, she rose up as if lifted by magic, blood oozing from her leg, her feet never touching the ground. She floated there for a moment, and then the entire warehouse went dark.

Rufus lit a match, throwing a dim light into the huge room. Nash and the angel were gone, the back door was wide open, and Cyril was struggling against the gag in Enzo's mouth.

Ben looked to him for permission to leave the circle. Cyril nodded urgently. Ben hurried across the warehouse, taking care to avoid stepping on the lines of either circle. He pulled the gag down and began untying Enzo's hands.

"What have I done?" Cyril said, shaking his head.

"You tell me," Ben said, freeing his other hand and stepping back so Cyril could untie his feet.

He stood, looked Ben in the eye, and nodded in resignation.

"I've unleashed a named demon onto the world."

"So what can we do about it?" Ben asked.

"We must kill Nash," Cyril said. "Though that may be more difficult to do with Magoth pulling her strings."

"Won't he just possess someone else if we kill her?"

"Maybe, if he can find a willing host."

"Why would anyone want to be possessed?"

"Power," Cyril said with a shrug. "Right now, we have other things to worry about. I'll clean this mess up after I get my grandson back."

He went to his comatose body and took the drone ring and a couple of knives, one for his belt, the other for his boot. Then he took the egg and handed it to Ben.

"Take good care of this for me. Stay here and try to remain undetected. You can watch my progress through the drone feed."

"What if Magoth comes back?"

"He won't, at least not until he's ready, and that won't be for a while. Even with his demonic powers, it's going to take some time for Nash's legs to heal—good shot, by the way."

"Thanks."

Cyril put a hand on Ben's shoulder. "Take care of everyone. Be ready to leave as soon as I return."

"We'll be ready," Ben said. "Be careful."

Chapter 37

Ben sat down with his eyes closed, pretending to meditate while he watched the drone feed. He saw Enzo's body walking through the streets, Cyril taking great care to avoid detection by anyone or anything until he reached the more populated areas, where he walked briskly and purposefully toward the main gate of the inner city.

He reached the outer wall in short order where he was stopped by a guard holding up his hand.

"The inner city is closed until the intruders can be found," the guard said.

"Well then, there shouldn't be any harm in letting me in, should there?"

"Huh?"

"You're searching for intruders within the inner wall," Cyril said a bit slowly. "I'm outside the wall, so I can't be the one you're searching for, can I?"

"Well … I guess not."

"So letting me in shouldn't be a problem, should it?" Cyril asked, pulling aside his coat to let the guard see the Gervais House badge and then flipping a gold coin into the air.

"I suppose not," the guard said, catching the coin and turning toward the tower. "Open the gate," he called out.

Cyril offered him a thin smile before slipping into the city and heading directly for the temple. Pairs of Dragon Guard were patrolling every street. Cyril flashed Enzo's badge when they approached, and they waved him along.

Ben started to feel a bit more at ease about the situation.

Then Cyril reached the temple gate, which was guarded by two priests backed up by six Dragon Guard.

He opened his coat, revealing the house badge. The demeanor of the priests changed visibly when they saw it.

"The temple is closed," the first priest said.

"I know," Cyril said. "But my son is inside and I'm worried about him."

"I'm sure he's safe."

"Oh, I am too, but he's young and probably very frightened," Cyril said. "It would mean a lot to me if I could make sure he's all right."

The priest seemed to hesitate until Cyril lifted his belt pouch and let it fall against his leg, the muffled clinking of coins tipping the scales. He nodded, motioning to a Dragon Guard to open the gate.

"I will speak to my father about your generosity," Cyril said. "He will be most pleased." He slipped the priest a handful of gold coins.

"Follow this guard. He'll take you to a waiting room. An attendant will be with you shortly."

"Thank you again," Cyril said, following the Dragon Guard into the austere temple, the drone trailing a dozen feet behind him along the ceiling. After a few hallways and turns, the Dragon Guard stopped at an open door, motioning with his head for Cyril to enter.

"Thank you," Cyril said, smiling graciously.

"Wait here," the Dragon Guard said before leaving.

The drone did a quick scan of the corridor and then shot down the hallway searching for the nearest staircase leading to the upper levels. After a few dead ends, Cyril found one, carefully retracing his path before peeking out of the room and scanning the hallway again.

When he saw an acolyte coming around the corner, Cyril pulled his head back quickly and went to a chair. He was sitting patiently when the man entered the room.

"Can I help you?" the young man asked.

"Yes, my name is Enzo Gervais and I'd like to see my son."

"And why is the child in the temple?"

"I made an arrangement with the high priest," Cyril said.

The acolyte flinched slightly. "The high priest is dead."

"Yes, I heard," Cyril said. "That's why I'm here. I wanted to make sure my son is all right since the high priest was his guardian."

"I see," he said, putting his hand to his chin. "Perhaps my superior will be better able to help you. Please come with me."

"Of course," Cyril said, nodding deferentially and following behind the acolyte.

He led Cyril several levels upstairs before taking him toward an office with a double door at the end of the main hall.

Ben started to feel the tension seep back into his shoulders.

"Please, wait here," the acolyte said, stopping at the door to a small antechamber adjacent to the office.

Cyril nodded his thanks and took a seat, settling in comfortably.

A few moments later a priest and the acolyte entered through a door in the side of the room.

"Mr. Gervais, welcome to the temple. I am the acting high priest until our master can elevate his choice for successor to his rightful place."

"Congratulations," Cyril said, "though we all wish your ascension hadn't been the result of such a tragedy."

"Thank you. My assistant tells me that you've made an arrangement with the former high priest concerning your son and that you'd like to see him."

"Precisely," Cyril said.

"This is highly unusual. Surely you understand the permanent nature of the transaction when a child is involved."

"Yes, but I worry," Cyril said. "I just want to look in on him—make sure he's all right."

The priest pursed his lips for a moment before shaking his head.

"First, let me say that we're grateful for the all of the contributions your family has made and continues to make to our cause. Unfortunately, I can't allow you to see the child until I review the file and I simply don't have time right now, given the threat we're under."

"I understand completely," Cyril said, drawing a knife from his belt and cutting the man's throat with one smooth stroke, then stepping into the surprised acolyte and stabbing him in the heart before he could even cry out.

Ben was a bit surprised by the sudden turn of events. Such quick violence—two dead in as many seconds.

Cyril quickly dragged the bodies behind the desk, moved a chair to cover the stains left by the blood, and put out the lamp. Then he sent the drone to scout for a staircase leading up to the next level.

He walked with a purpose, like the temple was his home and he knew exactly where he was going. The first acolyte he encountered nodded respectfully in passing. Cyril smiled politely without breaking stride. When he reached the next level, he found that the staircase to the level above was on the other end of the temple.

As he passed an open door, someone called out, "Excuse me."

Cyril kept walking.

A priest came out of the room at a trot. "Excuse me, you're not allowed to be here without an escort," he said.

Cyril stopped, turning with an embarrassed smile. "I'm lost," he said. "My escort was taking me to the nursery so I could see my son and he got called away. He gave me directions but I got turned around. Can you help me?"

The priest cocked his head, frowning skeptically. "That is highly unusual. Any acolyte knows better than to leave a guest unattended."

Cyril shrugged helplessly. "I don't know what happened. The priest who called him away was pretty angry, though. It seemed like the acolyte was in trouble."

"Be that as it may, you can't be on this level without an escort. Follow me to the guard room and I'll send for another acolyte."

"Thank you," Cyril said, nodding in gratitude.

Two steps after the priest turned his back, Cyril grabbed his mouth with his left hand and stabbed him in the lower back, pulling the blade out to the side, slashing through the width of the man's kidney, then bringing the bloody blade up and cutting his throat. He didn't let him hit the floor, instead walking him toward the nearest room.

Without dropping the body, he cracked the door and sent the drone in to scout the room. Finding an empty office, he quickly dragged the priest inside and laid him down behind the desk. Sending the drone out ahead of him, he hurried down the hallway toward the far end of the temple and the stairs leading up to the top levels.

He could hear several Dragon Guard playing cards behind the door at the end of the hall. He took two steps up the nearby staircase to conceal himself from anyone coming down the hallway and sent the drone up to the next level. A Dragon Guard stood sentry in the hallway, a few feet from the top of the stairs.

Cyril panned around and picked out another Dragon Guard at the far end of the hallway, staring right back at his partner. The nursery was two levels up. Moving along the corner of the ceiling, the drone floated up the next staircase, finding another Dragon Guard at either end of the long corridor running the length of that level. Cyril moved the drone slowly to the nursery, carefully floating underneath the door and finding the child sleeping quietly in his crib.

Ben smiled to himself when he saw the image of his tiny nephew. Cyril was close, but there was still a lot in his way. Worse still, he couldn't afford to raise the alarm or the chances of getting out alive would diminish rapidly.

Suddenly, a roar shook the world.

Ben felt visceral fear course through him, the kind of fear prey feel in the presence of their natural predator. The drone turned toward the window and accelerated, hitting the glass at high speed and breaking a small hole through it without shattering the pane. It sped away from the temple, making a beeline for the tallest building nearby and landing on top of its chimney.

The view from the feed instantly changed, looking back at the temple.

The dragon glided in gracefully, landing on the topmost platform, tipping his head back and roaring again. All the world fell deathly silent. The drone feed went dark.

When Ben opened his eyes, everyone was looking at him, their faces deathly pale.

"Was that the dragon?" Imogen asked, her voice trembling.

Ben nodded. Even without the benefit of the augment, he knew that he would never forget what he'd just seen. Black as sackcloth, the wyrm had leathery batlike wings, a huge snout that opened into a maw filled with needle-sharp teeth, a long tail ending in a single barb, and eyes like those of a gigantic cat. The creature was enormous—sixty feet from nose to tail with a wingspan to match.

"That isn't possible," the augment said.

"Show me the footage," Ben said.

There was a moment's hesitation before the image appeared in his mind's eye. He was starting to get used to the split reality the augment created for him, one set of images coming through his eyes, the other through his mind. As the image played out again, Ben noticed the rider.

"Stop ... go back and stop."

The image slowly reversed and then stopped at the best angle to see the rider.

"Can you magnify that image?" Ben asked.

The augment zoomed in quickly, revealing a rider that wasn't human, at least not anymore. He was humanoid, but distinctly dragonlike, with a snout, horns, wings, and catlike eyes. His skin was scaled, and his fingers ended in inch-long black talons.

"What are we going to do?" Imogen asked, her voice sounding very small.

"We wait," Ben said. "It's all we can do."

He went to his aunt and gave her a hug. She buried her face on his shoulder and wept.

The dragon roared again, this time more in anger than in announcement of his presence.

The drone feed abruptly resumed, shifting view rapidly until it had acquired the dragon again, flying toward the north end of town.

A streak of light suddenly shot up from the ground, brilliantly illuminating the early morning sky. The dragon rolled out of the way effortlessly, tucking his wings back and falling into a dive toward the place where the light had originated, breathing a gout of flame as he neared the ground, flaring his wings to break his fall and coming to a momentary hover in an instant.

For several seconds, fire roared forth from the dragon, thoroughly engulfing the ground. Then he turned away and began to gain altitude, craning his neck to see his kill. He roared again.

The drone shot straight up into the air, gaining several thousand feet in a matter of seconds, the image zooming in to view the spot where the dragon had breathed fire. The Warlock stood on a perfectly circular scrap of dirt that was entirely unscathed. Fire raged all around him, but within a radius of ten feet, the area was untouched.

He had a single Dragon Guard with him, the man clearly enchanted by his magic. The dragon roared again, banking for another attack when the drone refocused on the temple and darted forward, returning to the floor where Cyril was hiding, entering through a window that he'd opened. He sent it out into the hall and watched the guards run by, all of them heading for the lower levels.

After several moments of quiet, he sent the drone to the stairs and scouted the route to the nursery again. Only one guard remained on each of the floors above. He crept out into the hall, moving quickly but quietly.

A roar in the distance stopped him in his tracks for a moment, but then he continued on to the staircase. He waited at the bottom of the stairs, sending the drone up, moving it along the floor close to the wall until it came to the first door. The drone slipped under it and scanned the room, which looked like a small ritual chamber.

The drone rose several inches and then accelerated into the door causing a loud click when it hit. It backed up and did it again, and then again. Ben waited, wondering what was happening until the door opened and Cyril dragged a dead Dragon Guard inside and laid him down behind the altar, taking his sword.

When he opened the door to the hall, both he and Ben were startled to see a Dragon Guard standing there looking at the blood on the floor.

"Intruder!" the Dragon Guard yelled, going for his sword. Cyril stabbed him in the face, driving the point of his blade into the man's skull, only stopping once it hit the inside of the man's helmet.

"Shit," Cyril muttered, catching the man's body and dragging him into the ritual room.

He waited and listened, sending the drone into the hall to watch for approaching guards, but all was quiet, save for the battle raging in the distance.

Sword in hand, he quietly closed the door and went to the stairs, following his drone into a long empty hallway. On tiptoes he moved toward the nursery. Approaching an open door, he slowed and sent his drone to look inside.

Two priests stood on the balcony, watching the battle between the dragon and the Warlock.

Cyril crept past, only moving more quickly once he was certain that they wouldn't hear him. He reached the nursery without being noticed and carefully opened the door. The room was dark, the early morning light casting a very dim glow through the curtains.

Cyril smiled down at his sleeping grandson. "There you are, my little namesake, I've come to take you home," he whispered, reaching down to pick the child up.

"Hello, Cyril," an oddly familiar, yet strangely inhuman voice said from off to the side. "I knew you'd come here eventually."

He whirled, leveling his sword at the voice.

As the drone panned to take in the scene, Ben felt a jolt of horror course through him.

Britney Harper stood in the shadows, her hair dirty and disheveled, her face grimy, her clothes torn and tattered. She stepped into the dim light.

Her eyes were completely black.

"Oh God, Britney, what have they done to you?" Cyril whispered.

She smiled, her once-beautiful teeth now yellow and stained.

"Britney doesn't live here anymore … but I can still feel her anger at you, at your family … I can still feel how betrayed she felt. That's why the high priest gave her to me. He knew I would feel her hatred for you and your family. He knew I would be able to track you anywhere."

"I can help you," Cyril said.

"Help me? How would you help me?"

"I can try to bring you back."

"You don't understand. If Britney came back, I would have to leave. Why would I want that? But you *can* help me. You can tell me where your grandsons are, especially Frank. He tricked Britney into helping you when she wasn't supposed to. That's why they did this to her."

Cyril stepped to the side, giving himself more room to work and to distance himself from his grandson.

Britney laughed. "Did you really think you could get out of here alive?"

"That was the plan," Cyril said. "Just out of curiosity, how did you know it was me?"

"I can always find my prey … it's like a sense of smell, only better. I'm drawn to your essence, the energy that animates you."

"Interesting," Cyril said. "I didn't know they could make a person into a stalker."

"When it suits them," she said, stepping into a low crouch.

"I don't want to hurt you, Britney, but I will if I have to."

"I told you … Britney doesn't live here anymore."

From a standstill, she leapt into the air and landed on Cyril. He had just enough time to run her through, driving the sword into her chest and out her back as she crashed down on top of him.

"I love you, Ben," Cyril shouted, as he struggled to throw Britney off of him. "Run!"

She screamed in rage, grabbing him by the shoulders and smashing his head into the floor over and over again until his eyes went blank and blood began to splatter. Enzo's body went limp and still.

Ben felt a kind of fear that he'd never known before. He raced to his grandfather's body, catching him as he slumped over.

"No, no, no," he said, fumbling for a pulse, shaking his head, trying to see through the tears streaming from his eyes. It felt like his insides were trying to claw their way out of his stomach. He laid Cyril down, listening for breath … but there was nothing.

"No," he said, laying his head down on Cyril's chest and weeping uncontrollably. Imogen was there a moment later, breaking down in hysterical sobbing and then letting out a blood-chilling scream a moment before she fainted and crumpled to the floor. Ben ignored everything except the grief that had so suddenly flooded into him, permeating every fiber of his being.

He didn't know that anything could hurt so deeply, a visceral pain that was all-encompassing. He was vaguely aware of Homer lying right beside him, whimpering quietly, his nose just inches from Cyril. Ben's whole world felt like it was crumbling out from underneath him.

And then there was nothing.

Chapter 38

He woke slowly at first, until he remembered. And then he was wide awake, rolling over and vomiting onto the floor by his bedroll.

"What happened?" Frank demanded. "I want to know everything and they won't tell me, so you're going to." He was standing over Ben, looking down at him with an expression of anger, disgust, and betrayal.

"Shut up, Frank." Ben curled into a ball and started to cry again, his whole world seeming to unravel. Cyril had been the center of his whole life—his parent, his teacher, and his friend all rolled into one ... and now he was gone.

"Get up and answer my questions," Frank said, hauling Ben to his feet.

He came up in a surge, his grief transforming into rage in an instant. He hit Frank hard in the center of the chest with an open palm. His brother staggered back, his mouth opening as if he were a fish out of water.

"All right, Frank, you want to know what happened, I'll fucking tell you. You killed Britney. You tricked her into getting us out of that jail cell and then the high priest turned her into a stalker. And then she killed our grandfather." Ben shoved him.

Frank staggered back a few more steps, a glimmer of fear in his eyes.

"Our grandfather was the Wizard ... yeah, that one, the one who fought the dragons and nearly won. He lost two wives and a daughter, our mother, in the bargain, so he took us into hiding, to protect us. But he couldn't tell us the truth because you're such a piece of shit that nobody trusts you.

"He hid the egg and he kept all of this from us because he knew that if he told you, you would betray him, you'd betray us all, just like you betrayed Britney."

"So where's the egg now?" Frank demanded.

Ben lunged into him, hitting him in the chest with his shoulder, knocking him to the ground.

"You just don't get it, do you? You killed Britney ... you killed our grandfather!"

"No, I didn't," Frank said, scrambling to regain his feet. "She helped me because I asked her to. And it got you out of prison."

"And it cost her everything ... but you don't even care, do you? All you want is the egg."

"It's rightfully mine," Frank said. "I'm the eldest—"

Ben's sword came free, pointing at Frank in a instant, just inches from his face.

He stopped talking, holding very still, looking at his brother with renewed fear.

"By a minute and a half," Ben said. "But that doesn't matter. You will never have that egg. Our grandfather left it to me."

Frank backed up, pushing himself across the floor with his feet. "Bullshit! He always gave you everything, but not this time."

"Stop," Hound said, stepping forward with a warning look to Frank. "Cyril made it crystal clear that the egg goes to Ben. That's just the way it is, so I suggest you get used to it."

"I thought you were my friend," Frank said.

Hound chuckled mirthlessly, shaking his head and sighing sadly. "Cyril was my friend. He hired me to watch over you, not to protect *you*, but to protect the world *from* you. He knew exactly what you are, Frank, and so do I. So let me say this clearly: If you try to take that egg from your brother, I'll put you in the dirt. Got it?" Hound said, with a very pointed look.

Frank regained his feet, shaking his head sadly, donning the mantle of the victim. "All my life, everyone I thought I knew has been lying to me."

Ben snorted derisively, sheathing his sword and shaking his head as he went to Cyril. He took his tech pistol and ammunition, sword, knives, and money, along with the last ex-plus charge and two grenades. His confrontation with Frank had shoved his grief into the distance. He'd detached from it for the moment, but it was like a monster stalking him in the night ... eventually it would catch up with him and crush him utterly, but right now he didn't have time.

"You're going to take everything else too, huh?"

"Yeah, I am," Ben said, turning to face his brother again. "I have a purpose for all of this other than buying whiskey and whores."

He strapped the revolver on and moved his shotgun to the other side behind his sword, then tossed his empty revolver to the ground at Frank's feet. "You can have that one ... it's out of bullets anyway."

"Hate to break up the family drama, but we should be going," Annabelle said.

Ben looked at her as if remembering that she was even present and nodded. "Are you still willing to take us to safety?"

"You're the Wizard now," she said. "My father will want to meet you as soon as possible."

"All right, what's your plan?" Ben said, numbness settling into his soul.

"We have a warehouse across town with a shipment bound for K Falls leaving today. They'll transport us to Rocky Point, where we have a boat waiting to take us across to the north end of the lake. From there, I have a contact with fresh horses. If all goes well, you'll be having dinner with my father in a few days."

"Fair enough, but we still have to get to your warehouse without attracting attention."

The dragon roared in the distance. Everyone stopped talking for a moment.

"I thought we'd go around town outside the markers," Annabelle said.

"Better than going through it," Ben said. It felt surreal. In the back of his mind, he knew that his grandfather was dead, a fact that would forever change his life, but he couldn't bring himself to feel anything at the moment except numbness and a dull-but-building fury.

He could see in a glance that his rising anger was easily matched by his brother's. Before, on the trail, when he'd considered killing Frank, he'd been revolted at the prospect. Now, detached, numb and cold-eyed, he knew that it might come to that if he was really going to confront the dragon.

"Get your gear, we're leaving," Ben said.

"What about my father?" Imogen asked through tears. "We can't just leave him here."

Ben felt a pang of guilt. She was right, Cyril deserved far better than they could give him.

"The best we can do is burn him," Frank said, all trace of his hostility and anger strangely gone. He walked over and picked up one of the dragon-fire rifles.

"I wouldn't do that," Hound said.

"Why not?" Frank said, not waiting for an answer as he pointed the rifle at Cyril and fired. A gout of flame erupted from the barrel, engulfing Cyril's body in fire and completely consuming him in a brilliant conflagration.

The moment Frank pulled the trigger, he cried out in pain, dropping the rifle and looking at his right hand in disbelief, his face a mask of agony, his whole body trembling from the sudden pain of a dragon rune burned into his hand. It was an angry welt, the flesh burned away, the wound cauterized by the sudden heat.

"That's why, dumb-ass," Hound said. "Come here, let me see that hand."

Frank didn't move, his face still a mask of shock and pain.

Hound grabbed him by the wrist and shook his head.

"We should probably get out of here," John said, gesturing to the growing fire as it started to lick at the back wall of the warehouse.

"Grab his pack and gun," Hound said to Ben, leading Frank out of the building.

"Zack, take my grandfather's pack," Ben said. "You'll need some gear."

They had just stepped out into the space between the warehouses when the dragon soared into view flying toward the temple. Everyone stood mesmerized by the sight. It was magnificent and terrifying all at once, a primordial creature of magic and ferocity. Somewhere in the back of his mind Ben's reason began to question the wisdom of attacking such a beast, but his building rage easily overpowered such rational thoughts.

"He has the Warlock's staff," John said, handing his monocular to Ben.

Sure enough, the winged man riding the dragon was carrying the dragon-claw staff. He handed the monocular back to John and hoisted his pack.

"So much for the Warlock," Hound said.

"What's a Warlock?" Zack asked.

"Someone you really don't want to meet," Ben said. "Let's go."

"Wait," John said. "Shit."

"What?"

John handed the monocular to Imogen and looked down, closing his eyes and shaking his head sadly.

Her face went white and she started to tremble as she looked at the dragon. "No," she whispered.

The dragon launched into the sky, the high priest on his back carrying a baby.

Imogen dropped the monocular and slumped to the ground.

Ben knelt in front of her, gently lifting her face by the chin. "I know it hurts. I know you're afraid, but I need you to set that aside for now. Once we're safe, once we have a chance to arm up and make a plan, I'm going after that goddamned wyrm, I'm going to kill it and I'm going to get my nephew back. But right now, we have to run."

Hound took a moment to quickly wrap Frank's hand in a bandage. Ben ignored his brother's whimpering and complaining, instead focusing on Imogen.

She clenched her jaw, wiped the tears from her face and nodded. "Promise?"

"I promise," he said, helping her up.

The trek to the markers and around the town was uneventful save for a few barking dogs. It was evident from the noise in the distance that the majority of the Dragon Guard had been deployed north of town where the dragon and the Warlock had done battle. A large swath of the city was burning—dozens of houses and businesses falling victim to the flames.

"Are you really going to kill the dragon?" Zack asked while they walked through the tall grass along the south edge of town.

"Yes," Ben said, though he didn't feel nearly as confident as he tried to sound.

Frank huffed in the background.

"I'm sorry about your grandfather," Zack said.

"Me too," Ben said, patting his friend on the back.

They reached the warehouse by midmorning, Annabelle going in first to make sure everything was in order before waving the rest of them in. Each of them was put inside a crate, which was then nailed shut. Homer rode with Ben, a bit cramped but neither of them minded. The crates were loaded into a series of wagons, other crates filled with all manner of supplies loaded on top of them.

The ride was uncomfortable and Ben found himself holding his breath every time they reached a checkpoint, but they got through without any problems.

"Perhaps I am in need of repair," the augment said at one point during their journey.

"I doubt it," Ben said.

"I have carefully reviewed the footage of recent events and I cannot reconcile what I have seen with what I know to be true—a clear indication that I am malfunctioning."

"You're not malfunctioning … you're just stubborn. The dragon is real. Magic is real. And I really can talk to my dog."

"None of those things are possible."

"Nope … but they're real just the same."

The augment went silent. Ben returned to his meditation, focusing on his lucky coin. The single-mindedness of the practice didn't leave room for anything else, not thought, not emotion … it was the perfect refuge from his grief. He knew he couldn't afford to open that door until he was safe. To do so would paralyze him and leave him and everyone he cared about vulnerable.

"System diagnostics indicate that I'm functioning within acceptable parameters," the augment said a while later.

Ben felt a twinge of annoyance at being pulled out of his meditation.

"Like I said, you're not broken, you're just stubborn."

"I need to connect to the NACC network to confirm my diagnostic results."

"That's going to have to wait," Ben said. "No EM emissions of any kind. Consider that a standing order unless I direct you otherwise."

The augment went silent again. Ben returned to his meditation.

Sometime later, the wagon stopped. The muffled voices of workers unloading the cargo filtered through the crate. It took a while for them to unload all of the real freight, then the workers left and things went quiet for a few minutes.

Abruptly, he heard the lid of his crate being pried off, then Adam helped Ben to his feet. He climbed out and stretched his legs a bit before lifting Homer out.

"Somebody want to open the door?" Homer said. "I've got business with a tree."

Ben opened the warehouse door and let his dog out, peering this way and that and feeling a bit of relief that there weren't any Dragon Guard in sight, just people working the docks.

"Where are you going from here?" Zack asked.

"North."

"I think I should come with you. If I go home, I'm afraid the Dragon Guard will find me and hurt my parents."

Ben closed his eyes and nodded, adding another couple of names to his mental list of the people in his life victimized by the wyrm.

"The Dragon Guard might harass them anyway trying to find out where you went."

"Shit. I hadn't though about that," Zack said. "Maybe I could warn them—send them a letter."

"Annabelle might have something to write with."

Homer nosed the door open enough to squeeze through and the three of them walked back to the group.

"The boat will take a few minutes to prepare," Adam said. "We should wait here until the last minute."

The door opened behind them. Everyone turned to see Britney standing in the doorway, smiling at them with her grimy yellow teeth.

"Found you," she said, strolling toward them.

Kat shot her three times.

Britney smiled at her momentarily before turning her attention to Frank.

Hound shot her with Bertha. She took the hit to the chest and staggered back, smiling at him for a moment before she lunged into a sprint. He fired again, but the shot passed under her as she leapt into the air and landed on Hound's chest, knocking him over onto his back. Rather than press her attack, she rolled forward the moment he hit the ground, coming to her feet fluidly and hitting Frank in the chest with both hands, knocking him back a dozen feet.

He landed flat on his back, gasping for breath. She strolled toward him, seemingly oblivious to everyone else in the room. An arrow hit her in the back at an angle, coming out of her side. She ignored it, barely flinching at the wound.

"You tricked me, Frank. You lied to me and manipulated me. You pretended to care about me when you didn't."

Frank tried to say something but nothing came out.

A knife hit her in the back, just left of the spine—a perfect strike to the heart. She ignored it. Ben saw the look of fear in Annabelle's eyes when she glanced at her husband.

Ben approached her from behind, sword drawn.

"Britney," he said.

"I'll be with you in a moment, dear Ben," she said over her shoulder. "You really are the nice one—shame your lying brother killed you, too."

She leapt onto Frank's chest, grabbing him by the face and raising his head to slam it into the floor. Ben was moving the moment she leapt, reaching her a moment later, swinging his blade with everything he had. Time slowed. Emotions crashed into him like a tsunami. He'd had a crush on Britney for months—he'd dreamt about her, imagined a life with her … he could have loved her. Frank had betrayed him so totally that he didn't even care if she killed him, yet his indifference to the well-being of his brother nagged at his conscience.

Above all, a rage fueled by loss and grief drove him, carried his blade into her neck, cleaving her head from her body with a single stroke. Frank shoved her aside, stripping off his shirt quickly to get her black blood off of him as he staggered to his feet, looking at Ben with a mixture of gratitude and confusion.

Ben ignored him. He stared at Britney's body, dark blood oozing from her neck into a pool on the floor. He'd never killed anyone before. Cyril had always protected him from that.

And now, his first kill was the woman he wanted to love.

He tried to tell himself that she was already dead, that the stalker's spirit had possessed her, that her body was just a vessel for a creature of deliberate malice, but none of that removed the fact that he'd just decapitated the woman that he had intended to court as his wife.

In the face of an emotional onslaught that threatened to undo his sanity, he stepped back from his emotions, detaching and distancing himself from the things he was feeling, cutting himself off from the unbearable pain and loss and horror. Deliberately embracing the numbness, he cleaned his blade and returned it to its scabbard.

"Is the boat ready?" he asked quietly.

Imogen laid a hand on his shoulder.

"Are you okay?"

"No," he said calmly.

"Time to go," Adam said from the door.

"Why?" Frank asked, before anyone could move. "Why did you save me? You obviously hate me, so why not let her kill me?"

Ben looked at him for a moment before answering with a helpless shrug. "You're my brother," he said, holding his eyes for a moment before turning toward the door.

The boat ride to the north end of the lake was quiet, everyone content to wrestle with their own thoughts. When Ben stepped off the boat, something caught his eye. He frowned as he bent down and picked up a gold coin. Smiling to himself, he slipped it into his pocket.

True to her word, Annabelle had horses ready for them. Within a few minutes of making landfall, they were riding north along old Highway 95 toward the Deschutes Territory and the promise of sanctuary.

Ben kept to himself during the trip, focusing his mind on meditation, trying to keep the grief at bay. Three days later, they rounded a bend and saw their new home—an idyllic vineyard nestled into the east slope of the Cascade Mountains.

"This place smells good," Homer said.

Ben smiled down at his best friend trotting along beside him.

"You'll be safe here," Annabelle said.

She spurred her horse, leading the way up the winding path to the top of the hill and the home of the Dragon Slayer.

Here Ends
The Dragon's Egg
Dragonfall: Book One

Look for The Dragon's Codex
Dragonfall: Book Two
Coming Spring 2016

Made in the USA
Columbia, SC
29 November 2021

49967239R00146